This Book
Was Donated By

Enzo
Earet

2019

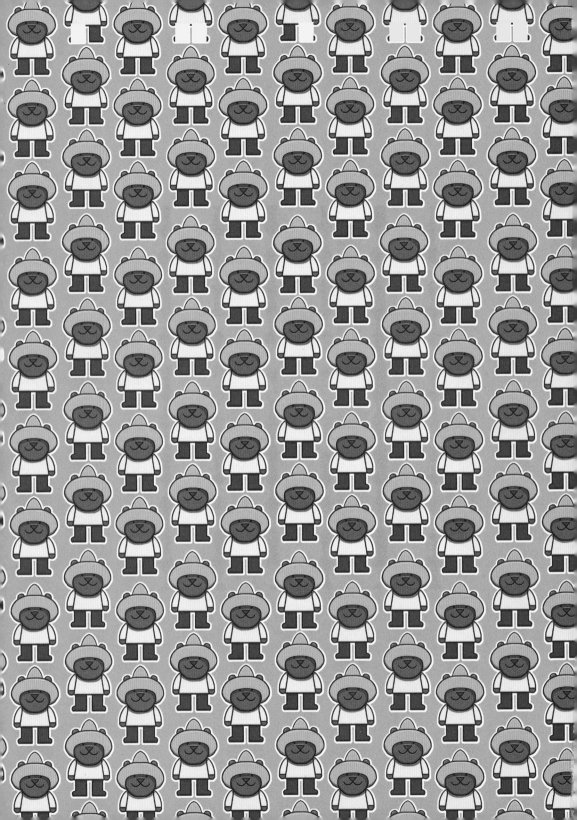

APOCALYPSE

A GRAPHIC NOVEL BY
NATHAN HALE

AMULET BOOKS
NEW YORK

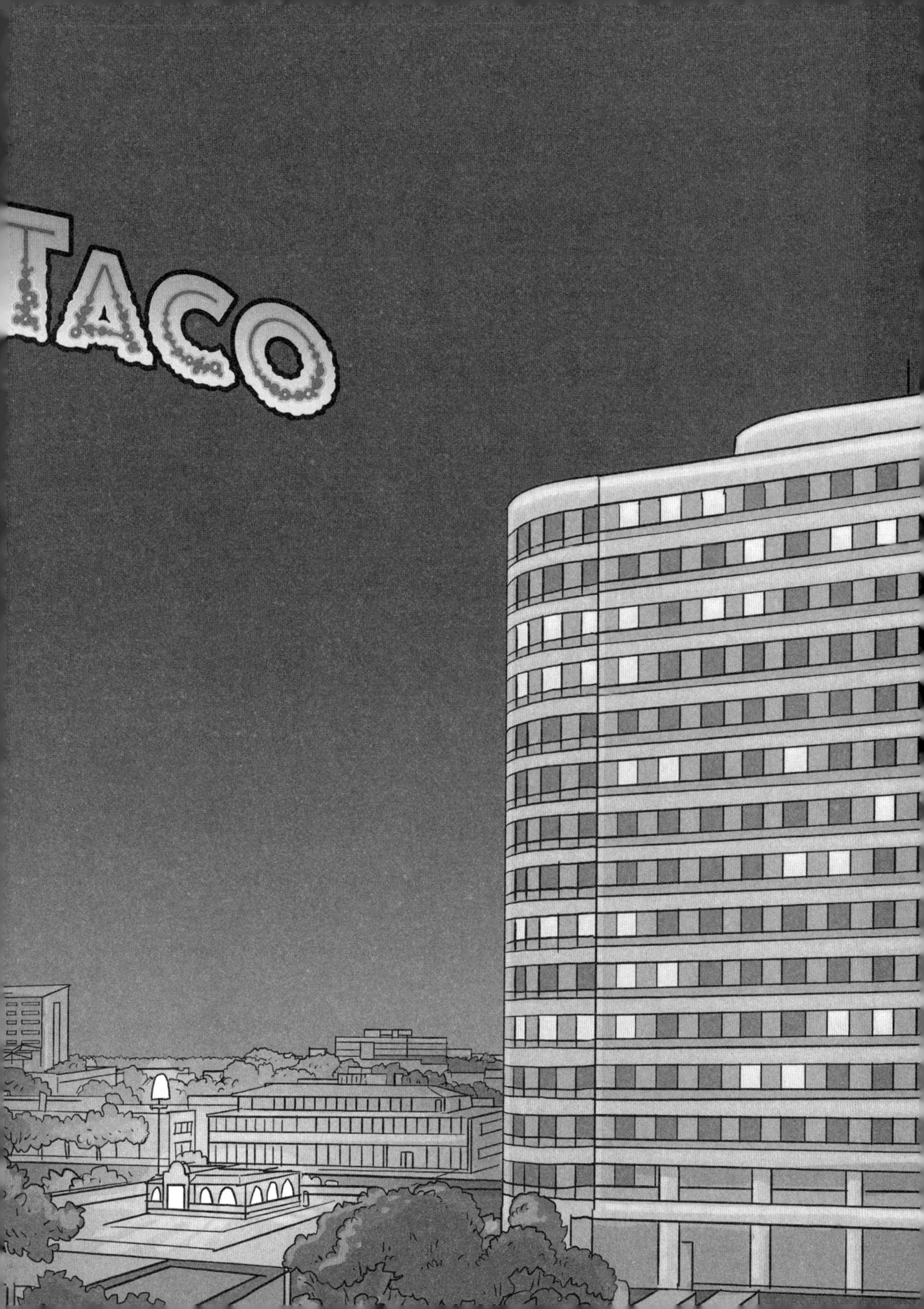
TACO

PUBLISHER'S NOTE: THIS IS A WORK OF FICTION. NAMES, CHARACTERS, PLACES, AND INCIDENTS ARE EITHER THE PRODUCT OF THE AUTHOR'S IMAGINATION OR USED FICTITIOUSLY, AND ANY RESEMBLANCE TO ACTUAL PERSONS, LIVING OR DEAD, BUSINESS ESTABLISHMENTS, EVENTS, OR LOCALES IS ENTIRELY COINCIDENTAL.

CATALOGING--IN--PUBLICATION DATA HAS BEEN APPLIED FOR AND MAY BE OBTAINED FROM THE LIBRARY OF CONGRESS.

ISBN 978-1-4197-3373-4

TEXT AND ILLUSTRATIONS COPYRIGHT © 2019 NATHAN HALE
BOOK DESIGN BY CHAD W. BECKERMAN

PRINTED AND BOUND IN USA
10 9 8 7 6 5 4 3 2 1

AMULET BOOKS ARE AVAILABLE AT SPECIAL DISCOUNTS WHEN PURCHASED IN QUANTITY FOR PREMIUMS AND PROMOTIONS AS WELL AS FUNDRAISING OR EDUCATIONAL USE. SPECIAL EDITIONS CAN ALSO BE CREATED TO SPECIFICATION. FOR DETAILS, CONTACT SPECIALSALES@ABRAMSBOOKS.COM OR THE ADDRESS BELOW.

AMULET BOOKS® IS A REGISTERED TRADEMARK OF HARRY N. ABRAMS, INC.

ABRAMS The Art of Books
195 Broadway, New York, NY 10007
abramsbooks.com

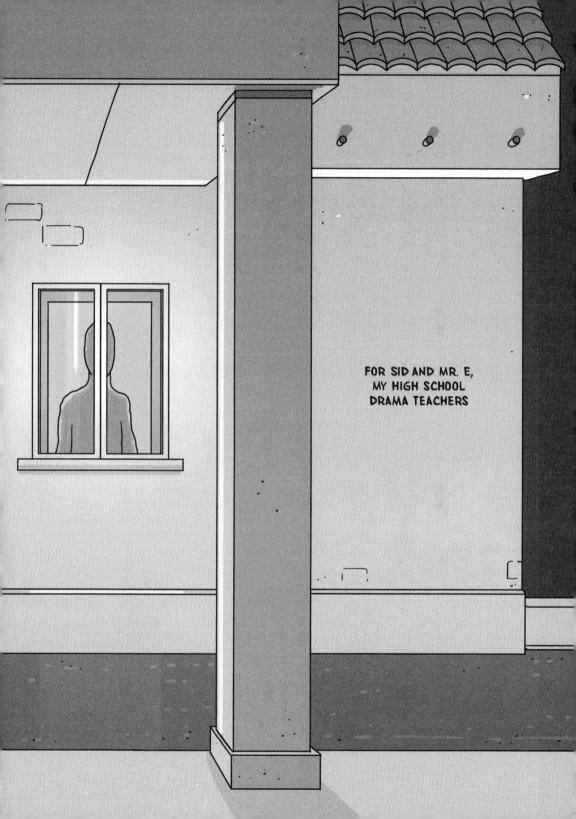

FOR SID AND MR. E,
MY HIGH SCHOOL
DRAMA TEACHERS

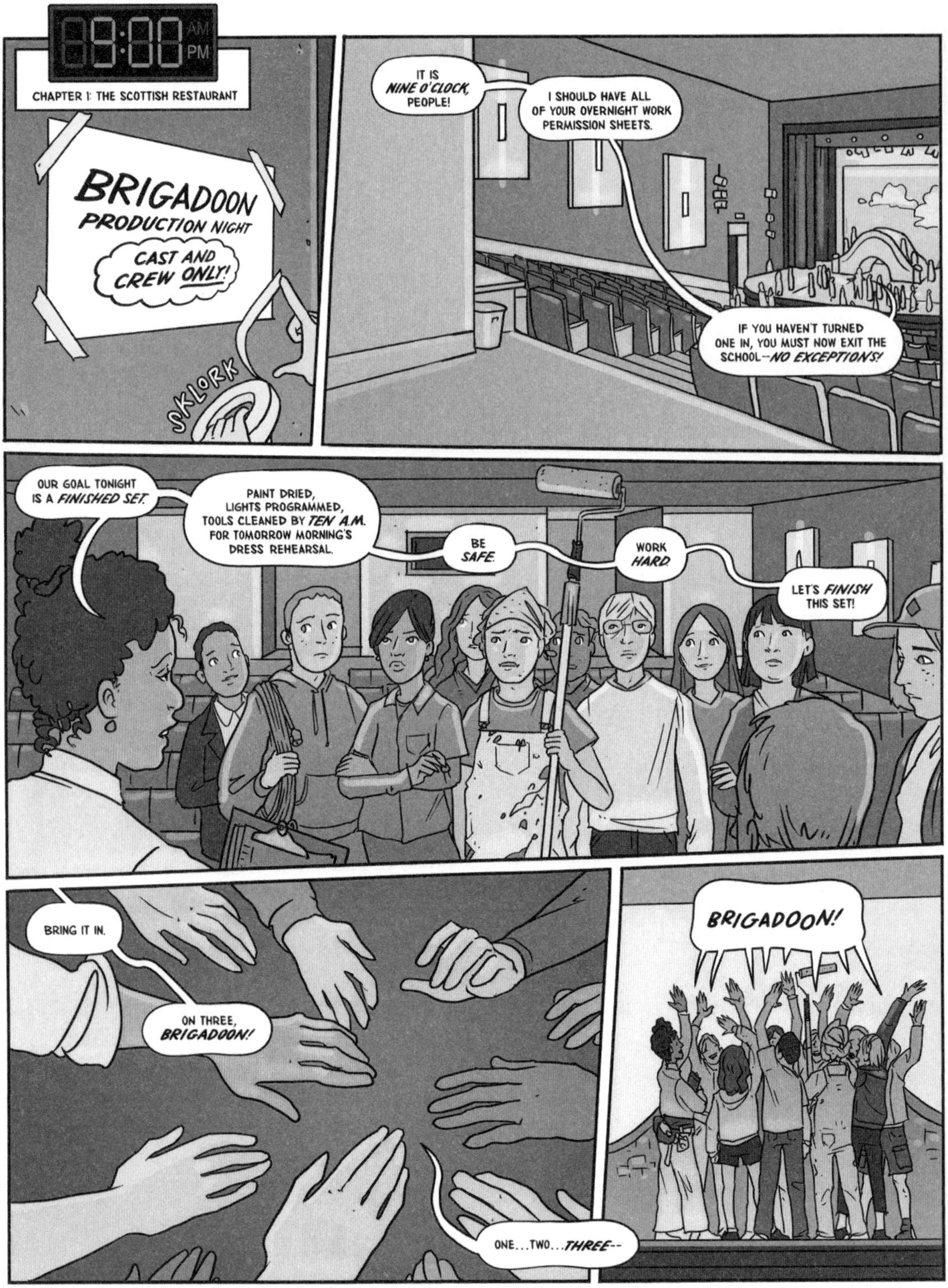
9:00 AM PM
CHAPTER 1: THE SCOTTISH RESTAURANT
BRIGADOON PRODUCTION NIGHT
CAST AND CREW ONLY!
SKLORK
IT IS NINE O'CLOCK, PEOPLE!
I SHOULD HAVE ALL OF YOUR OVERNIGHT WORK PERMISSION SHEETS.
IF YOU HAVEN'T TURNED ONE IN, YOU MUST NOW EXIT THE SCHOOL--NO EXCEPTIONS!
OUR GOAL TONIGHT IS A FINISHED SET.
PAINT DRIED, LIGHTS PROGRAMMED, TOOLS CLEANED BY TEN A.M. FOR TOMORROW MORNING'S DRESS REHEARSAL.
BE SAFE.
WORK HARD.
LET'S FINISH THIS SET!
BRING IT IN.
ON THREE, BRIGADOON!
ONE...TWO...THREE--
BRIGADOON!

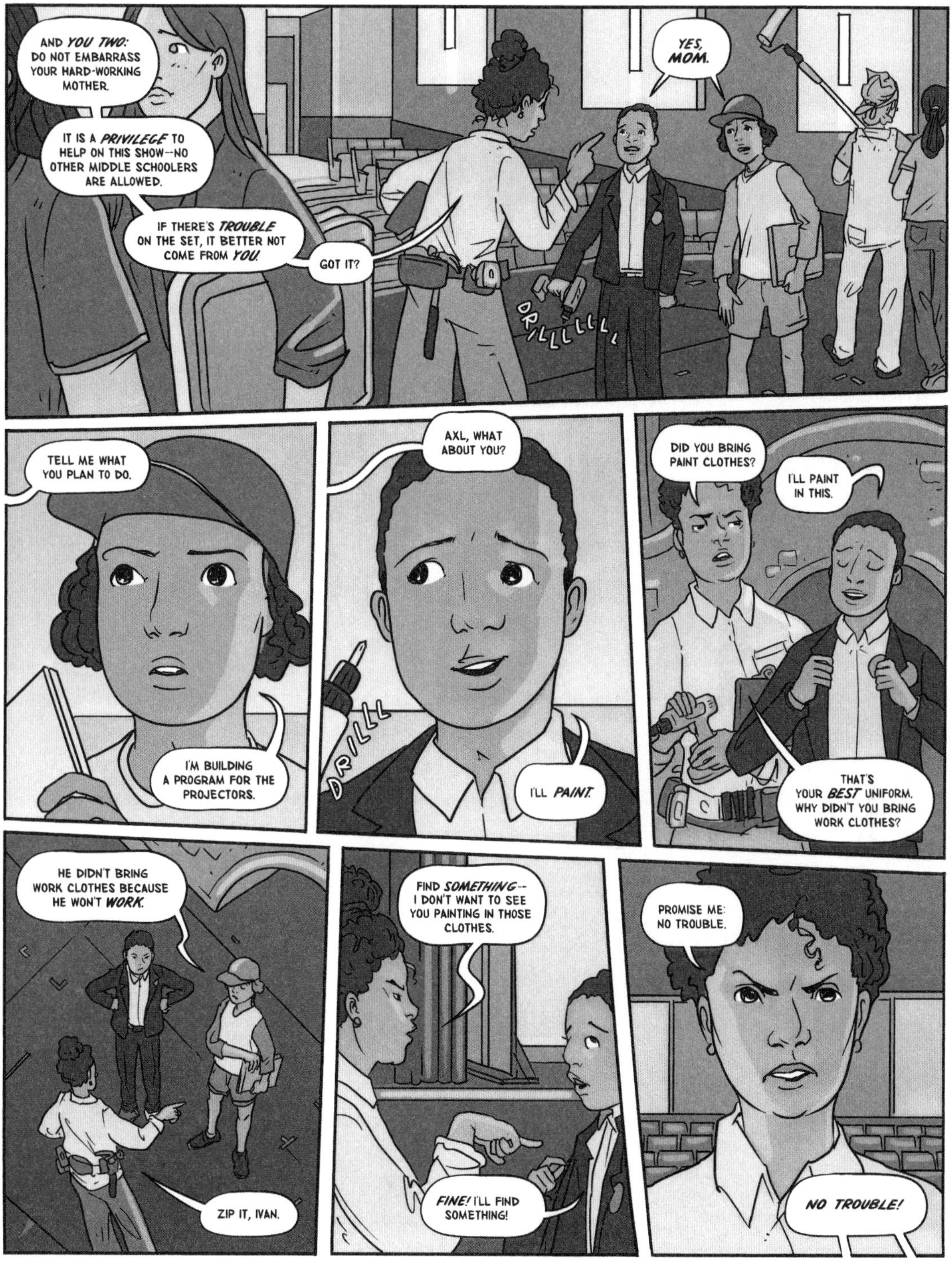
AND YOU TWO: DO NOT EMBARRASS YOUR HARD-WORKING MOTHER.
IT IS A PRIVILEGE TO HELP ON THIS SHOW--NO OTHER MIDDLE SCHOOLERS ARE ALLOWED.
IF THERE'S TROUBLE ON THE SET, IT BETTER NOT COME FROM YOU.
GOT IT?
YES, MOM.
DRILLLLLL
TELL ME WHAT YOU PLAN TO DO.
I'M BUILDING A PROGRAM FOR THE PROJECTORS.
AXL, WHAT ABOUT YOU?
DRILLL
I'LL PAINT.
DID YOU BRING PAINT CLOTHES?
I'LL PAINT IN THIS.
THAT'S YOUR BEST UNIFORM. WHY DIDN'T YOU BRING WORK CLOTHES?
HE DIDN'T BRING WORK CLOTHES BECAUSE HE WON'T WORK.
ZIP IT, IVAN.
FIND SOMETHING-- I DON'T WANT TO SEE YOU PAINTING IN THOSE CLOTHES.
FINE! I'LL FIND SOMETHING!
PROMISE ME: NO TROUBLE.
NO TROUBLE!

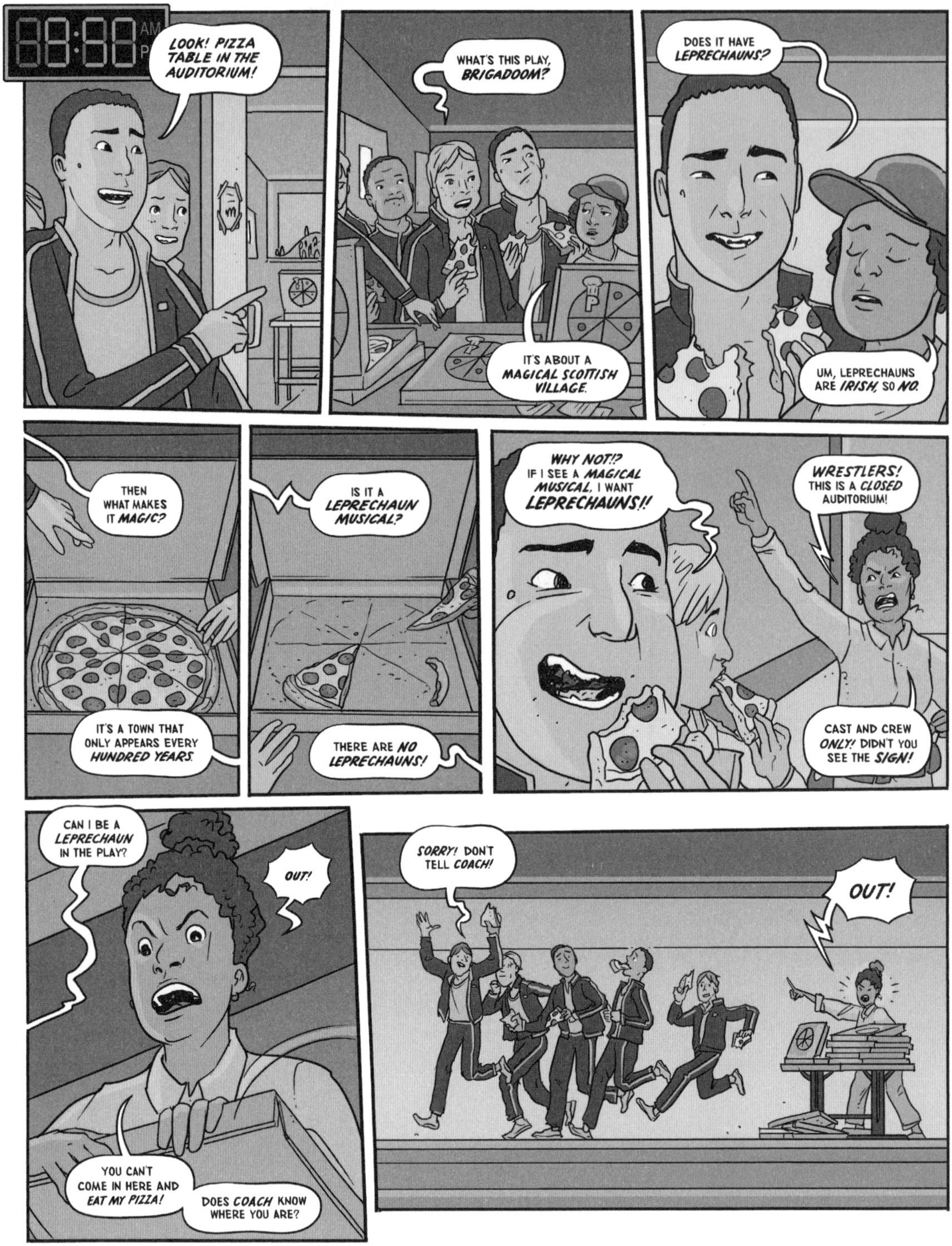
LOOK! PIZZA TABLE IN THE AUDITORIUM!
WHAT'S THIS PLAY, BRIGADOOM?
IT'S ABOUT A MAGICAL SCOTTISH VILLAGE.
DOES IT HAVE LEPRECHAUNS?
UM, LEPRECHAUNS ARE IRISH, SO NO.
THEN WHAT MAKES IT MAGIC?
IT'S A TOWN THAT ONLY APPEARS EVERY HUNDRED YEARS.
IS IT A LEPRECHAUN MUSICAL?
THERE ARE NO LEPRECHAUNS!
WHY NOT!? IF I SEE A MAGICAL MUSICAL, I WANT LEPRECHAUNS!!
WRESTLERS! THIS IS A CLOSED AUDITORIUM!
CAST AND CREW ONLY! DIDN'T YOU SEE THE SIGN!
CAN I BE A LEPRECHAUN IN THE PLAY?
OUT!
YOU CAN'T COME IN HERE AND EAT MY PIZZA!
DOES COACH KNOW WHERE YOU ARE?
SORRY! DON'T TELL COACH!
OUT!

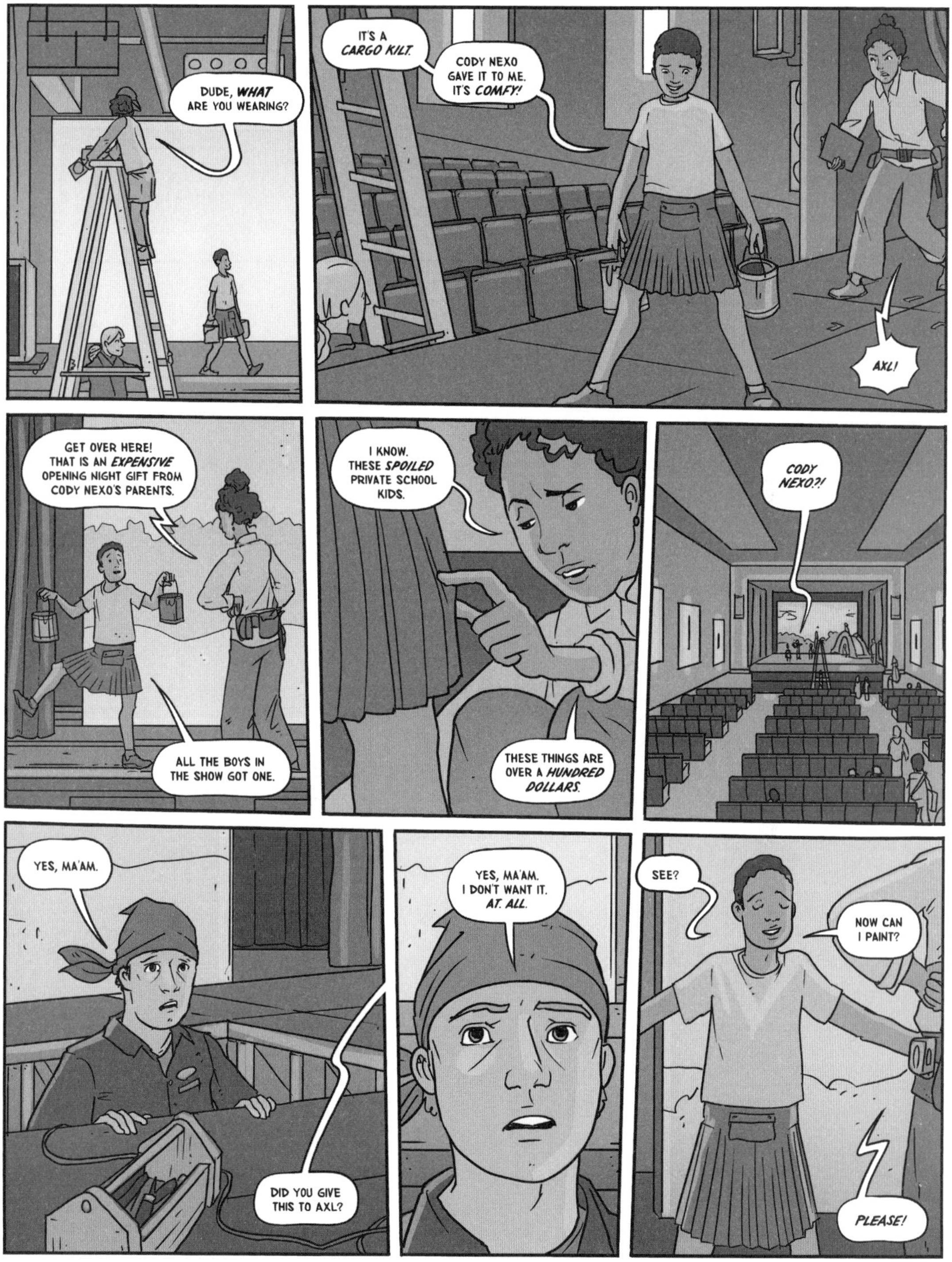
DUDE, WHAT ARE YOU WEARING?
IT'S A CARGO KILT.
CODY NEXO GAVE IT TO ME. IT'S COMFY!
AXL!
GET OVER HERE! THAT IS AN EXPENSIVE OPENING NIGHT GIFT FROM CODY NEXO'S PARENTS.
ALL THE BOYS IN THE SHOW GOT ONE.
I KNOW. THESE SPOILED PRIVATE SCHOOL KIDS.
THESE THINGS ARE OVER A HUNDRED DOLLARS.
CODY NEXO?!
YES, MA'AM.
DID YOU GIVE THIS TO AXL?
YES, MA'AM. I DON'T WANT IT. AT. ALL.
SEE?
NOW CAN I PAINT?
PLEASE!

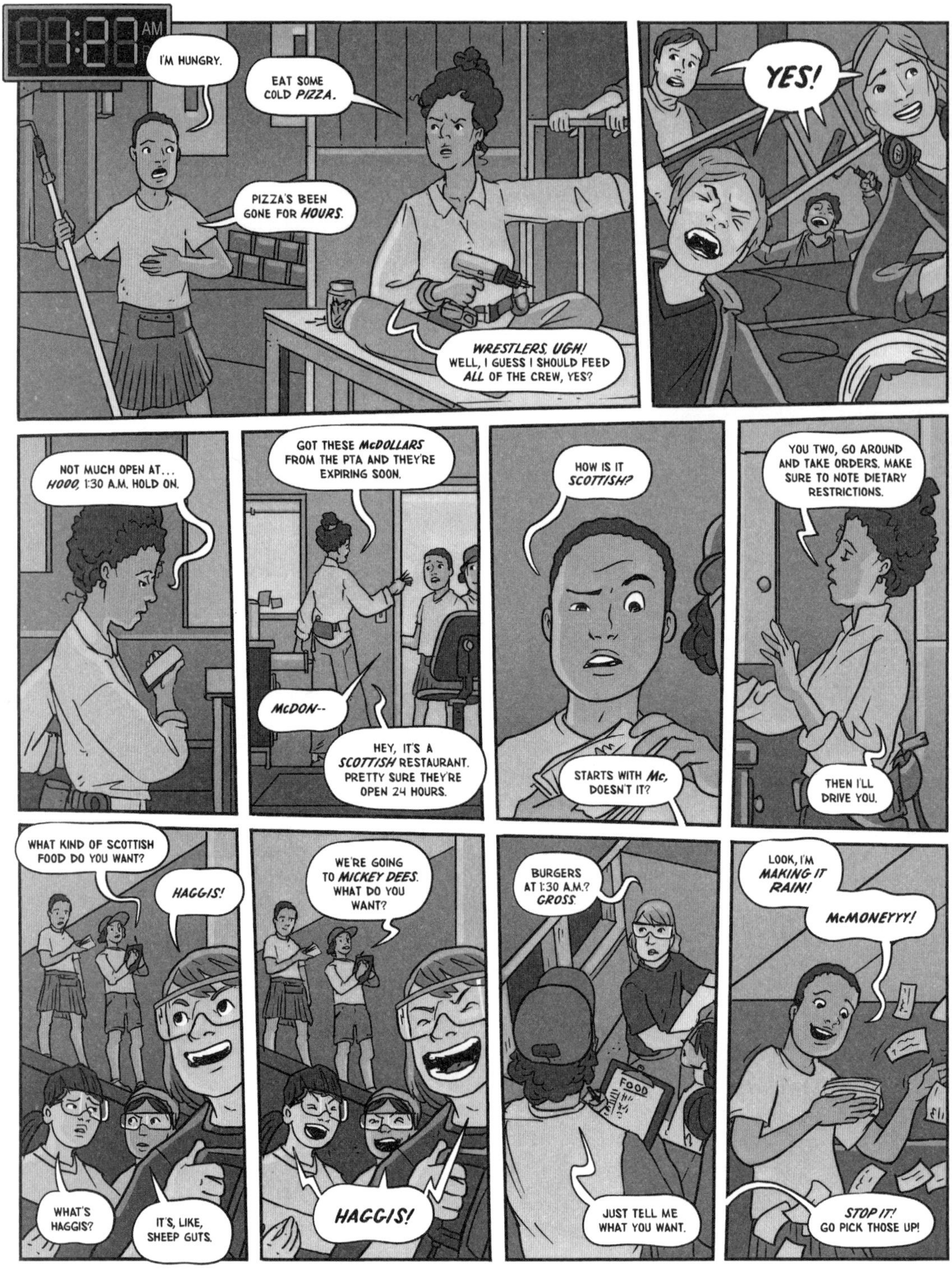
11:21 AM
I'M HUNGRY.
EAT SOME COLD *PIZZA*.
PIZZA'S BEEN GONE FOR *HOURS*.
WRESTLERS, UGH! WELL, I GUESS I SHOULD FEED *ALL* OF THE CREW, YES?
YES!
NOT MUCH OPEN AT... *HOOO*, 1:30 A.M. HOLD ON.
GOT THESE *McDOLLARS* FROM THE PTA AND THEY'RE EXPIRING SOON.
McDON--
HEY, IT'S A *SCOTTISH* RESTAURANT. PRETTY SURE THEY'RE OPEN 24 HOURS.
HOW IS IT *SCOTTISH?*
STARTS WITH *Mc*, DOESN'T IT?
YOU TWO, GO AROUND AND TAKE ORDERS. MAKE SURE TO NOTE DIETARY RESTRICTIONS.
THEN I'LL DRIVE YOU.
WHAT KIND OF SCOTTISH FOOD DO YOU WANT?
HAGGIS!
WHAT'S HAGGIS?
IT'S, LIKE, SHEEP GUTS.
WE'RE GOING TO *MICKEY DEES*. WHAT DO YOU WANT?
HAGGIS!
BURGERS AT 1:30 A.M.? *GROSS*.
FOOD
JUST TELL ME WHAT YOU WANT.
LOOK, I'M *MAKING IT RAIN!*
McMONEYYY!
STOP IT! GO PICK THOSE UP!

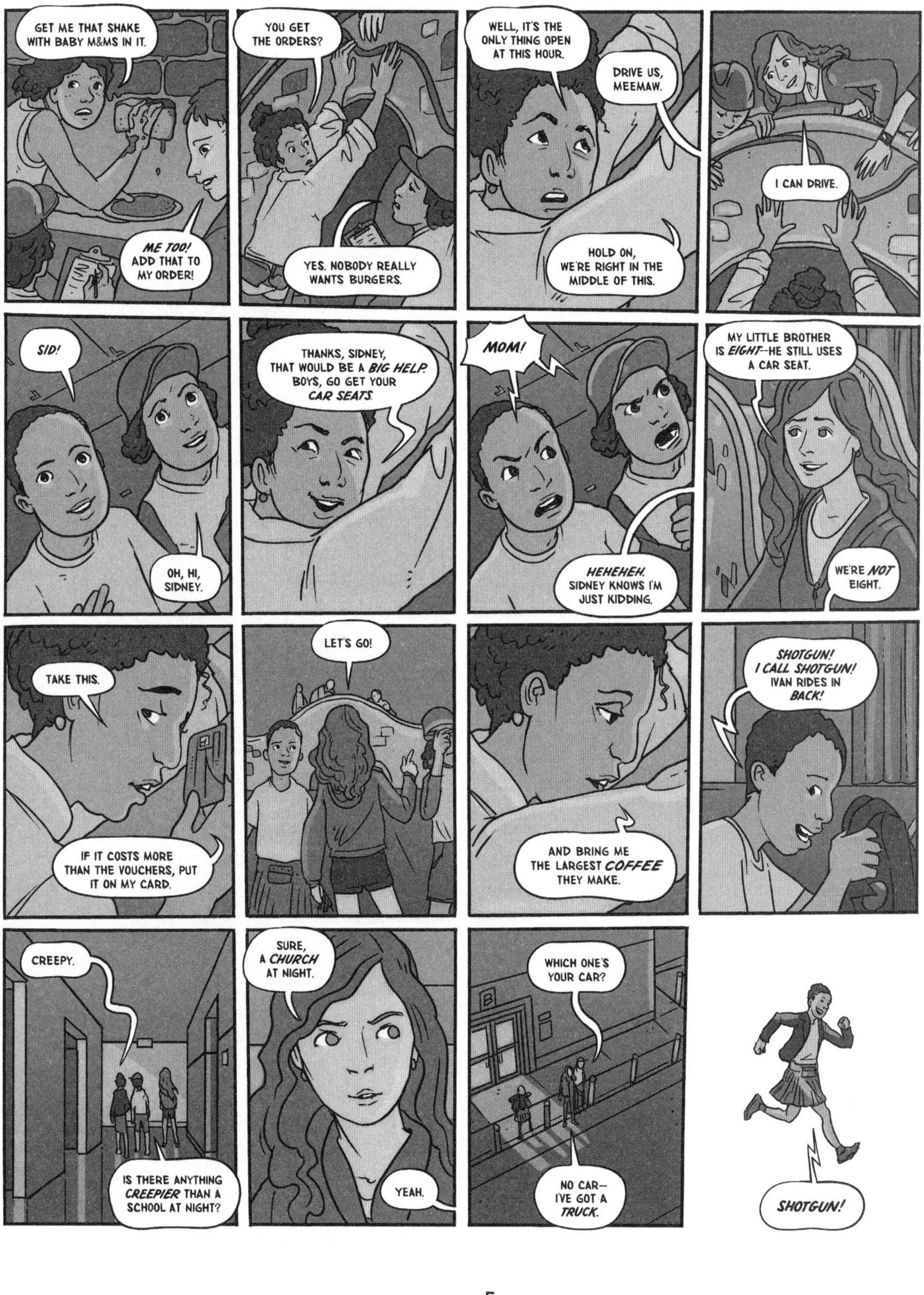
GET ME THAT SHAKE WITH BABY M&MS IN IT.
ME TOO! ADD THAT TO MY ORDER!
YOU GET THE ORDERS?
YES. NOBODY REALLY WANTS BURGERS.
WELL, IT'S THE ONLY THING OPEN AT THIS HOUR.
DRIVE US, MEEMAW.
HOLD ON, WE'RE RIGHT IN THE MIDDLE OF THIS.
I CAN DRIVE.
SID!
OH, HI, SIDNEY.
THANKS, SIDNEY, THAT WOULD BE A BIG HELP. BOYS, GO GET YOUR CAR SEATS.
MOM!
HEHEHEH. SIDNEY KNOWS I'M JUST KIDDING.
MY LITTLE BROTHER IS EIGHT--HE STILL USES A CAR SEAT.
WE'RE NOT EIGHT.
TAKE THIS.
IF IT COSTS MORE THAN THE VOUCHERS, PUT IT ON MY CARD.
LET'S GO!
AND BRING ME THE LARGEST COFFEE THEY MAKE.
SHOTGUN! I CALL SHOTGUN! IVAN RIDES IN BACK!
CREEPY.
IS THERE ANYTHING CREEPIER THAN A SCHOOL AT NIGHT?
SURE, A CHURCH AT NIGHT.
YEAH.
WHICH ONE'S YOUR CAR?
NO CAR— I'VE GOT A TRUCK.
SHOTGUN!

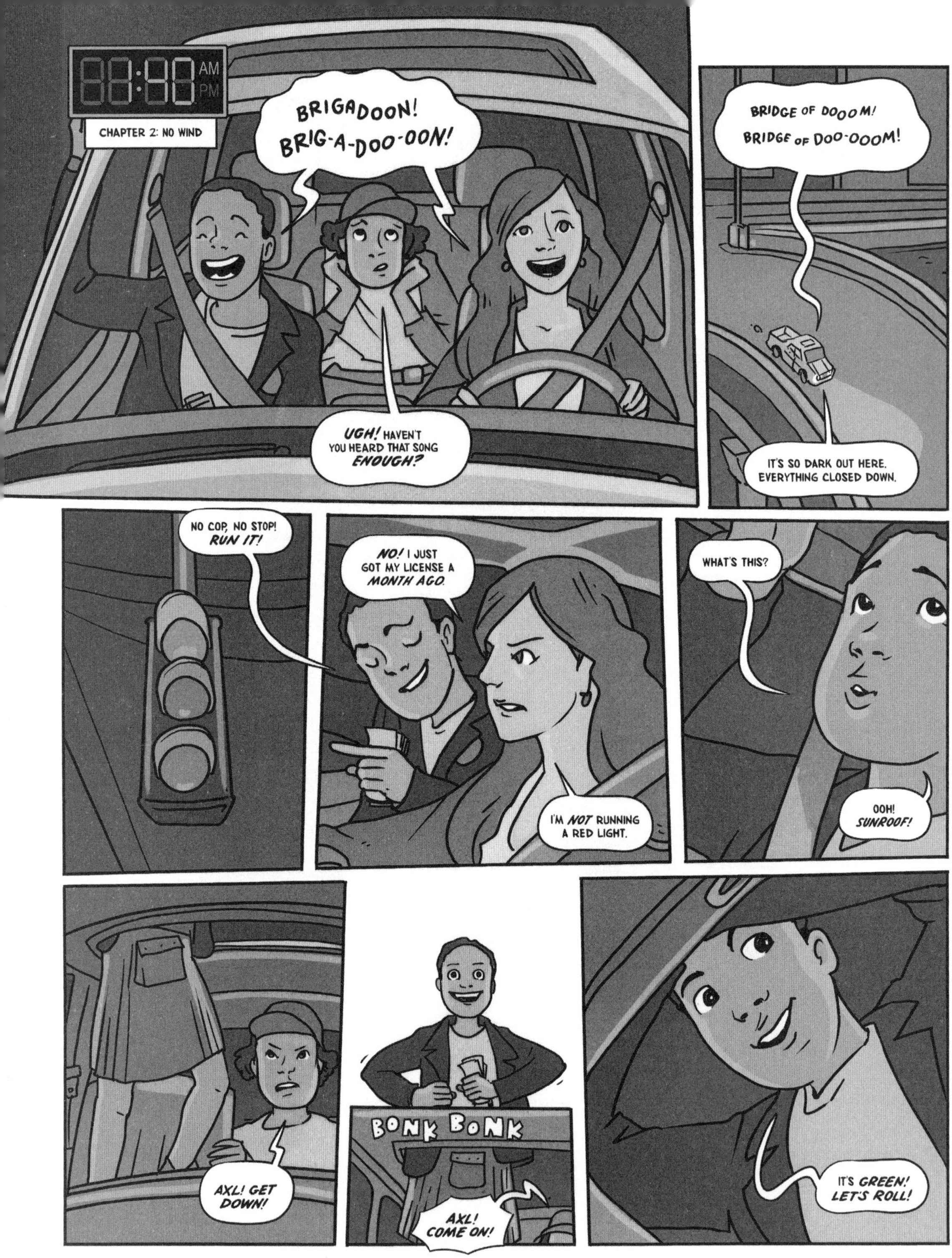

CHAPTER 2: NO WIND
BRIGADOON! BRIG-A-DOO-OON!
UGH! HAVEN'T YOU HEARD THAT SONG ENOUGH?
BRIDGE OF DOOOM! BRIDGE OF DOO-OOOM!
IT'S SO DARK OUT HERE. EVERYTHING CLOSED DOWN.
NO COP, NO STOP! RUN IT!
NO! I JUST GOT MY LICENSE A MONTH AGO.
I'M NOT RUNNING A RED LIGHT.
WHAT'S THIS?
OOH! SUNROOF!
AXL! GET DOWN!
BONK BONK
AXL! COME ON!
IT'S GREEN! LET'S ROLL!

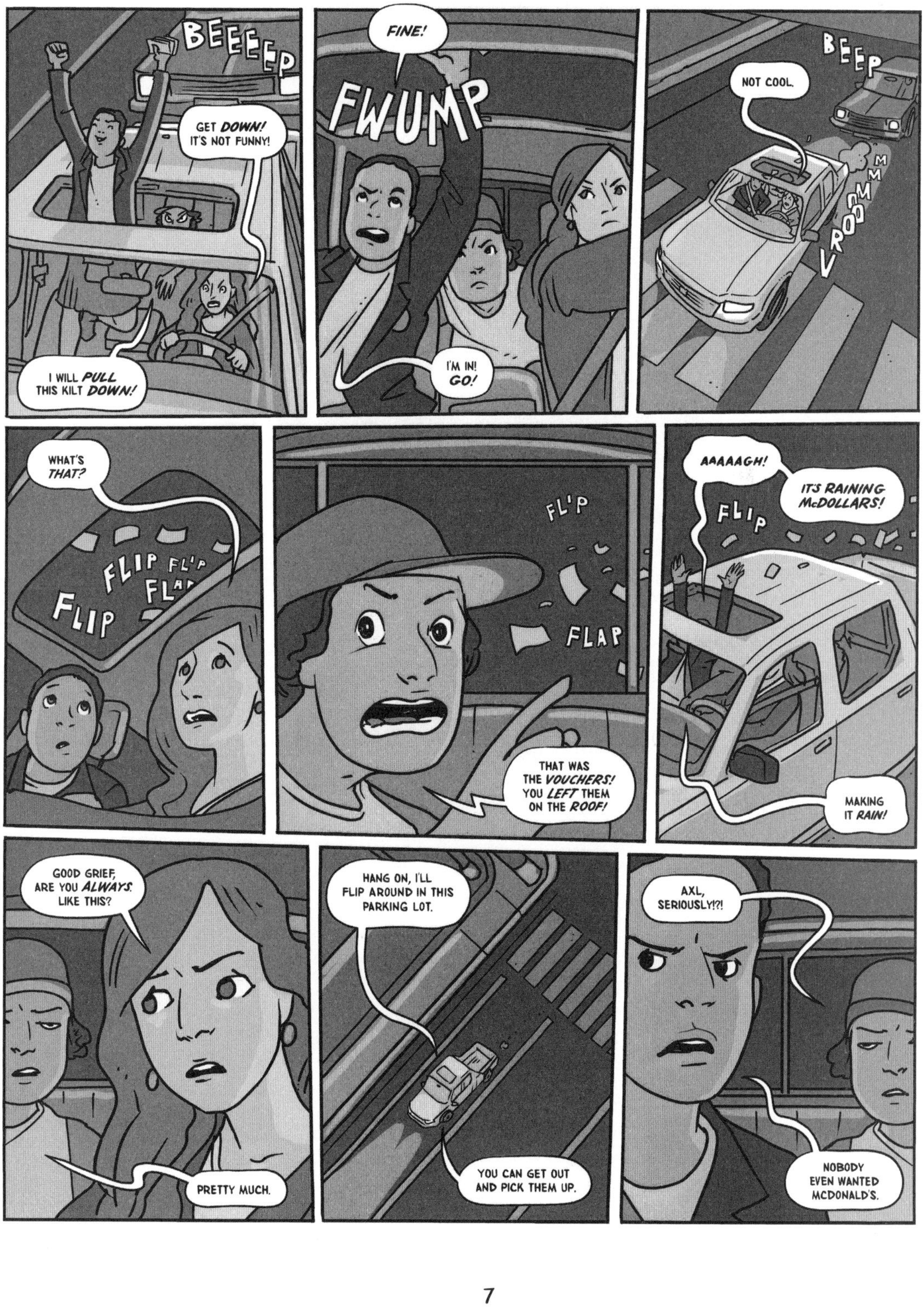
BEEEEEP
GET DOWN! IT'S NOT FUNNY!
I WILL PULL THIS KILT DOWN!
FINE!
FWUMP
I'M IN! GO!
BEEP
NOT COOL.
VROOMMM
WHAT'S THAT?
FLIP FLIP FL'P
FL'P
FLAP
THAT WAS THE VOUCHERS! YOU LEFT THEM ON THE ROOF!
AAAAAGH!
IT'S RAINING McDOLLARS!
FLIP
MAKING IT RAIN!
GOOD GRIEF, ARE YOU ALWAYS LIKE THIS?
PRETTY MUCH.
HANG ON, I'LL FLIP AROUND IN THIS PARKING LOT.
YOU CAN GET OUT AND PICK THEM UP.
AXL, SERIOUSLY!?!
NOBODY EVEN WANTED MCDONALD'S.

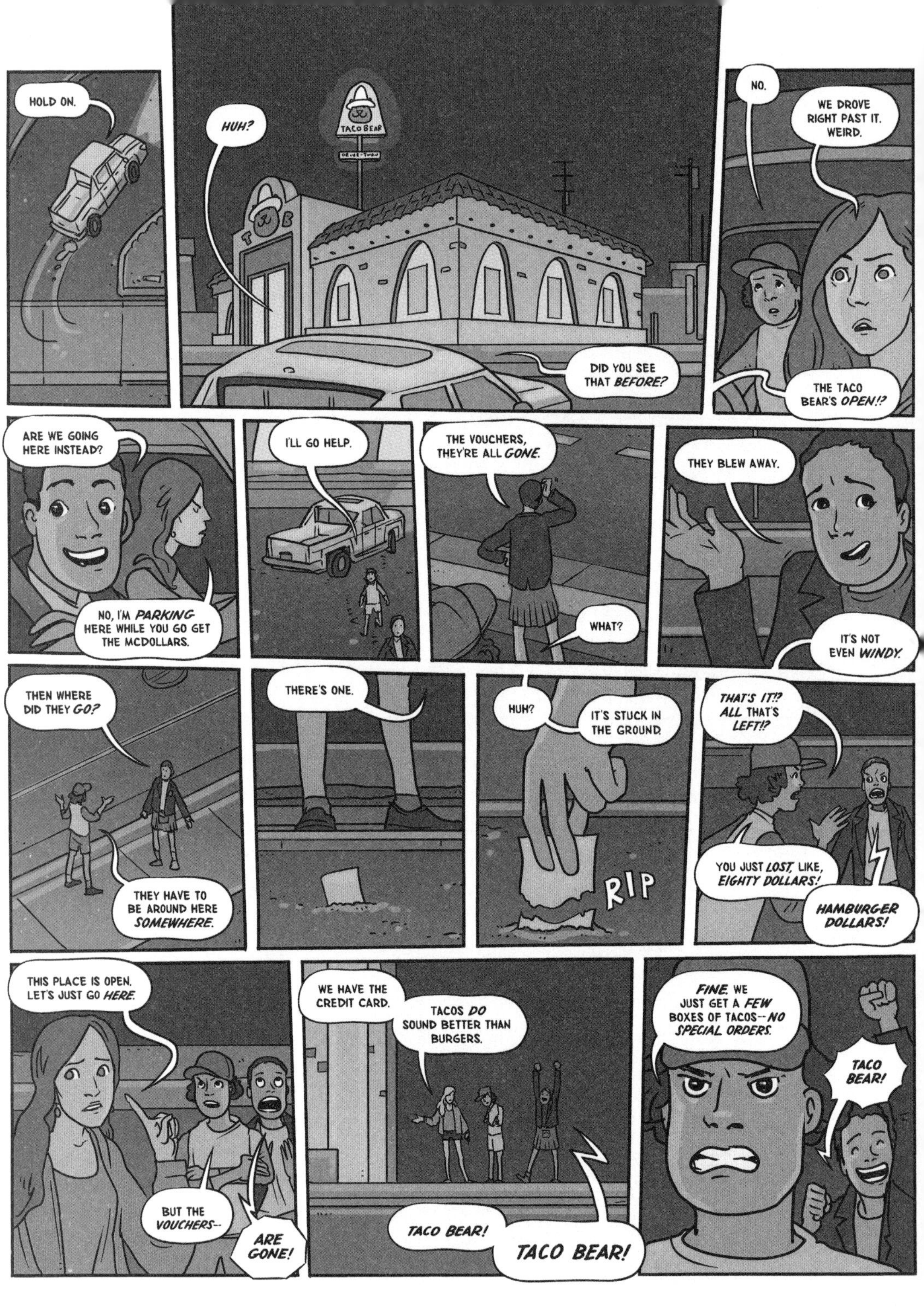
HOLD ON.
HUH?
TACO BEAR
DRIVE-THRU
DID YOU SEE THAT *BEFORE?*
NO.
WE DROVE RIGHT PAST IT. WEIRD.
THE TACO BEAR'S *OPEN!?*
ARE WE GOING HERE INSTEAD?
NO, I'M *PARKING* HERE WHILE YOU GO GET THE MCDOLLARS.
I'LL GO HELP.
THE VOUCHERS, THEY'RE ALL *GONE.*
WHAT?
THEY BLEW AWAY.
IT'S NOT EVEN *WINDY.*
THEN WHERE DID THEY *GO?*
THEY HAVE TO BE AROUND HERE *SOMEWHERE.*
THERE'S ONE.
HUH?
IT'S STUCK IN THE GROUND.
RIP
THAT'S IT!? ALL THAT'S LEFT!?
YOU JUST *LOST,* LIKE, *EIGHTY DOLLARS!*
HAMBURGER DOLLARS!
THIS PLACE IS OPEN. LET'S JUST GO *HERE.*
BUT THE *VOUCHERS--*
ARE GONE!
WE HAVE THE CREDIT CARD.
TACOS *DO* SOUND BETTER THAN BURGERS.
TACO BEAR!
TACO BEAR!
FINE. WE JUST GET A *FEW* BOXES OF TACOS--*NO SPECIAL ORDERS.*
TACO BEAR!

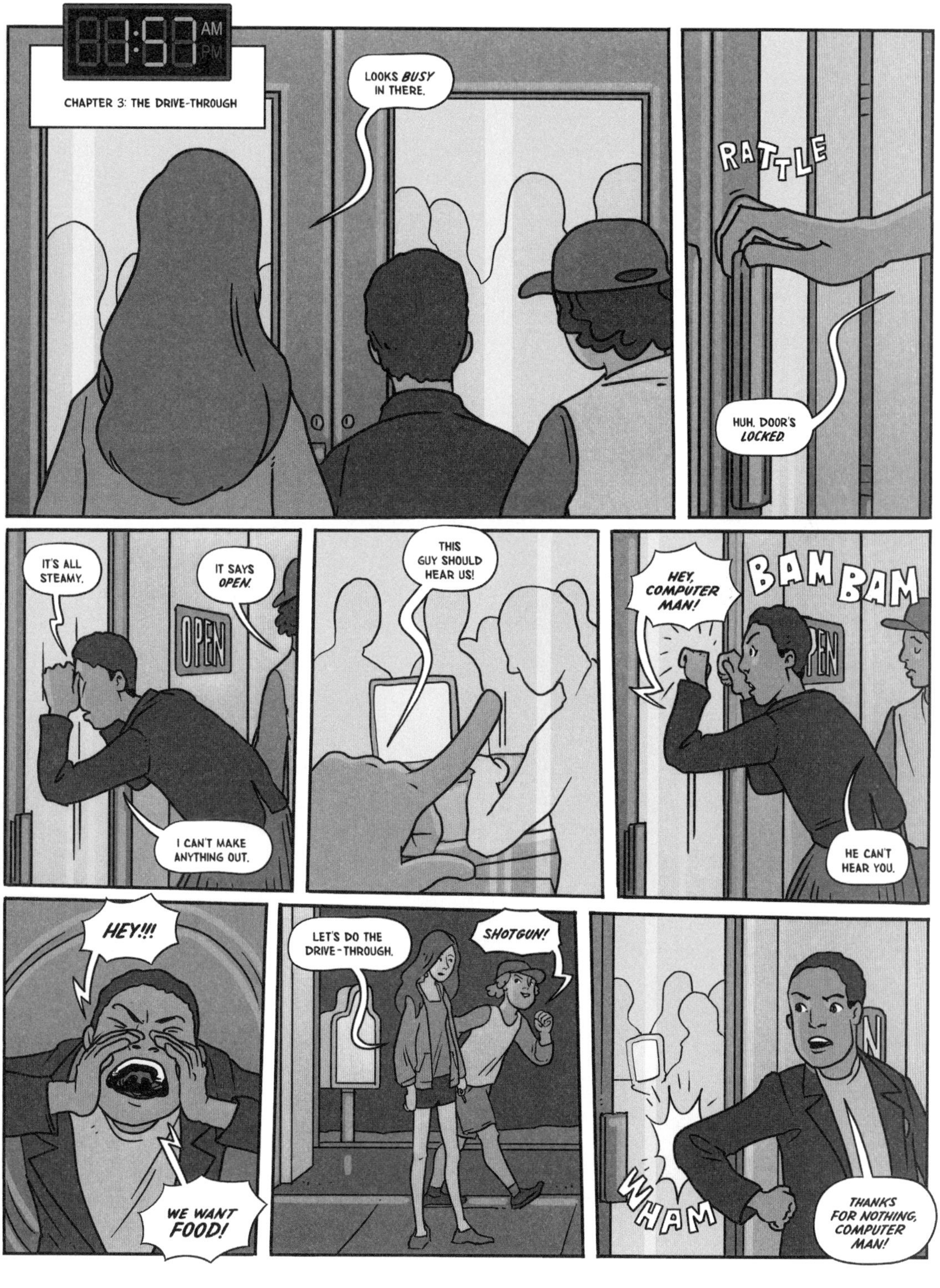
11:57 AM PM
CHAPTER 3: THE DRIVE-THROUGH
LOOKS BUSY IN THERE.
RATTLE
HUH. DOOR'S LOCKED.
IT'S ALL STEAMY.
IT SAYS OPEN.
OPEN
I CAN'T MAKE ANYTHING OUT.
THIS GUY SHOULD HEAR US!
HEY, COMPUTER MAN!
BAM BAM
HE CAN'T HEAR YOU.
HEY!!!
WE WANT FOOD!
LET'S DO THE DRIVE-THROUGH.
SHOTGUN!
WHAM
THANKS FOR NOTHING, COMPUTER MAN!

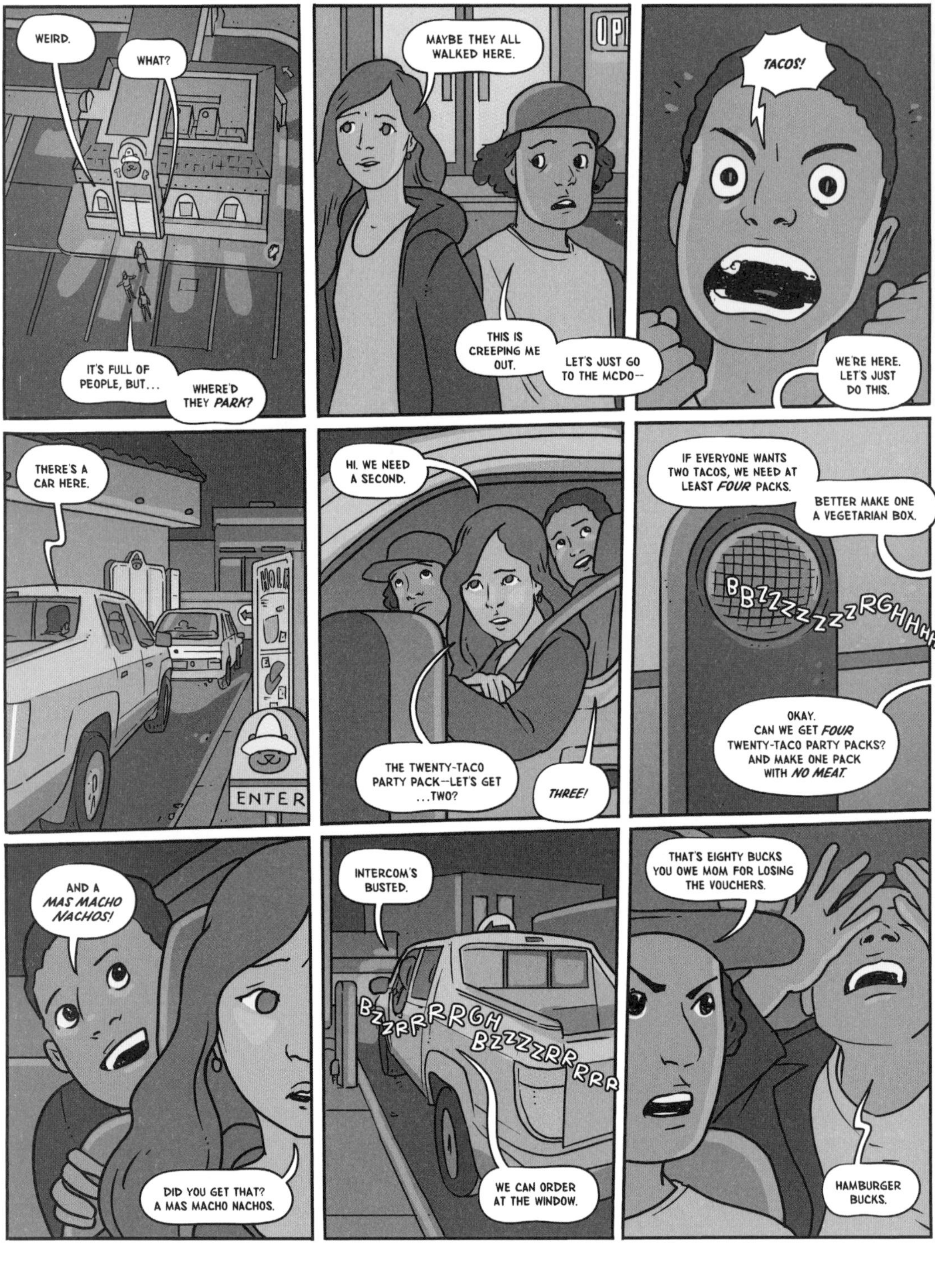
WEIRD.
WHAT?
IT'S FULL OF PEOPLE, BUT...
WHERE'D THEY *PARK?*
OPE
MAYBE THEY ALL WALKED HERE.
THIS IS CREEPING ME OUT.
LET'S JUST GO TO THE MCDO--
TACOS!
WE'RE HERE. LET'S JUST DO THIS.
THERE'S A CAR HERE.
ENTER
HI, WE NEED A SECOND.
THE TWENTY-TACO PARTY PACK--LET'S GET ...TWO?
THREE!
IF EVERYONE WANTS TWO TACOS, WE NEED AT LEAST *FOUR* PACKS.
BETTER MAKE ONE A VEGETARIAN BOX.
BBZZZZZZZZRGHHHH
OKAY. CAN WE GET *FOUR* TWENTY-TACO PARTY PACKS? AND MAKE ONE PACK WITH *NO MEAT.*
AND A *MAS MACHO NACHOS!*
DID YOU GET THAT? A MAS MACHO NACHOS.
INTERCOM'S BUSTED.
BZZRRRRGH BZZZZRRRRRR
WE CAN ORDER AT THE WINDOW.
THAT'S EIGHTY BUCKS YOU OWE MOM FOR LOSING THE VOUCHERS.
HAMBURGER BUCKS.

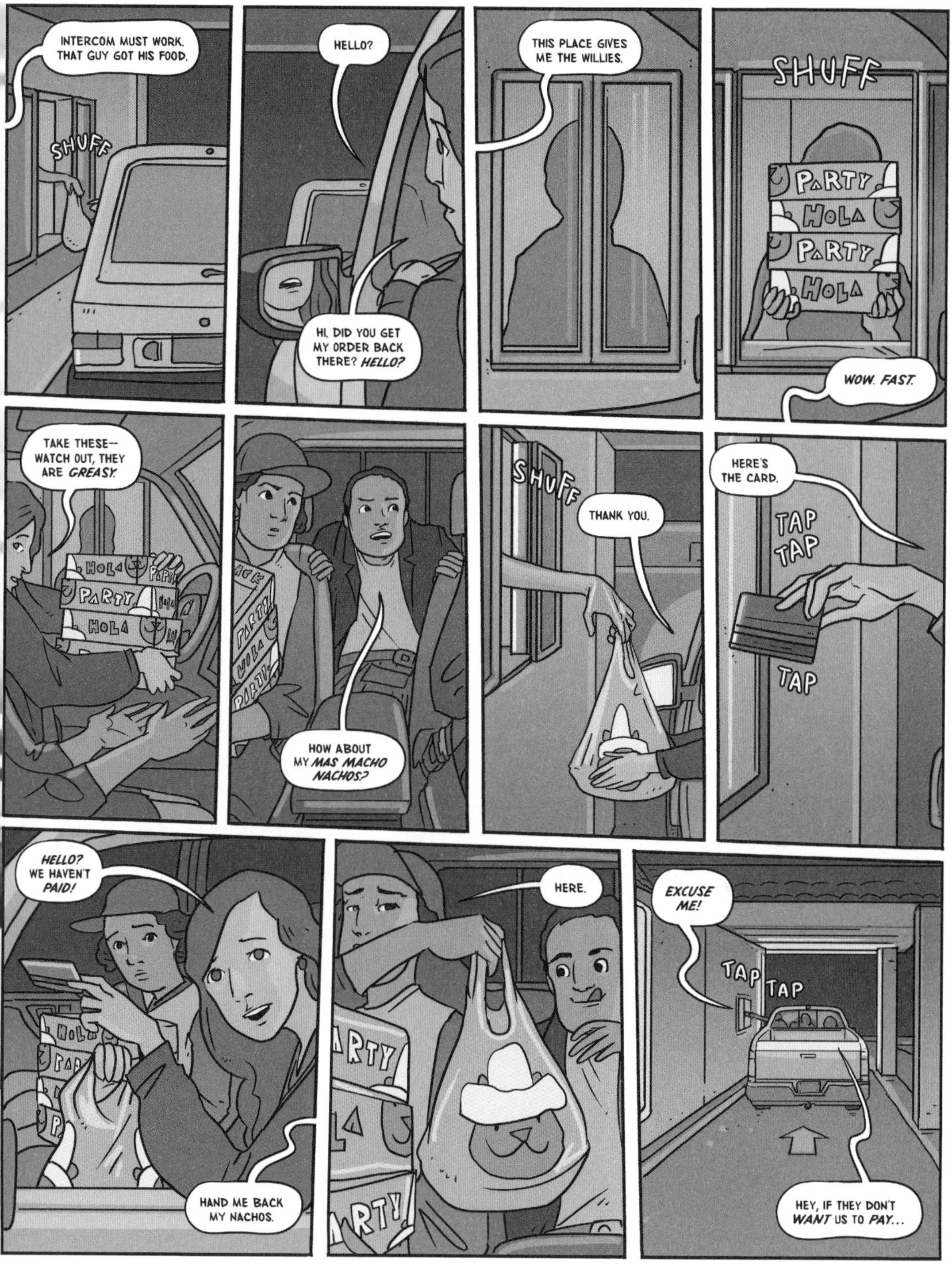
INTERCOM MUST WORK. THAT GUY GOT HIS FOOD.
SHUFF
HELLO?
HI, DID YOU GET MY ORDER BACK THERE? HELLO?
THIS PLACE GIVES ME THE WILLIES.
SHUFF
PARTY HOLA PARTY HOLA
WOW. FAST.
TAKE THESE-- WATCH OUT, THEY ARE GREASY.
HOW ABOUT MY MAS MACHO NACHOS?
SHUFF
THANK YOU.
HERE'S THE CARD.
TAP TAP
TAP
HELLO? WE HAVEN'T PAID!
HAND ME BACK MY NACHOS.
HERE.
EXCUSE ME!
TAP TAP
HEY, IF THEY DON'T WANT US TO PAY...

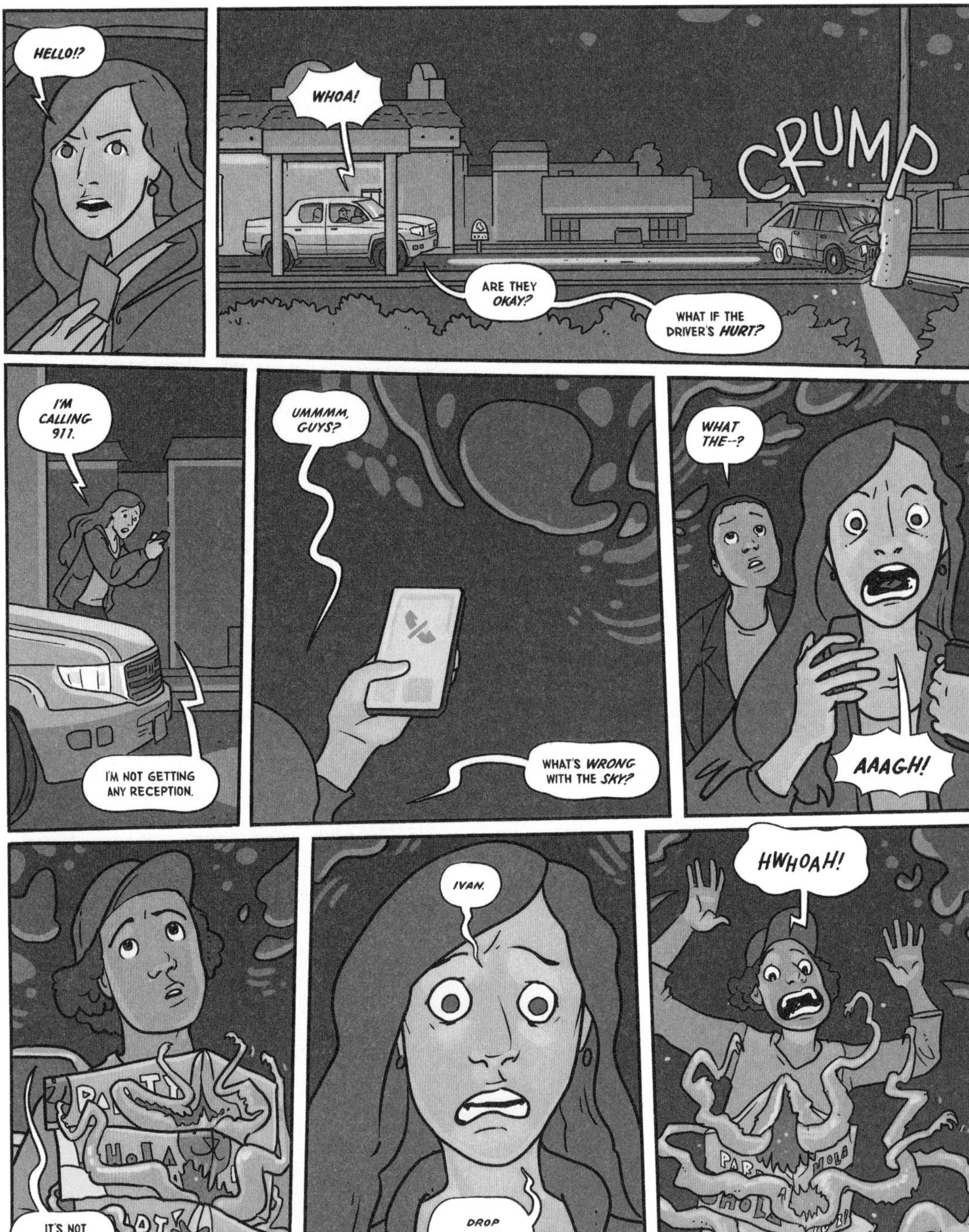
HELLO!?
WHOA!
CRUMP
ARE THEY OKAY?
WHAT IF THE DRIVER'S HURT?
I'M CALLING 911.
I'M NOT GETTING ANY RECEPTION.
UMMMM, GUYS?
WHAT'S WRONG WITH THE SKY?
WHAT THE--?
AAAGH!
IT'S NOT THAT WEIRD.
HUH?
IVAN.
DROP THOSE BOXES.
HWHOAH!

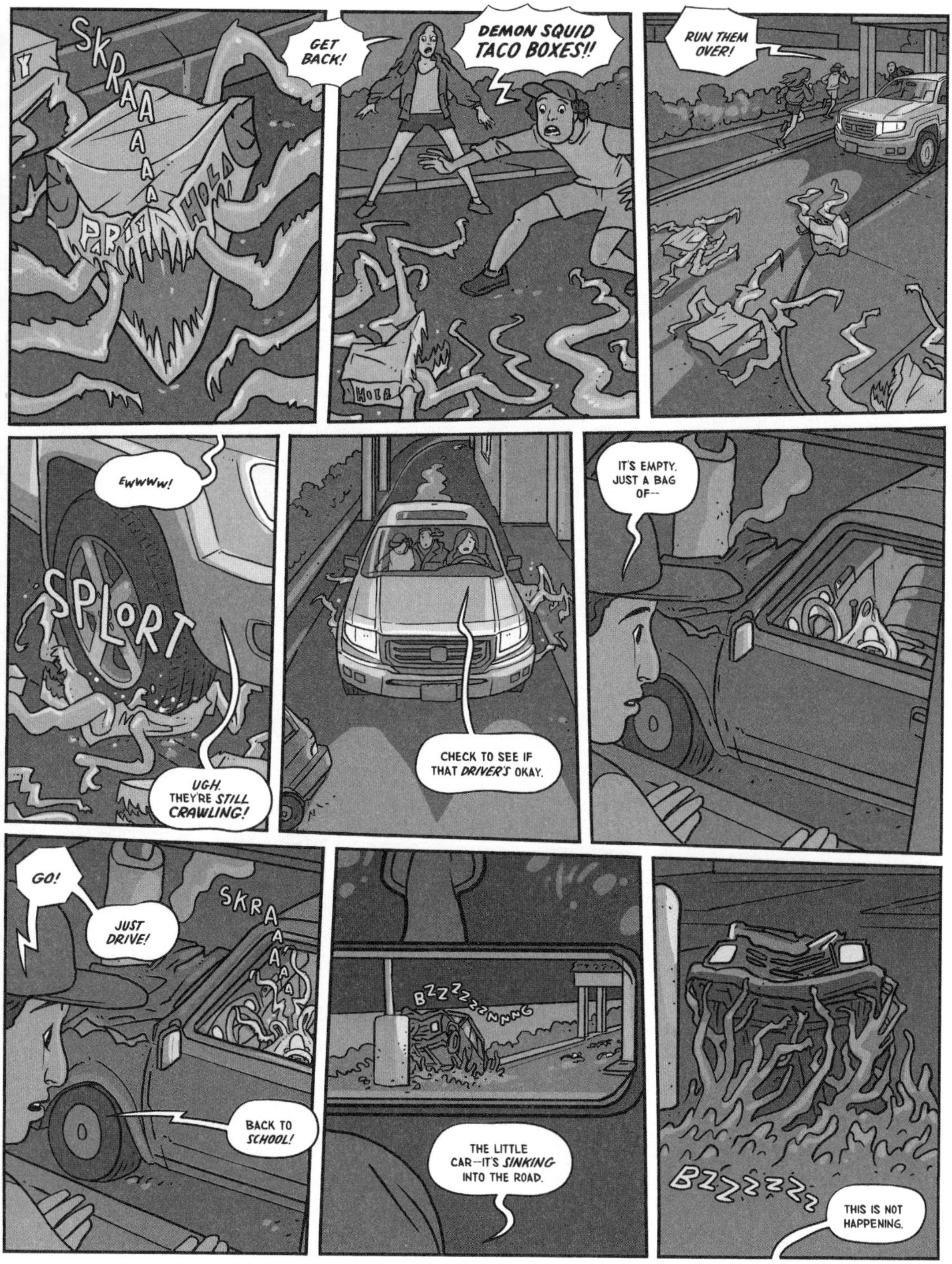
SKRAAAAAAA
PRÍY HOLA
GET BACK!
DEMON SQUID TACO BOXES!!
HOLA
RUN THEM OVER!
EWWWW!
SPLORT
UGH. THEY'RE STILL CRAWLING!
CHECK TO SEE IF THAT DRIVER'S OKAY.
IT'S EMPTY. JUST A BAG OF--
GO!
JUST DRIVE!
SKRAAAAA
BACK TO SCHOOL!
BZZZZZZNNNG
THE LITTLE CAR--IT'S SINKING INTO THE ROAD.
BZZZZZZ
THIS IS NOT HAPPENING.

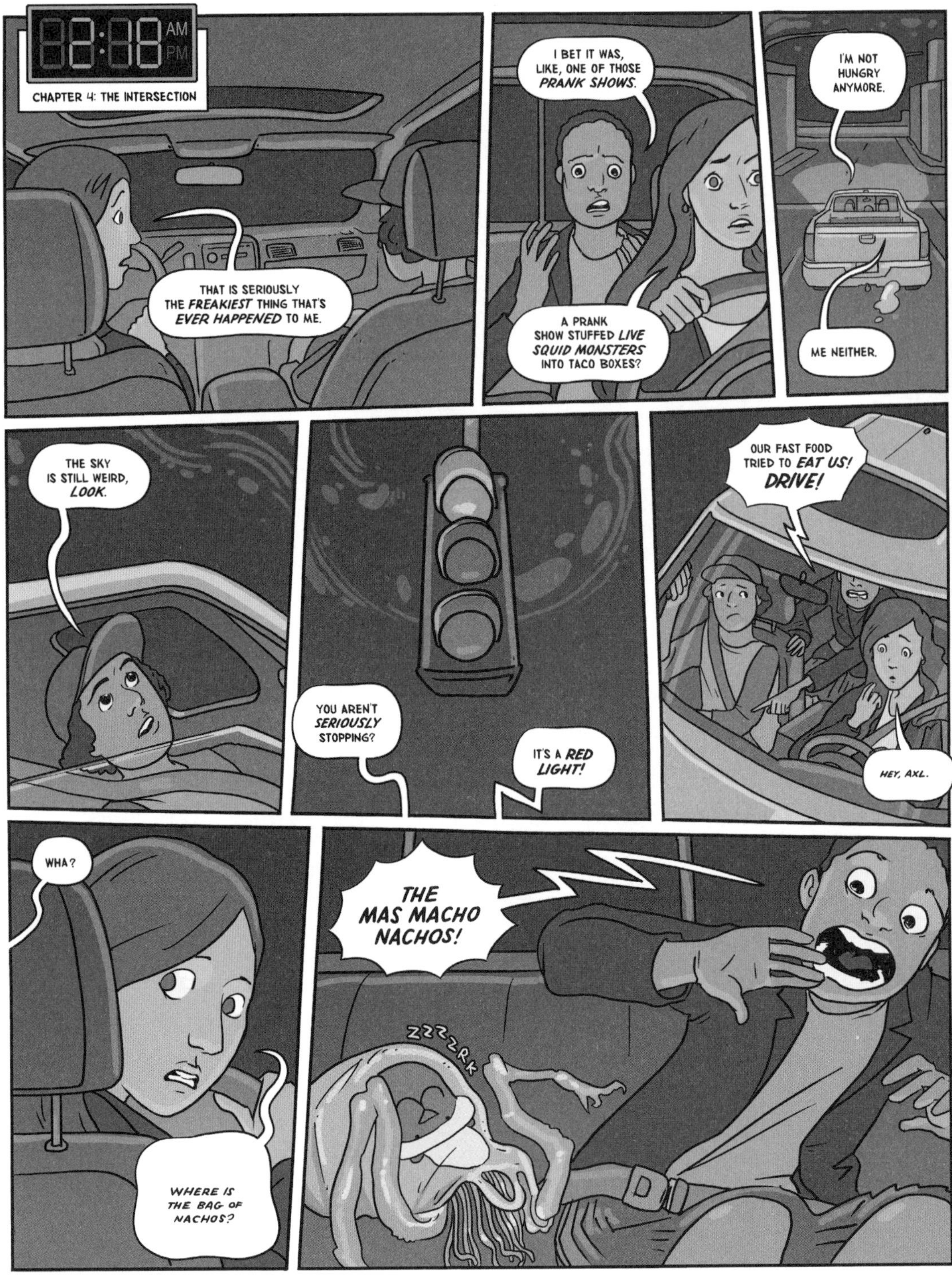
12:18 AM PM
CHAPTER 4: THE INTERSECTION
THAT IS SERIOUSLY THE FREAKIEST THING THAT'S EVER HAPPENED TO ME.
I BET IT WAS, LIKE, ONE OF THOSE PRANK SHOWS.
A PRANK SHOW STUFFED LIVE SQUID MONSTERS INTO TACO BOXES?
I'M NOT HUNGRY ANYMORE.
ME NEITHER.
THE SKY IS STILL WEIRD, LOOK.
YOU AREN'T SERIOUSLY STOPPING?
IT'S A RED LIGHT!
OUR FAST FOOD TRIED TO EAT US! DRIVE!
HEY, AXL.
WHA?
WHERE IS THE BAG OF NACHOS?
THE MAS MACHO NACHOS!
ZZZZRK

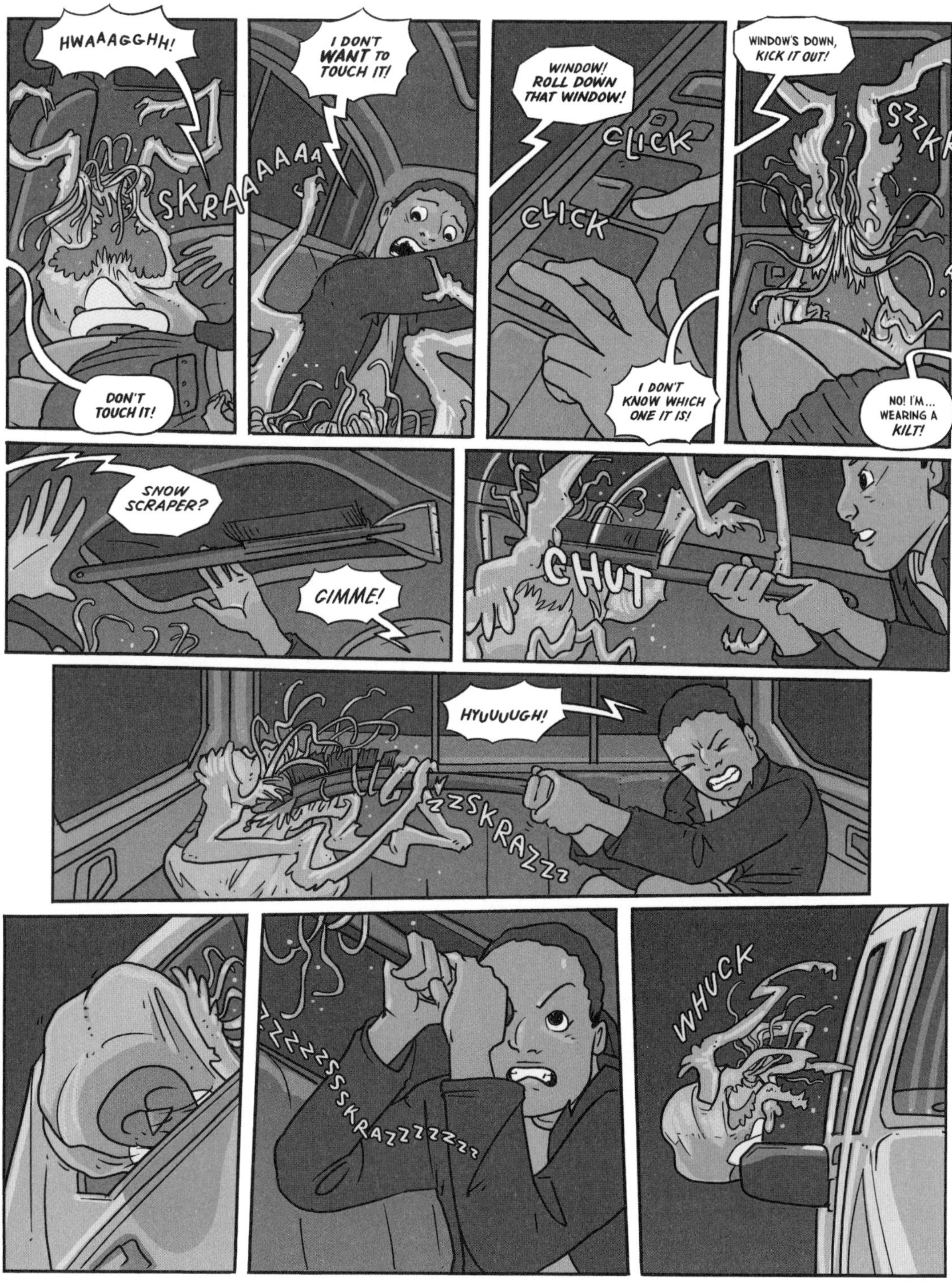
HWAAAGGHH!
SKRAAAAAAA
DON'T TOUCH IT!
I DON'T WANT TO TOUCH IT!
WINDOW! ROLL DOWN THAT WINDOW!
CLICK
CLICK
I DON'T KNOW WHICH ONE IT IS!
WINDOW'S DOWN, KICK IT OUT!
SZZKRAAAAA
NO! I'M... WEARING A KILT!
SNOW SCRAPER?
GIMME!
CHUT
HYUUUUGH!
ZZSKRAZZZZ
ZZZZZZSSSKRAZZZZZZZ
WHUCK

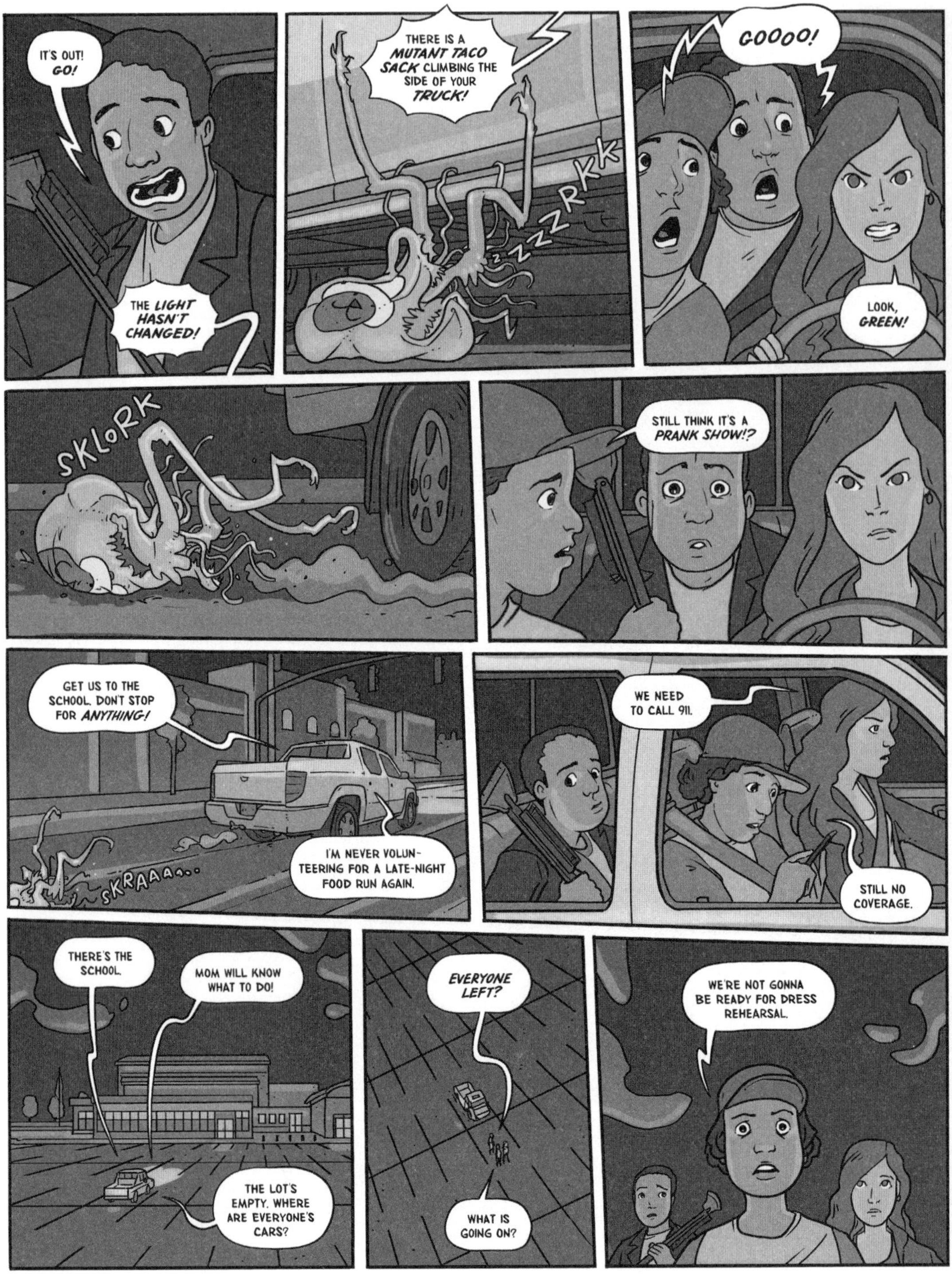
IT'S OUT! GO!
THE LIGHT HASN'T CHANGED!
THERE IS A MUTANT TACO SACK CLIMBING THE SIDE OF YOUR TRUCK!
ZZZZRKK
GOOOO!
LOOK, GREEN!
SKLORK
STILL THINK IT'S A PRANK SHOW!?
GET US TO THE SCHOOL. DON'T STOP FOR ANYTHING!
I'M NEVER VOLUNTEERING FOR A LATE-NIGHT FOOD RUN AGAIN.
SKRAAAa...
WE NEED TO CALL 911.
STILL NO COVERAGE.
THERE'S THE SCHOOL.
MOM WILL KNOW WHAT TO DO!
THE LOT'S EMPTY. WHERE ARE EVERYONE'S CARS?
EVERYONE LEFT?
WHAT IS GOING ON?
WE'RE NOT GONNA BE READY FOR DRESS REHEARSAL.

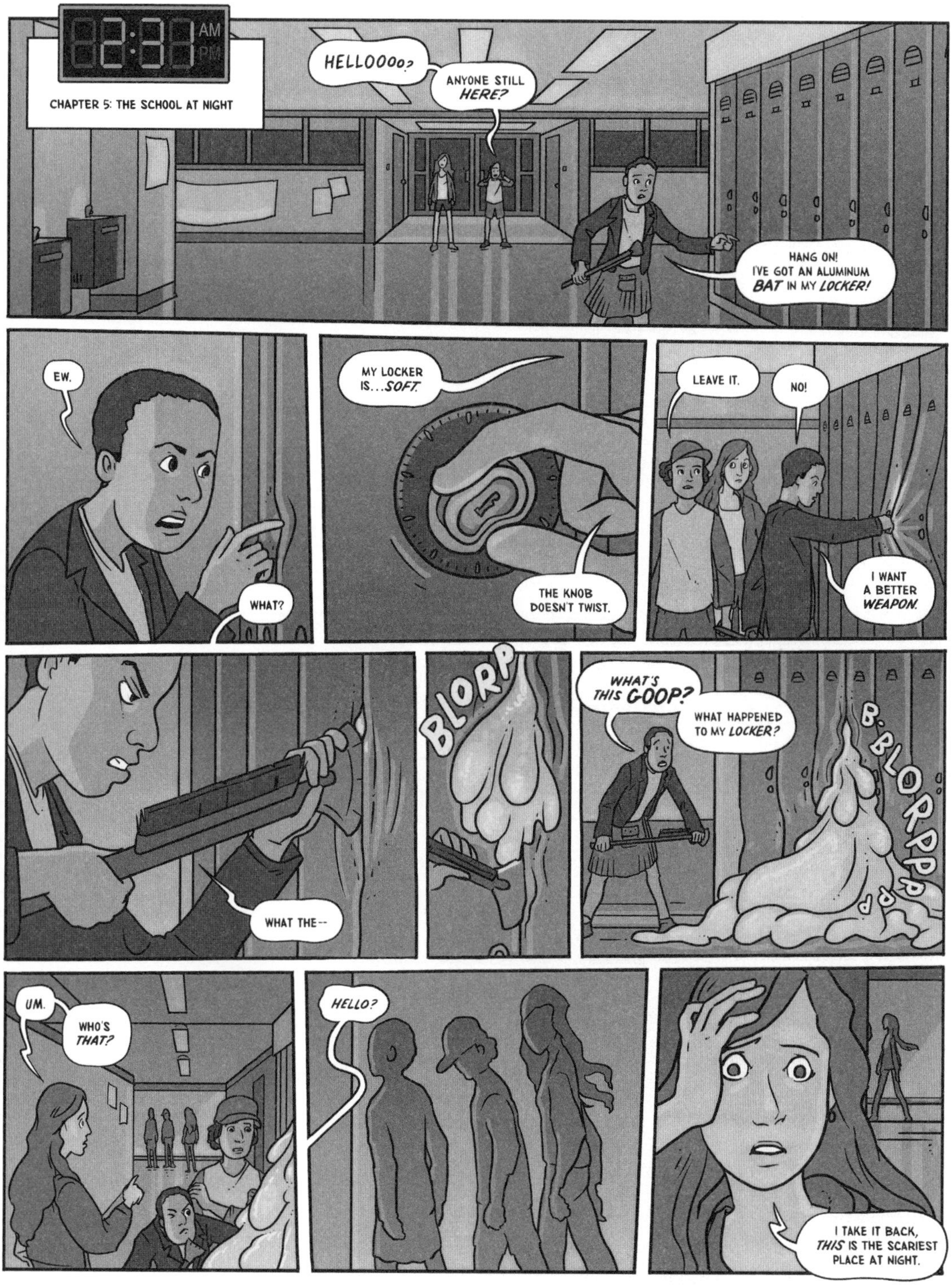

12:31 AM PM
CHAPTER 5: THE SCHOOL AT NIGHT
HELLOOOoo?
ANYONE STILL HERE?
HANG ON! I'VE GOT AN ALUMINUM BAT IN MY LOCKER!
EW.
WHAT?
MY LOCKER IS...SOFT.
THE KNOB DOESN'T TWIST.
LEAVE IT.
NO!
I WANT A BETTER WEAPON.
WHAT THE--
BLORP
WHAT'S THIS GOOP?
WHAT HAPPENED TO MY LOCKER?
B-BLORRPPP
UM.
WHO'S THAT?
HELLO?
I TAKE IT BACK, THIS IS THE SCARIEST PLACE AT NIGHT.

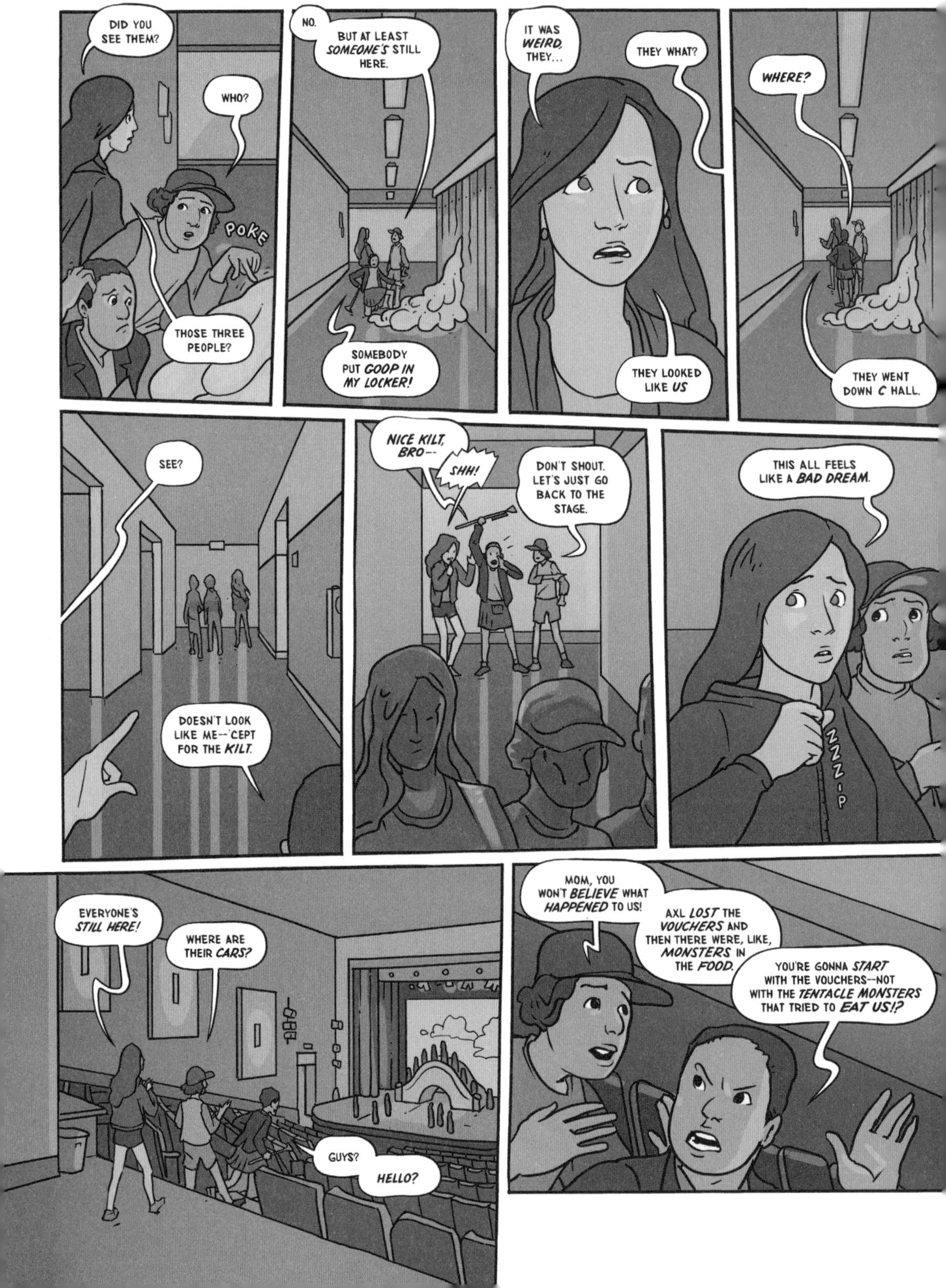

DID YOU SEE THEM?
WHO?
POKE
THOSE THREE PEOPLE?
NO.
BUT AT LEAST SOMEONE'S STILL HERE.
SOMEBODY PUT GOOP IN MY LOCKER!
IT WAS WEIRD, THEY...
THEY WHAT?
THEY LOOKED LIKE US
WHERE?
THEY WENT DOWN C HALL.
SEE?
DOESN'T LOOK LIKE ME--'CEPT FOR THE KILT.
NICE KILT, BRO--
SHH!
DON'T SHOUT. LET'S JUST GO BACK TO THE STAGE.
THIS ALL FEELS LIKE A BAD DREAM.
ZZZIP
EVERYONE'S STILL HERE!
WHERE ARE THEIR CARS?
GUYS?
HELLO?
MOM, YOU WON'T BELIEVE WHAT HAPPENED TO US!
AXL LOST THE VOUCHERS AND THEN THERE WERE, LIKE, MONSTERS IN THE FOOD.
YOU'RE GONNA START WITH THE VOUCHERS--NOT WITH THE TENTACLE MONSTERS THAT TRIED TO EAT US!?

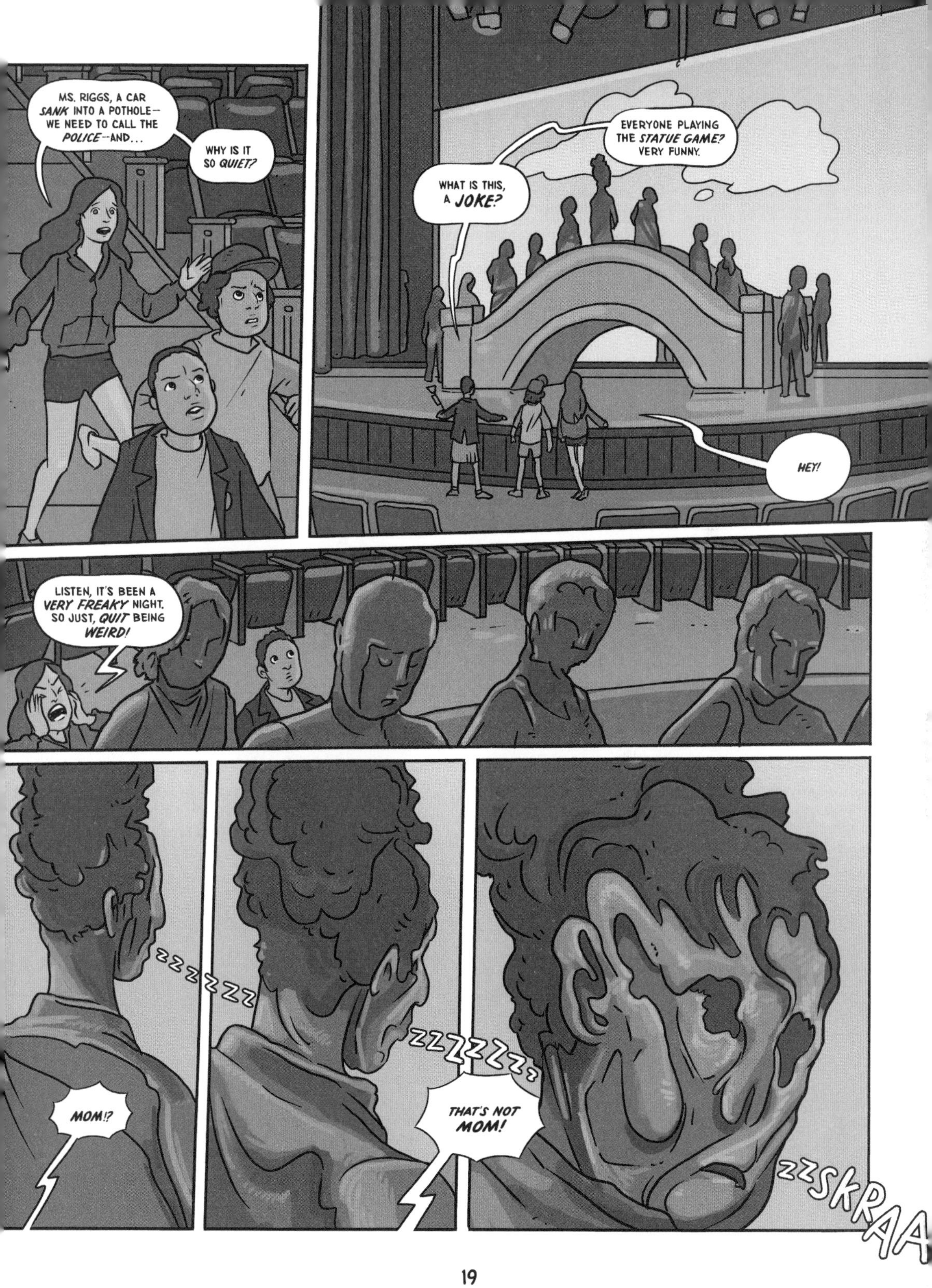
MS. RIGGS, A CAR SANK INTO A POTHOLE--WE NEED TO CALL THE POLICE--AND...
WHY IS IT SO QUIET?
EVERYONE PLAYING THE STATUE GAME? VERY FUNNY.
WHAT IS THIS, A JOKE?
HEY!
LISTEN, IT'S BEEN A VERY FREAKY NIGHT. SO JUST, QUIT BEING WEIRD!
ZZZZZZZ
MOM!?
ZZZZZZZZ
THAT'S NOT MOM!
ZZSKRAA

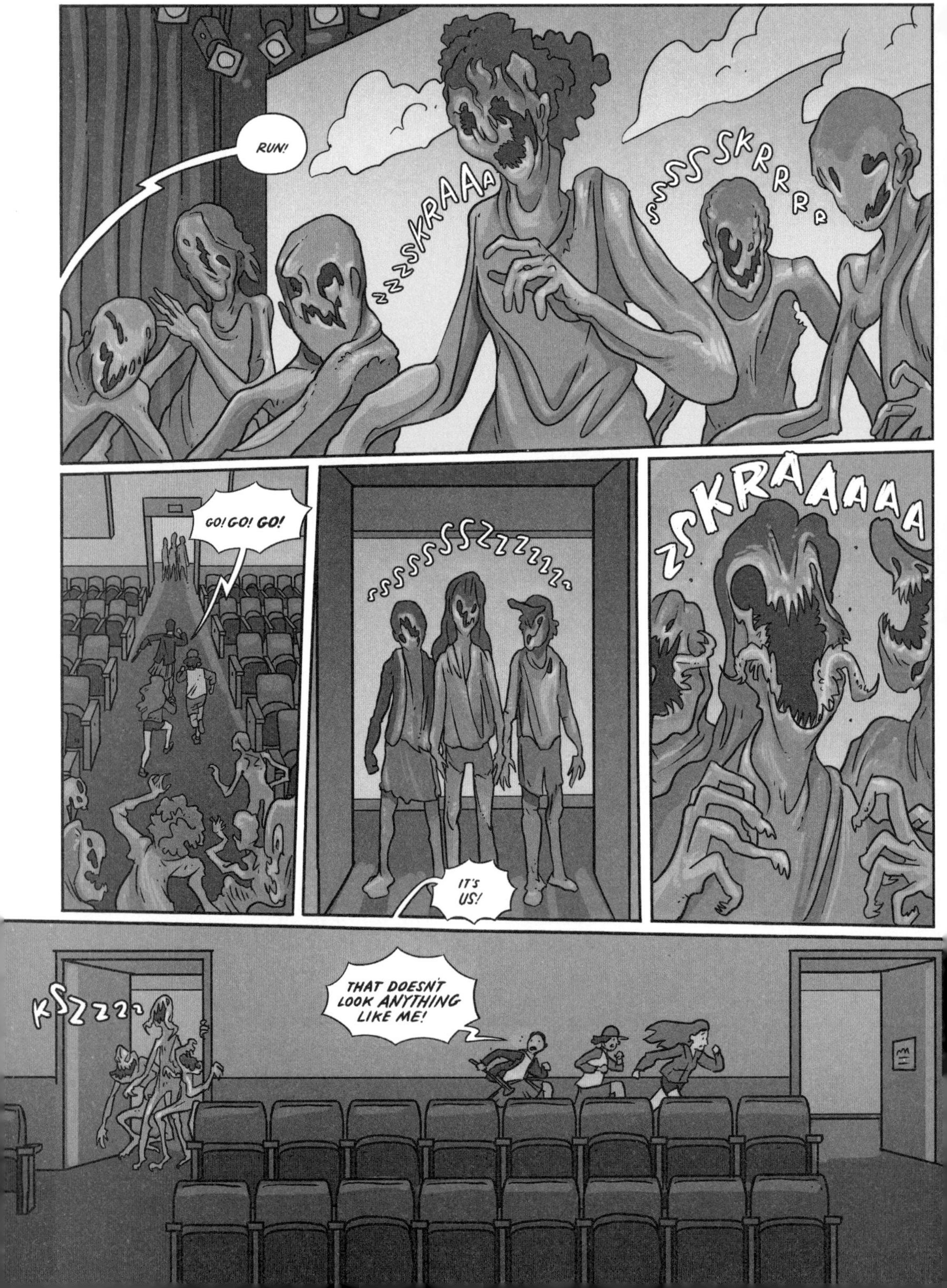
RUN!
ZZZSKRAAAA
SSSSSKRRRRR
GO! GO! GO!
SSSSSSSZZZZZZ
IT'S US!
ZZSKRAAAAAA
KSZZZZZ
THAT DOESN'T LOOK ANYTHING LIKE ME!

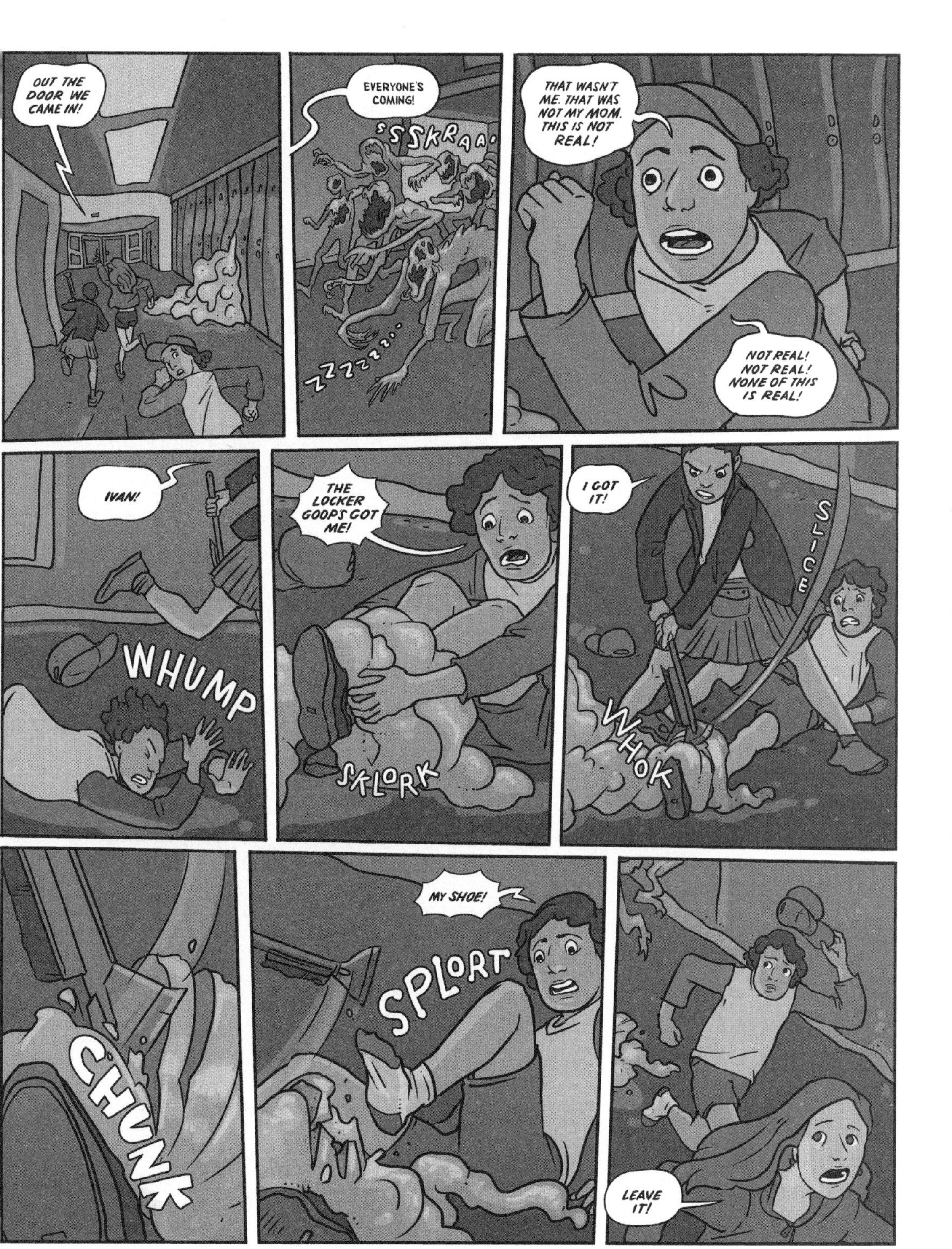
OUT THE DOOR WE CAME IN!
EVERYONE'S COMING!
SSSKRAAA
ZZZZZZZ
THAT WASN'T ME. THAT WAS NOT MY MOM. THIS IS NOT REAL!
NOT REAL! NOT REAL! NONE OF THIS IS REAL!
IVAN!
WHUMP
THE LOCKER GOOP'S GOT ME!
SKLORK
I GOT IT!
SLICE
WHOK
CHUNK
MY SHOE!
SPLORT
LEAVE IT!

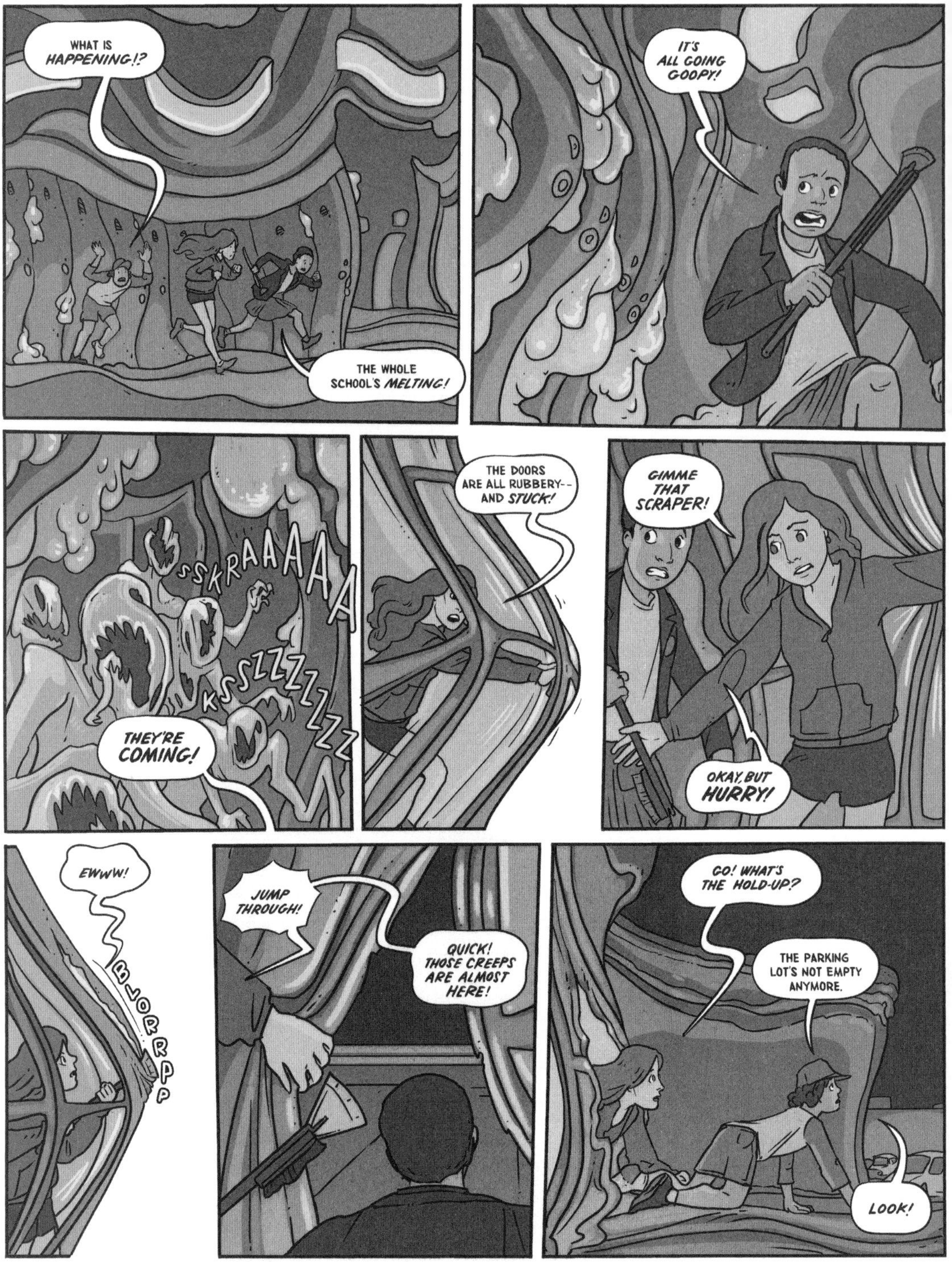
WHAT IS HAPPENING!?
THE WHOLE SCHOOL'S MELTING!
IT'S ALL GOING GOOPY!
SSKRAAAAAA
KSSZZZZZZZZ
THEY'RE COMING!
THE DOORS ARE ALL RUBBERY-- AND STUCK!
GIMME THAT SCRAPER!
OKAY, BUT HURRY!
EWWW!
BLORRRPP
JUMP THROUGH!
QUICK! THOSE CREEPS ARE ALMOST HERE!
GO! WHAT'S THE HOLD-UP?
THE PARKING LOT'S NOT EMPTY ANYMORE.
LOOK!

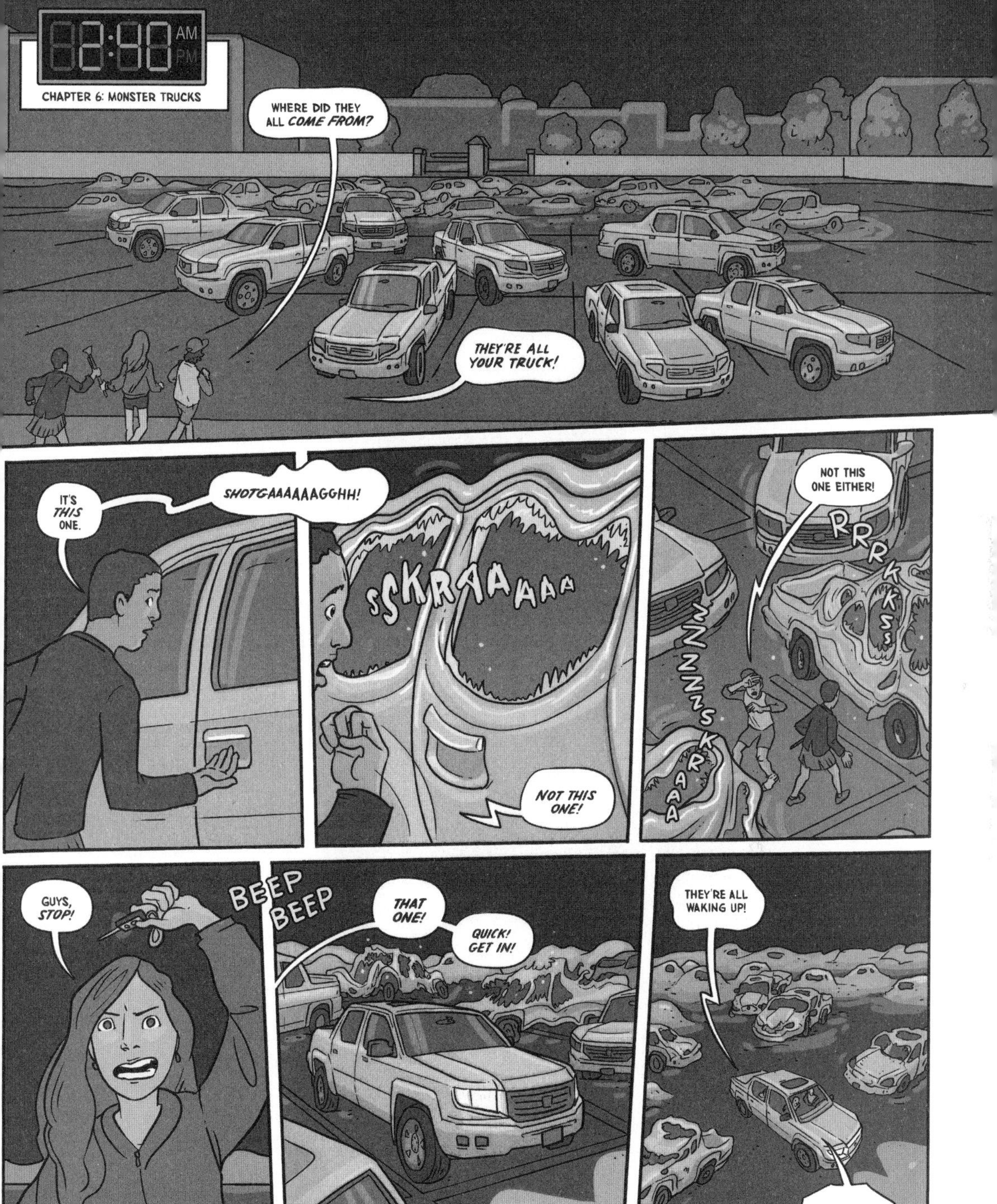
2:40 AM
CHAPTER 6: MONSTER TRUCKS
WHERE DID THEY ALL *COME FROM?*
THEY'RE ALL YOUR TRUCK!
IT'S *THIS* ONE.
SHOTGAAAAAAGGHH!
SSKRAAAAAAA
NOT THIS ONE!
NOT THIS ONE EITHER!
RRRKKSS
ZZZZZSKRAAA
GUYS, *STOP!*
BEEP BEEP
THAT ONE!
QUICK! GET IN!
THEY'RE ALL WAKING UP!
DRIVE!!!

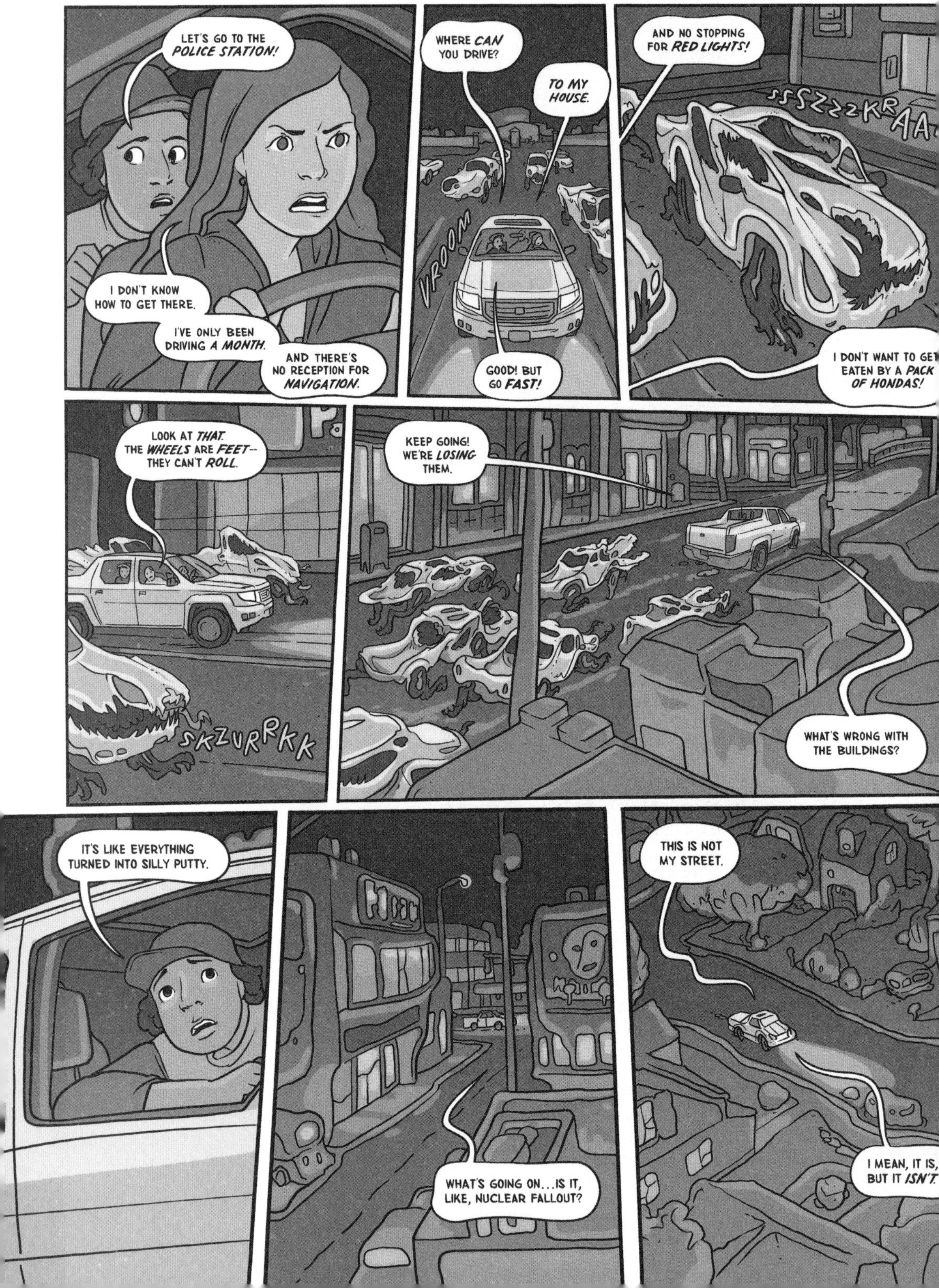
LET'S GO TO THE POLICE STATION!
I DON'T KNOW HOW TO GET THERE.
I'VE ONLY BEEN DRIVING A MONTH.
AND THERE'S NO RECEPTION FOR NAVIGATION.
WHERE CAN YOU DRIVE?
TO MY HOUSE.
VROOOM
GOOD! BUT GO FAST!
AND NO STOPPING FOR RED LIGHTS!
SSSZZZZKRAAA
I DON'T WANT TO GET EATEN BY A PACK OF HONDAS!
LOOK AT THAT. THE WHEELS ARE FEET-- THEY CAN'T ROLL.
SKZURRKK
KEEP GOING! WE'RE LOSING THEM.
WHAT'S WRONG WITH THE BUILDINGS?
IT'S LIKE EVERYTHING TURNED INTO SILLY PUTTY.
WHAT'S GOING ON...IS IT, LIKE, NUCLEAR FALLOUT?
THIS IS NOT MY STREET.
I MEAN, IT IS, BUT IT ISN'T.

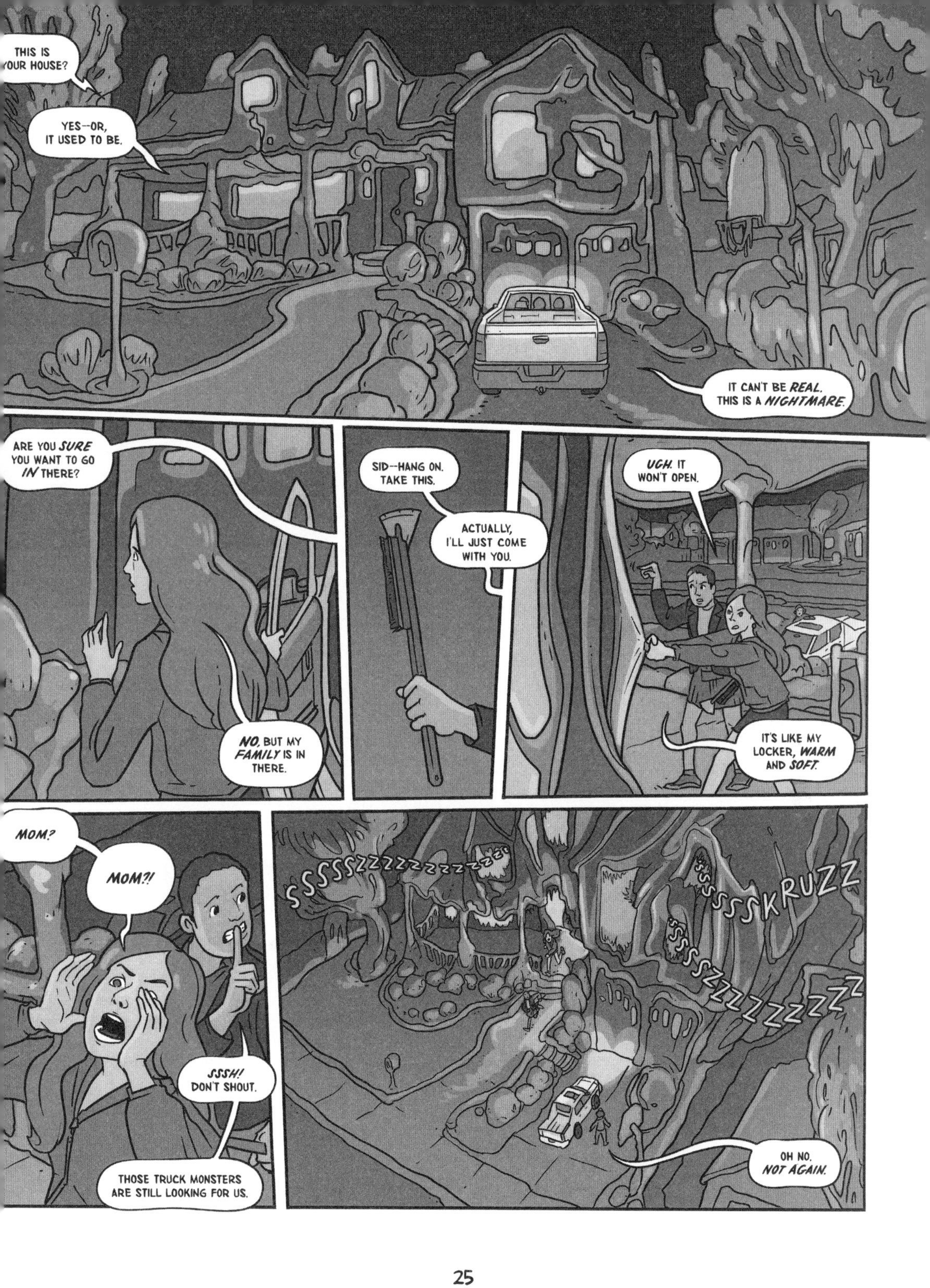
THIS IS YOUR HOUSE?
YES--OR, IT USED TO BE.
IT CAN'T BE REAL. THIS IS A NIGHTMARE.
ARE YOU SURE YOU WANT TO GO IN THERE?
NO, BUT MY FAMILY IS IN THERE.
SID--HANG ON. TAKE THIS.
ACTUALLY, I'LL JUST COME WITH YOU.
UGH. IT WON'T OPEN.
IT'S LIKE MY LOCKER, WARM AND SOFT.
MOM?
MOM?!
SSSH! DON'T SHOUT.
THOSE TRUCK MONSTERS ARE STILL LOOKING FOR US.
SSSSSZZZZZZZZZZZZZ
SSSSSSKRUZZ
SSSSSZZZZZZZZZ
OH NO. NOT AGAIN.

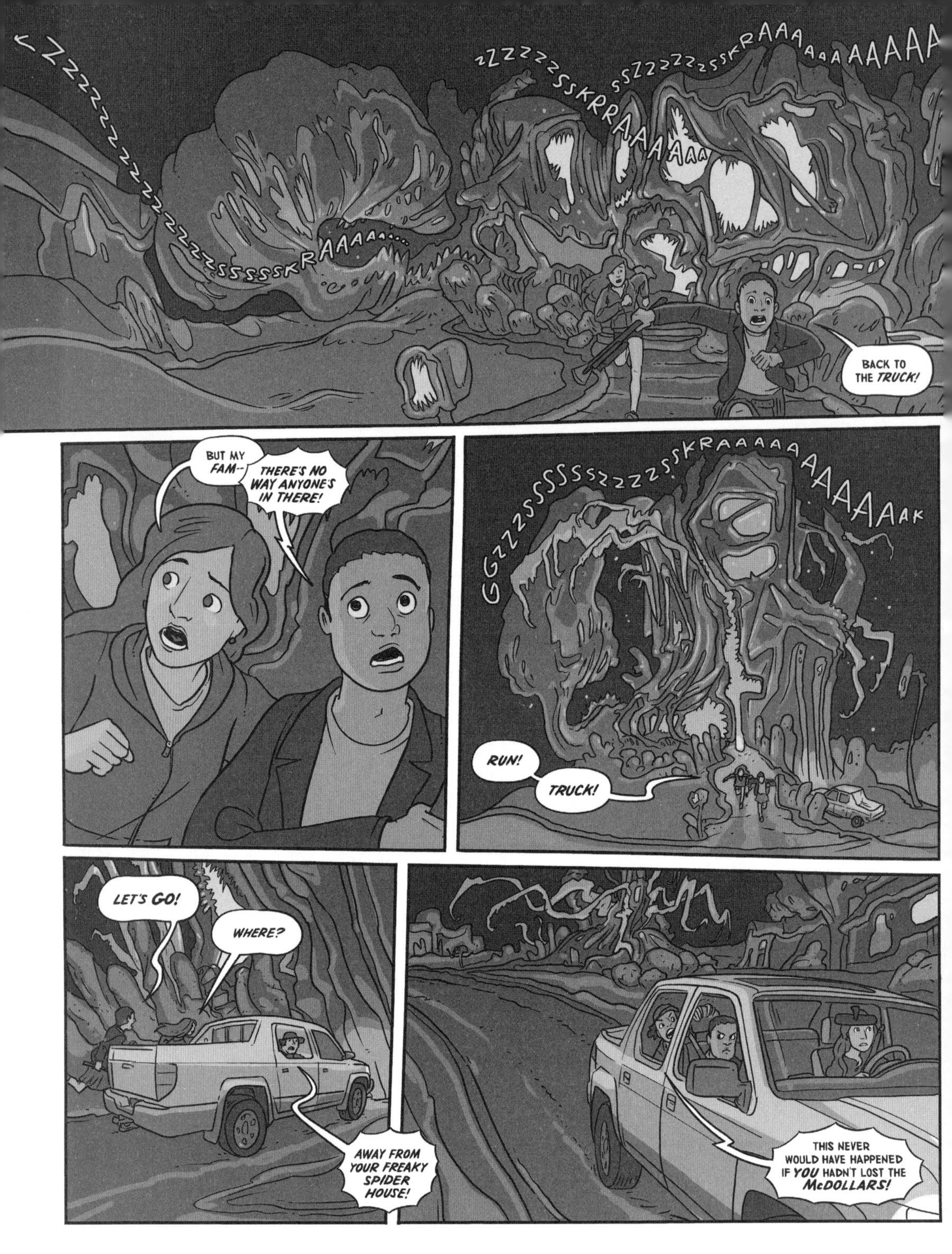

ZZZZZZZZZZZZZZZZZZZSSSSSSKRAAAAA....
ZZZZZZSSKRAAAAAAA
SSZZZZZZSSKRAAAAAAAAAA
BACK TO THE *TRUCK!*
BUT MY *FAM*--
THERE'S NO WAY ANYONE'S IN THERE!
GGZZZSSSSSSZZZZSSKRAAAAAAAAAAAAK
RUN!
TRUCK!
LET'S GO!
WHERE?
AWAY FROM YOUR FREAKY SPIDER HOUSE!
THIS NEVER WOULD HAVE HAPPENED IF *YOU* HADN'T LOST THE *McDOLLARS!*

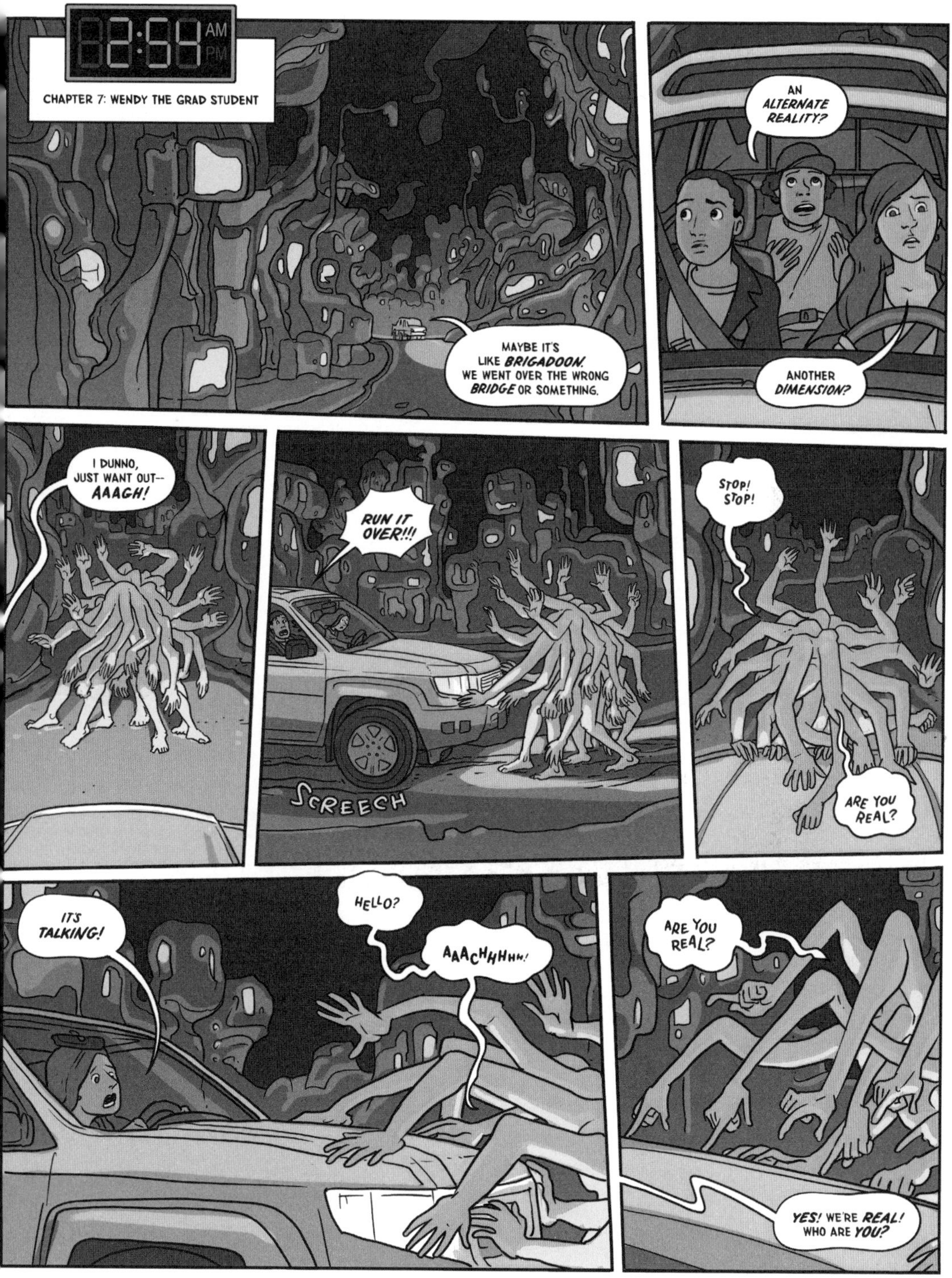
2:59 AM PM
CHAPTER 7: WENDY THE GRAD STUDENT
MAYBE IT'S LIKE BRIGADOON. WE WENT OVER THE WRONG BRIDGE OR SOMETHING.
AN ALTERNATE REALITY?
ANOTHER DIMENSION?
I DUNNO, JUST WANT OUT-- AAAGH!
RUN IT OVER!!!
SCREECH
STOP! STOP!
ARE YOU REAL?
IT'S TALKING!
HELLO?
AAACHHHHH!
ARE YOU REAL?
YES! WE'RE REAL! WHO ARE YOU?

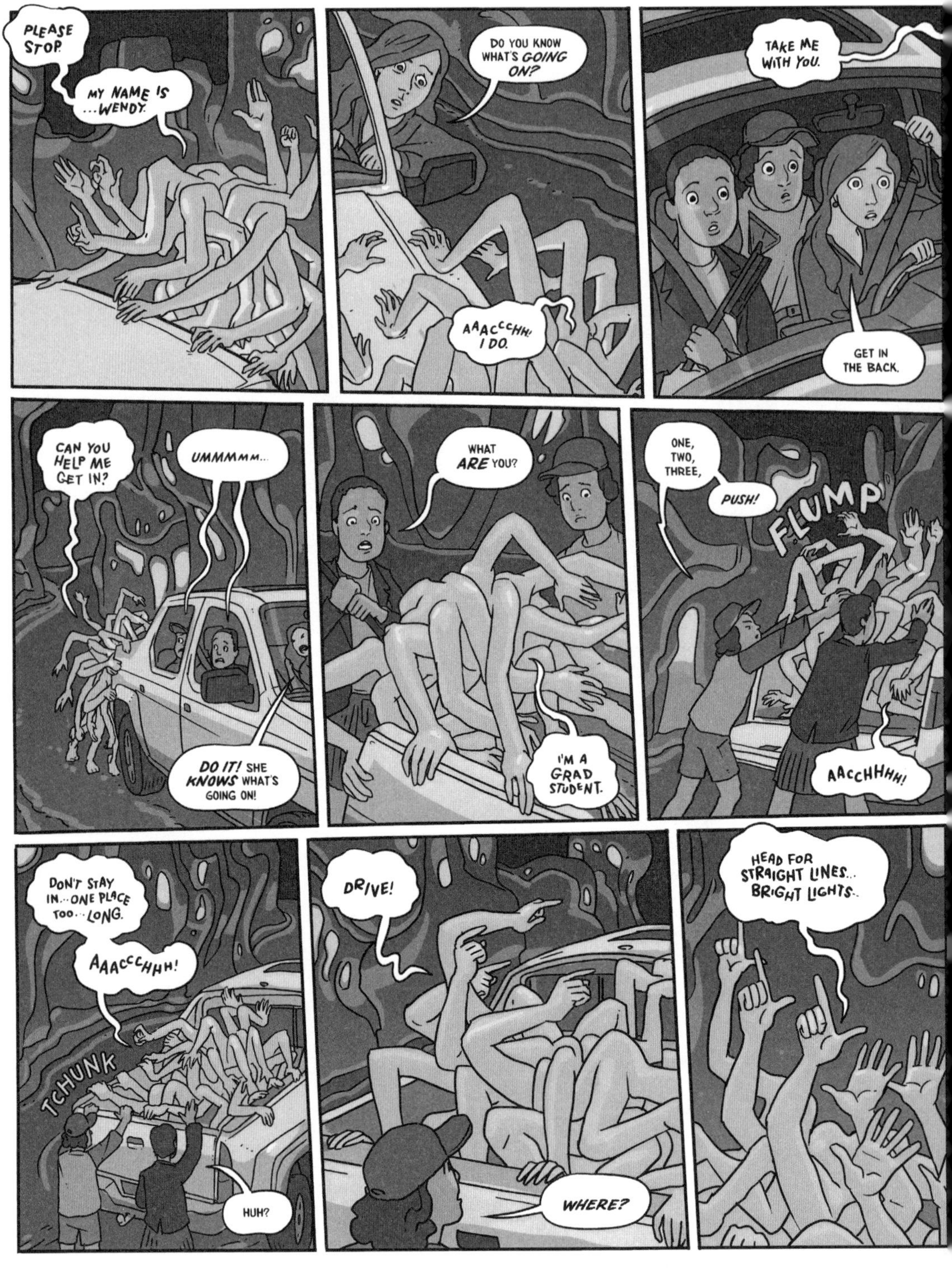
PLEASE STOP.
MY NAME IS ...WENDY.
DO YOU KNOW WHAT'S GOING ON?
AAACCCHH! I DO.
TAKE ME WITH YOU.
GET IN THE BACK.
CAN YOU HELP ME GET IN?
UMMMMM...
DO IT! SHE KNOWS WHAT'S GOING ON!
WHAT ARE YOU?
I'M A GRAD STUDENT.
ONE, TWO, THREE,
PUSH!
FLUMP
AACCHHHH!
DON'T STAY IN... ONE PLACE TOO... LONG.
AAACCCHHH!
TCHUNK
HUH?
DRIVE!
WHERE?
HEAD FOR STRAIGHT LINES... BRIGHT LIGHTS...

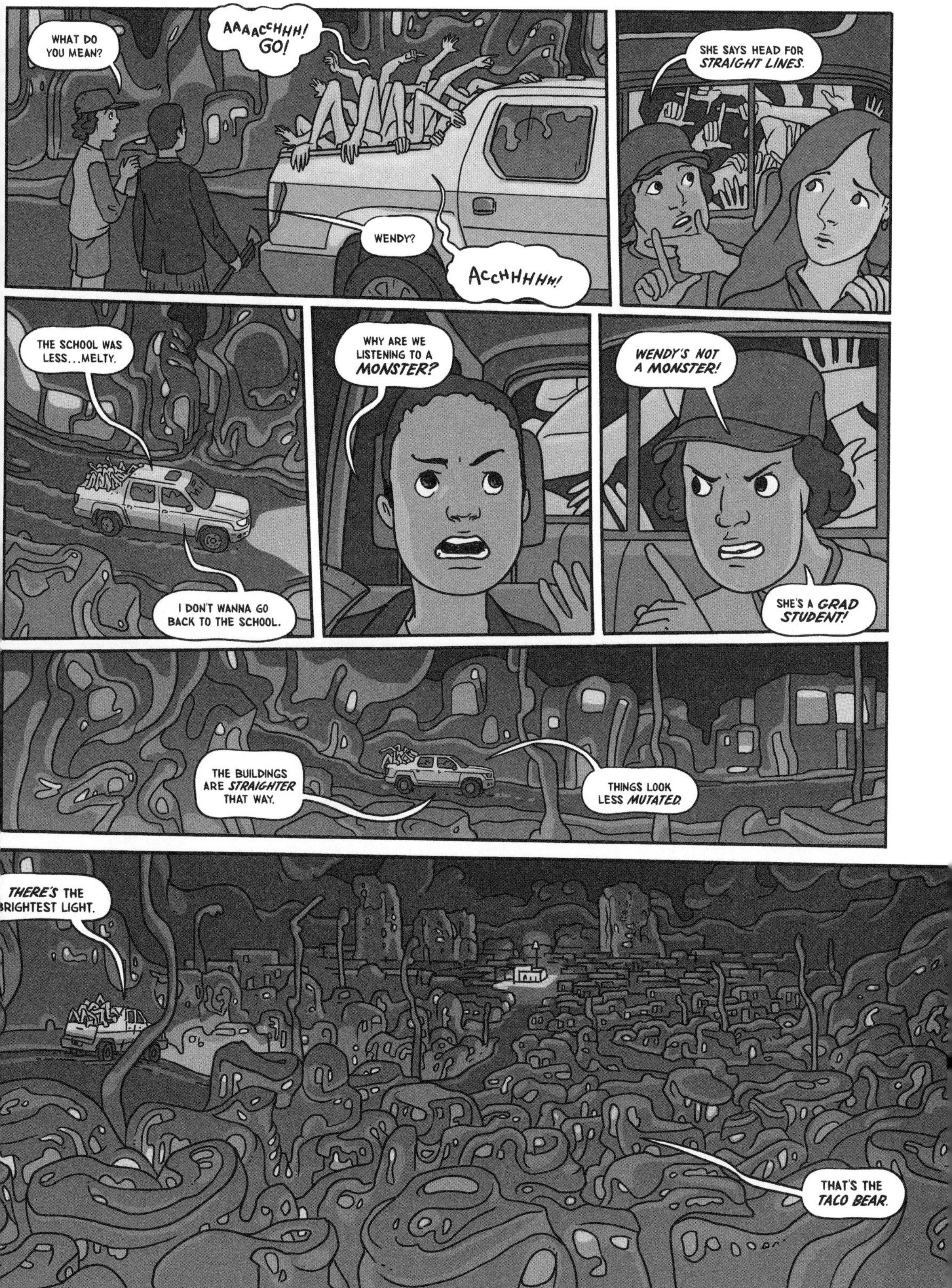
WHAT DO YOU MEAN?
AAAACCHHH! GO!
WENDY?
ACCHHHHH!
SHE SAYS HEAD FOR *STRAIGHT LINES*.
THE SCHOOL WAS LESS. . . MELTY.
I DON'T WANNA GO BACK TO THE SCHOOL.
WHY ARE WE LISTENING TO A *MONSTER?*
WENDY'S NOT A MONSTER!
SHE'S A *GRAD STUDENT!*
THE BUILDINGS ARE *STRAIGHTER* THAT WAY.
THINGS LOOK LESS *MUTATED*.
THERE'S THE BRIGHTEST LIGHT.
THAT'S THE *TACO BEAR*.

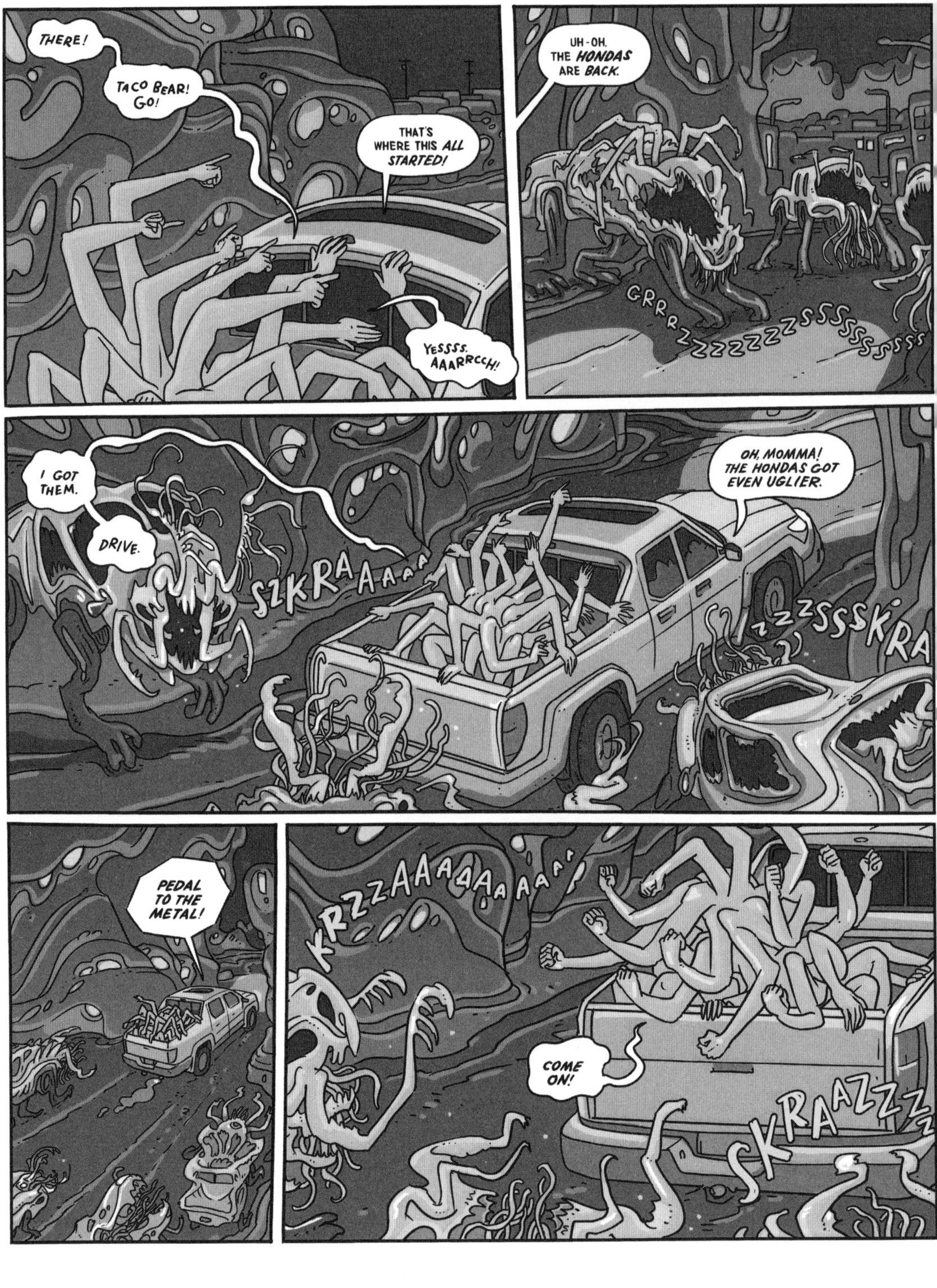

THERE!
TACO BEAR! GO!
THAT'S WHERE THIS ALL STARTED!
YESSSS. AAARRCCH!
UH-OH. THE HONDAS ARE BACK.
GRRRZZZZZZZZSSSSSSSSSSS
I GOT THEM.
DRIVE.
SZKRAAAAA
OH, MOMMA! THE HONDAS GOT EVEN UGLIER.
ZZZSSSSKRA
PEDAL TO THE METAL!
KRZZAAAAAAAAAA
COME ON!
SKRAAZZZZ

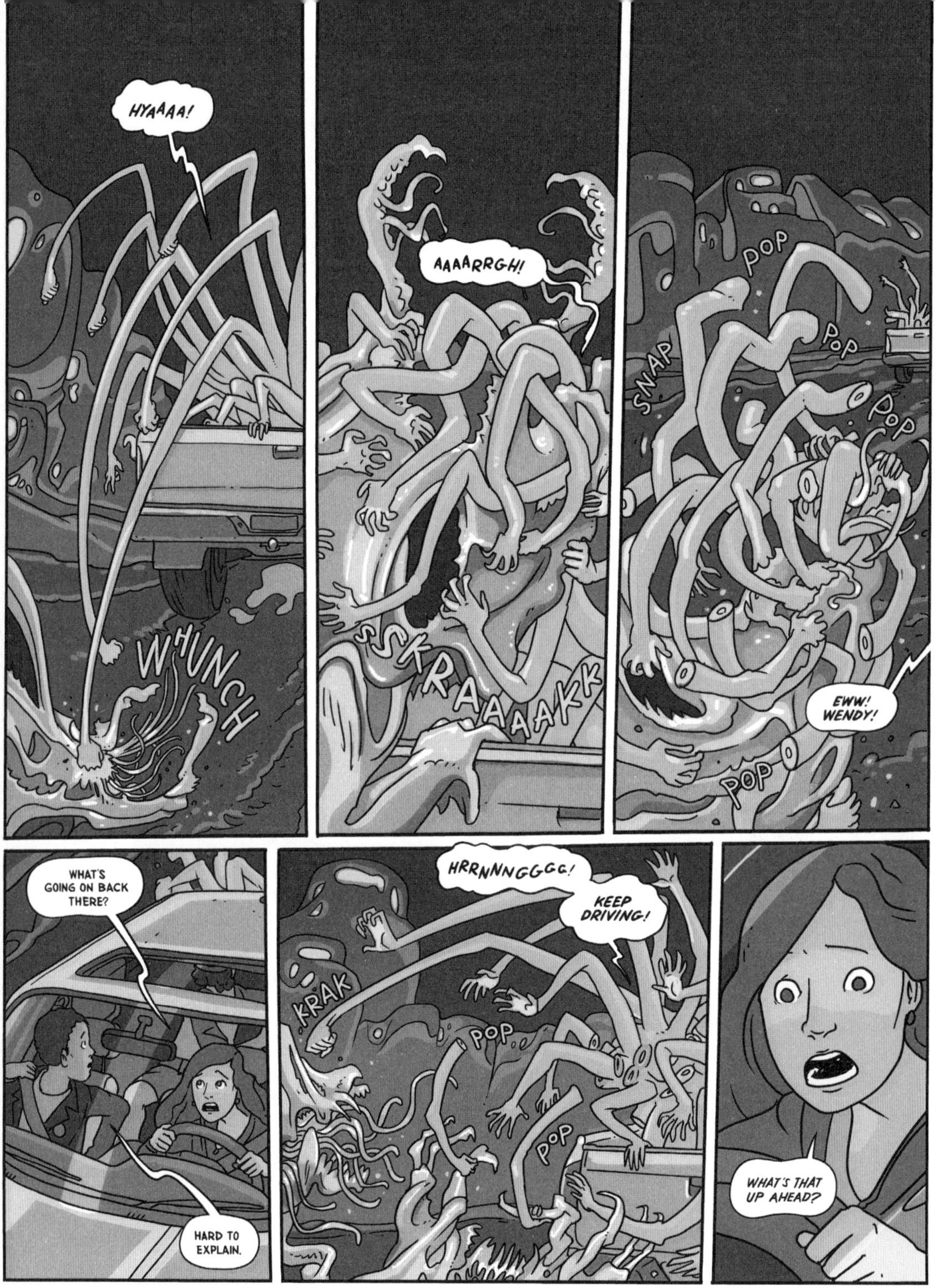
HYAAAA!
WHUNCH
AAAARRGH!
SSKRAAAAAKK
POP
SNAP
POP
POP
EWW! WENDY!
POP
WHAT'S GOING ON BACK THERE?
HARD TO EXPLAIN.
HRRNNNGGGG!
KEEP DRIVING!
KRAK
POP
POP
WHAT'S THAT UP AHEAD?

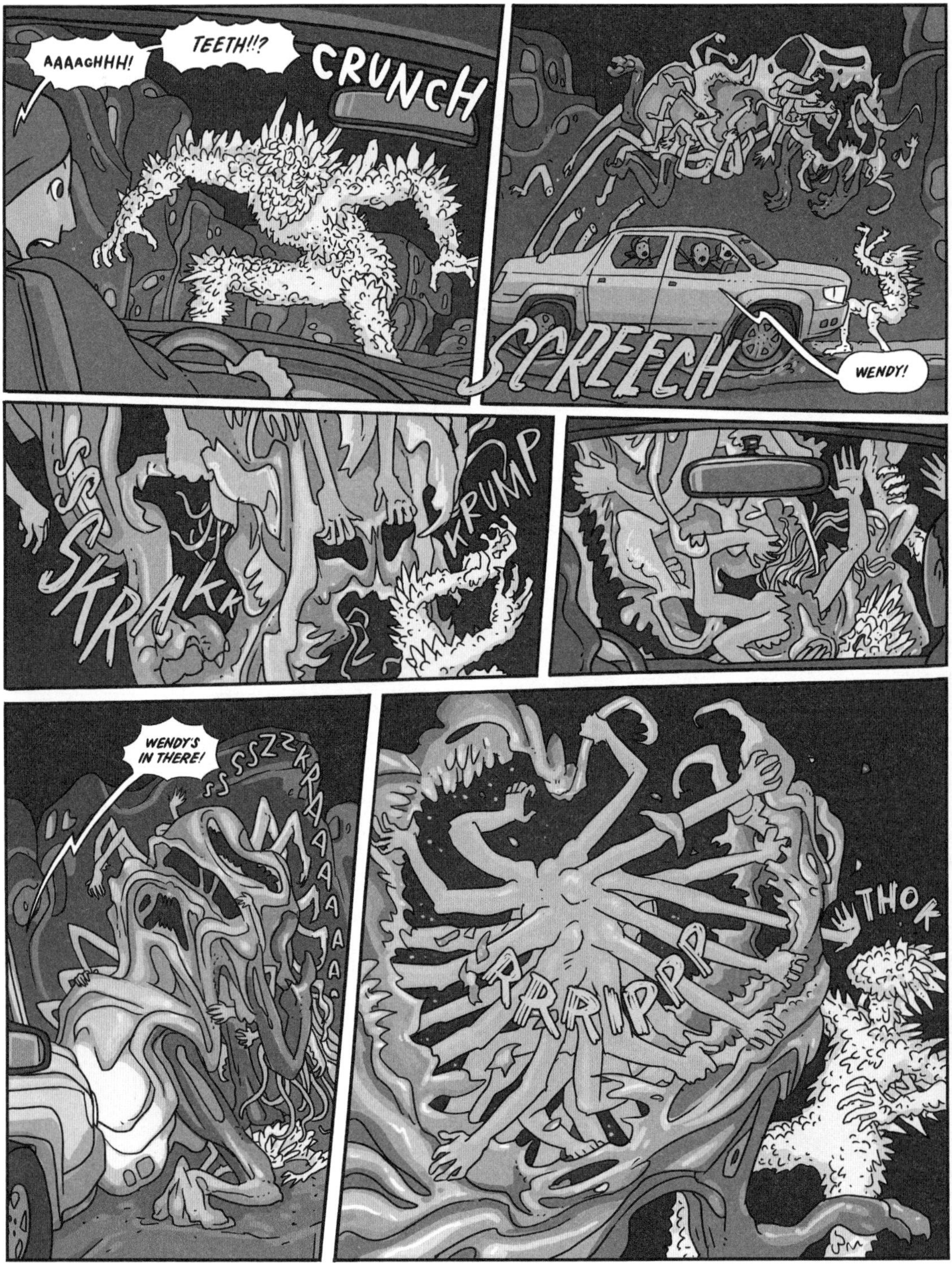
AAAAGHHH!
TEETH!!?
CRUNCH
SCREECH
WENDY!
SKRAKK
KRUMP
WENDY'S IN THERE!
SSSZZKRAAAAAAA
RRRIPP
THOK

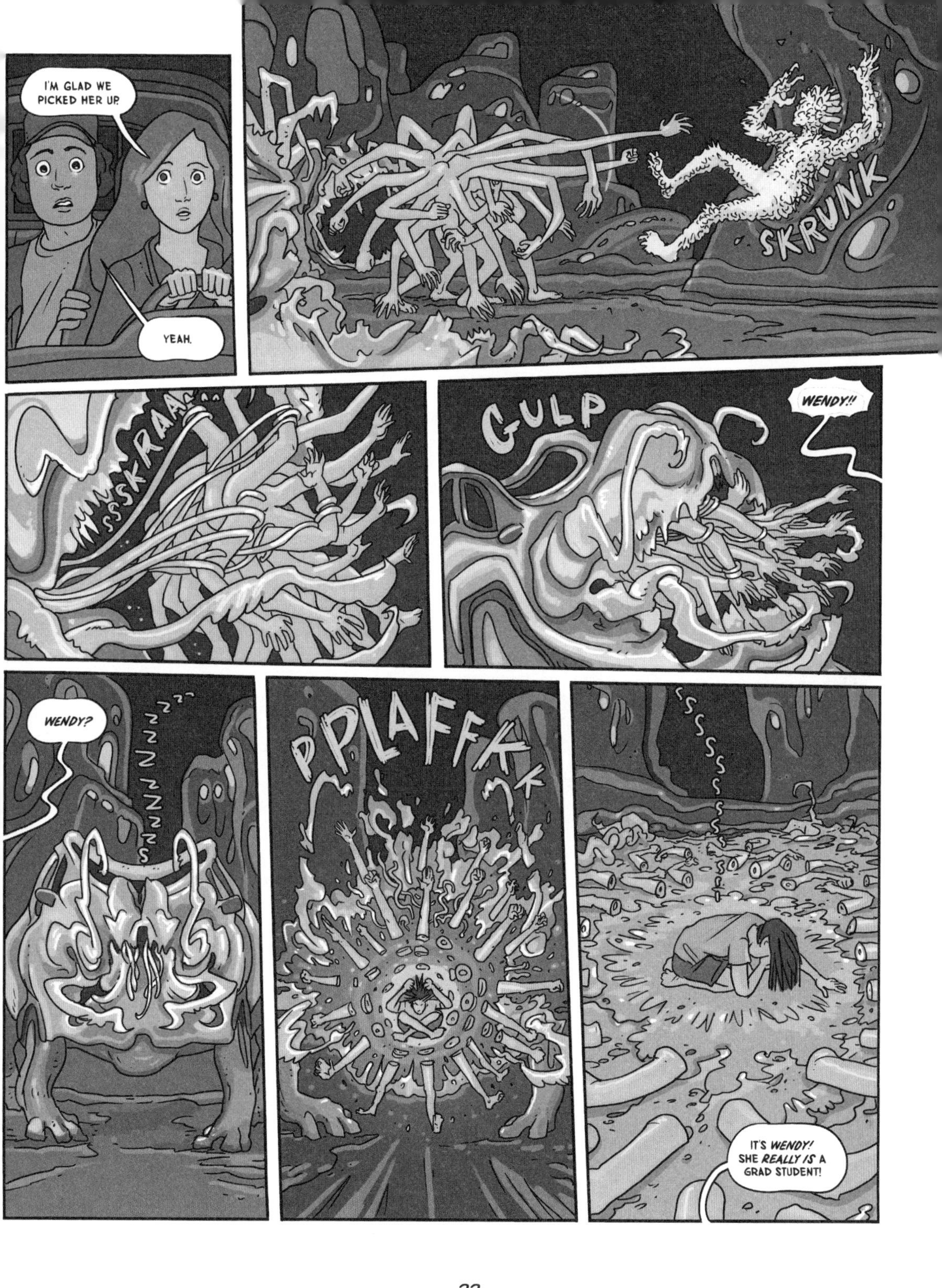
I'M GLAD WE PICKED HER UP.
YEAH.
SKRUNK
SSSKRAAA
GULP
WENDY!!
WENDY?
PPLAFFKK
IT'S WENDY! SHE REALLY IS A GRAD STUDENT!

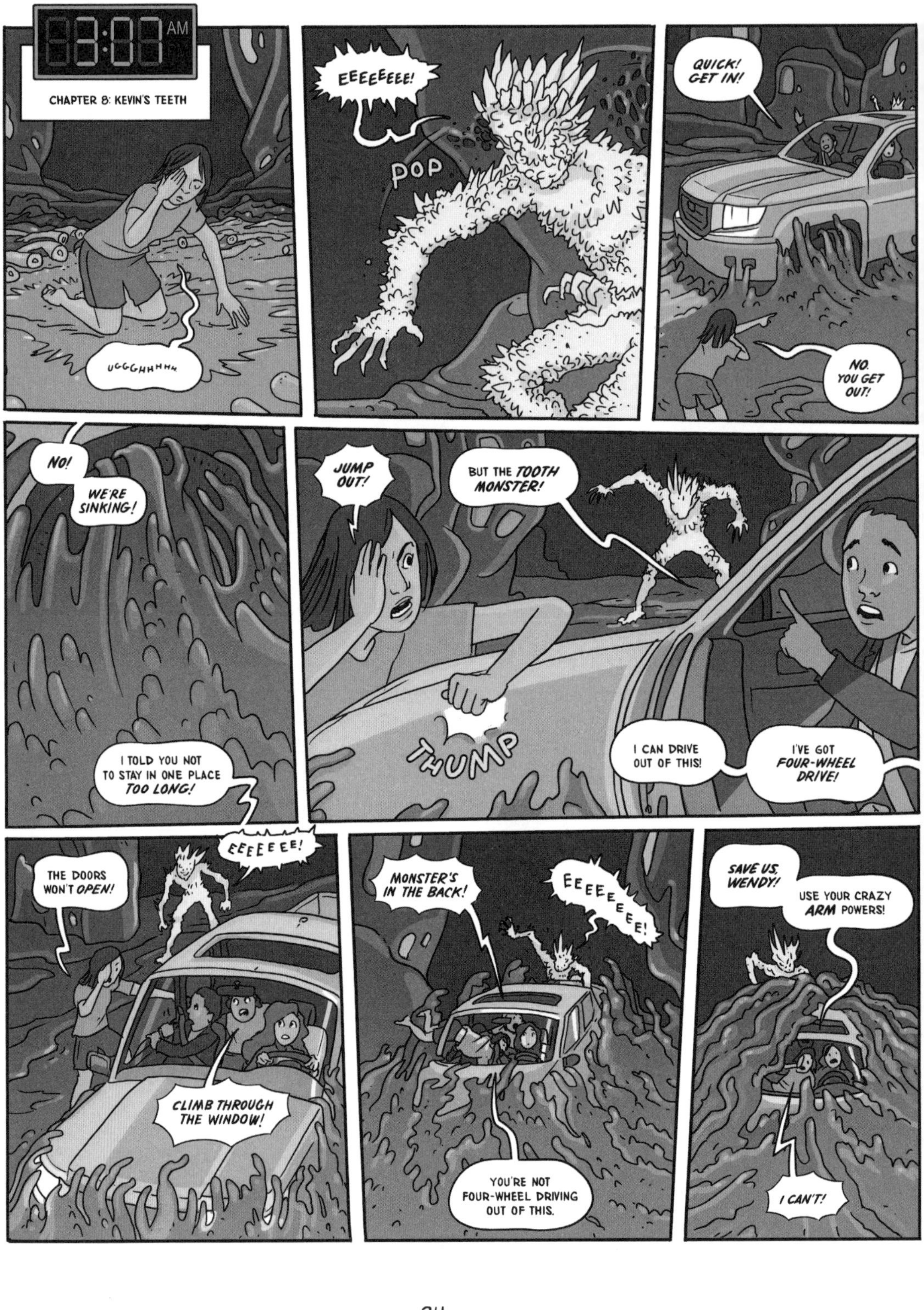
3:03 AM
CHAPTER 8: KEVIN'S TEETH
UGGGHHHHH
EEEEEEEE!
POP
QUICK! GET IN!
NO. YOU GET OUT!
NO!
WE'RE SINKING!
I TOLD YOU NOT TO STAY IN ONE PLACE TOO LONG!
JUMP OUT!
BUT THE TOOTH MONSTER!
THUMP
I CAN DRIVE OUT OF THIS!
I'VE GOT FOUR-WHEEL DRIVE!
THE DOORS WON'T OPEN!
EEEEEEE!
CLIMB THROUGH THE WINDOW!
MONSTER'S IN THE BACK!
EEEEEEEE!
YOU'RE NOT FOUR-WHEEL DRIVING OUT OF THIS.
SAVE US, WENDY!
USE YOUR CRAZY ARM POWERS!
I CAN'T!

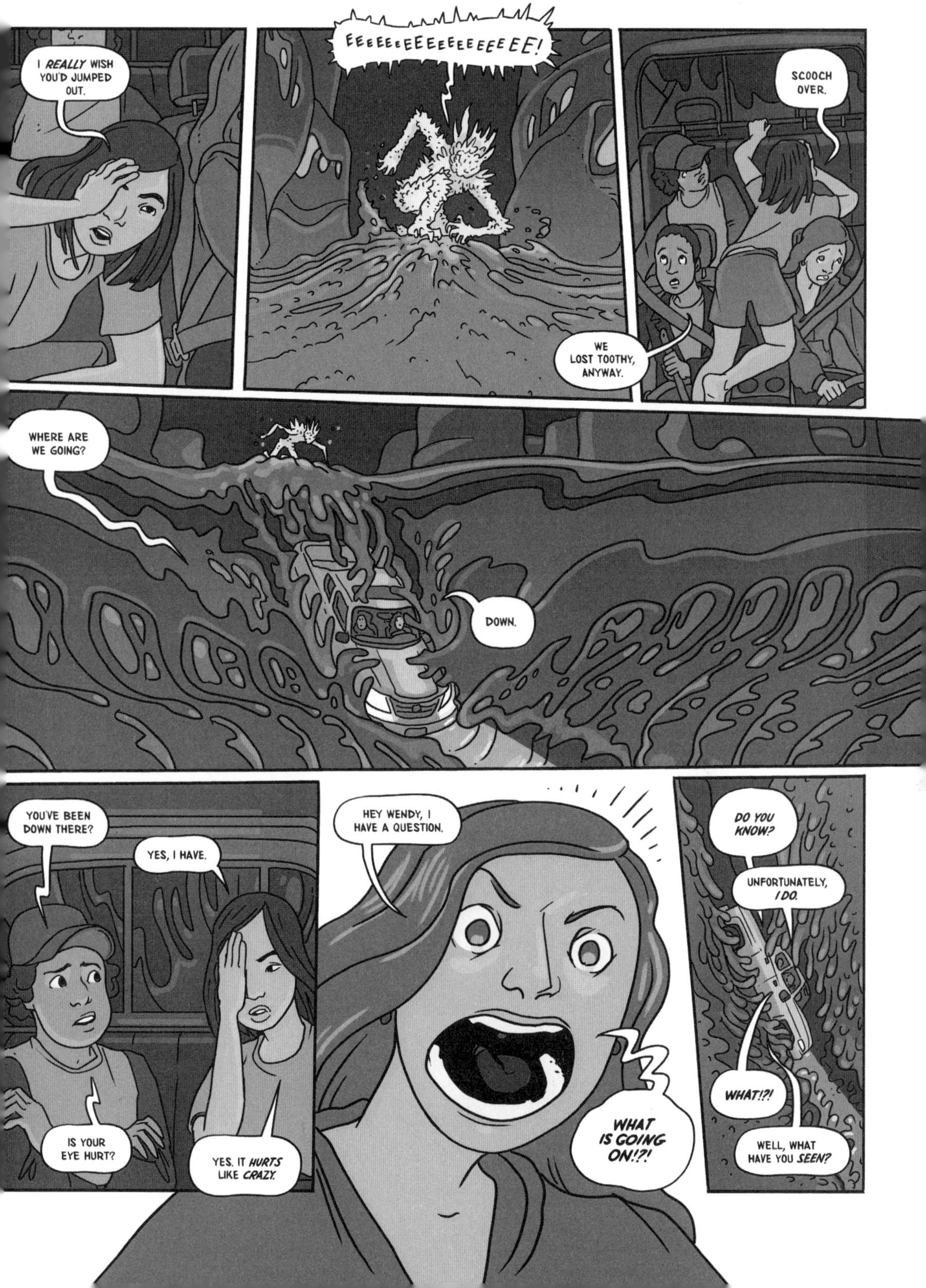
I REALLY WISH YOU'D JUMPED OUT.
EEEEEEEEEEEEEEEEE!
SCOOCH OVER.
WE LOST TOOTHY, ANYWAY.
WHERE ARE WE GOING?
DOWN.
YOU'VE BEEN DOWN THERE?
YES, I HAVE.
IS YOUR EYE HURT?
YES. IT HURTS LIKE CRAZY.
HEY WENDY, I HAVE A QUESTION.
WHAT IS GOING ON!?!
DO YOU KNOW?
UNFORTUNATELY, I DO.
WHAT!?!
WELL, WHAT HAVE YOU SEEN?

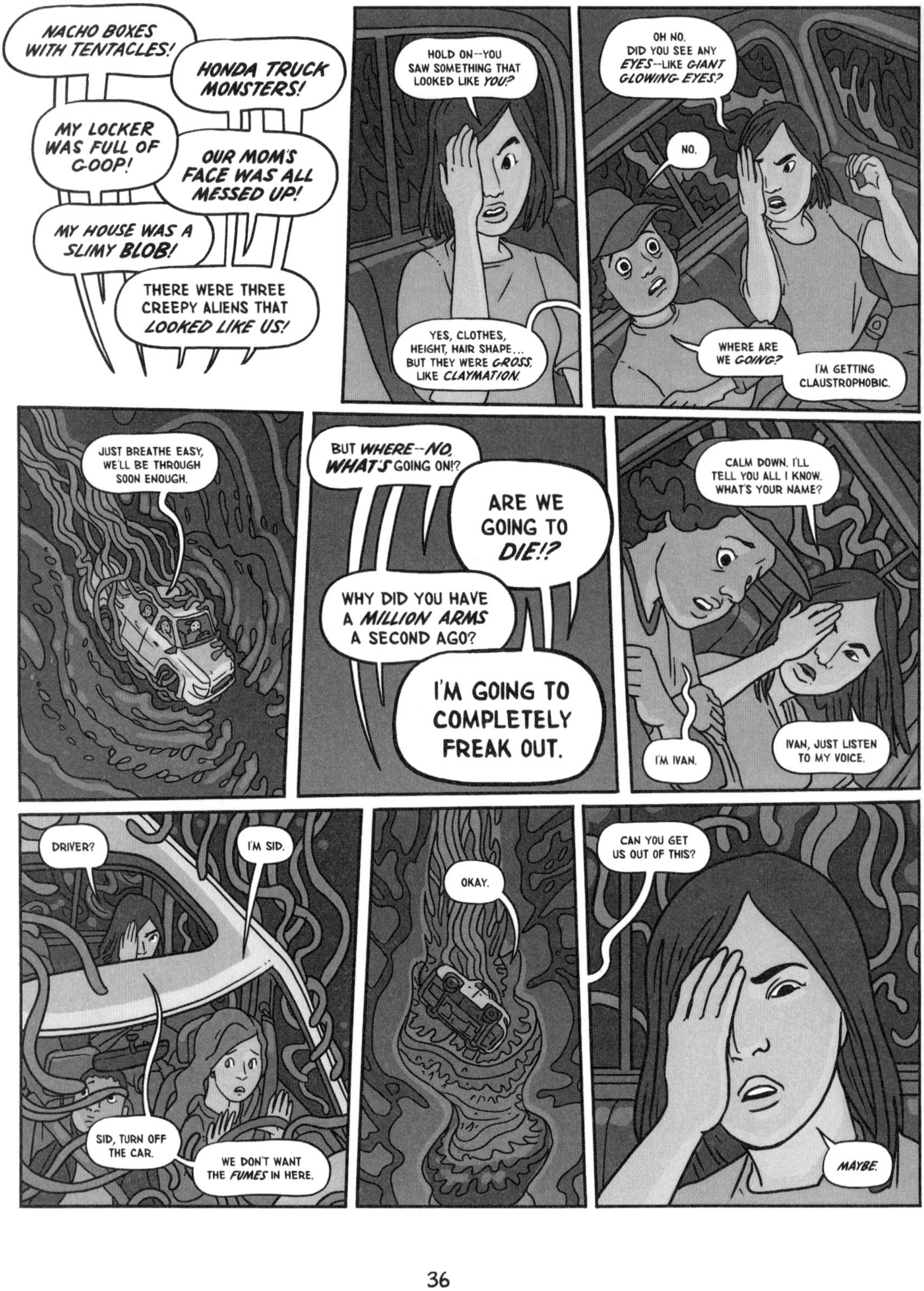
NACHO BOXES WITH TENTACLES!
HONDA TRUCK MONSTERS!
MY LOCKER WAS FULL OF GOOP!
OUR MOM'S FACE WAS ALL MESSED UP!
MY HOUSE WAS A SLIMY BLOB!
THERE WERE THREE CREEPY ALIENS THAT LOOKED LIKE US!
HOLD ON--YOU SAW SOMETHING THAT LOOKED LIKE YOU?
YES, CLOTHES, HEIGHT, HAIR SHAPE... BUT THEY WERE GROSS. LIKE CLAYMATION.
OH NO. DID YOU SEE ANY EYES--LIKE GIANT GLOWING EYES?
NO.
WHERE ARE WE GOING?
I'M GETTING CLAUSTROPHOBIC.
JUST BREATHE EASY, WE'LL BE THROUGH SOON ENOUGH.
BUT WHERE--NO, WHAT'S GOING ON!?
ARE WE GOING TO DIE!?
WHY DID YOU HAVE A MILLION ARMS A SECOND AGO?
I'M GOING TO COMPLETELY FREAK OUT.
CALM DOWN. I'LL TELL YOU ALL I KNOW. WHAT'S YOUR NAME?
I'M IVAN.
IVAN, JUST LISTEN TO MY VOICE.
DRIVER?
I'M SID.
SID, TURN OFF THE CAR.
WE DON'T WANT THE FUMES IN HERE.
OKAY.
CAN YOU GET US OUT OF THIS?
MAYBE.

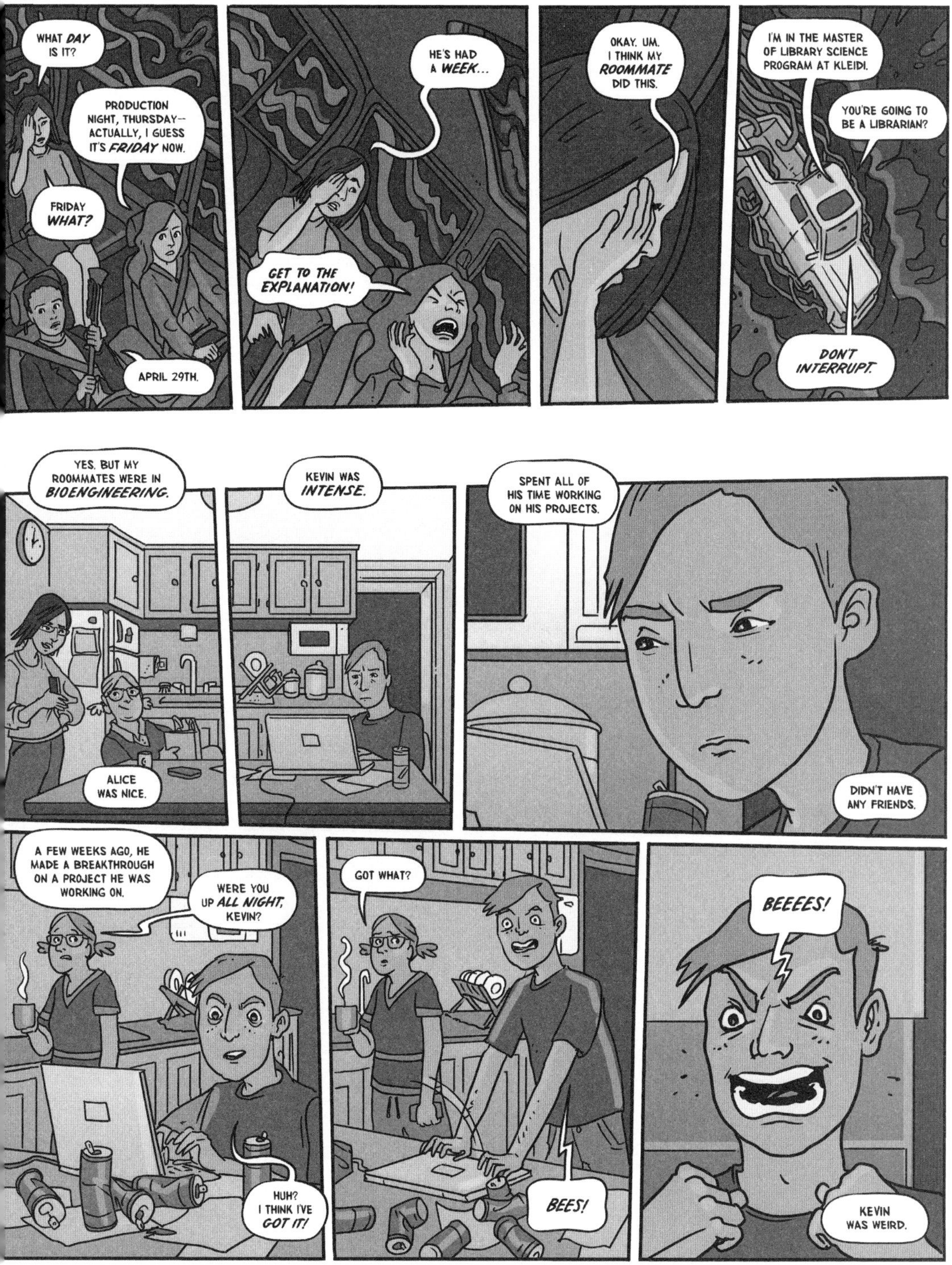
WHAT DAY IS IT?
PRODUCTION NIGHT, THURSDAY--ACTUALLY, I GUESS IT'S FRIDAY NOW.
FRIDAY WHAT?
APRIL 29TH.
HE'S HAD A WEEK...
GET TO THE EXPLANATION!
OKAY. UM. I THINK MY ROOMMATE DID THIS.
I'M IN THE MASTER OF LIBRARY SCIENCE PROGRAM AT KLEIDI.
YOU'RE GOING TO BE A LIBRARIAN?
DON'T INTERRUPT.
YES. BUT MY ROOMMATES WERE IN BIOENGINEERING.
ALICE WAS NICE.
KEVIN WAS INTENSE.
SPENT ALL OF HIS TIME WORKING ON HIS PROJECTS.
DIDN'T HAVE ANY FRIENDS.
A FEW WEEKS AGO, HE MADE A BREAKTHROUGH ON A PROJECT HE WAS WORKING ON.
WERE YOU UP ALL NIGHT, KEVIN?
HUH? I THINK I'VE GOT IT!
GOT WHAT?
BEES!
BEEEES!
KEVIN WAS WEIRD.

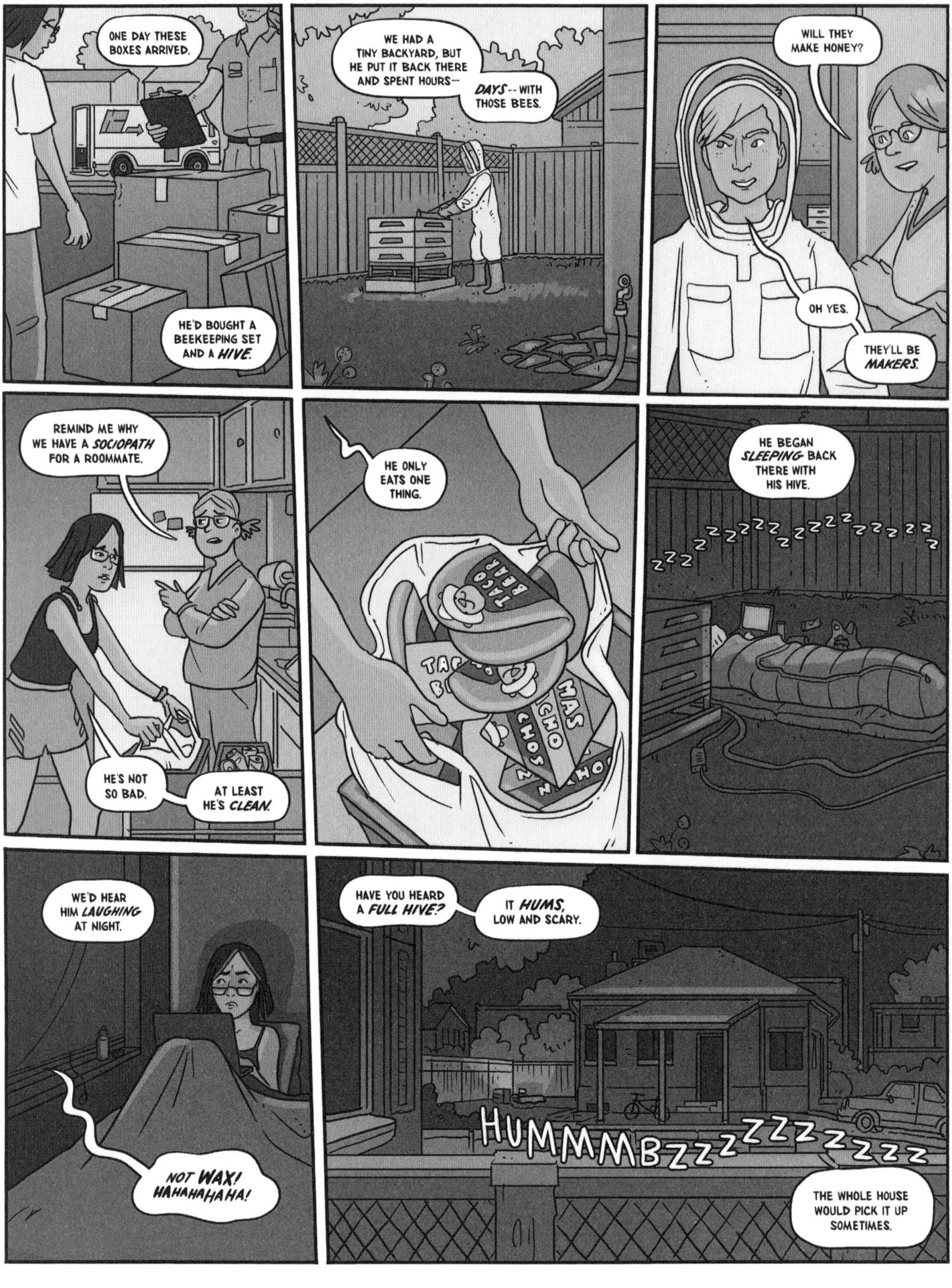
ONE DAY THESE BOXES ARRIVED.
HE'D BOUGHT A BEEKEEPING SET AND A *HIVE*.
WE HAD A TINY BACKYARD, BUT HE PUT IT BACK THERE AND SPENT HOURS--
DAYS--WITH THOSE BEES.
WILL THEY MAKE HONEY?
OH YES.
THEY'LL BE *MAKERS*.
REMIND ME WHY WE HAVE A *SOCIOPATH* FOR A ROOMMATE.
HE'S NOT SO BAD.
AT LEAST HE'S *CLEAN*.
HE ONLY EATS ONE THING.
TACO BEEF
MAS NACHO NACHOS
HE BEGAN *SLEEPING* BACK THERE WITH HIS HIVE.
ZZZZZZZZZZZZZZZZZ
WE'D HEAR HIM *LAUGHING* AT NIGHT.
NOT WAX! HAHAHAHAHA!
HAVE YOU HEARD A *FULL HIVE?*
IT *HUMS*, LOW AND SCARY.
HUMMMMBZZZZZZZZZZZZ
THE WHOLE HOUSE WOULD PICK IT UP SOMETIMES.

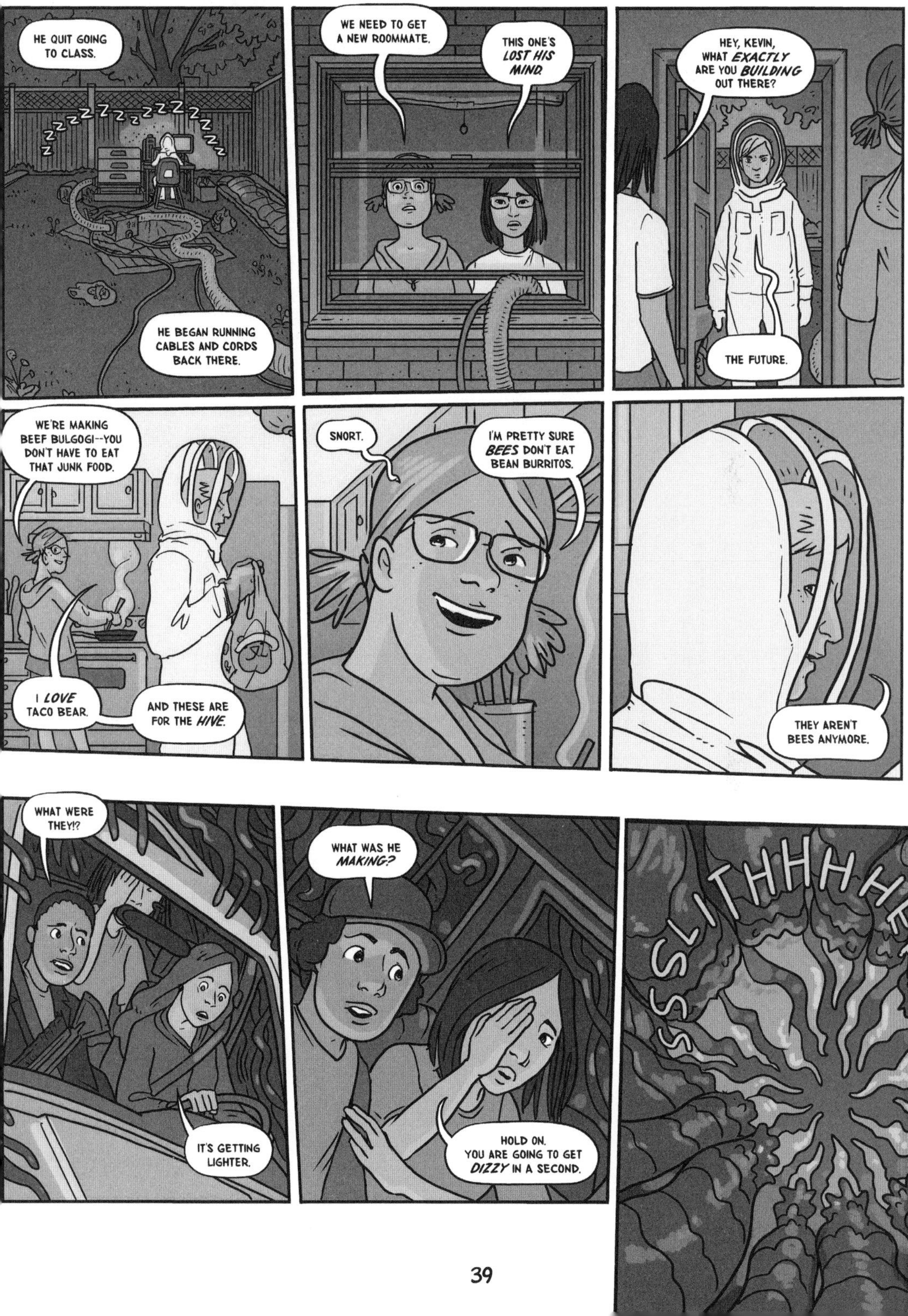
HE QUIT GOING TO CLASS.
ZZZZZZZZZZZZZZZ
HE BEGAN RUNNING CABLES AND CORDS BACK THERE.
WE NEED TO GET A NEW ROOMMATE.
THIS ONE'S *LOST HIS MIND.*
HEY, KEVIN, WHAT *EXACTLY* ARE YOU *BUILDING* OUT THERE?
THE FUTURE.
WE'RE MAKING BEEF BULGOGI--YOU DON'T HAVE TO EAT THAT JUNK FOOD.
I *LOVE* TACO BEAR.
AND THESE ARE FOR THE *HIVE.*
SNORT.
I'M PRETTY SURE *BEES* DON'T EAT BEAN BURRITOS.
THEY AREN'T BEES ANYMORE.
WHAT WERE THEY!?
IT'S GETTING LIGHTER.
WHAT WAS HE *MAKING?*
HOLD ON. YOU ARE GOING TO GET *DIZZY* IN A SECOND.
SSSLITHHHHHERRR

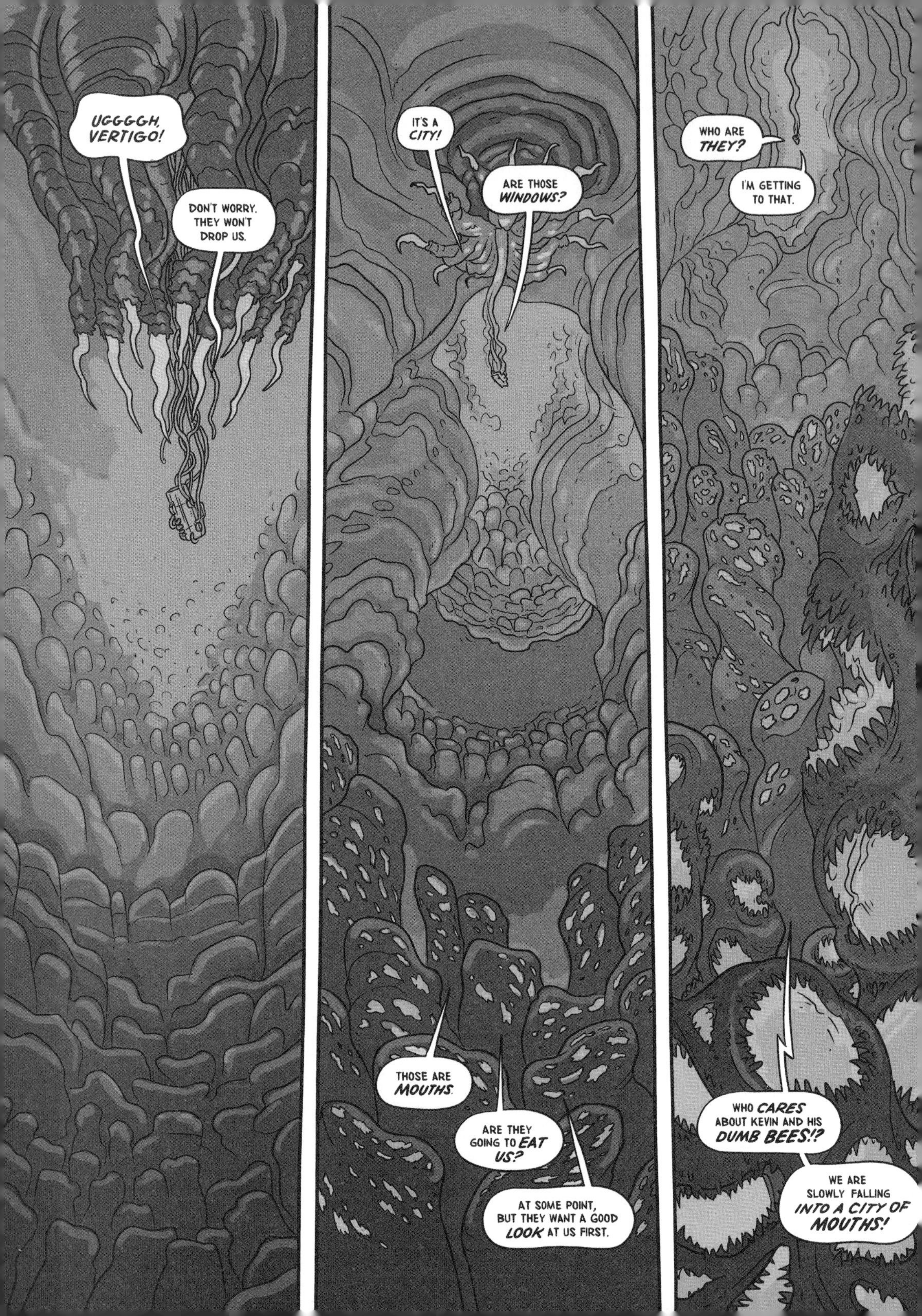
UGGGGH, VERTIGO!
DON'T WORRY. THEY WON'T DROP US.
IT'S A CITY!
ARE THOSE WINDOWS?
THOSE ARE MOUTHS.
ARE THEY GOING TO EAT US?
AT SOME POINT, BUT THEY WANT A GOOD LOOK AT US FIRST.
WHO ARE THEY?
I'M GETTING TO THAT.
WHO CARES ABOUT KEVIN AND HIS DUMB BEES!?
WE ARE SLOWLY FALLING INTO A CITY OF MOUTHS!

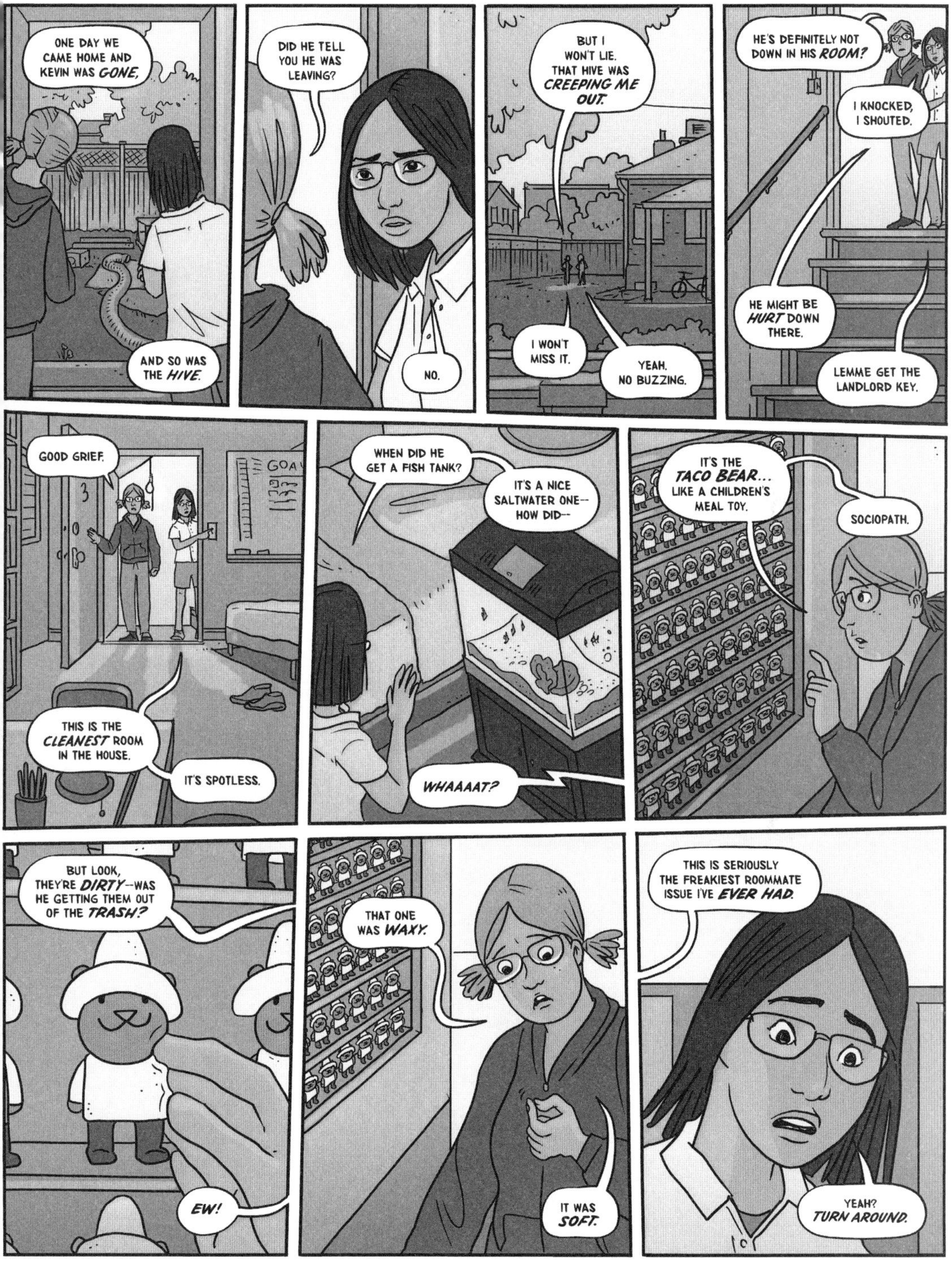
ONE DAY WE CAME HOME AND KEVIN WAS *GONE,*
AND SO WAS THE *HIVE.*
DID HE TELL YOU HE WAS LEAVING?
NO.
BUT I WON'T LIE. THAT HIVE WAS *CREEPING ME OUT.*
I WON'T MISS IT.
YEAH. NO BUZZING.
HE'S DEFINITELY NOT DOWN IN HIS *ROOM?*
I KNOCKED, I SHOUTED.
HE MIGHT BE *HURT* DOWN THERE.
LEMME GET THE LANDLORD KEY.
GOOD GRIEF.
THIS IS THE *CLEANEST* ROOM IN THE HOUSE.
IT'S SPOTLESS.
WHEN DID HE GET A FISH TANK?
IT'S A NICE SALTWATER ONE--HOW DID--
WHAAAAT?
IT'S THE *TACO BEAR...* LIKE A CHILDREN'S MEAL TOY.
SOCIOPATH.
BUT LOOK, THEY'RE *DIRTY*--WAS HE GETTING THEM OUT OF THE *TRASH?*
EW!
THAT ONE WAS *WAXY.*
IT WAS *SOFT.*
THIS IS SERIOUSLY THE FREAKIEST ROOMMATE ISSUE I'VE *EVER HAD.*
YEAH? *TURN AROUND.*

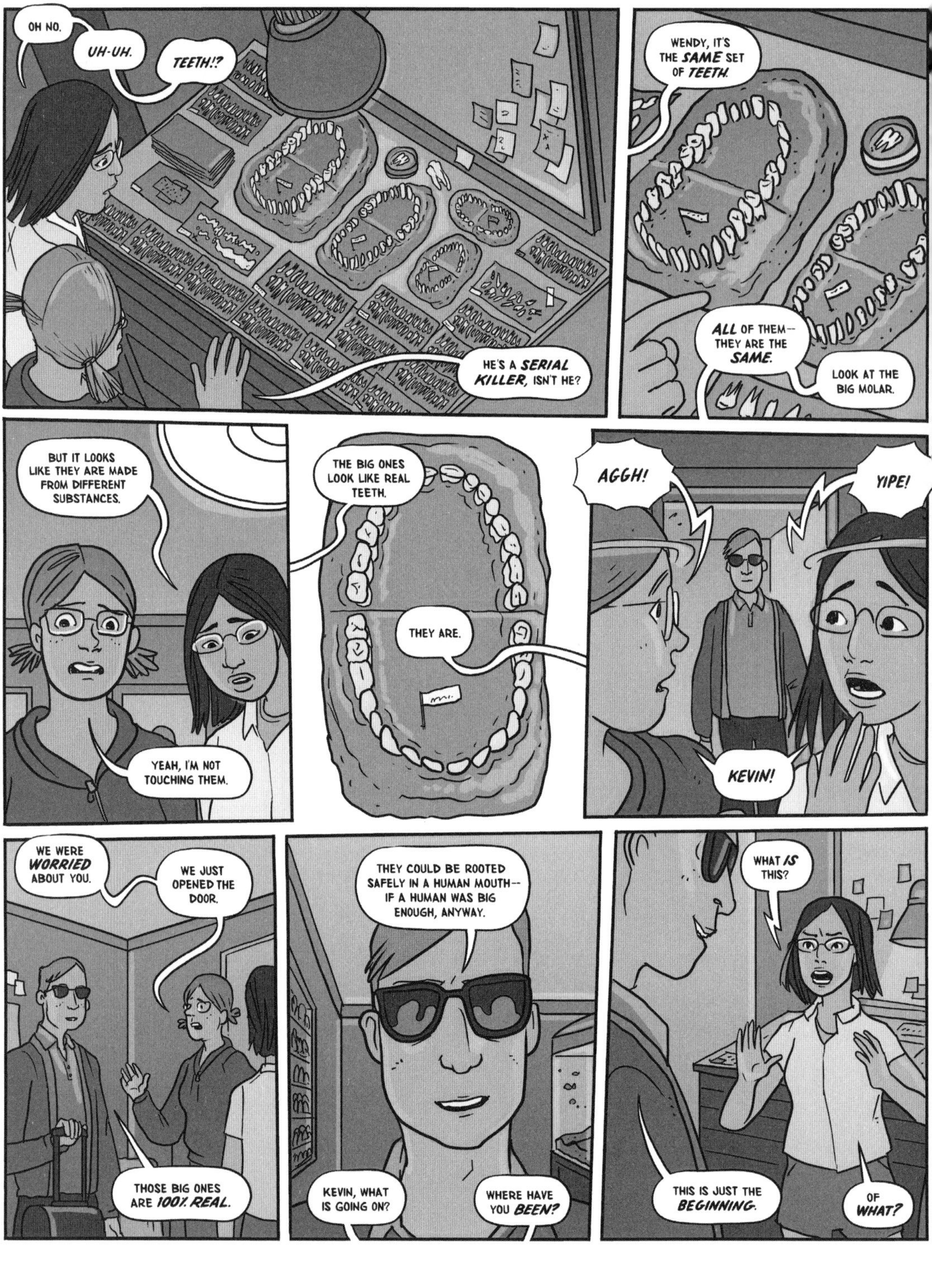
OH NO.
UH-UH.
TEETH!?
HE'S A SERIAL KILLER, ISN'T HE?
WENDY, IT'S THE SAME SET OF TEETH.
ALL OF THEM-- THEY ARE THE SAME.
LOOK AT THE BIG MOLAR.
BUT IT LOOKS LIKE THEY ARE MADE FROM DIFFERENT SUBSTANCES.
YEAH, I'M NOT TOUCHING THEM.
THE BIG ONES LOOK LIKE REAL TEETH.
THEY ARE.
AGGH!
YIPE!
KEVIN!
WE WERE WORRIED ABOUT YOU.
WE JUST OPENED THE DOOR.
THOSE BIG ONES ARE 100% REAL.
THEY COULD BE ROOTED SAFELY IN A HUMAN MOUTH-- IF A HUMAN WAS BIG ENOUGH, ANYWAY.
KEVIN, WHAT IS GOING ON?
WHERE HAVE YOU BEEN?
WHAT IS THIS?
THIS IS JUST THE BEGINNING.
OF WHAT?

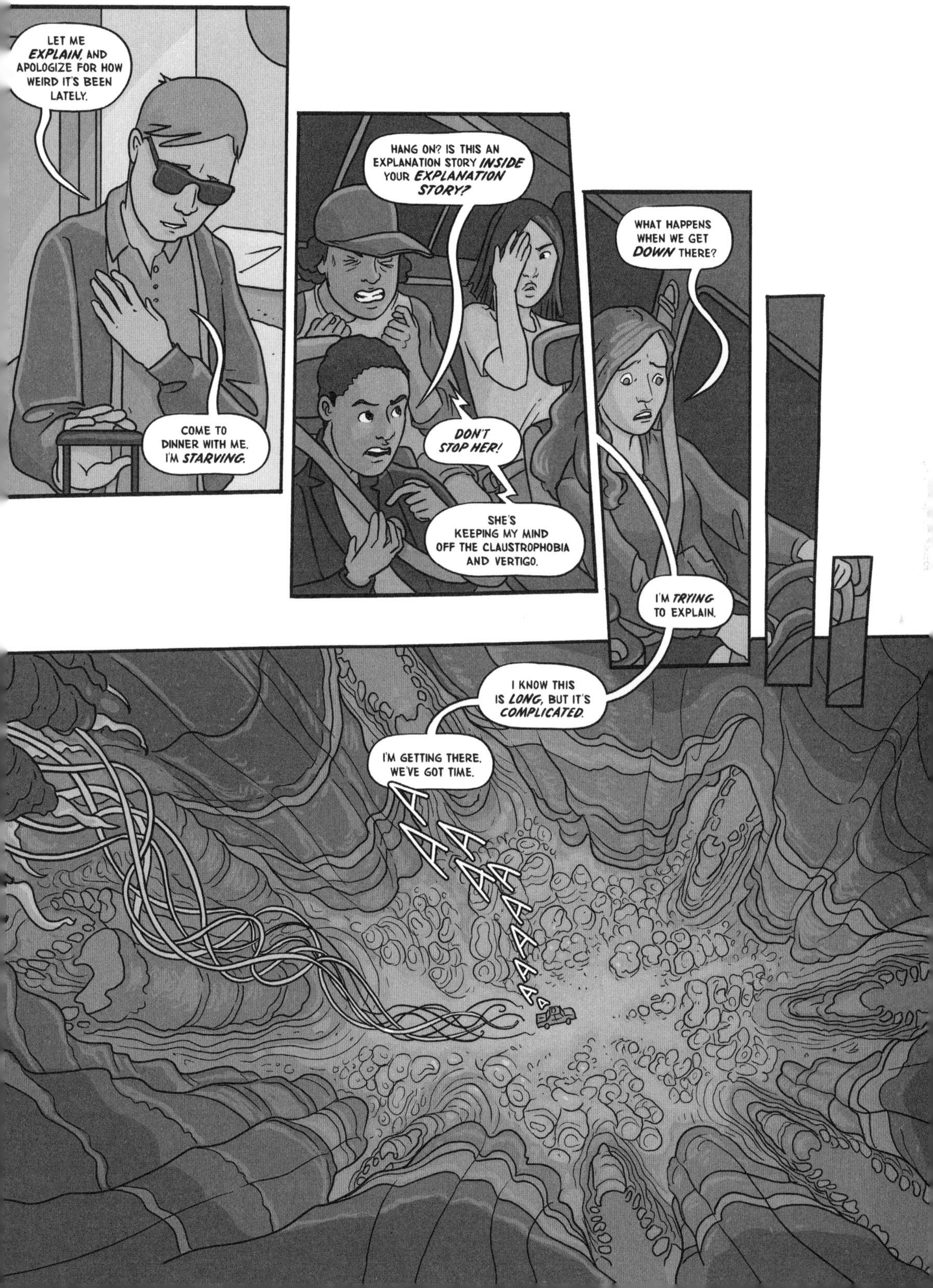
LET ME *EXPLAIN*, AND APOLOGIZE FOR HOW WEIRD IT'S BEEN LATELY.
COME TO DINNER WITH ME. I'M *STARVING*.
HANG ON? IS THIS AN EXPLANATION STORY *INSIDE* YOUR *EXPLANATION STORY?*
DON'T STOP HER!
SHE'S KEEPING MY MIND OFF THE CLAUSTROPHOBIA AND VERTIGO.
WHAT HAPPENS WHEN WE GET *DOWN* THERE?
I'M *TRYING* TO EXPLAIN.
I KNOW THIS IS *LONG*, BUT IT'S *COMPLICATED*.
I'M GETTING THERE. WE'VE GOT TIME.
AAAAAAAAAAAA

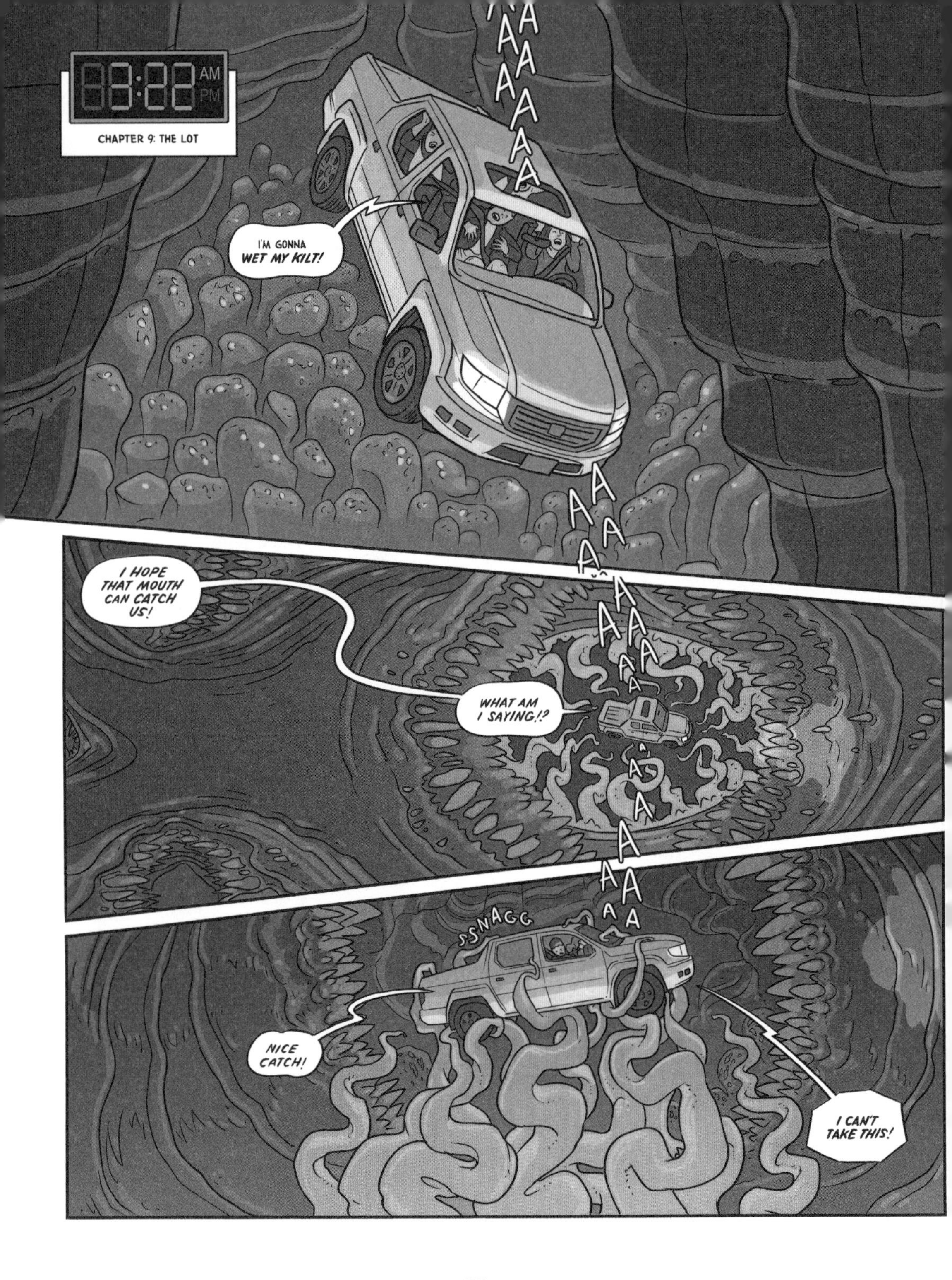
CHAPTER 9: THE LOT
I'M GONNA WET MY KILT!
I HOPE THAT MOUTH CAN CATCH US!
WHAT AM I SAYING!?
NICE CATCH!
I CAN'T TAKE THIS!

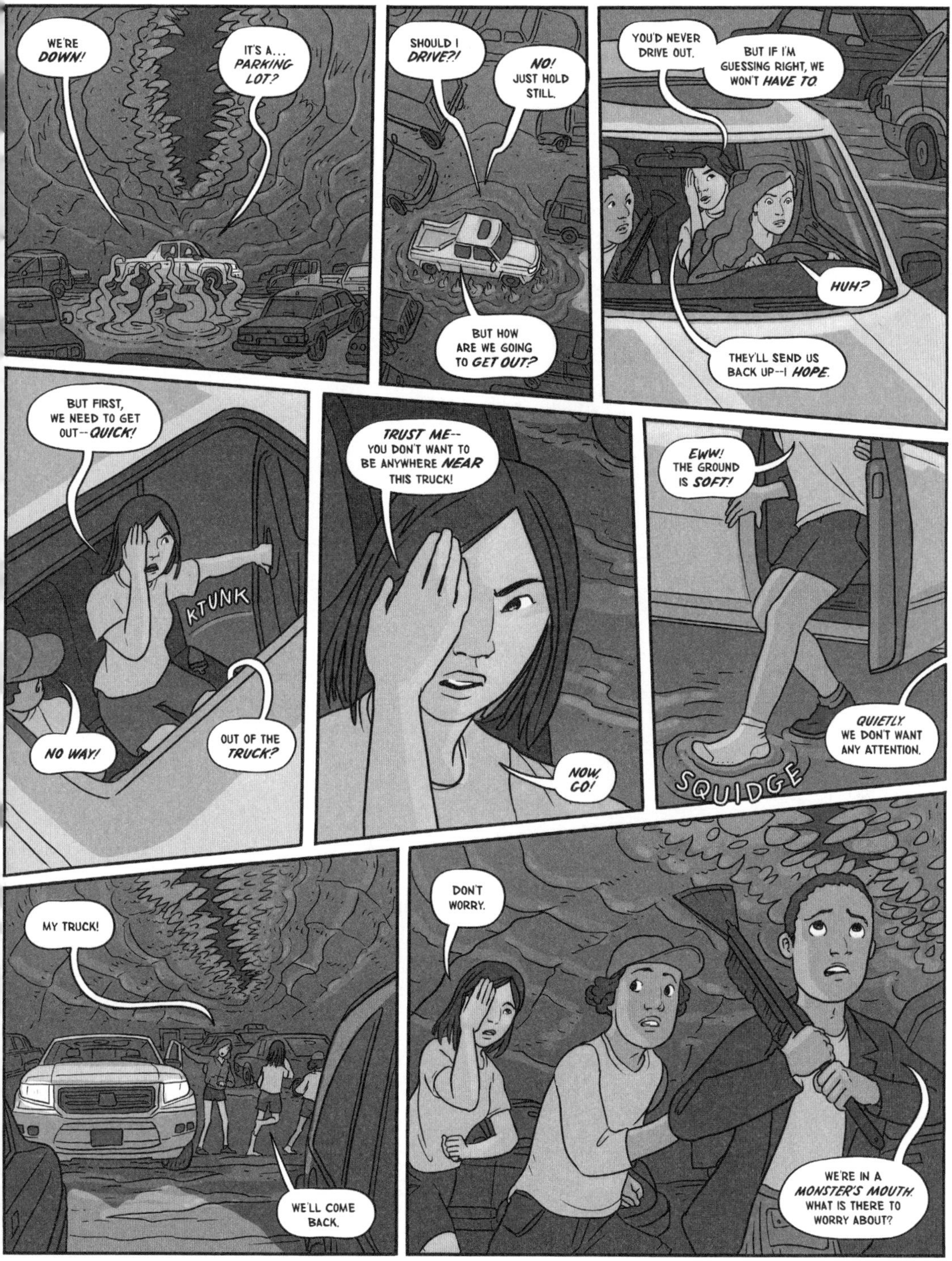
WE'RE DOWN!
IT'S A... PARKING LOT?
SHOULD I DRIVE?!
NO! JUST HOLD STILL.
BUT HOW ARE WE GOING TO GET OUT?
YOU'D NEVER DRIVE OUT.
BUT IF I'M GUESSING RIGHT, WE WON'T HAVE TO.
HUH?
THEY'LL SEND US BACK UP--I HOPE.
BUT FIRST, WE NEED TO GET OUT--QUICK!
KTUNK
NO WAY!
OUT OF THE TRUCK?
TRUST ME--YOU DON'T WANT TO BE ANYWHERE NEAR THIS TRUCK!
NOW, GO!
EWW! THE GROUND IS SOFT!
QUIETLY. WE DON'T WANT ANY ATTENTION.
SQUIDGE
MY TRUCK!
WE'LL COME BACK.
DON'T WORRY.
WE'RE IN A MONSTER'S MOUTH. WHAT IS THERE TO WORRY ABOUT?

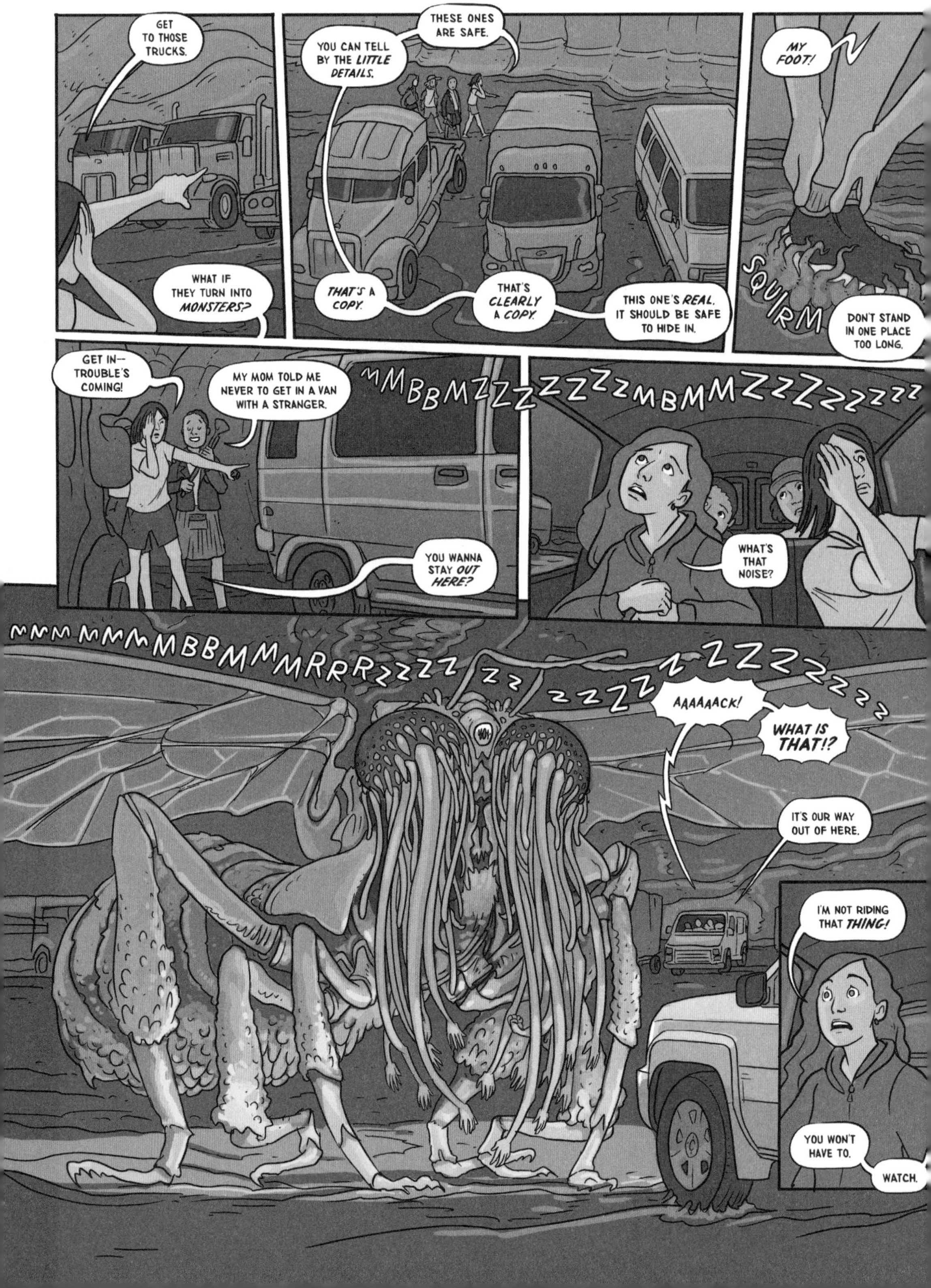
GET TO THOSE TRUCKS.
WHAT IF THEY TURN INTO MONSTERS?
YOU CAN TELL BY THE LITTLE DETAILS.
THESE ONES ARE SAFE.
THAT'S A COPY.
THAT'S CLEARLY A COPY.
THIS ONE'S REAL. IT SHOULD BE SAFE TO HIDE IN.
MY FOOT!
SQUIRM
DON'T STAND IN ONE PLACE TOO LONG.
GET IN-- TROUBLE'S COMING!
MY MOM TOLD ME NEVER TO GET IN A VAN WITH A STRANGER.
YOU WANNA STAY OUT HERE?
MMBBMZZZZZZZZMBMMZZZZZZZZZ
WHAT'S THAT NOISE?
MMMMMMMBBMMMMRRRZZZZZZZZZZZZZZZZZZZZZZ
AAAAAACK!
WHAT IS THAT!?
IT'S OUR WAY OUT OF HERE.
I'M NOT RIDING THAT THING!
YOU WON'T HAVE TO.
WATCH.

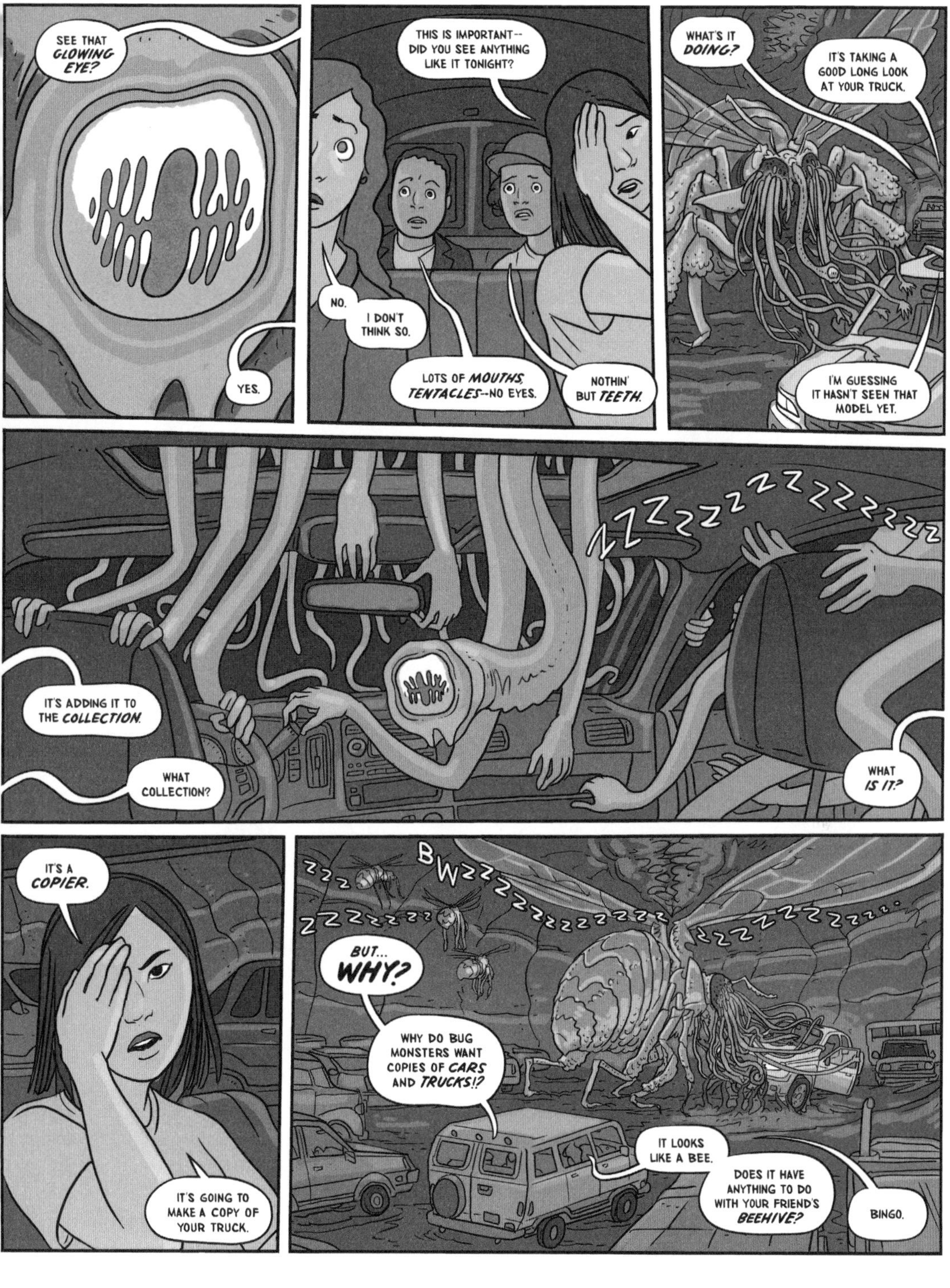
SEE THAT GLOWING EYE?
YES.
THIS IS IMPORTANT--DID YOU SEE ANYTHING LIKE IT TONIGHT?
NO.
I DON'T THINK SO.
LOTS OF MOUTHS, TENTACLES--NO EYES.
NOTHIN' BUT TEETH.
WHAT'S IT DOING?
IT'S TAKING A GOOD LONG LOOK AT YOUR TRUCK.
I'M GUESSING IT HASN'T SEEN THAT MODEL YET.
ZZZZZZZZZZZZZZZZZ
IT'S ADDING IT TO THE COLLECTION.
WHAT COLLECTION?
WHAT IS IT?
IT'S A COPIER.
IT'S GOING TO MAKE A COPY OF YOUR TRUCK.
BWZZZZZZZZZZZZZ
BUT... WHY?
WHY DO BUG MONSTERS WANT COPIES OF CARS AND TRUCKS!?
IT LOOKS LIKE A BEE.
DOES IT HAVE ANYTHING TO DO WITH YOUR FRIEND'S BEEHIVE?
BINGO.

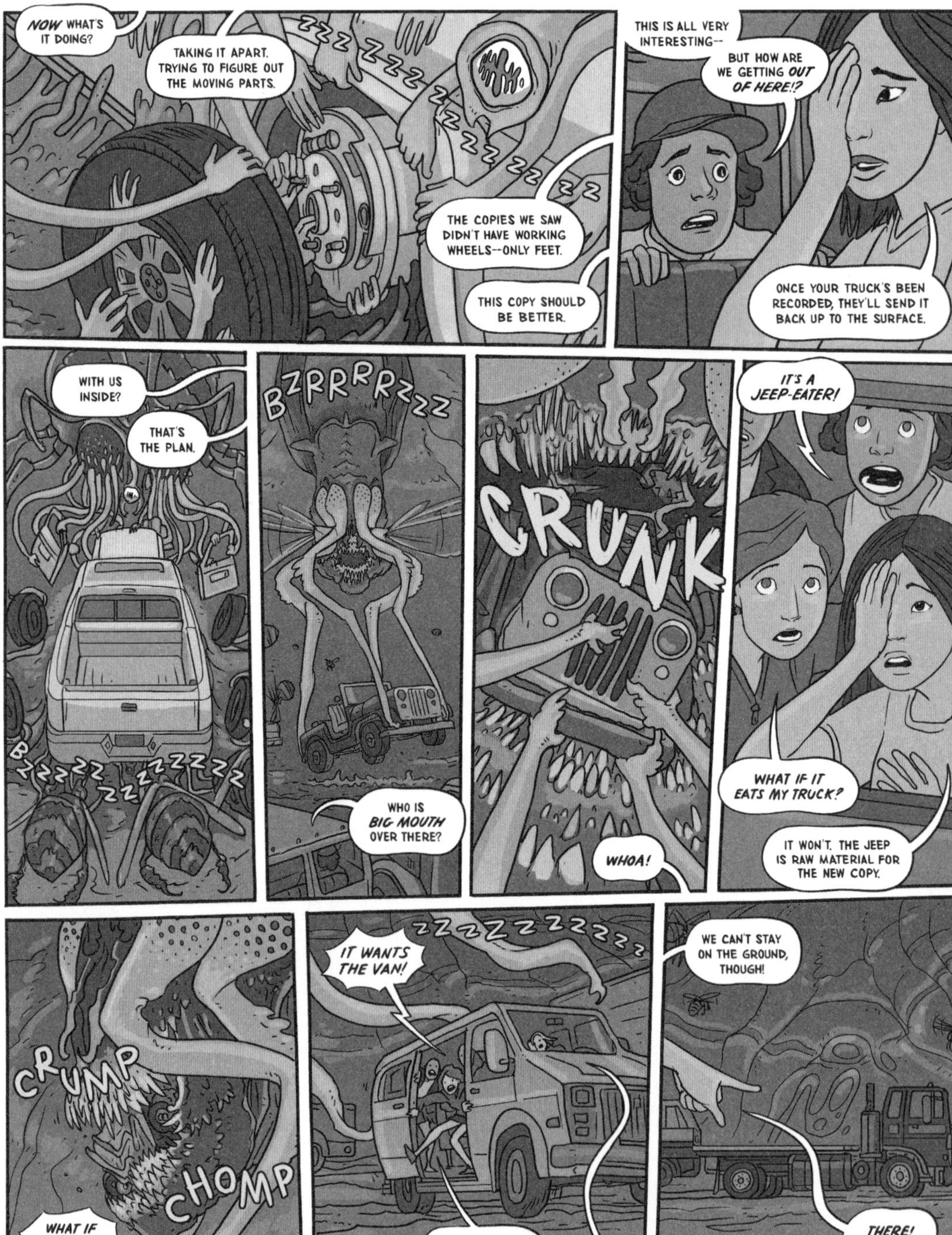
NOW WHAT'S IT DOING?
TAKING IT APART. TRYING TO FIGURE OUT THE MOVING PARTS.
ZZZZZZZZZZZZZZZZZ
THE COPIES WE SAW DIDN'T HAVE WORKING WHEELS--ONLY FEET.
THIS COPY SHOULD BE BETTER.
THIS IS ALL VERY INTERESTING--
BUT HOW ARE WE GETTING OUT OF HERE!?
ONCE YOUR TRUCK'S BEEN RECORDED, THEY'LL SEND IT BACK UP TO THE SURFACE.
WITH US INSIDE?
THAT'S THE PLAN.
BZZZZZZZZZZZZ
BZRRRRZZZ
WHO IS BIG MOUTH OVER THERE?
CRUNK
WHOA!
IT'S A JEEP-EATER!
WHAT IF IT EATS MY TRUCK?
IT WON'T. THE JEEP IS RAW MATERIAL FOR THE NEW COPY.
CRUMP
CHOMP
WHAT IF IT EATS THIS VAN?
ZZZZZZZZZZZZZ
IT WANTS THE VAN!
I THOUGHT THESE CARS WERE SAFE!
I DID TOO!
WE CAN'T STAY ON THE GROUND, THOUGH!
THERE! FLATBED!

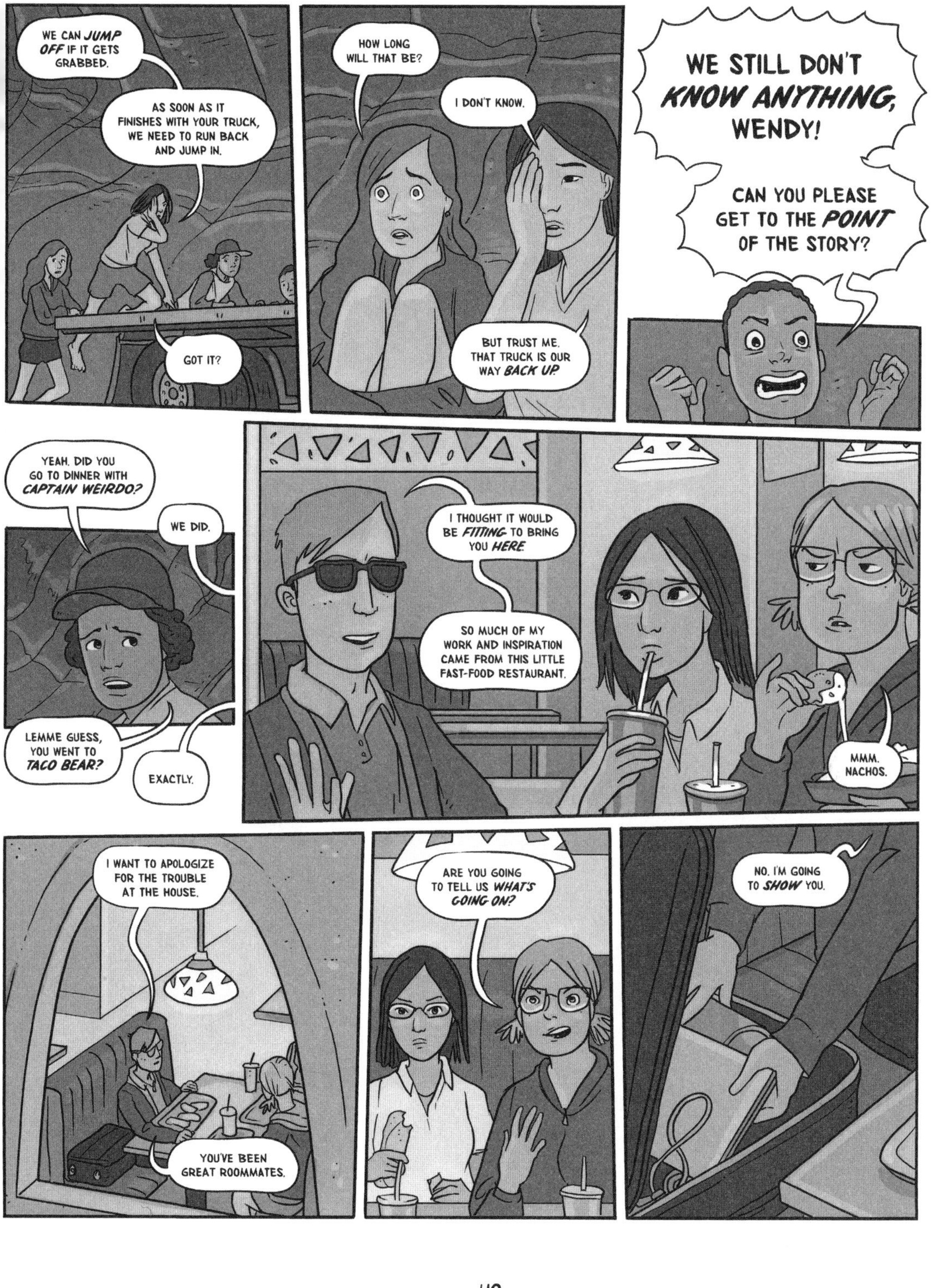
WE CAN *JUMP OFF* IF IT GETS GRABBED.
AS SOON AS IT FINISHES WITH YOUR TRUCK, WE NEED TO RUN BACK AND JUMP IN.
GOT IT?
HOW LONG WILL THAT BE?
I DON'T KNOW.
BUT TRUST ME. THAT TRUCK IS OUR WAY *BACK UP.*
WE STILL DON'T *KNOW ANYTHING,* WENDY!
CAN YOU PLEASE GET TO THE *POINT* OF THE STORY?
YEAH. DID YOU GO TO DINNER WITH *CAPTAIN WEIRDO?*
WE DID.
LEMME GUESS, YOU WENT TO *TACO BEAR?*
EXACTLY.
I THOUGHT IT WOULD BE *FITTING* TO BRING YOU *HERE.*
SO MUCH OF MY WORK AND INSPIRATION CAME FROM THIS LITTLE FAST-FOOD RESTAURANT.
MMM. NACHOS.
I WANT TO APOLOGIZE FOR THE TROUBLE AT THE HOUSE.
YOU'VE BEEN GREAT ROOMMATES.
ARE YOU GOING TO TELL US *WHAT'S GOING ON?*
NO. I'M GOING TO *SHOW* YOU.

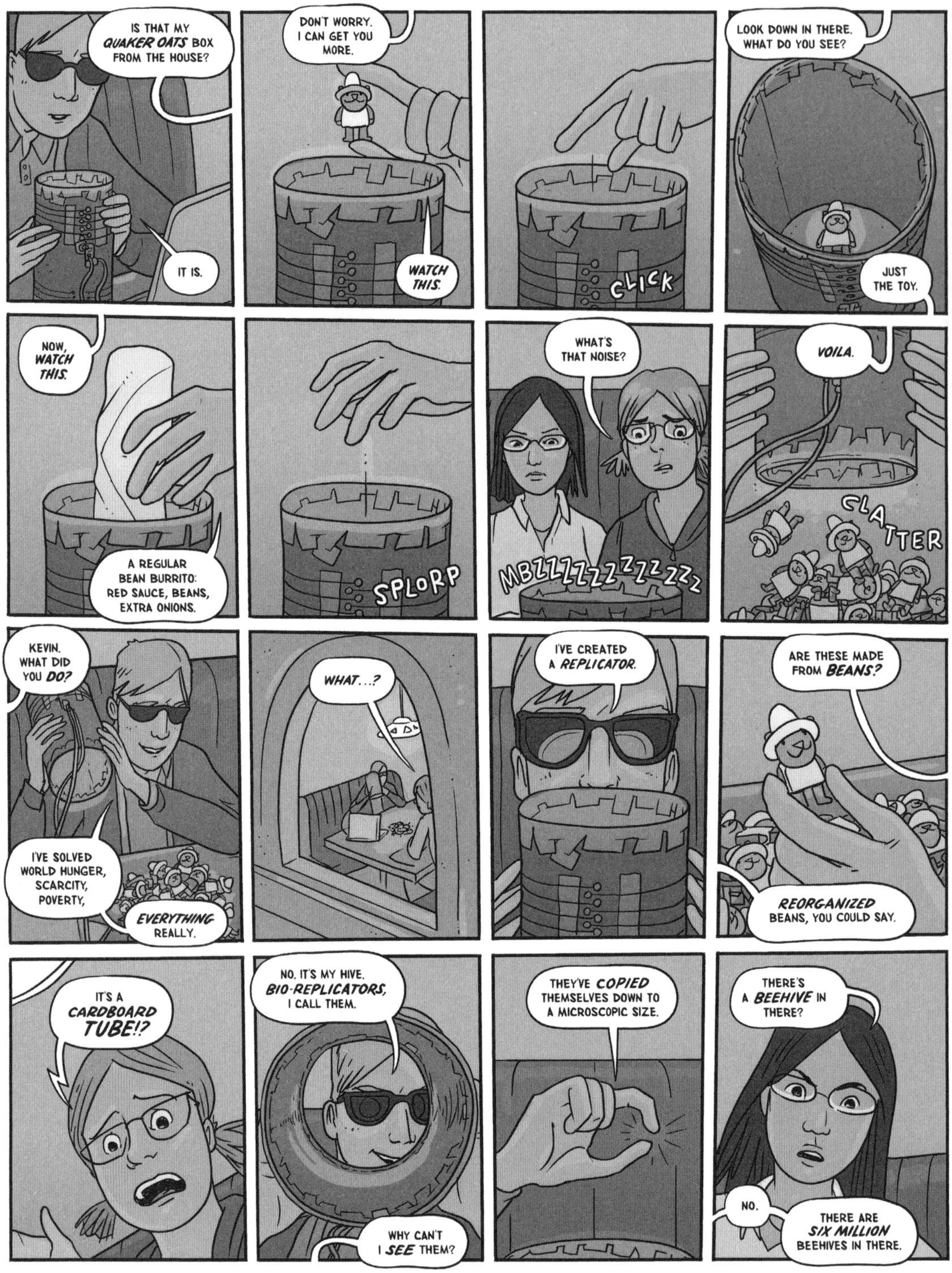
IS THAT MY QUAKER OATS BOX FROM THE HOUSE?
IT IS.
DON'T WORRY. I CAN GET YOU MORE.
WATCH THIS.
CLICK
LOOK DOWN IN THERE. WHAT DO YOU SEE?
JUST THE TOY.
NOW, WATCH THIS.
A REGULAR BEAN BURRITO: RED SAUCE, BEANS, EXTRA ONIONS.
SPLORP
WHAT'S THAT NOISE?
MBZZZZZZZZZZZZ
VOILA.
CLATTER
KEVIN. WHAT DID YOU DO?
I'VE SOLVED WORLD HUNGER, SCARCITY, POVERTY,
EVERYTHING REALLY.
WHAT...?
I'VE CREATED A REPLICATOR.
ARE THESE MADE FROM BEANS?
REORGANIZED BEANS, YOU COULD SAY.
IT'S A CARDBOARD TUBE!?
NO, IT'S MY HIVE. BIO-REPLICATORS, I CALL THEM.
WHY CAN'T I SEE THEM?
THEY'VE COPIED THEMSELVES DOWN TO A MICROSCOPIC SIZE.
THERE'S A BEEHIVE IN THERE?
NO.
THERE ARE SIX MILLION BEEHIVES IN THERE.

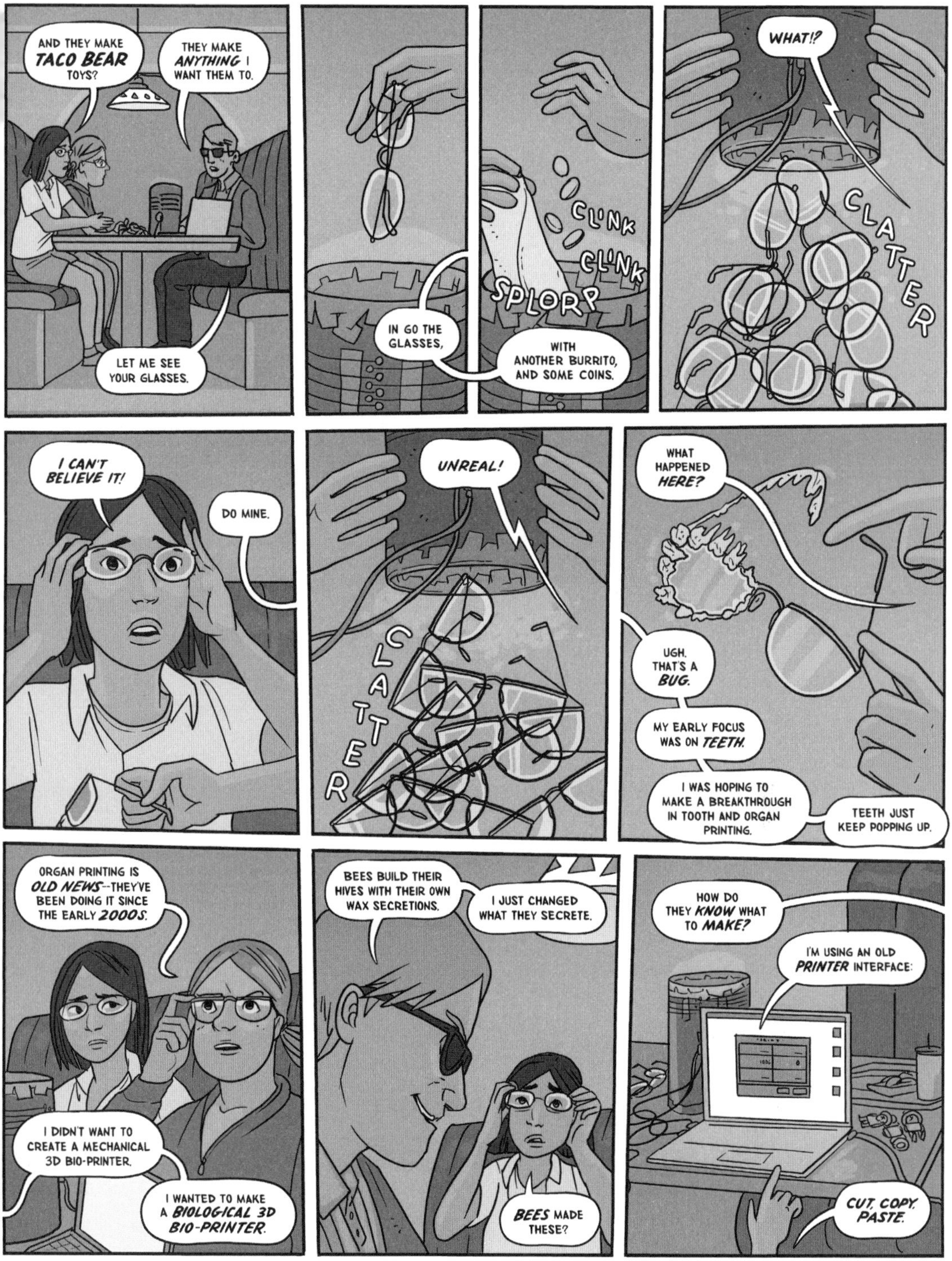
AND THEY MAKE TACO BEAR TOYS?
THEY MAKE ANYTHING I WANT THEM TO.
LET ME SEE YOUR GLASSES.
IN GO THE GLASSES,
CLINK
CLINK
SPLORP
WITH ANOTHER BURRITO, AND SOME COINS.
WHAT!?
CLATTER
I CAN'T BELIEVE IT!
DO MINE.
UNREAL!
CLATTER
WHAT HAPPENED HERE?
UGH. THAT'S A BUG.
MY EARLY FOCUS WAS ON TEETH.
I WAS HOPING TO MAKE A BREAKTHROUGH IN TOOTH AND ORGAN PRINTING.
TEETH JUST KEEP POPPING UP.
ORGAN PRINTING IS OLD NEWS--THEY'VE BEEN DOING IT SINCE THE EARLY 2000S.
I DIDN'T WANT TO CREATE A MECHANICAL 3D BIO-PRINTER.
I WANTED TO MAKE A BIOLOGICAL 3D BIO-PRINTER.
BEES BUILD THEIR HIVES WITH THEIR OWN WAX SECRETIONS.
I JUST CHANGED WHAT THEY SECRETE.
BEES MADE THESE?
HOW DO THEY KNOW WHAT TO MAKE?
I'M USING AN OLD PRINTER INTERFACE:
CUT, COPY, PASTE.

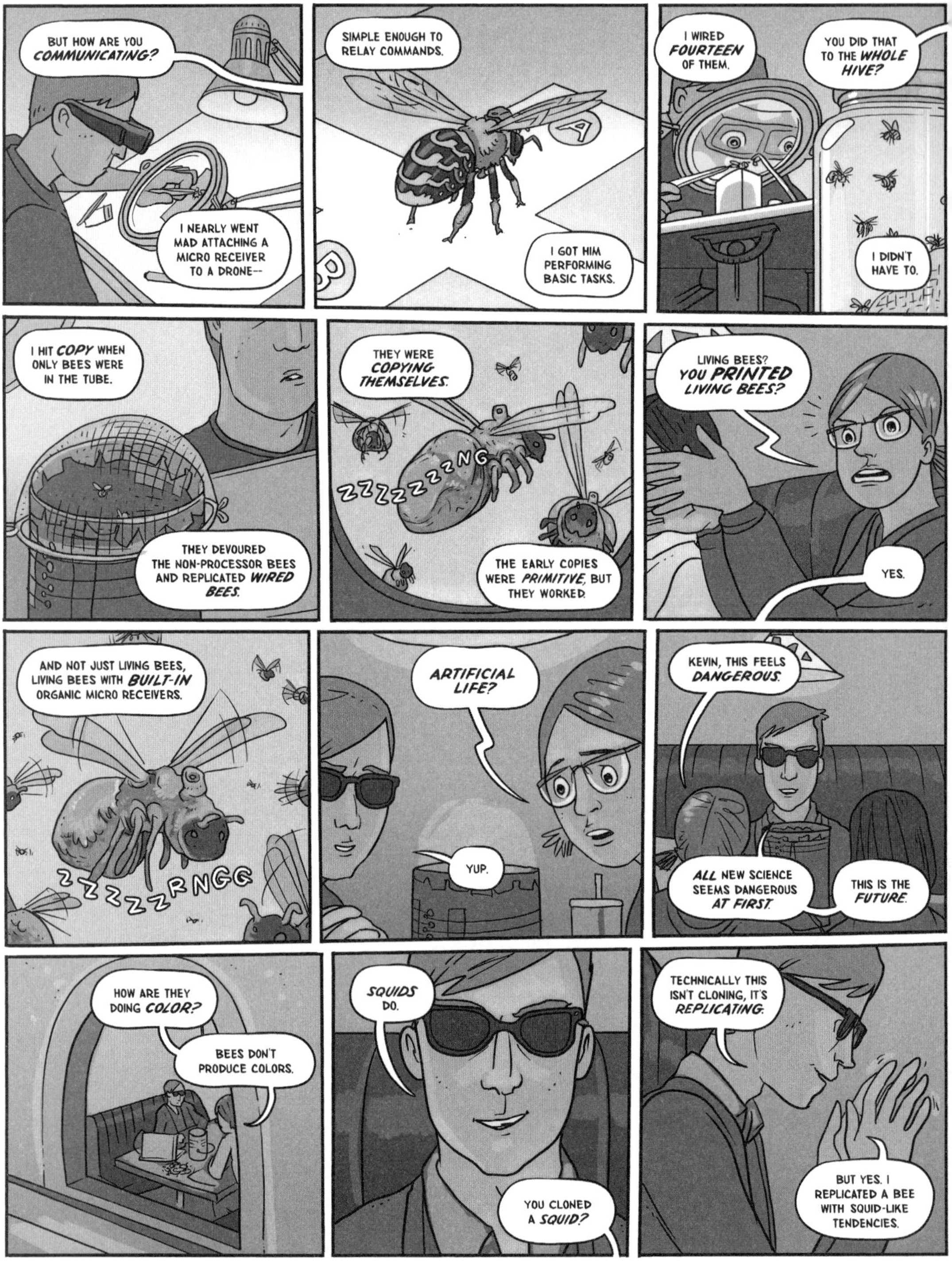

BUT HOW ARE YOU COMMUNICATING?
I NEARLY WENT MAD ATTACHING A MICRO RECEIVER TO A DRONE--
SIMPLE ENOUGH TO RELAY COMMANDS.
I GOT HIM PERFORMING BASIC TASKS.
I WIRED FOURTEEN OF THEM.
YOU DID THAT TO THE WHOLE HIVE?
I DIDN'T HAVE TO.
I HIT COPY WHEN ONLY BEES WERE IN THE TUBE.
THEY DEVOURED THE NON-PROCESSOR BEES AND REPLICATED WIRED BEES.
THEY WERE COPYING THEMSELVES.
ZZZZZZZZNG
THE EARLY COPIES WERE PRIMITIVE, BUT THEY WORKED.
LIVING BEES? YOU PRINTED LIVING BEES?
YES.
AND NOT JUST LIVING BEES, LIVING BEES WITH BUILT-IN ORGANIC MICRO RECEIVERS.
ZZZZZZRNGG
ARTIFICIAL LIFE?
YUP.
KEVIN, THIS FEELS DANGEROUS.
ALL NEW SCIENCE SEEMS DANGEROUS AT FIRST.
THIS IS THE FUTURE.
HOW ARE THEY DOING COLOR?
BEES DON'T PRODUCE COLORS.
SQUIDS DO.
YOU CLONED A SQUID?
TECHNICALLY THIS ISN'T CLONING, IT'S REPLICATING.
BUT YES. I REPLICATED A BEE WITH SQUID-LIKE TENDENCIES.

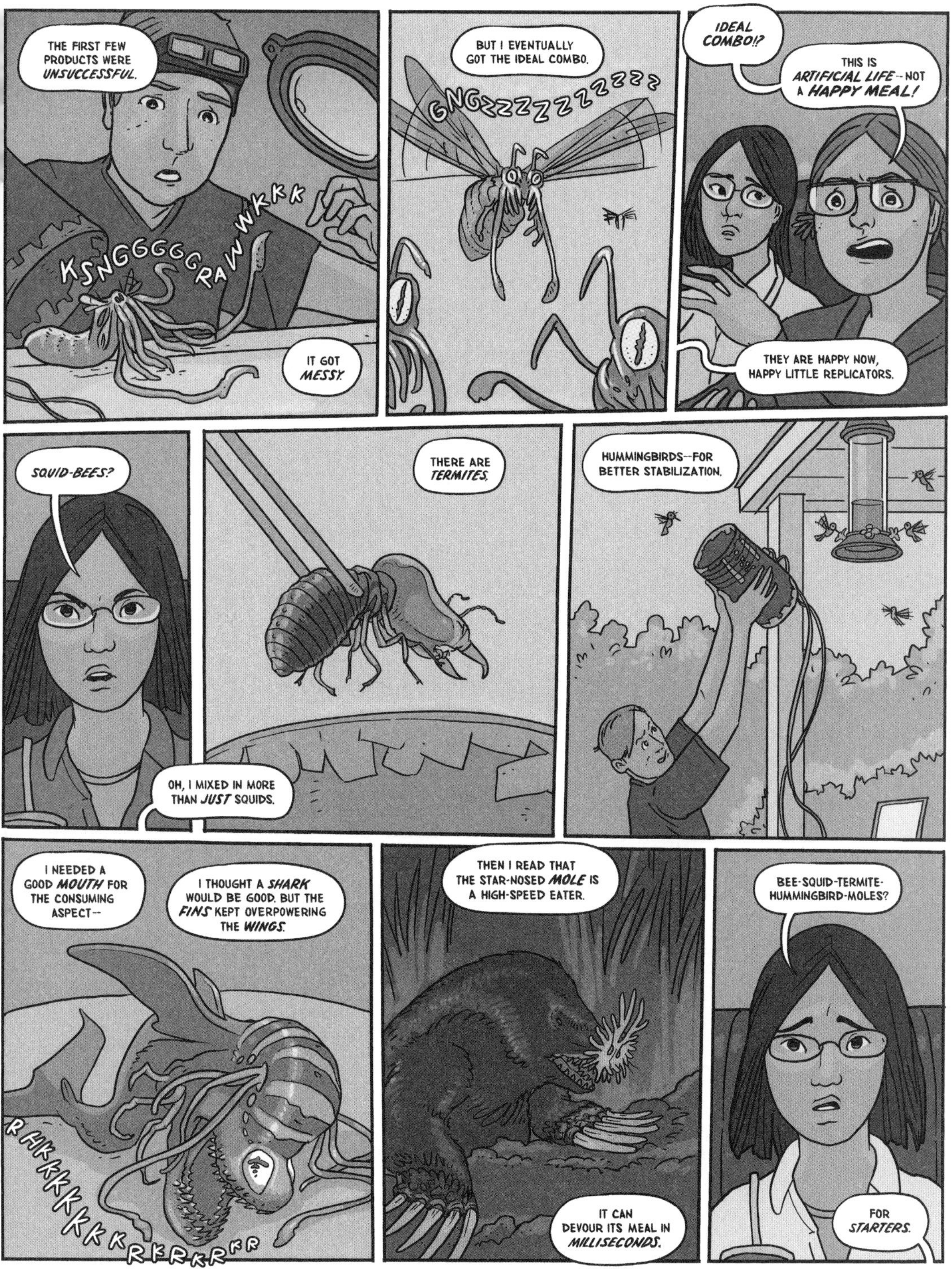
THE FIRST FEW PRODUCTS WERE *UNSUCCESSFUL.*
KSNGGGGGGRAWWKKK
IT GOT *MESSY.*
BUT I EVENTUALLY GOT THE IDEAL COMBO.
GNGZZZZZZZZZZZ
IDEAL COMBO!?
THIS IS *ARTIFICIAL LIFE*--NOT A *HAPPY MEAL!*
THEY ARE HAPPY NOW, HAPPY LITTLE REPLICATORS.
SQUID-BEES?
THERE ARE *TERMITES.*
OH, I MIXED IN MORE THAN *JUST* SQUIDS.
HUMMINGBIRDS--FOR BETTER STABILIZATION.
I NEEDED A GOOD *MOUTH* FOR THE CONSUMING ASPECT--
I THOUGHT A *SHARK* WOULD BE GOOD. BUT THE *FINS* KEPT OVERPOWERING THE *WINGS.*
RAKKKKKKKKKRRRRRRR
THEN I READ THAT THE STAR-NOSED *MOLE* IS A HIGH-SPEED EATER.
IT CAN DEVOUR ITS MEAL IN *MILLISECONDS.*
BEE-SQUID-TERMITE-HUMMINGBIRD-MOLES?
FOR *STARTERS.*

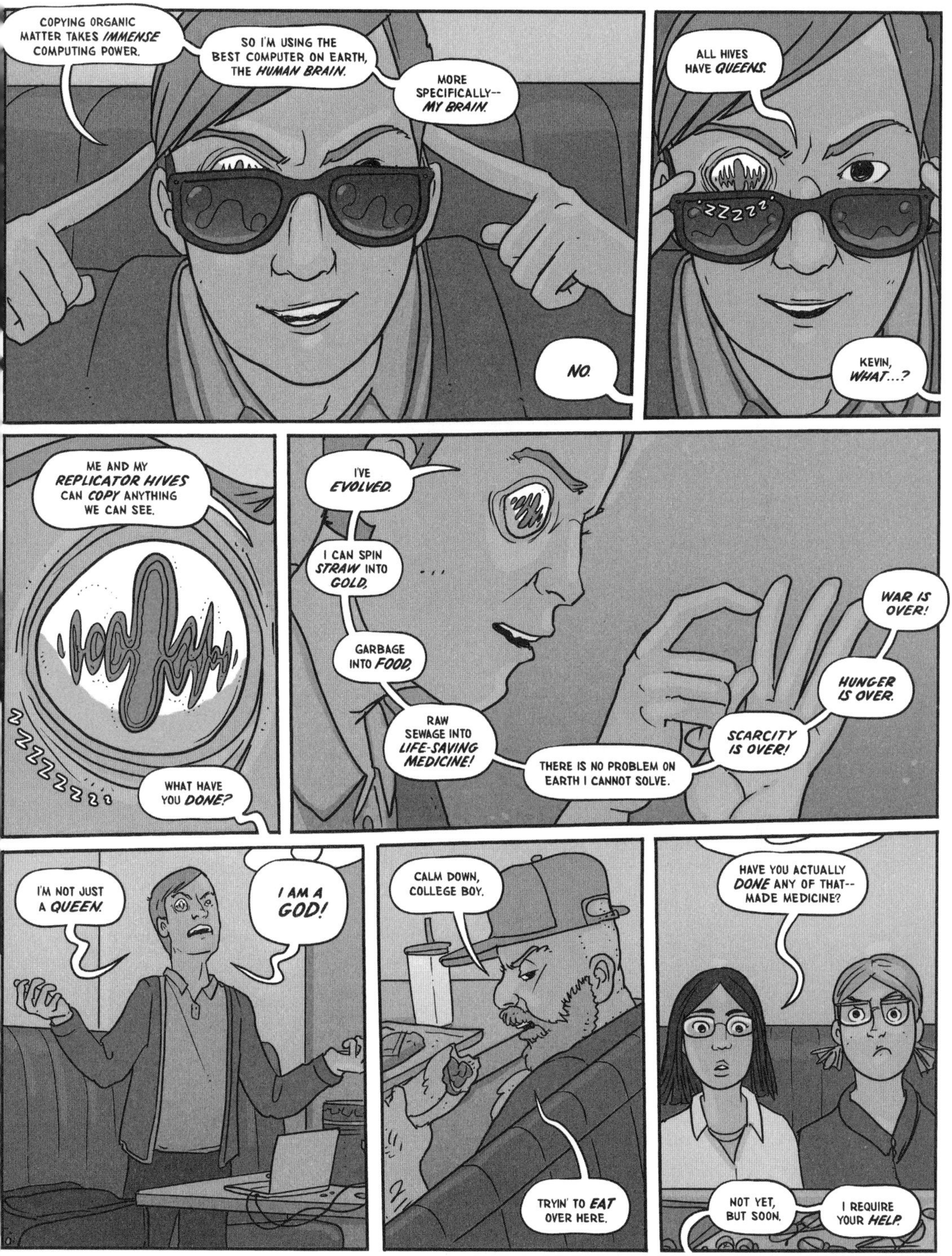
COPYING ORGANIC MATTER TAKES IMMENSE COMPUTING POWER.
SO I'M USING THE BEST COMPUTER ON EARTH, THE HUMAN BRAIN.
MORE SPECIFICALLY-- MY BRAIN.
NO.
ALL HIVES HAVE QUEENS.
ZZZZZ
KEVIN, WHAT...?
ME AND MY REPLICATOR HIVES CAN COPY ANYTHING WE CAN SEE.
ZZZZZZZZ
WHAT HAVE YOU DONE?
I'VE EVOLVED.
I CAN SPIN STRAW INTO GOLD,
GARBAGE INTO FOOD,
RAW SEWAGE INTO LIFE-SAVING MEDICINE!
THERE IS NO PROBLEM ON EARTH I CANNOT SOLVE.
SCARCITY IS OVER!
HUNGER IS OVER.
WAR IS OVER!
I'M NOT JUST A QUEEN.
I AM A GOD!
CALM DOWN, COLLEGE BOY.
TRYIN' TO EAT OVER HERE.
HAVE YOU ACTUALLY DONE ANY OF THAT-- MADE MEDICINE?
NOT YET, BUT SOON.
I REQUIRE YOUR HELP.

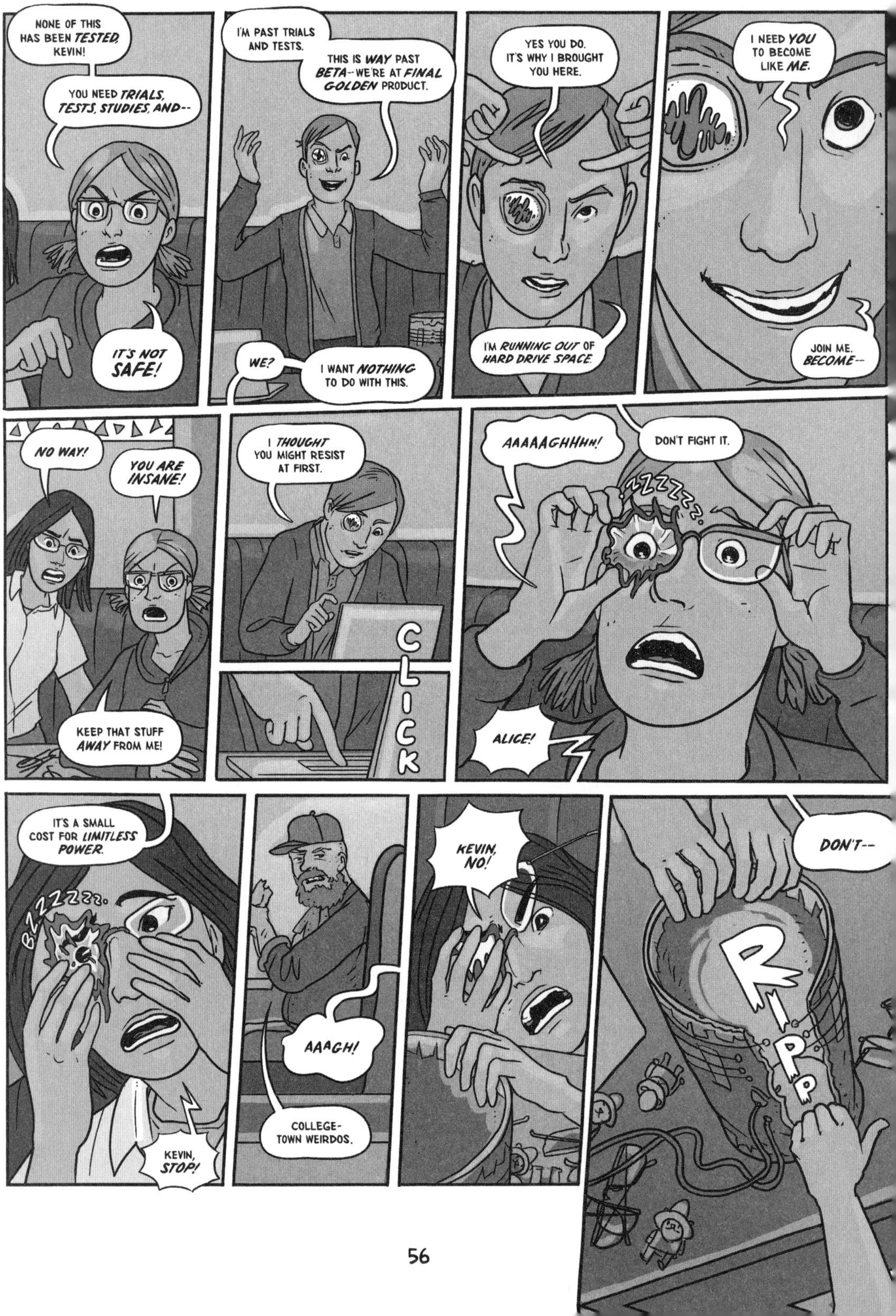
NONE OF THIS HAS BEEN TESTED, KEVIN!
YOU NEED TRIALS, TESTS, STUDIES, AND--
IT'S NOT SAFE!
I'M PAST TRIALS AND TESTS.
THIS IS WAY PAST BETA--WE'RE AT FINAL GOLDEN PRODUCT.
WE?
I WANT NOTHING TO DO WITH THIS.
YES YOU DO. IT'S WHY I BROUGHT YOU HERE.
I'M RUNNING OUT OF HARD DRIVE SPACE.
I NEED YOU TO BECOME LIKE ME.
JOIN ME. BECOME--
NO WAY!
YOU ARE INSANE!
KEEP THAT STUFF AWAY FROM ME!
I THOUGHT YOU MIGHT RESIST AT FIRST.
CLICK
AAAAAGHHHH!
DON'T FIGHT IT.
ZZZZZZ...
ALICE!
IT'S A SMALL COST FOR LIMITLESS POWER.
BZZZZZZ...
KEVIN, STOP!
AAAGH!
COLLEGE-TOWN WEIRDOS.
KEVIN, NO!
DON'T--
RIPP

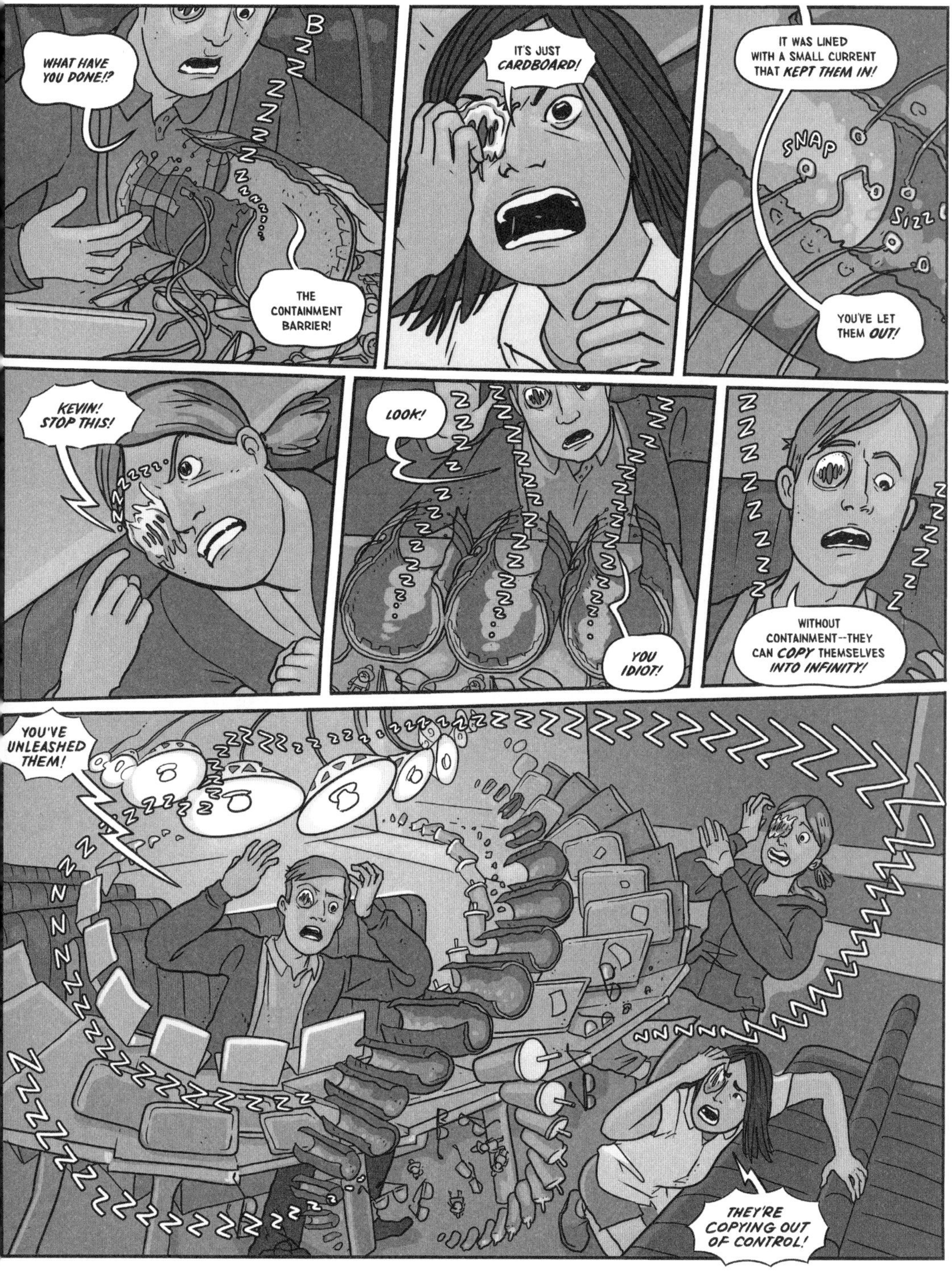
WHAT HAVE YOU DONE!?
THE CONTAINMENT BARRIER!
IT'S JUST CARDBOARD!
IT WAS LINED WITH A SMALL CURRENT THAT KEPT THEM IN!
SNAP
SIZZ
YOU'VE LET THEM OUT!
KEVIN! STOP THIS!
LOOK!
YOU IDIOT!
WITHOUT CONTAINMENT--THEY CAN COPY THEMSELVES INTO INFINITY!
YOU'VE UNLEASHED THEM!
THEY'RE COPYING OUT OF CONTROL!

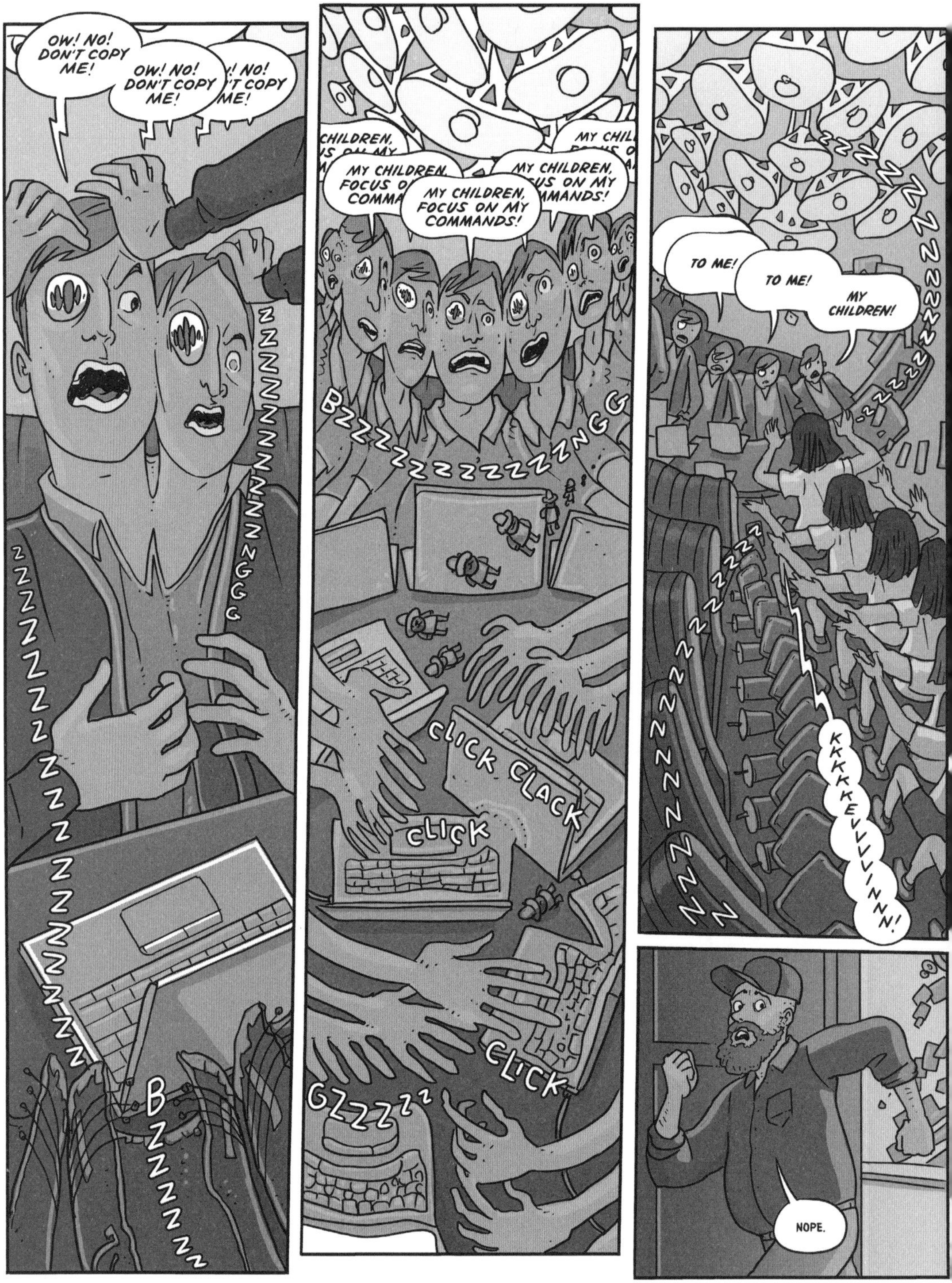
OW! NO! DON'T COPY ME!
OW! NO! DON'T COPY ME!
MY CHILDREN, FOCUS ON MY COMMANDS!
MY CHILDREN, FOCUS ON MY COMMANDS!
MY CHILDREN, FOCUS ON MY COMMANDS!
BZZZZZZZZZZZZZZZNGG
CLICK CLACK
CLICK
CLICK
GZZZZZZ
TO ME!
TO ME!
MY CHILDREN!
KKKKEVVVINNN!
NOPE.

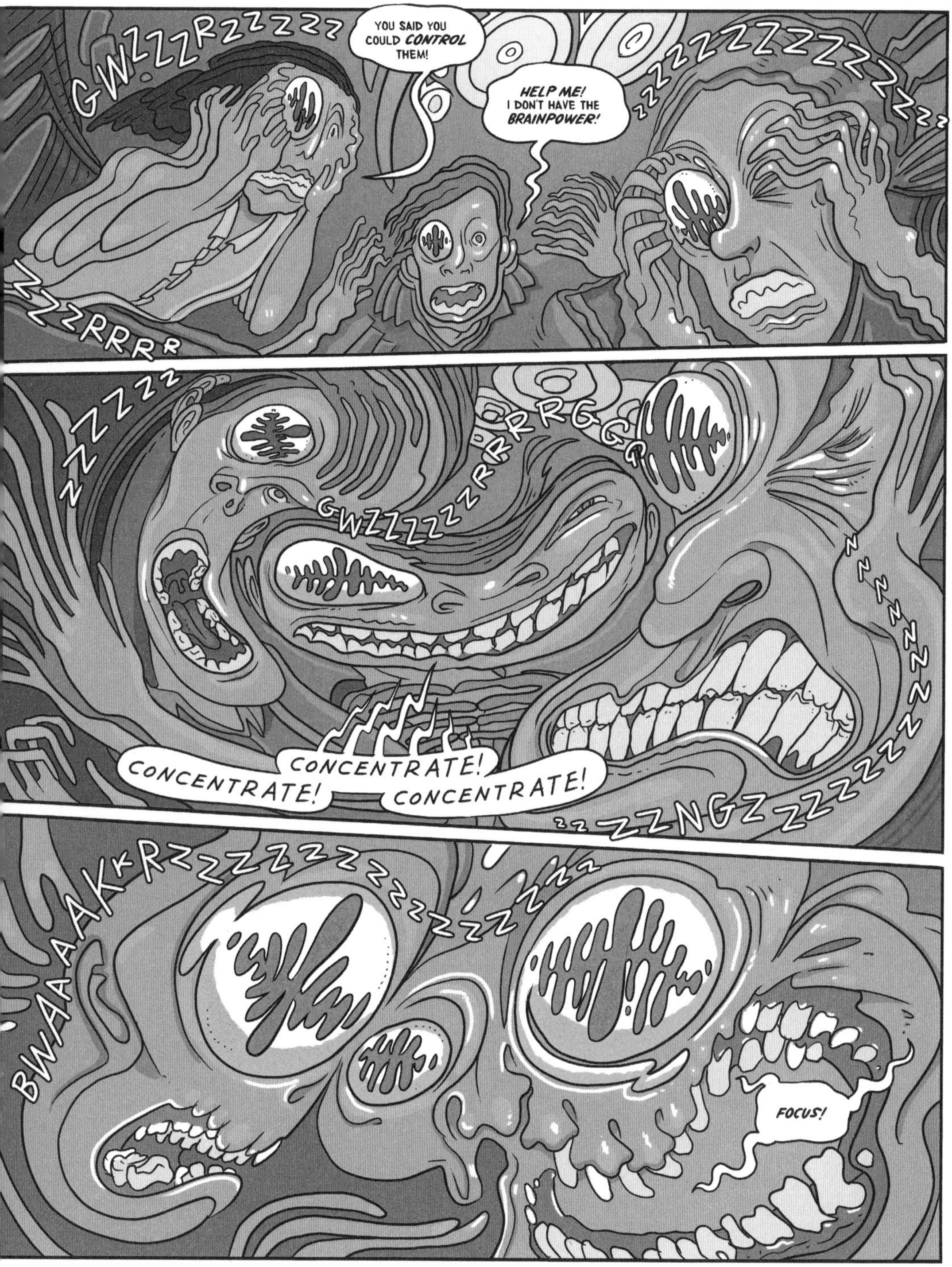
GWZZZRZZZZZZ
YOU SAID YOU COULD CONTROL THEM!
HELP ME! I DON'T HAVE THE BRAINPOWER!
ZZZZZZZZZZZZZZZ
ZZZRRRRR
ZZZZZZZZ
RRRRGGGG
GWZZZZZZZ
ZZZZZZZZZ
CONCENTRATE!
CONCENTRATE!
CONCENTRATE!
ZZZZNGZZZZZZZZZ
BWAAAKKRZZZZZZZZZZZZZZZZ
FOCUS!

QUEENS!

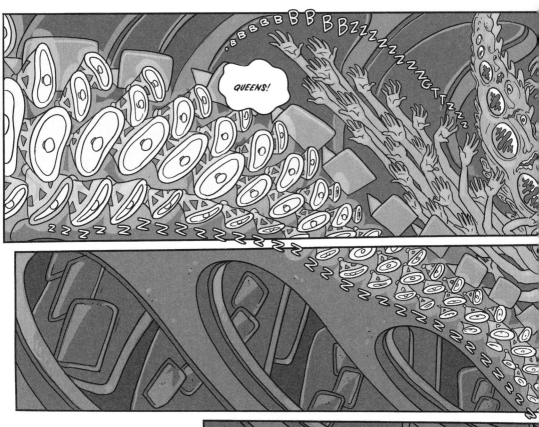

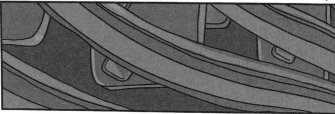

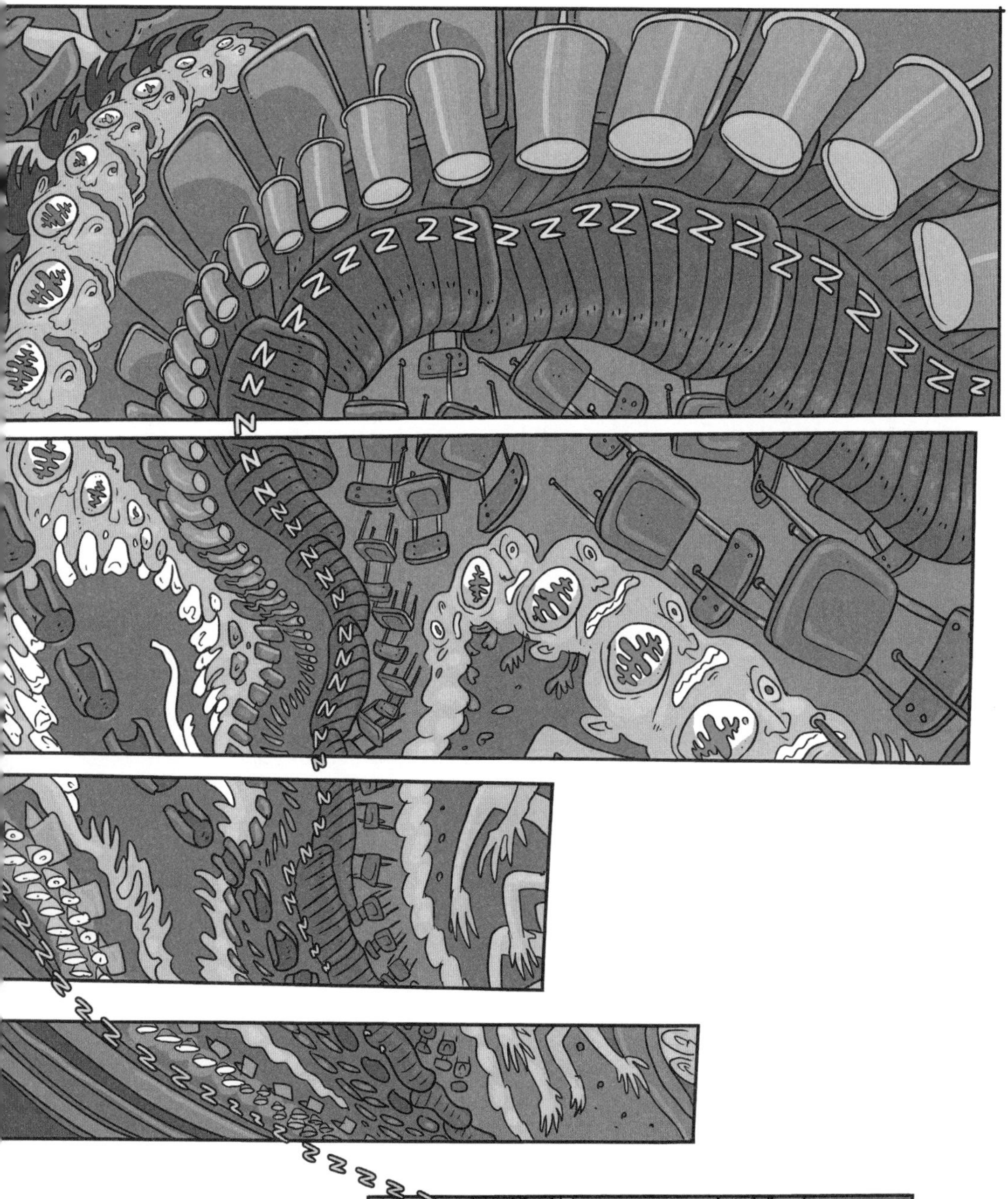

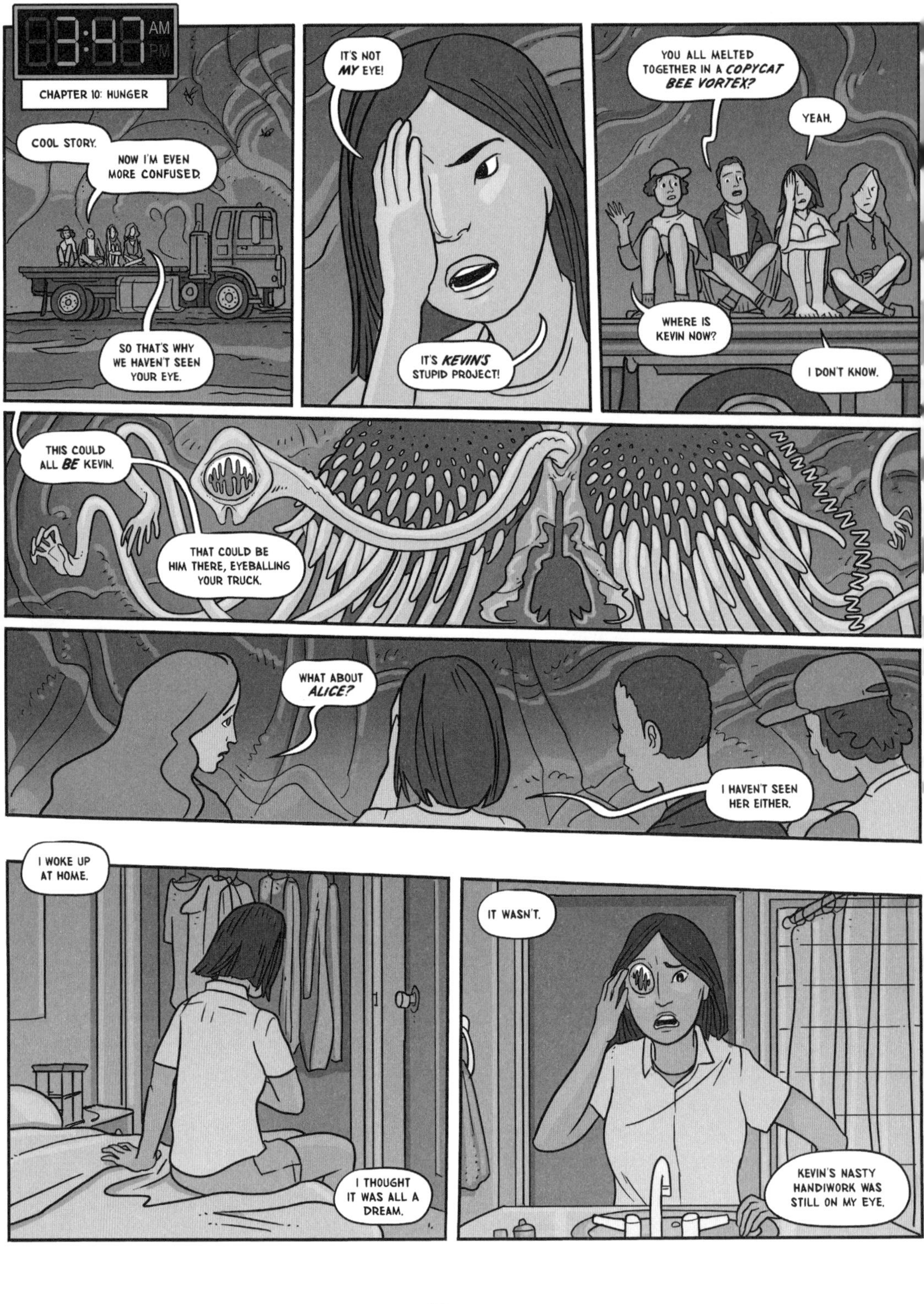
3:43 AM PM
CHAPTER 10: HUNGER
COOL STORY.
NOW I'M EVEN MORE CONFUSED.
SO THAT'S WHY WE HAVEN'T SEEN YOUR EYE.
IT'S NOT MY EYE!
IT'S KEVIN'S STUPID PROJECT!
YOU ALL MELTED TOGETHER IN A COPYCAT BEE VORTEX?
YEAH.
WHERE IS KEVIN NOW?
I DON'T KNOW.
THIS COULD ALL BE KEVIN.
THAT COULD BE HIM THERE, EYEBALLING YOUR TRUCK.
ZNNNNNNNZZZZZZZ
WHAT ABOUT ALICE?
I HAVEN'T SEEN HER EITHER.
I WOKE UP AT HOME.
I THOUGHT IT WAS ALL A DREAM.
IT WASN'T.
KEVIN'S NASTY HANDIWORK WAS STILL ON MY EYE.

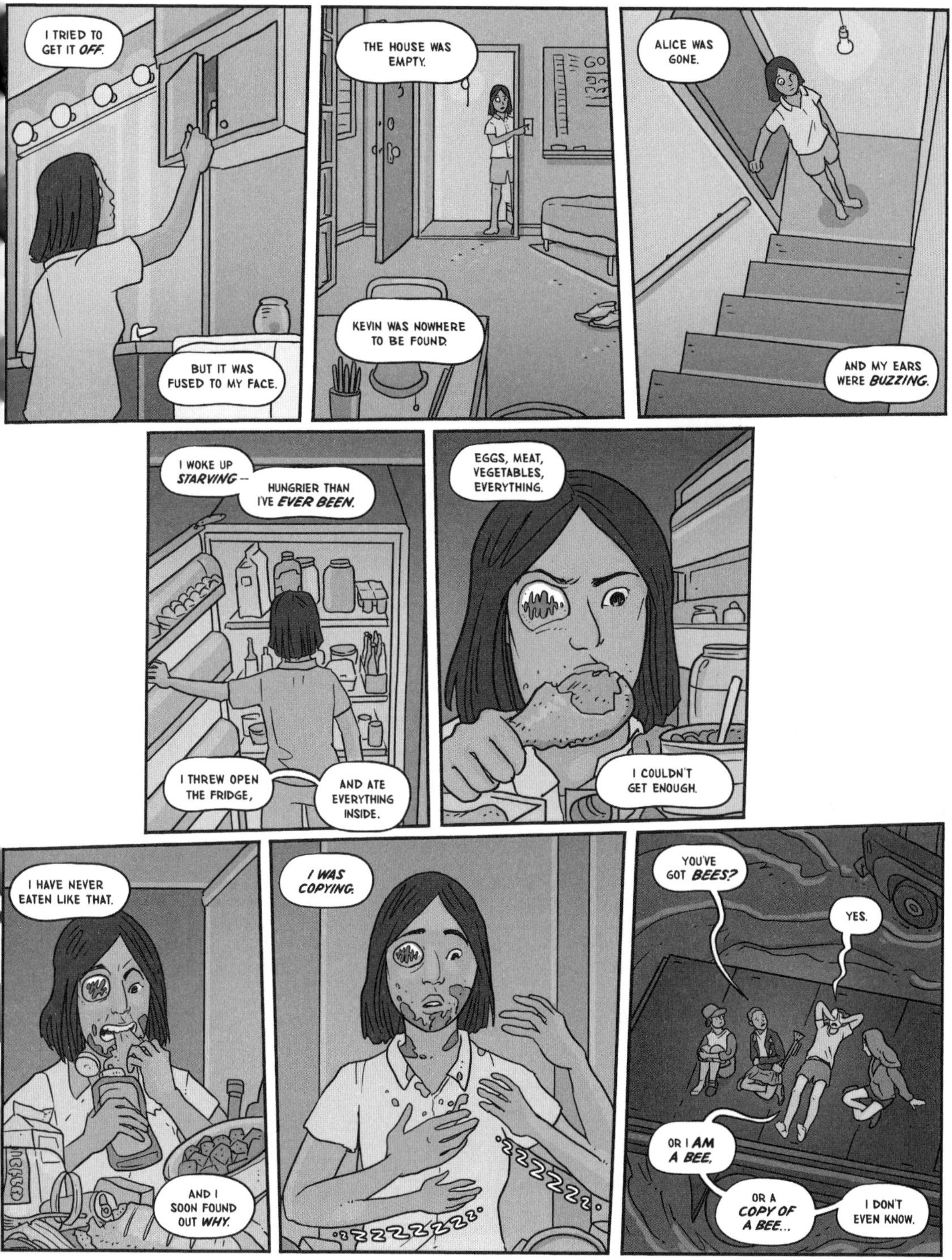
I TRIED TO GET IT OFF.
BUT IT WAS FUSED TO MY FACE.
THE HOUSE WAS EMPTY.
KEVIN WAS NOWHERE TO BE FOUND.
ALICE WAS GONE.
AND MY EARS WERE BUZZING.
I WOKE UP STARVING --
HUNGRIER THAN I'VE EVER BEEN.
I THREW OPEN THE FRIDGE,
AND ATE EVERYTHING INSIDE.
EGGS, MEAT, VEGETABLES, EVERYTHING.
I COULDN'T GET ENOUGH.
I HAVE NEVER EATEN LIKE THAT.
AND I SOON FOUND OUT WHY.
I WAS COPYING.
ZZZZZZZ
ZZZZZZZZZ
YOU'VE GOT BEES?
YES.
OR I AM A BEE,
OR A COPY OF A BEE...
I DON'T EVEN KNOW.

64

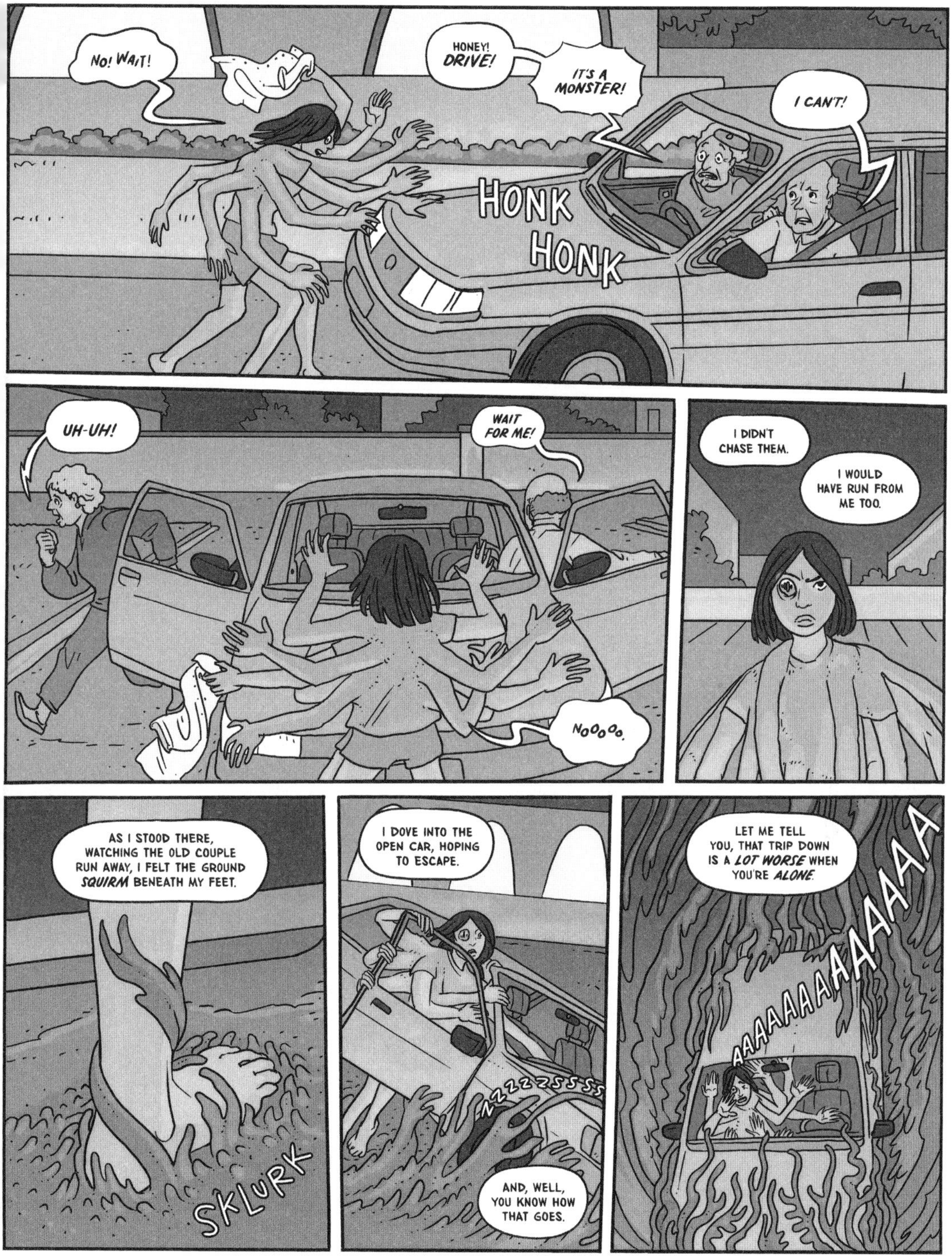
No! WAIT!
HONEY! DRIVE!
IT'S A MONSTER!
I CAN'T!
HONK
HONK
UH-UH!
WAIT FOR ME!
NOOOOO.
I DIDN'T CHASE THEM.
I WOULD HAVE RUN FROM ME TOO.
AS I STOOD THERE, WATCHING THE OLD COUPLE RUN AWAY, I FELT THE GROUND SQUIRM BENEATH MY FEET.
SKLURK
I DOVE INTO THE OPEN CAR, HOPING TO ESCAPE.
ZZZZZZSSSSS
AND, WELL, YOU KNOW HOW THAT GOES.
LET ME TELL YOU, THAT TRIP DOWN IS A LOT WORSE WHEN YOU'RE ALONE.
AAAAAAAAAAAAAAAAA

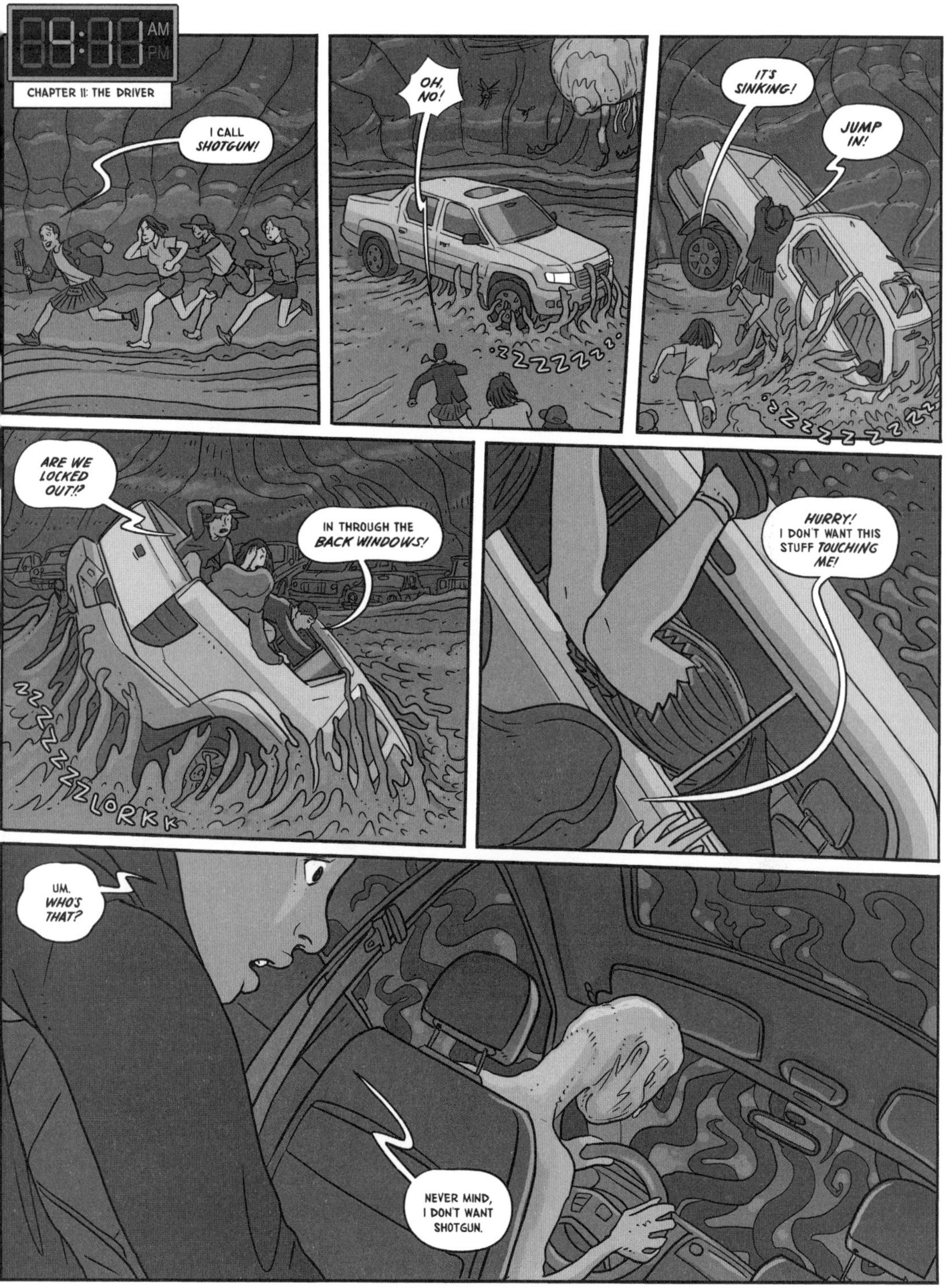

04:11 AM PM
CHAPTER 11: THE DRIVER
I CALL SHOTGUN!
OH, NO!
ZZZZZZZZZ
IT'S SINKING!
JUMP IN!
ZZZZZZZZZZ
ARE WE LOCKED OUT!?
IN THROUGH THE BACK WINDOWS!
ZZZZZZZZZLORKKK
HURRY! I DON'T WANT THIS STUFF TOUCHING ME!
UM. WHO'S THAT?
NEVER MIND, I DON'T WANT SHOTGUN.

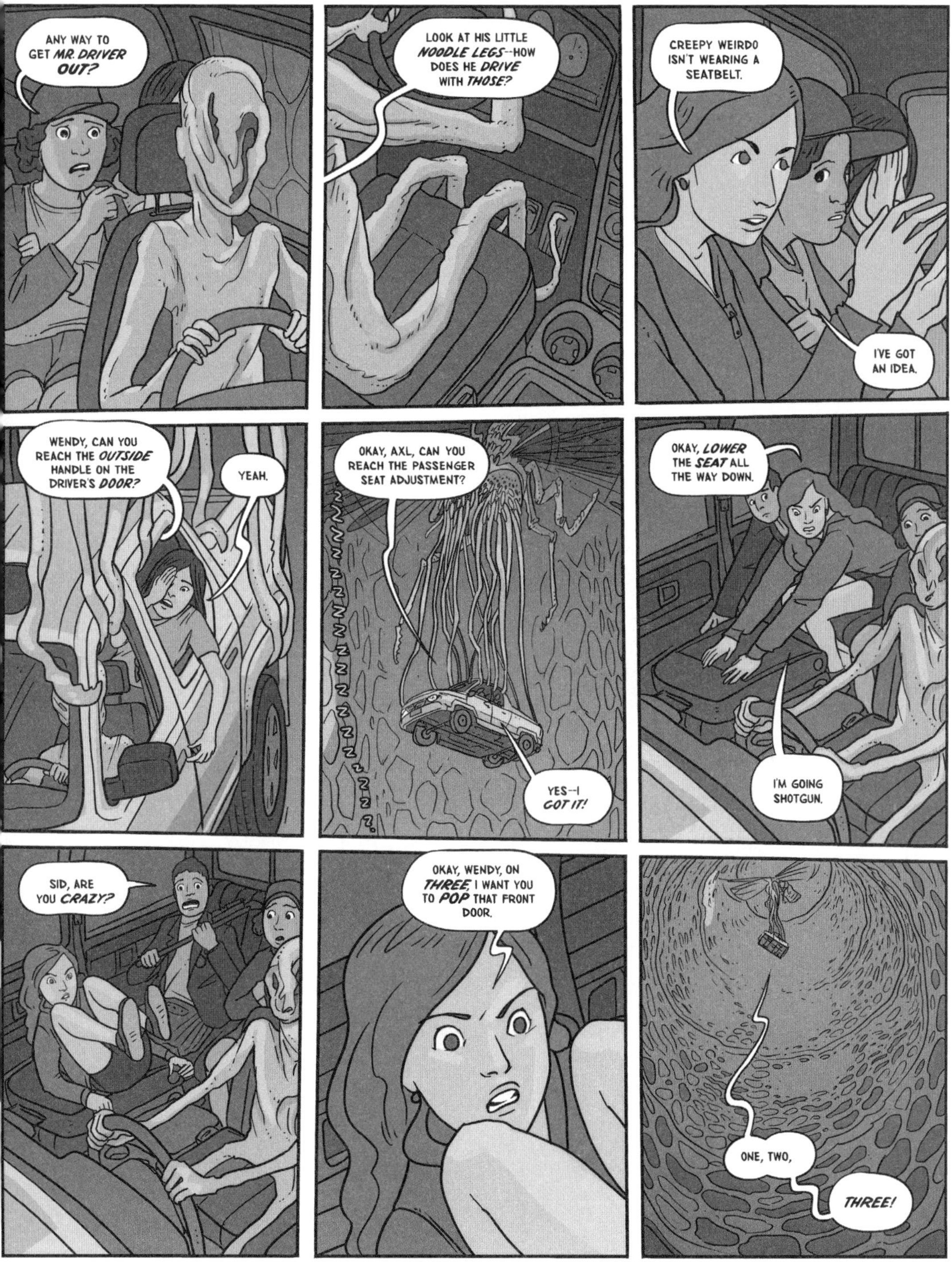
ANY WAY TO GET MR. DRIVER OUT?
LOOK AT HIS LITTLE NOODLE LEGS--HOW DOES HE DRIVE WITH THOSE?
CREEPY WEIRDO ISN'T WEARING A SEATBELT.
I'VE GOT AN IDEA.
WENDY, CAN YOU REACH THE OUTSIDE HANDLE ON THE DRIVER'S DOOR?
YEAH.
OKAY, AXL, CAN YOU REACH THE PASSENGER SEAT ADJUSTMENT?
YES--I GOT IT!
OKAY, LOWER THE SEAT ALL THE WAY DOWN.
I'M GOING SHOTGUN.
SID, ARE YOU CRAZY?
OKAY, WENDY, ON THREE, I WANT YOU TO POP THAT FRONT DOOR.
ONE, TWO,
THREE!

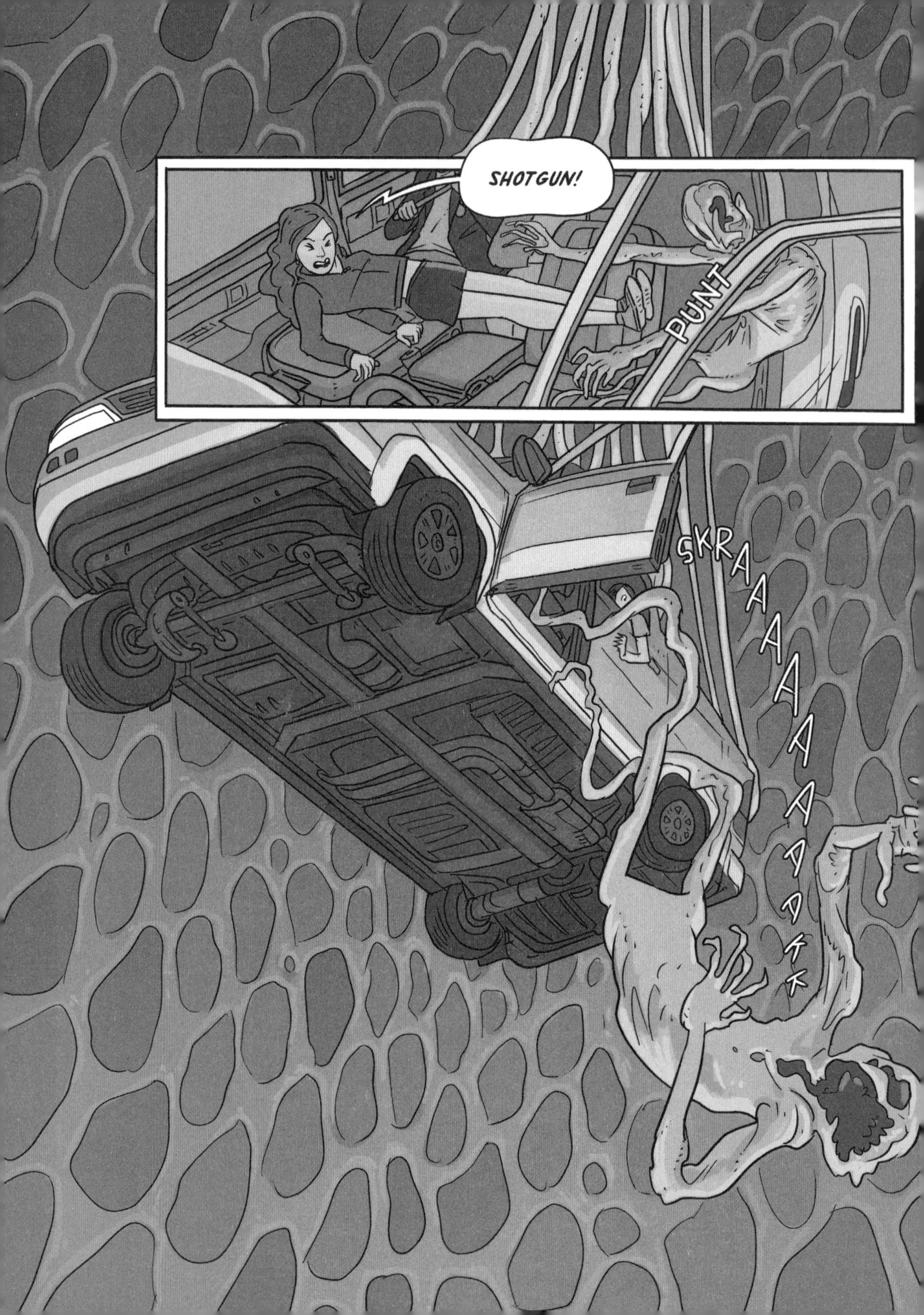
SHOTGUN!
PUNT
SKRAAAAAAAAAAAKK

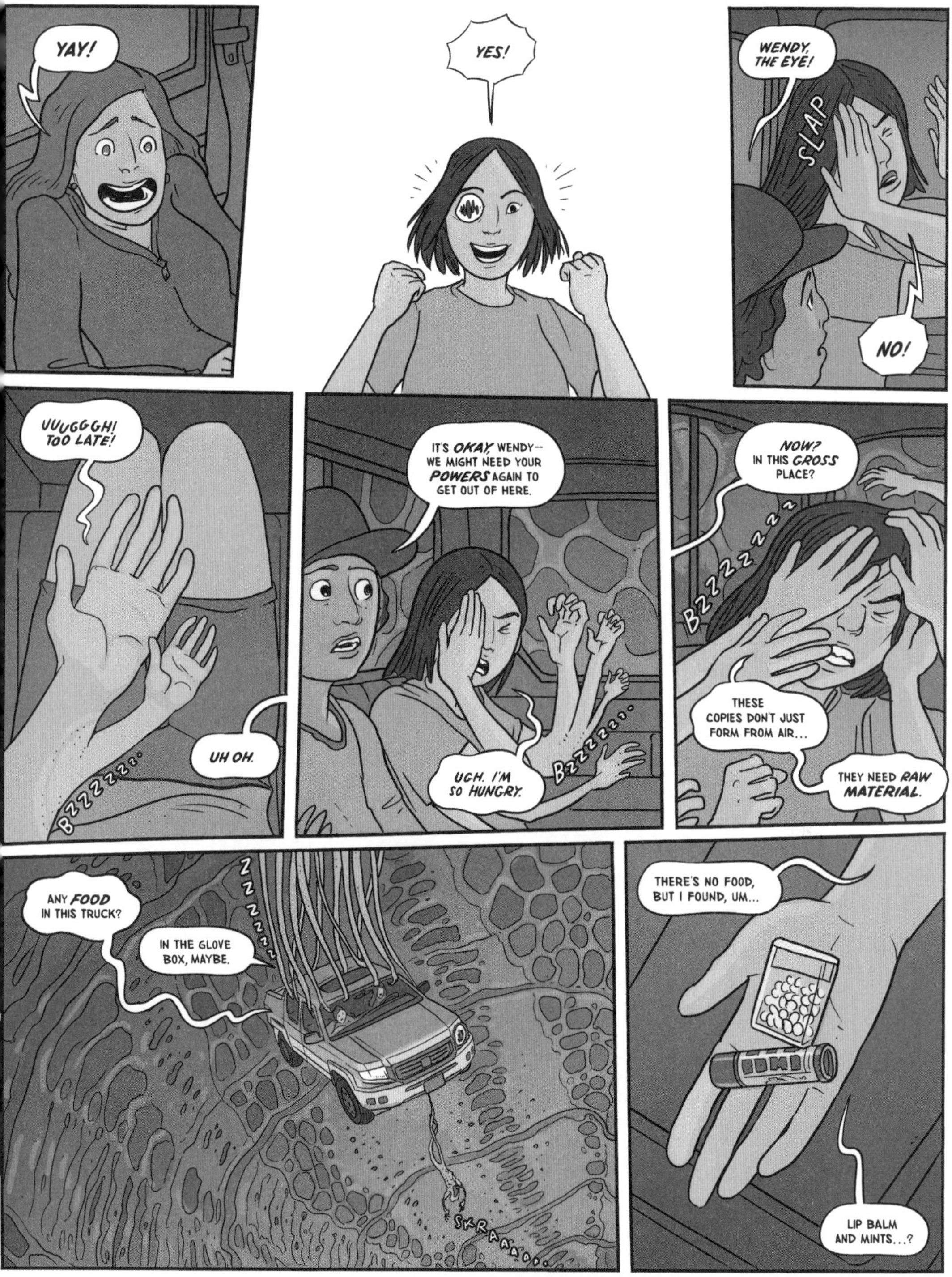
YAY!
YES!
WENDY, THE EYE!
SLAP
NO!
UUUGGGH! TOO LATE!
BZZZZZZZ...
UH OH.
IT'S OKAY, WENDY-- WE MIGHT NEED YOUR POWERS AGAIN TO GET OUT OF HERE.
UGH. I'M SO HUNGRY.
BZZZZZZ...
NOW? IN THIS GROSS PLACE?
BZZZZZZZZ
THESE COPIES DON'T JUST FORM FROM AIR...
THEY NEED RAW MATERIAL.
ANY FOOD IN THIS TRUCK?
IN THE GLOVE BOX, MAYBE.
ZZZZZZZ
SKRAAAAA...
THERE'S NO FOOD, BUT I FOUND, UM...
BOMB
LIP BALM AND MINTS...?

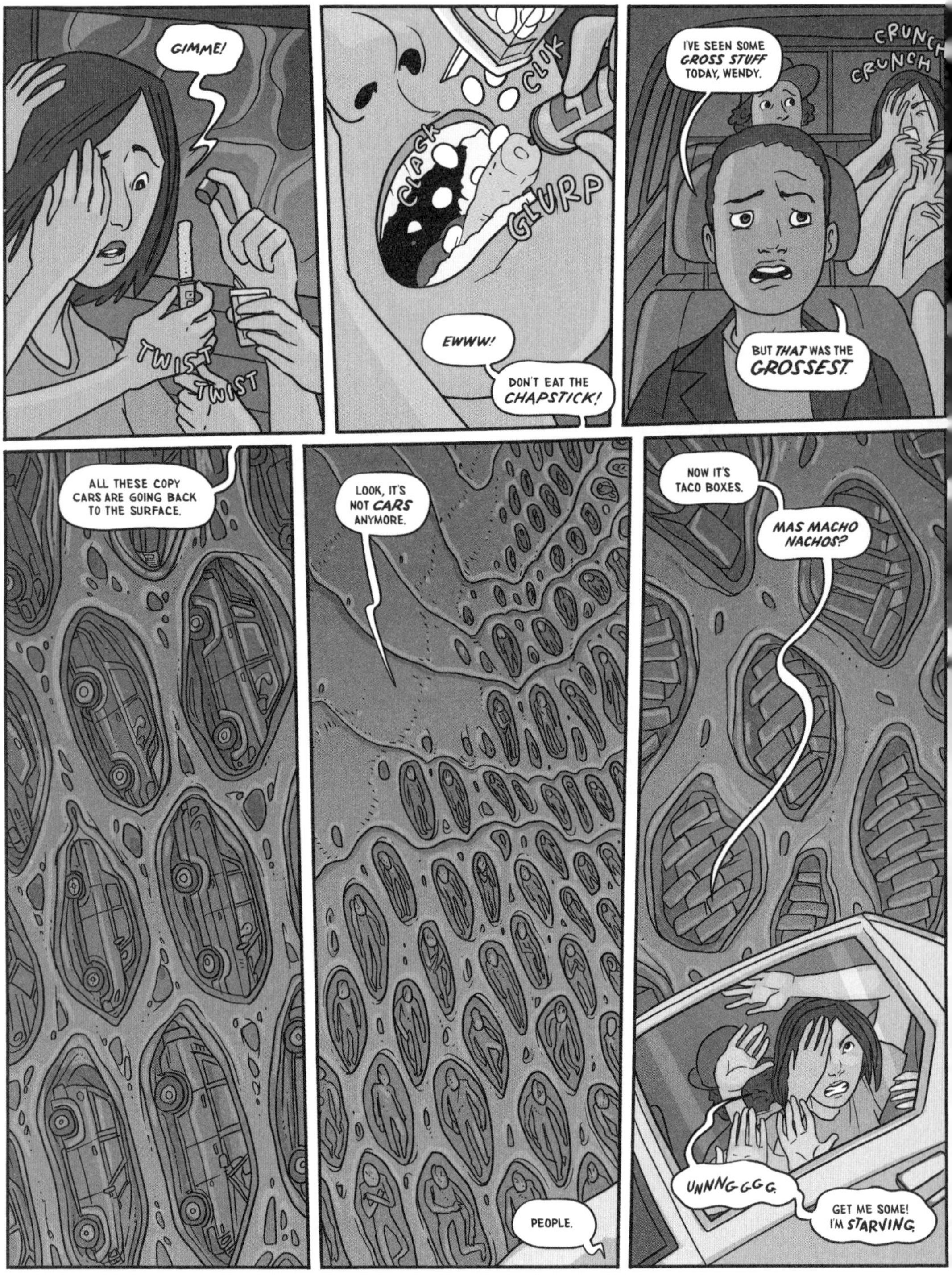
GIMME!
TWIST
TWIST
CLIK
CLACK
GLURP
EWWW!
DON'T EAT THE CHAPSTICK!
CRUNCH
CRUNCH
I'VE SEEN SOME GROSS STUFF TODAY, WENDY.
BUT THAT WAS THE GROSSEST.
ALL THESE COPY CARS ARE GOING BACK TO THE SURFACE.
LOOK, IT'S NOT CARS ANYMORE.
PEOPLE.
NOW IT'S TACO BOXES.
MAS MACHO NACHOS?
UNNNGGGG.
GET ME SOME! I'M STARVING.

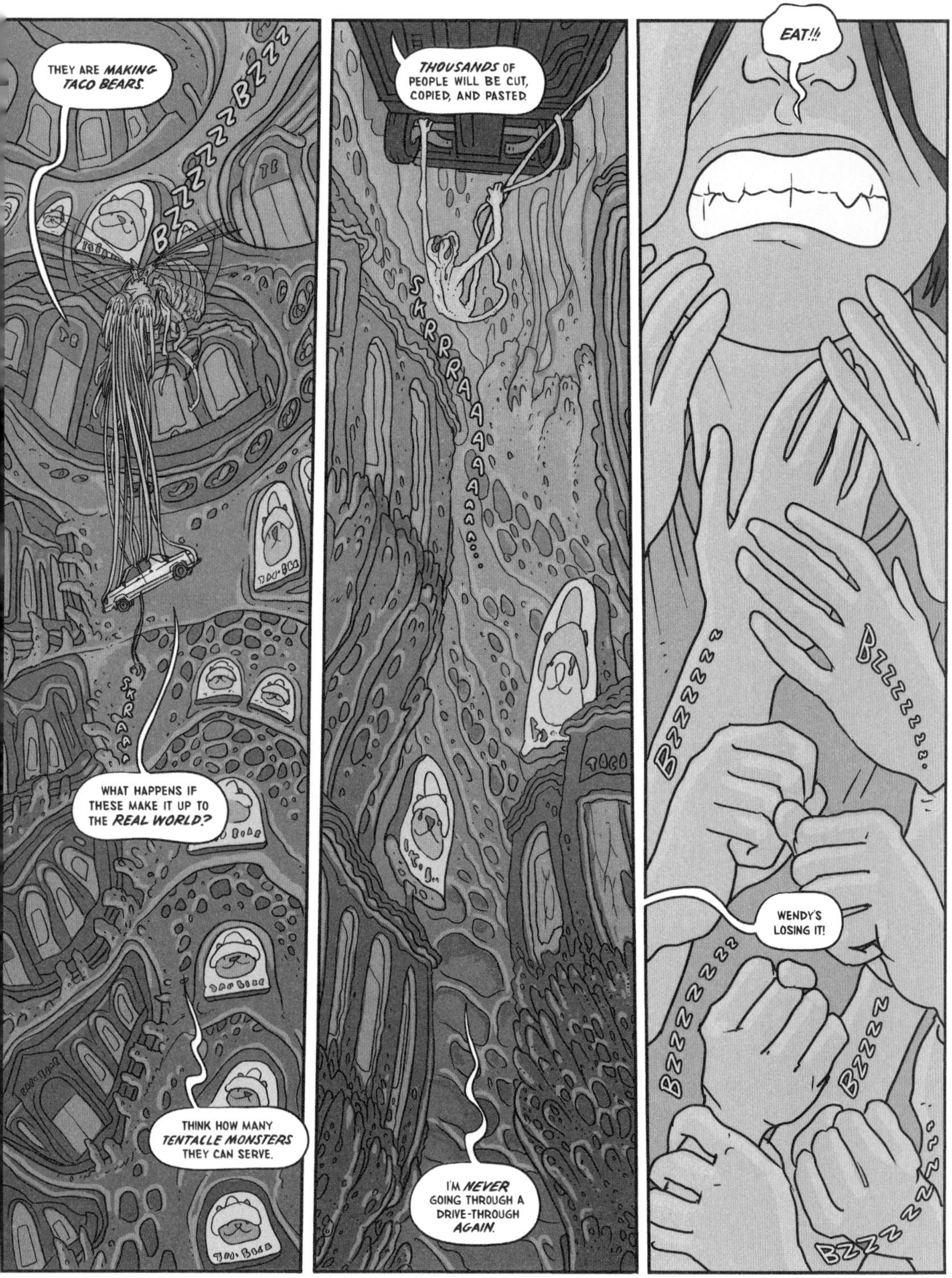
THEY ARE MAKING TACO BEARS.
WHAT HAPPENS IF THESE MAKE IT UP TO THE REAL WORLD?
THINK HOW MANY TENTACLE MONSTERS THEY CAN SERVE.
THOUSANDS OF PEOPLE WILL BE CUT, COPIED, AND PASTED.
I'M NEVER GOING THROUGH A DRIVE-THROUGH AGAIN.
EAT!!
WENDY'S LOSING IT!

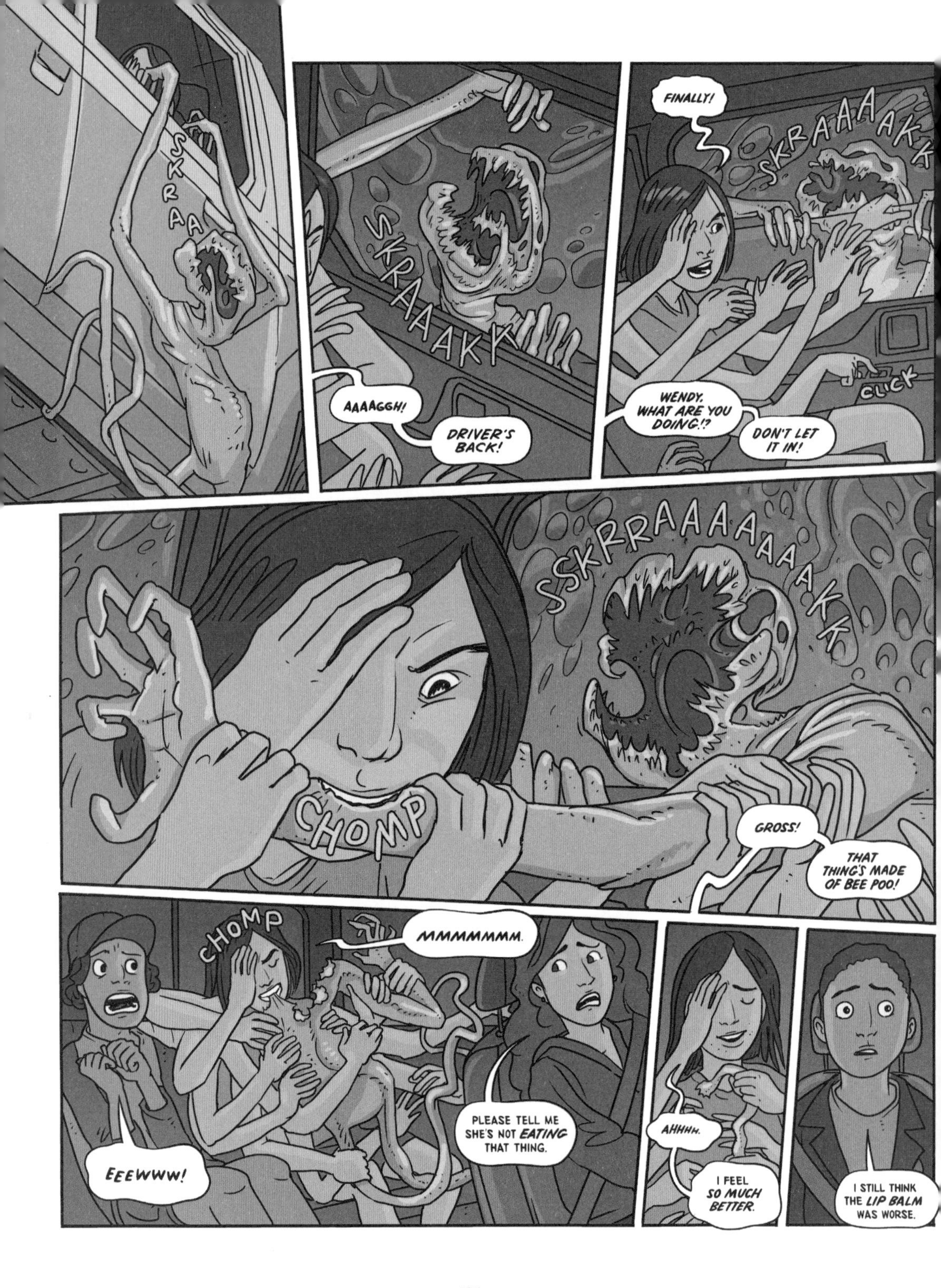
SKRAA
SKRAAAAKK
AAAAGGH!
DRIVER'S BACK!
FINALLY!
SKRAAAAKK
WENDY. WHAT ARE YOU DOING!?
DON'T LET IT IN!
CLICK
SSKRRAAAAAAAAKK
CHOMP
GROSS!
THAT THING'S MADE OF BEE POO!
CHOMP
MMMMMMMM.
EEEWWW!
PLEASE TELL ME SHE'S NOT *EATING* THAT THING.
AHHHH.
I FEEL *SO MUCH* BETTER.
I STILL THINK THE *LIP BALM* WAS WORSE.

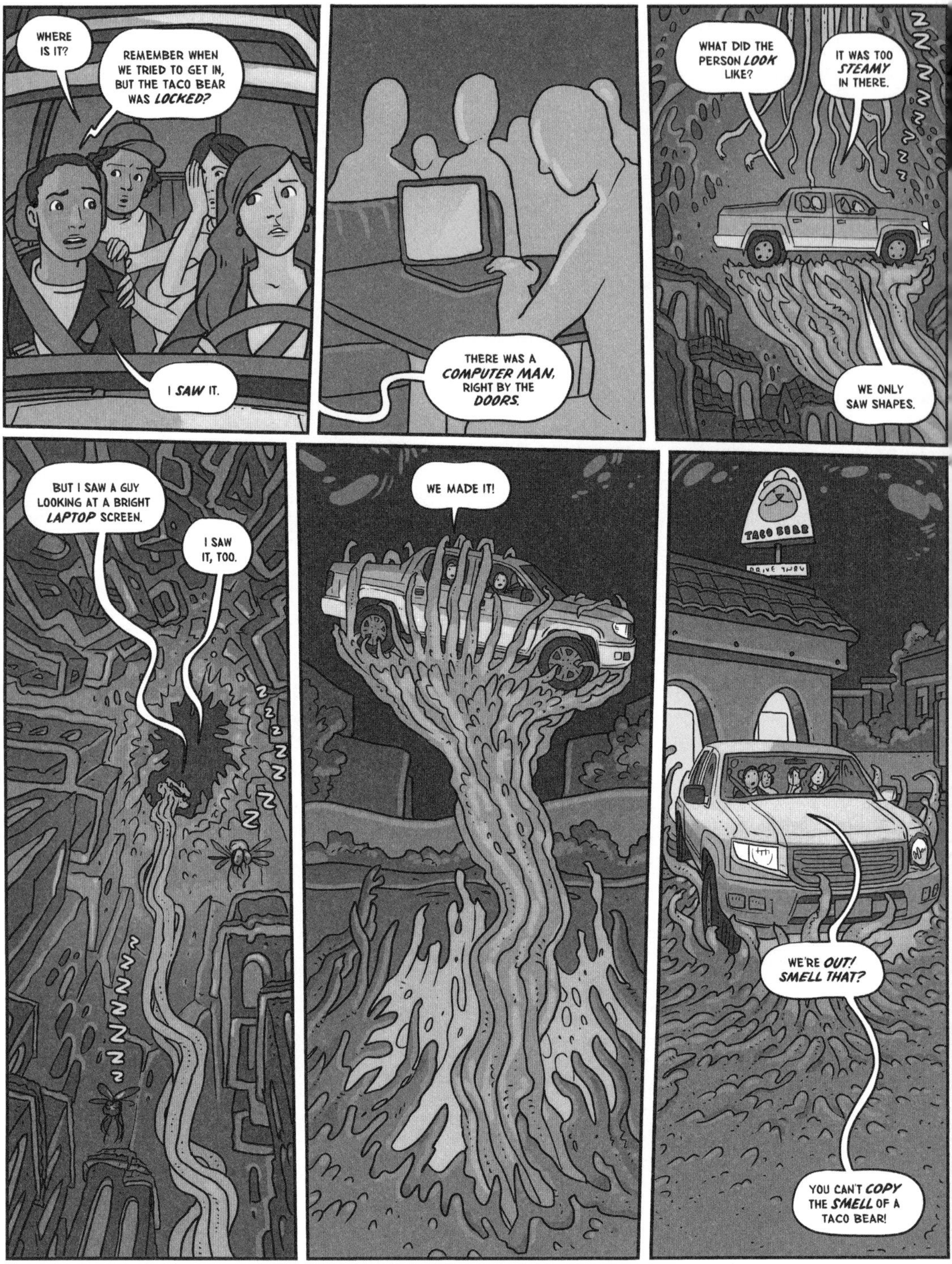
WHERE IS IT?
REMEMBER WHEN WE TRIED TO GET IN, BUT THE TACO BEAR WAS LOCKED?
I SAW IT.
THERE WAS A COMPUTER MAN, RIGHT BY THE DOORS.
WHAT DID THE PERSON LOOK LIKE?
IT WAS TOO STEAMY IN THERE.
WE ONLY SAW SHAPES.
BUT I SAW A GUY LOOKING AT A BRIGHT LAPTOP SCREEN.
I SAW IT, TOO.
WE MADE IT!
TACO BEAR
DRIVE THRU
WE'RE OUT! SMELL THAT?
YOU CAN'T COPY THE SMELL OF A TACO BEAR!

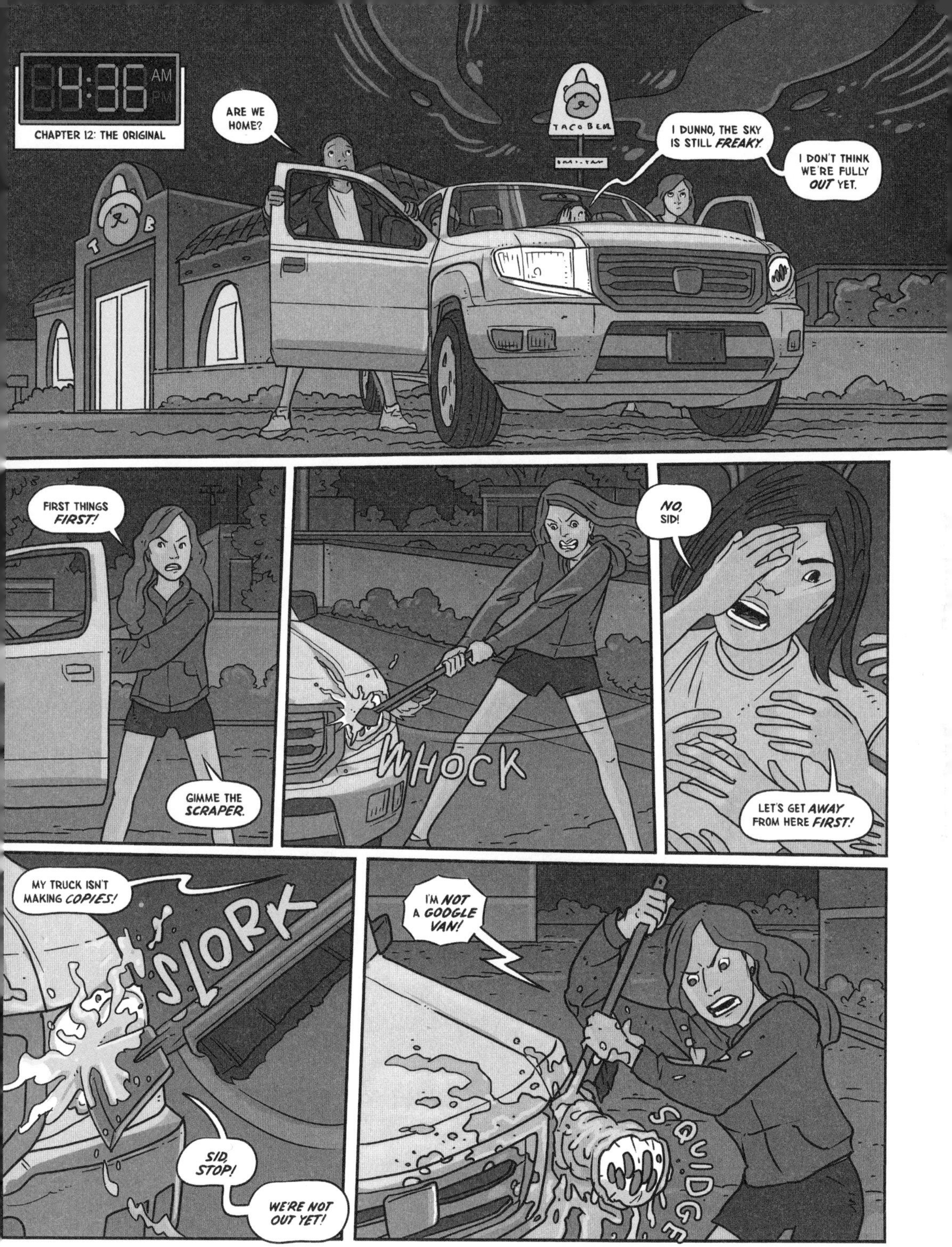
4:36 AM PM
CHAPTER 12: THE ORIGINAL
ARE WE HOME?
TACO BEAR
I DUNNO, THE SKY IS STILL FREAKY.
I DON'T THINK WE'RE FULLY OUT YET.
FIRST THINGS FIRST!
GIMME THE SCRAPER.
WHOCK
NO, SID!
LET'S GET AWAY FROM HERE FIRST!
MY TRUCK ISN'T MAKING COPIES!
SLORK
SID, STOP!
WE'RE NOT OUT YET!
I'M NOT A GOOGLE VAN!
SQUIDGE

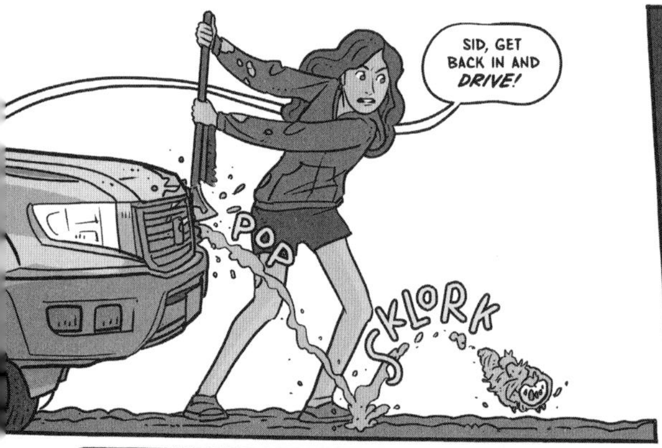
SID, GET BACK IN AND *DRIVE!*
POP
SKLORK

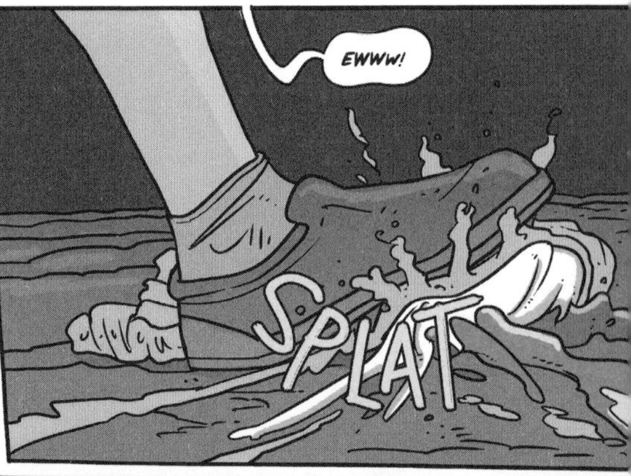
EWWW!
SPLAT

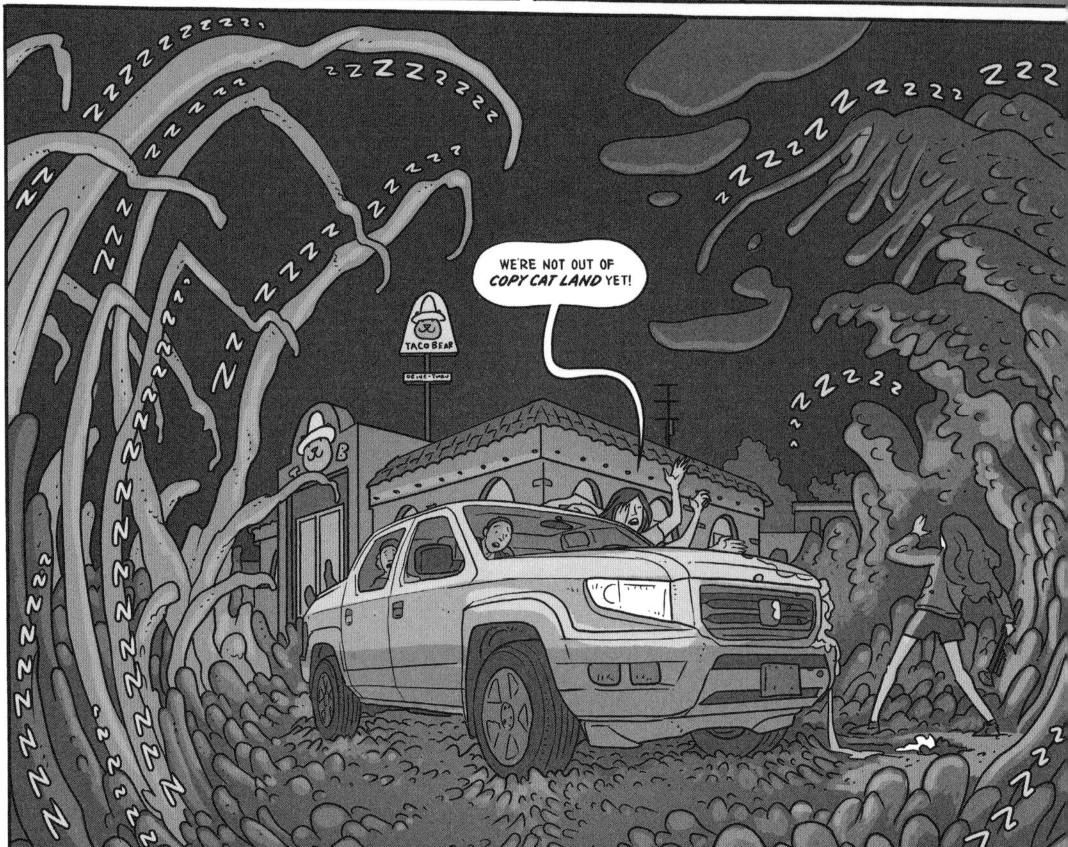
TACO BEAR
WE'RE NOT OUT OF *COPY CAT LAND* YET!

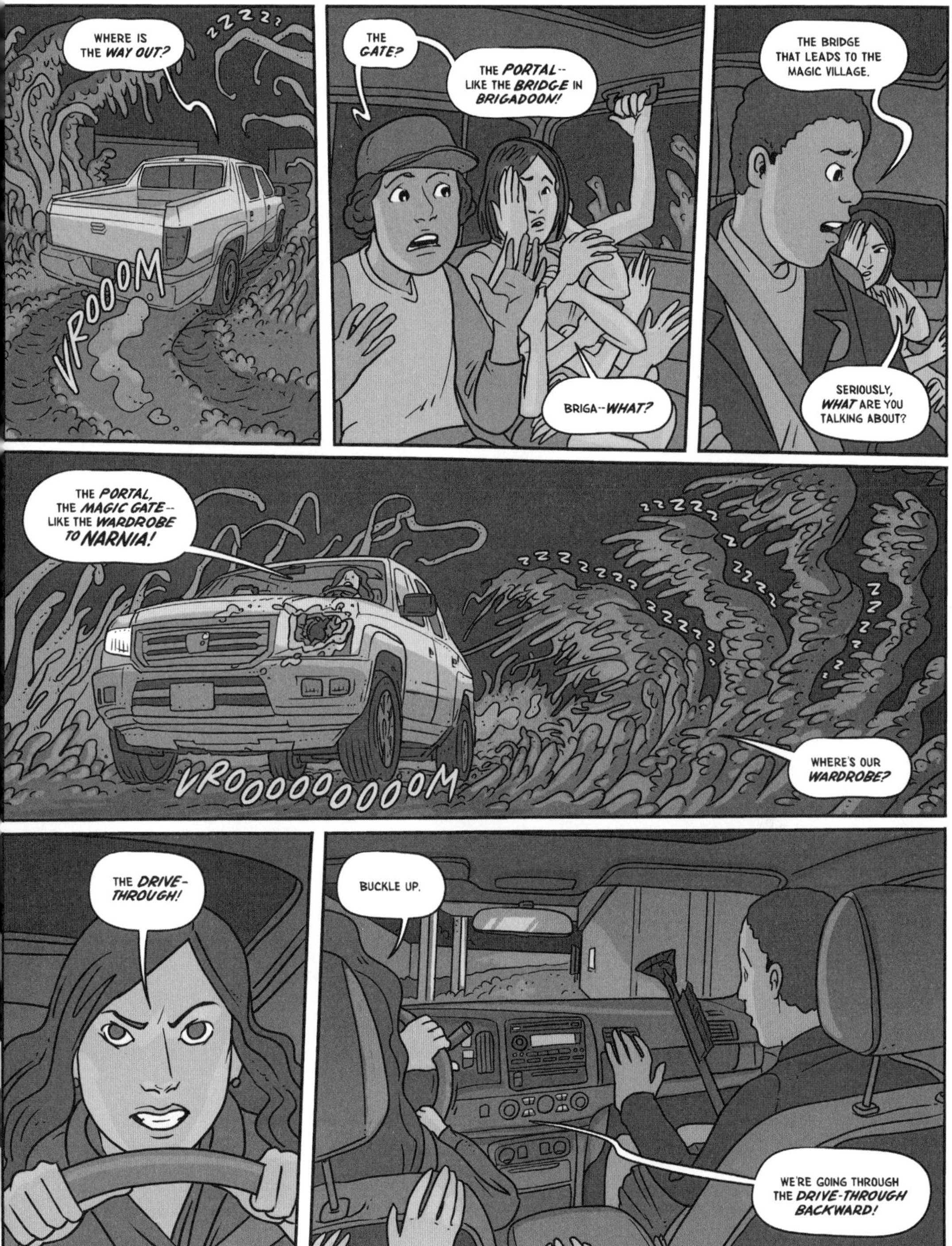
WHERE IS THE WAY OUT?
ZZZZZ
VROOOM
THE GATE?
THE PORTAL-- LIKE THE BRIDGE IN BRIGADOON!
BRIGA--WHAT?
THE BRIDGE THAT LEADS TO THE MAGIC VILLAGE.
SERIOUSLY, WHAT ARE YOU TALKING ABOUT?
THE PORTAL, THE MAGIC GATE-- LIKE THE WARDROBE TO NARNIA!
VROOOOOOOOOOM
WHERE'S OUR WARDROBE?
THE DRIVE-THROUGH!
BUCKLE UP.
WE'RE GOING THROUGH THE DRIVE-THROUGH BACKWARD!

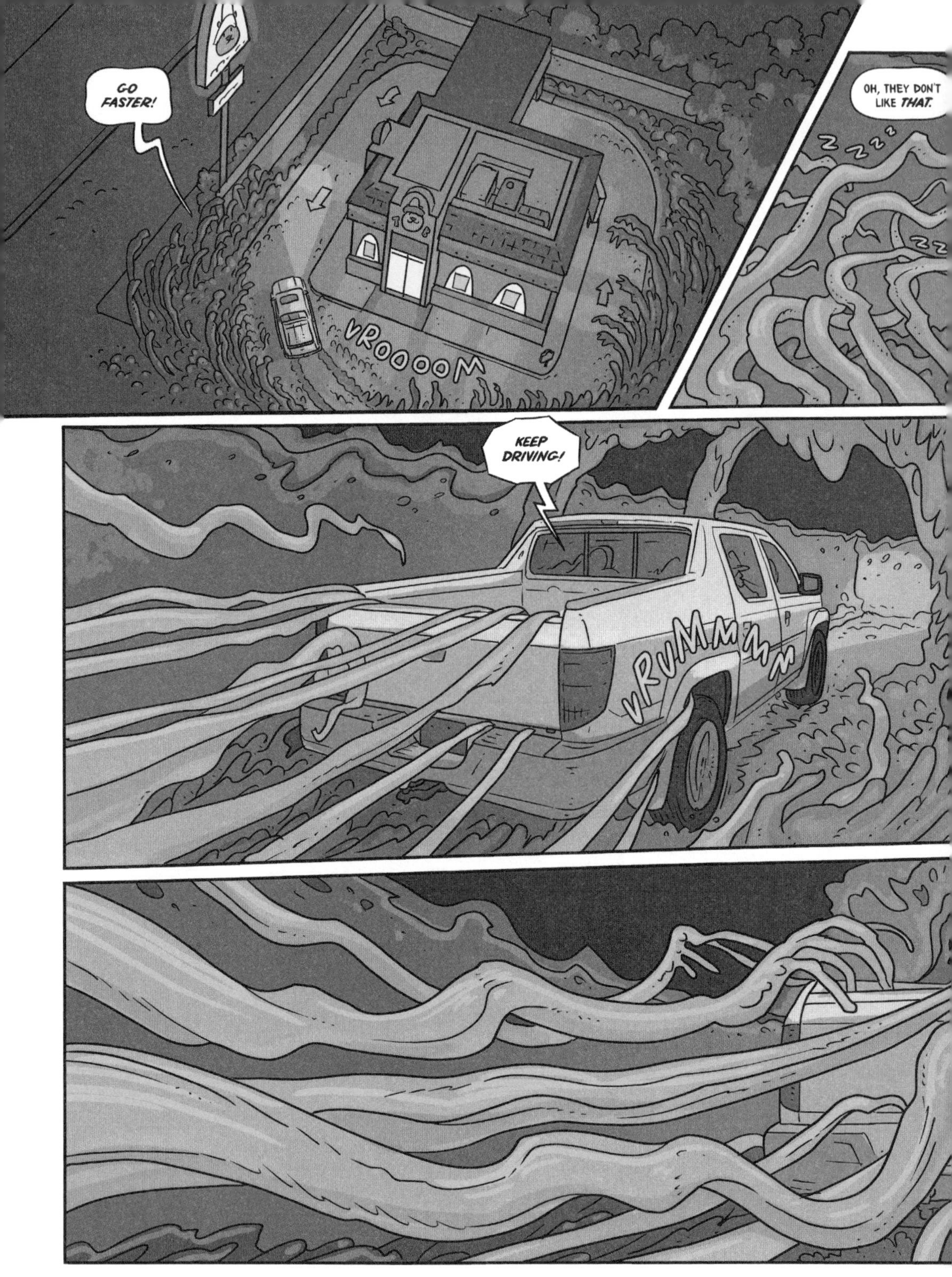
GO FASTER!
VROOOOM
OH, THEY DON'T LIKE THAT.
ZZZZ
ZZZ
KEEP DRIVING!
VRUMMMMM

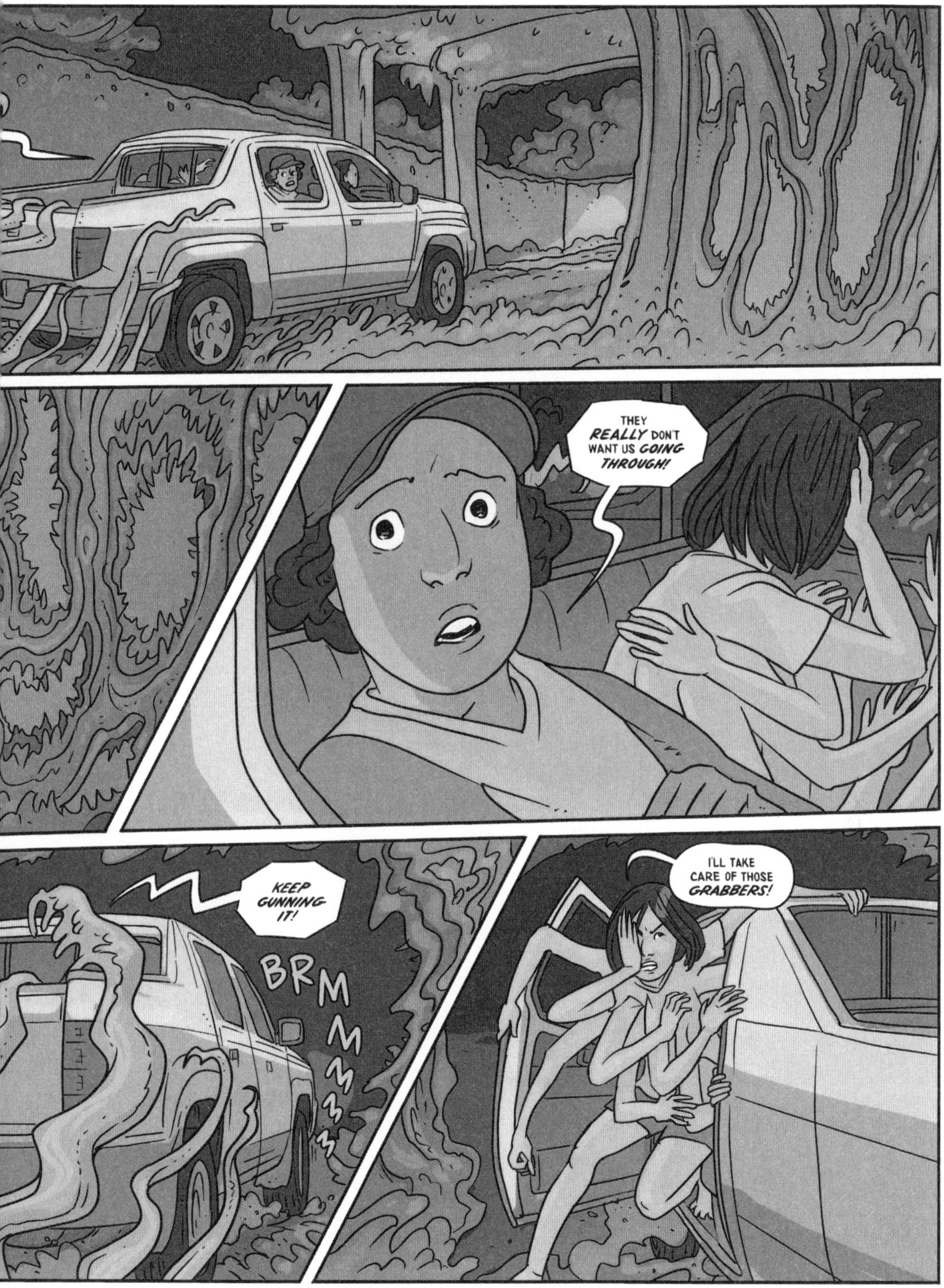
THEY REALLY DON'T WANT US GOING THROUGH!
KEEP GUNNING IT!
BRMMMMMM
I'LL TAKE CARE OF THOSE GRABBERS!

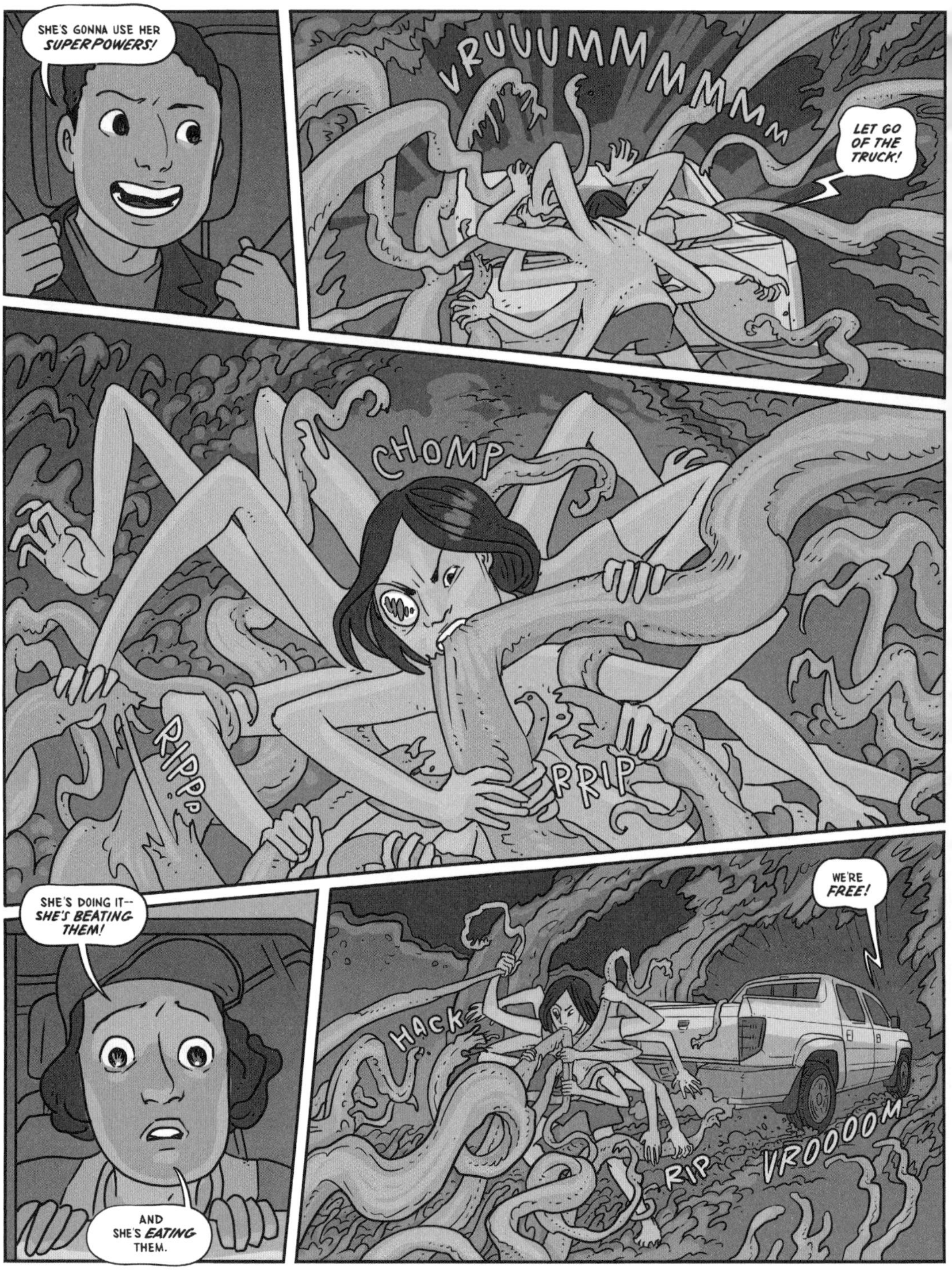
SHE'S GONNA USE HER SUPERPOWERS!
VRUUUMMMMMMM
LET GO OF THE TRUCK!
CHOMP
RIPPP
RRIP
SHE'S DOING IT-- SHE'S BEATING THEM!
AND SHE'S EATING THEM.
WE'RE FREE!
HACK
RIP
VROOOOM

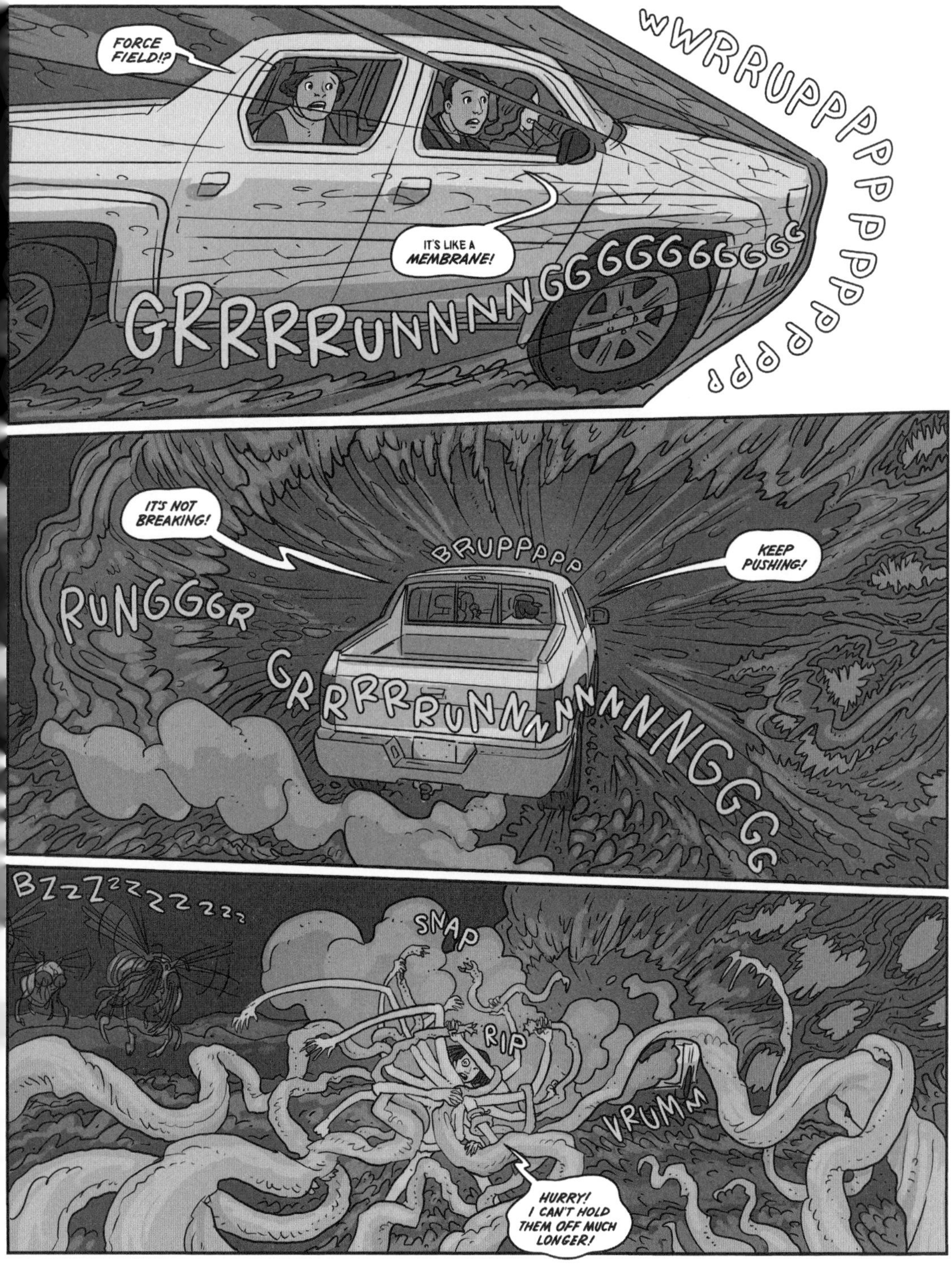
FORCE FIELD!?
wWRRUPPPPPPPPPPPP
IT'S LIKE A MEMBRANE!
GRRRRUNNNNNGGGGGGGGG
IT'S NOT BREAKING!
BRUPPPPPP
KEEP PUSHING!
RUNGGGR
GRRRRRUNNNNNNNNGGGGG
BZZZZZZZZZZ
SNAP
RIP
VRUMM
HURRY! I CAN'T HOLD THEM OFF MUCH LONGER!

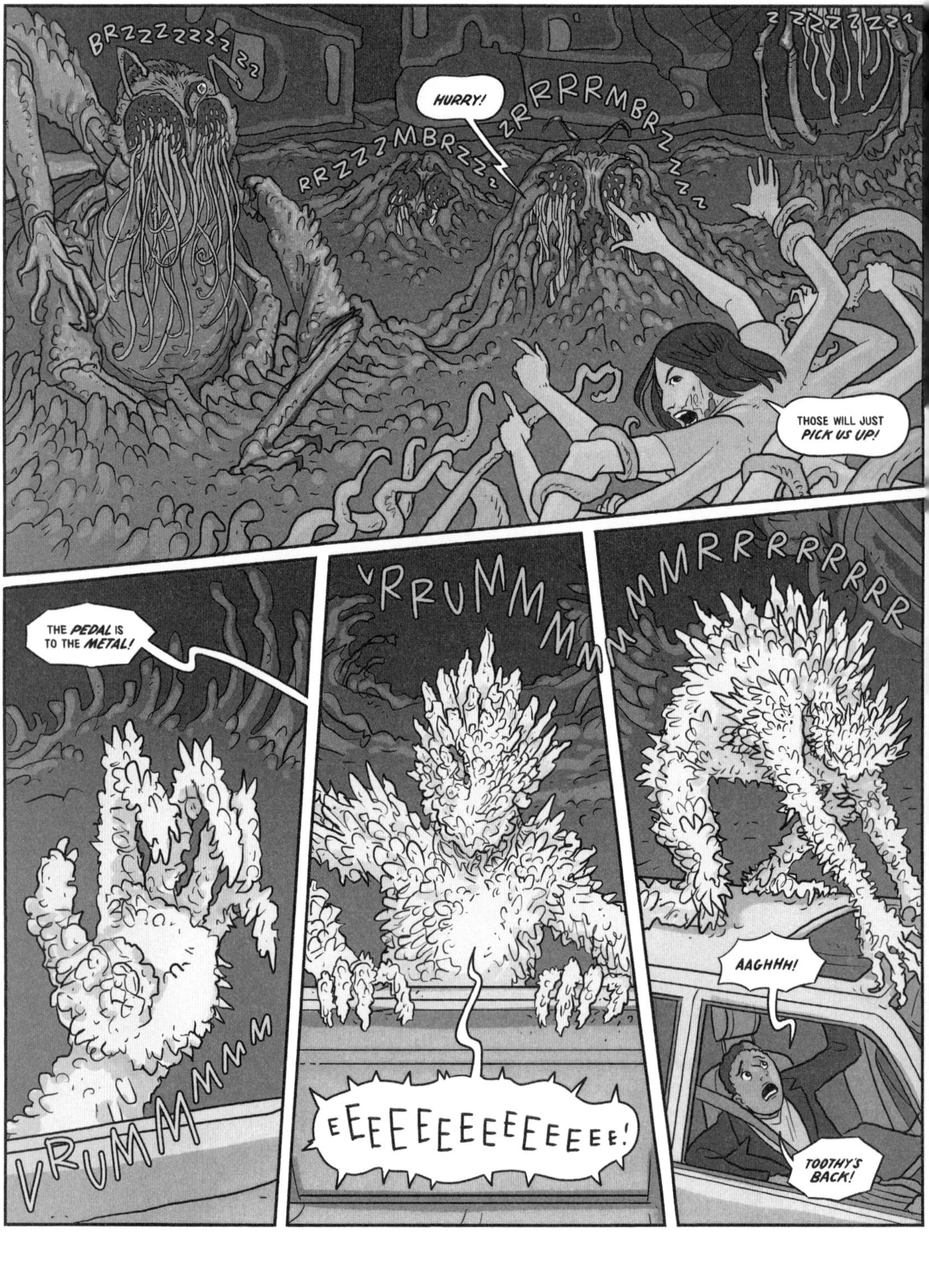
BRZZZZZZZZZZ
HURRY!
RRZZZMBRZZZ
ZRRRRMBRZZZZ
ZZZZZZZZZ
THOSE WILL JUST PICK US UP!
THE PEDAL IS TO THE METAL!
VRUMMMMMM
VRRUMMMMMMMMRRRRRRRRR
EEEEEEEEEEEEE!
AAGHHH!
TOOTHY'S BACK!

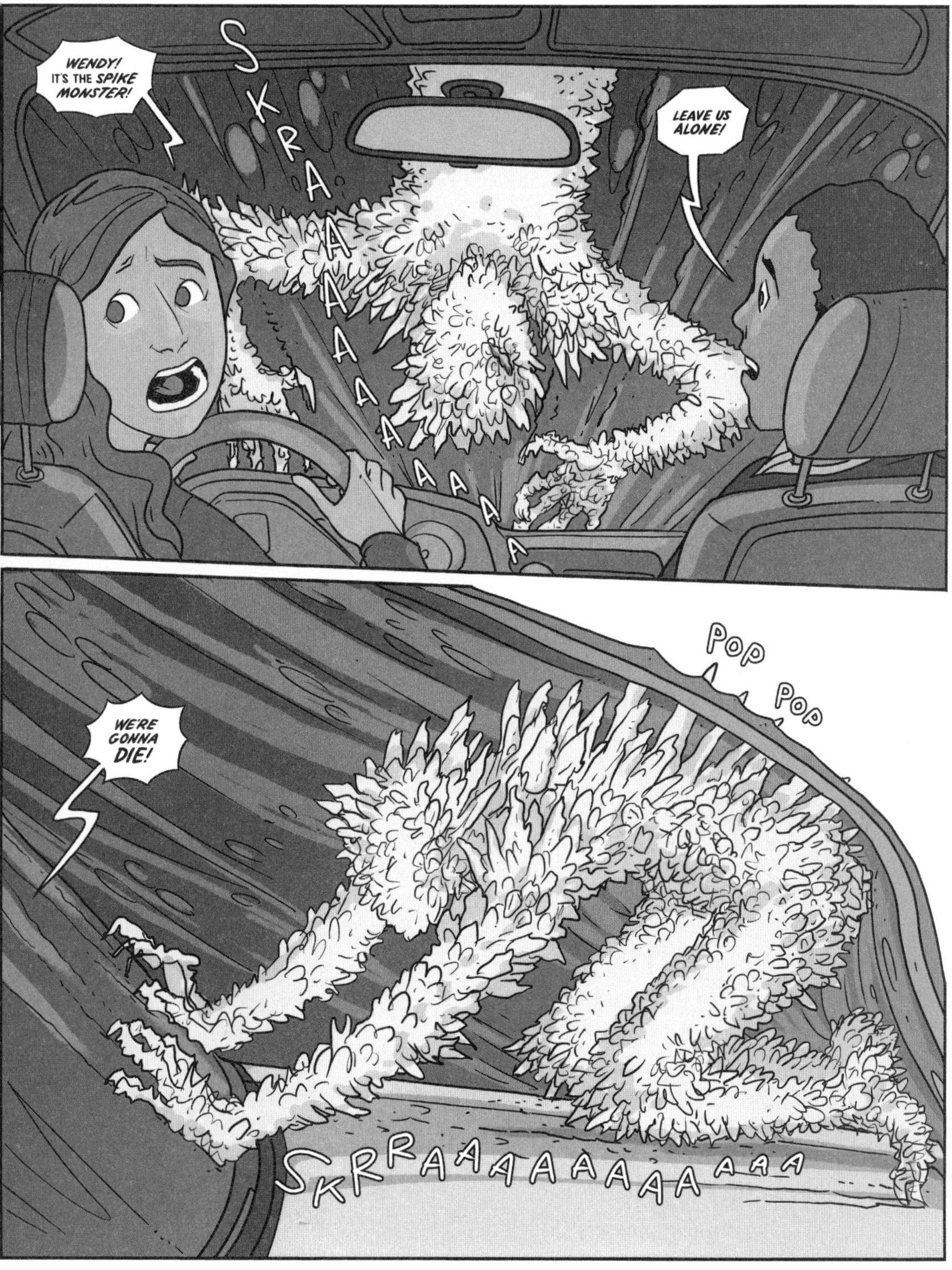
WENDY! IT'S THE SPIKE MONSTER!
SKRAAAAAAAAAAAA
LEAVE US ALONE!
WE'RE GONNA DIE!
POP
POP
SKRRAAAAAAAAAAAA

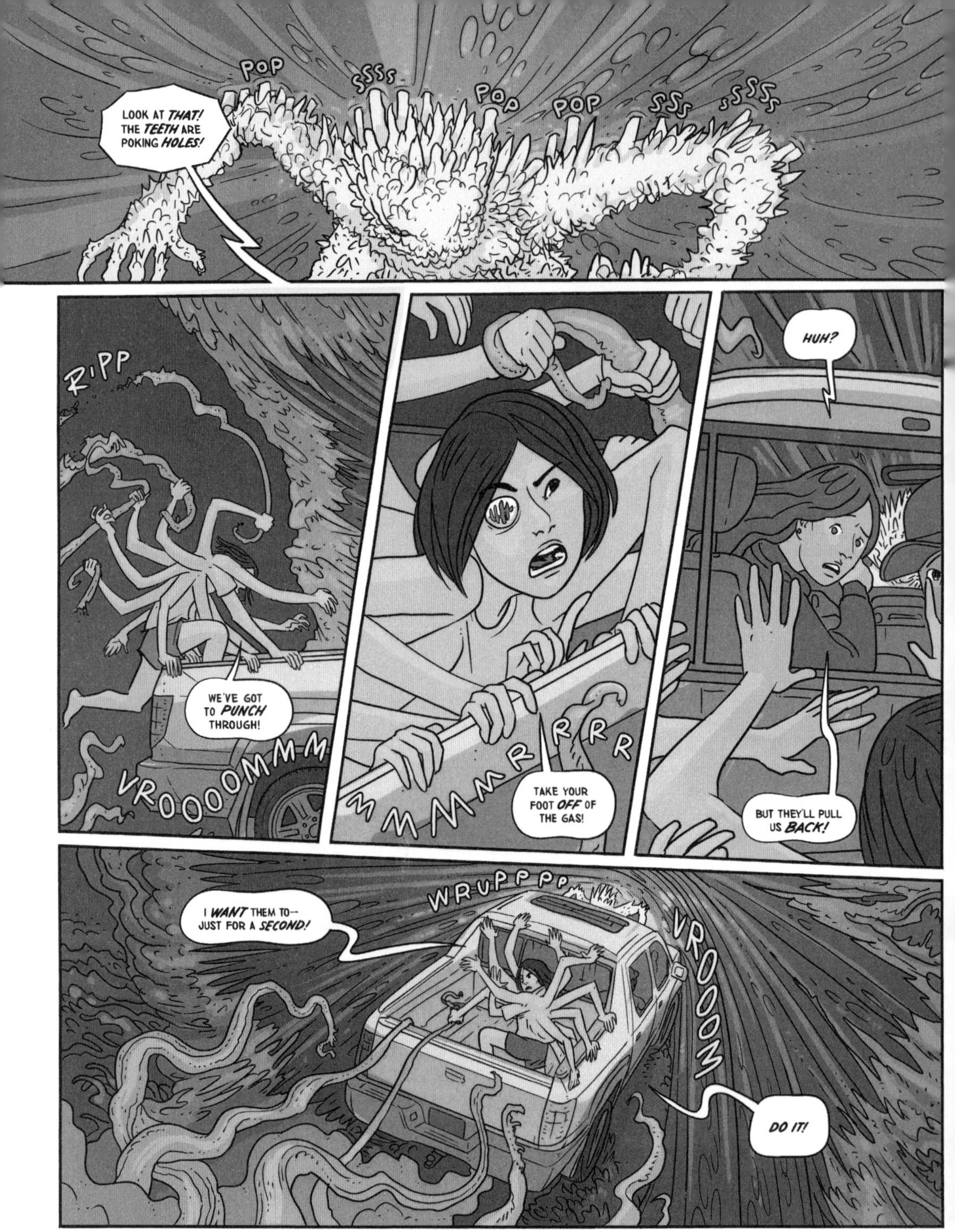
POP
SSSS
POP
POP
SSS
SSSS
LOOK AT THAT! THE TEETH ARE POKING HOLES!
RIPP
WE'VE GOT TO PUNCH THROUGH!
VROOOOMMMMMMMMMRRRRR
TAKE YOUR FOOT OFF OF THE GAS!
HUH?
BUT THEY'LL PULL US BACK!
WRUPPPPP
I WANT THEM TO-- JUST FOR A SECOND!
VROOOOM
DO IT!

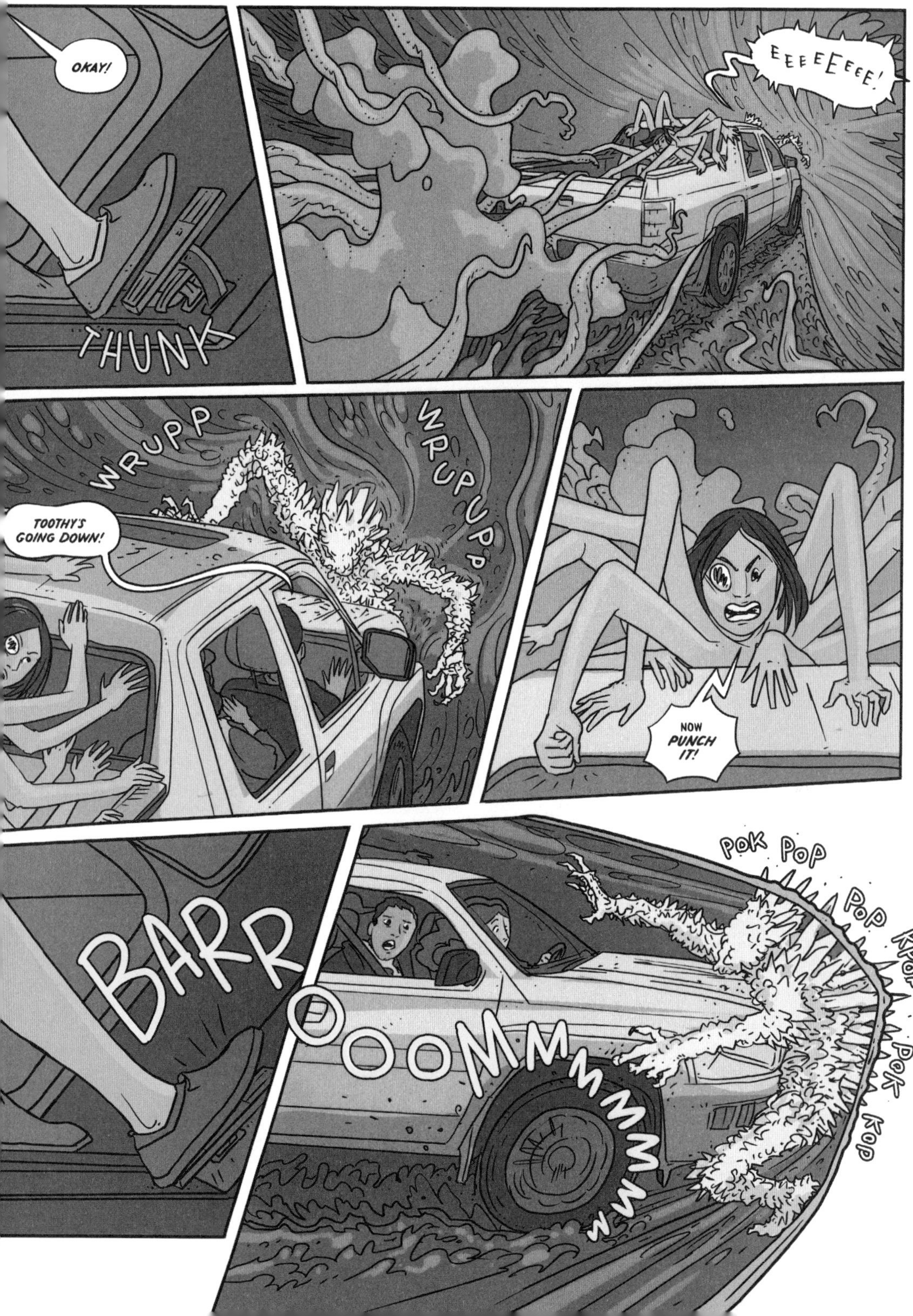
OKAY!
THUNK
EEEEEEEE!
WRUPP
WRUPUPUPP
TOOTHY'S GOING DOWN!
NOW PUNCH IT!
BARROOOOMMMMMMM
POK POP
POP KPOP
POK KOP

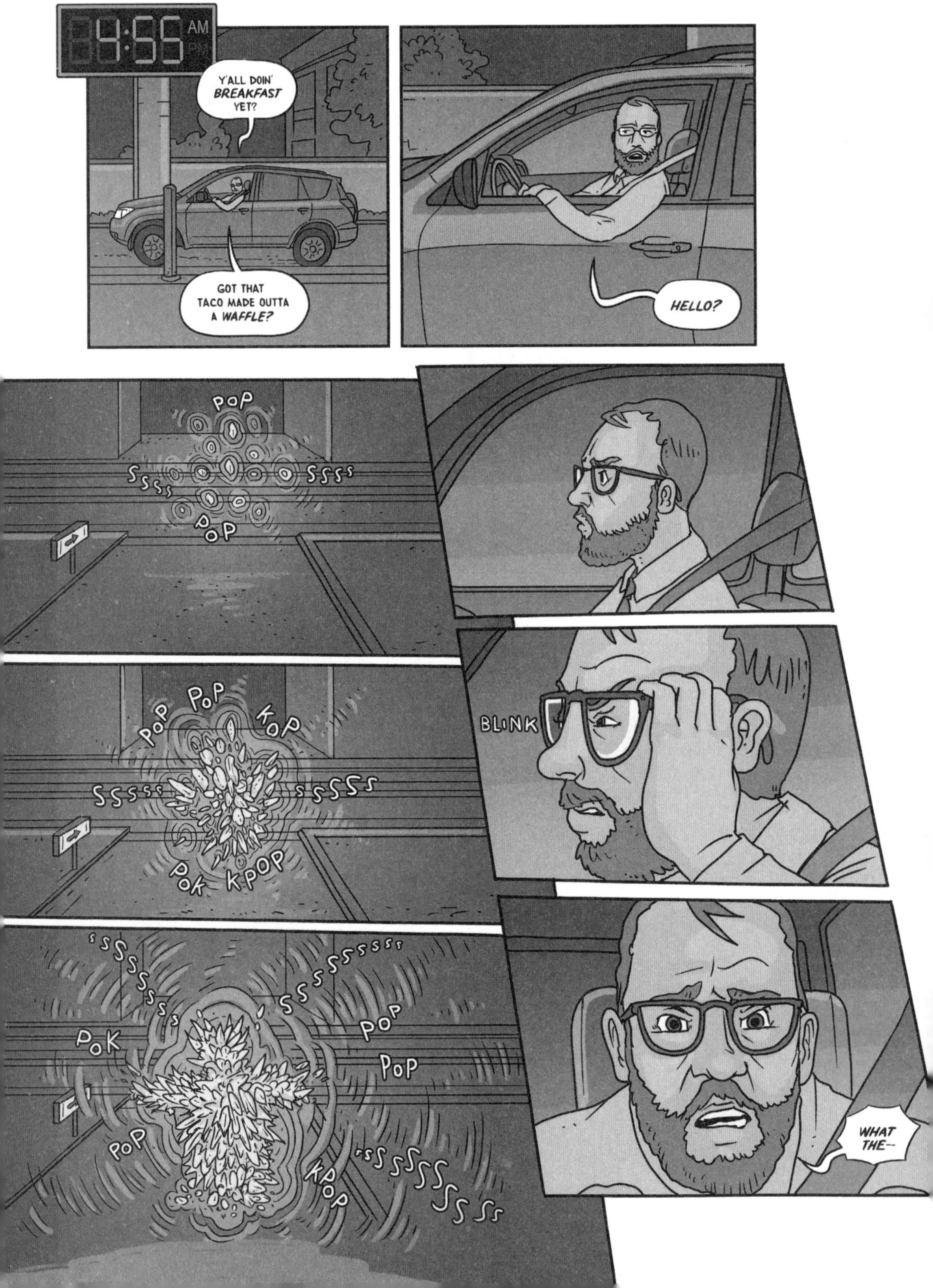
4:55 AM PM
Y'ALL DOIN' *BREAKFAST* YET?
GOT THAT TACO MADE OUTTA A *WAFFLE?*
HELLO?
POP
SSSSS
SSSS
POP
BLINK
POP POP KOP
SSSSS
SSSSS
POK KPOP
SSSSSSS
SSSSSSSSSS
POK
POP
POP
POP
KPOP
SSSSSSSSS
WHAT THE--

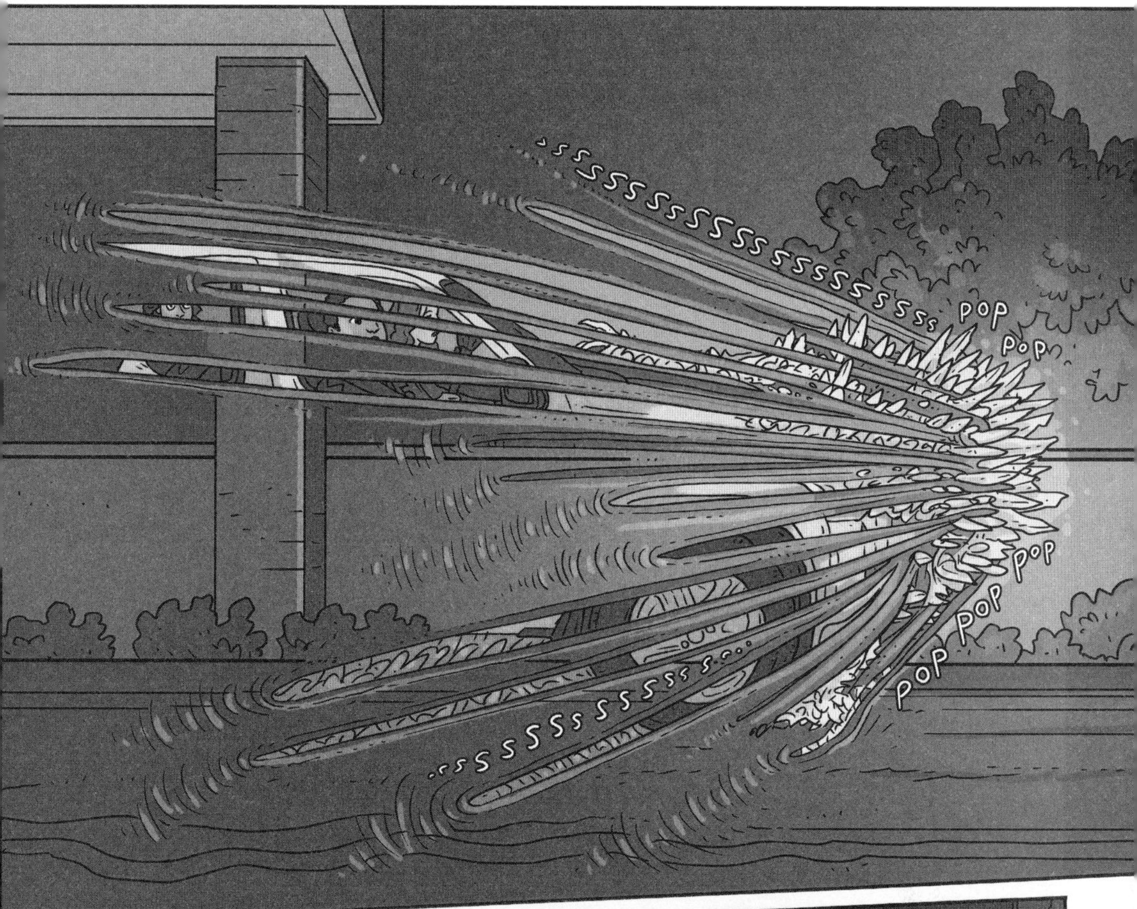
POP
POP
POP POP POP POP

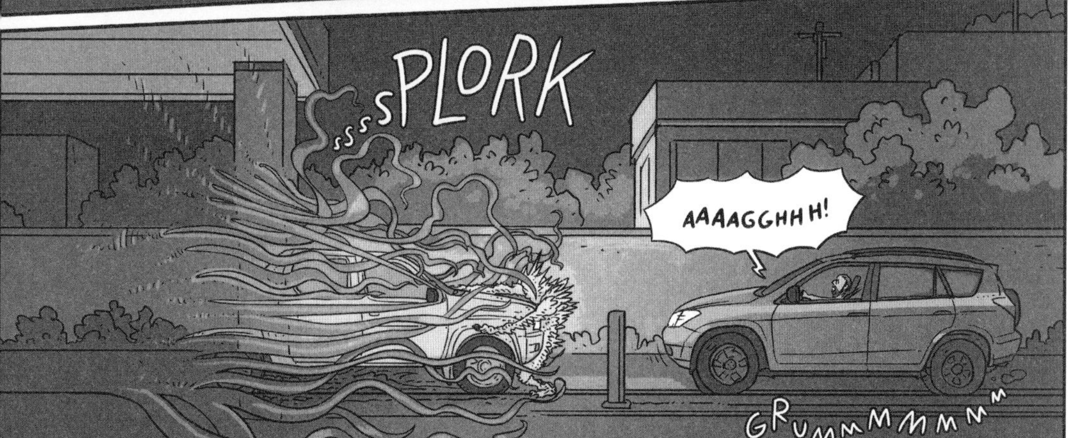
sssSPLORK
AAAAGGHHH!
GRUMMMMMMM

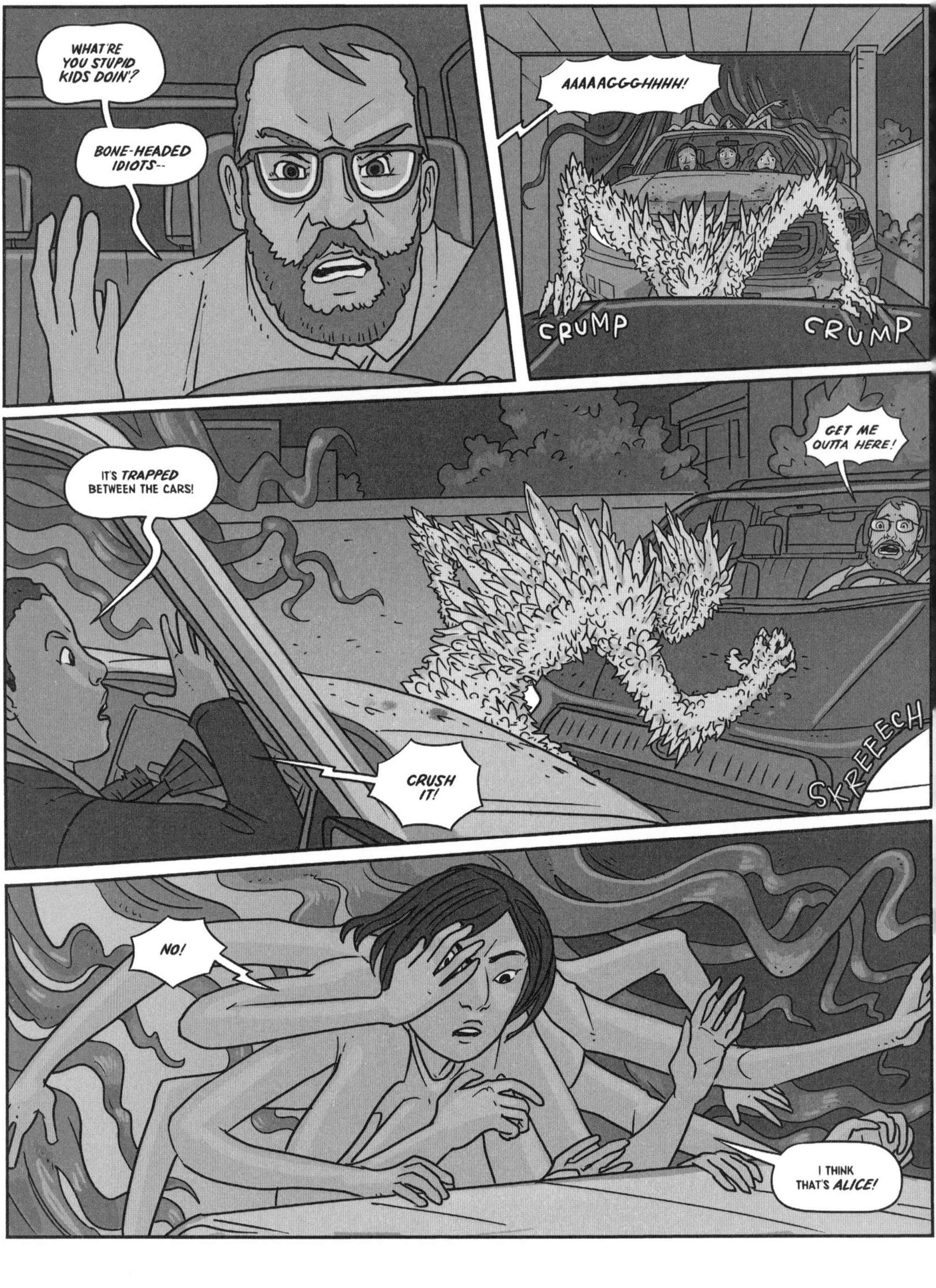
WHAT'RE YOU STUPID KIDS DOIN'?
BONE-HEADED IDIOTS--
AAAAAGGGHHHH!
CRUMP
CRUMP
IT'S TRAPPED BETWEEN THE CARS!
GET ME OUTTA HERE!
CRUSH IT!
SKREEECH
NO!
I THINK THAT'S ALICE!

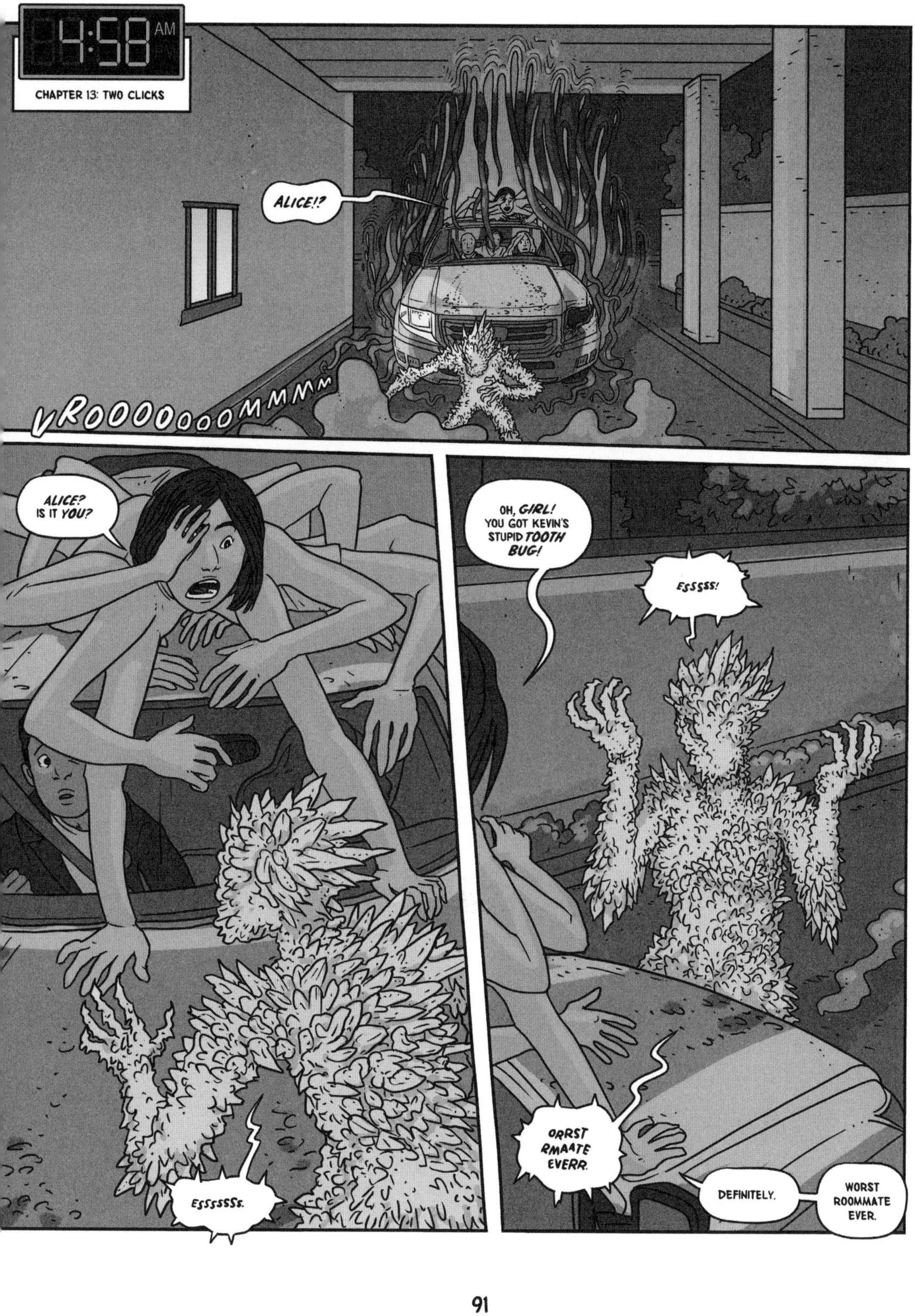
4:58 AM
CHAPTER 13: TWO CLICKS
ALICE!?
VROOOOOOOOMMMMM
ALICE? IS IT YOU?
ESSSSSSS.
OH, GIRL! YOU GOT KEVIN'S STUPID TOOTH BUG!
ESSSSS!
ORRST RMAATE EVERR.
DEFINITELY.
WORST ROOMMATE EVER.

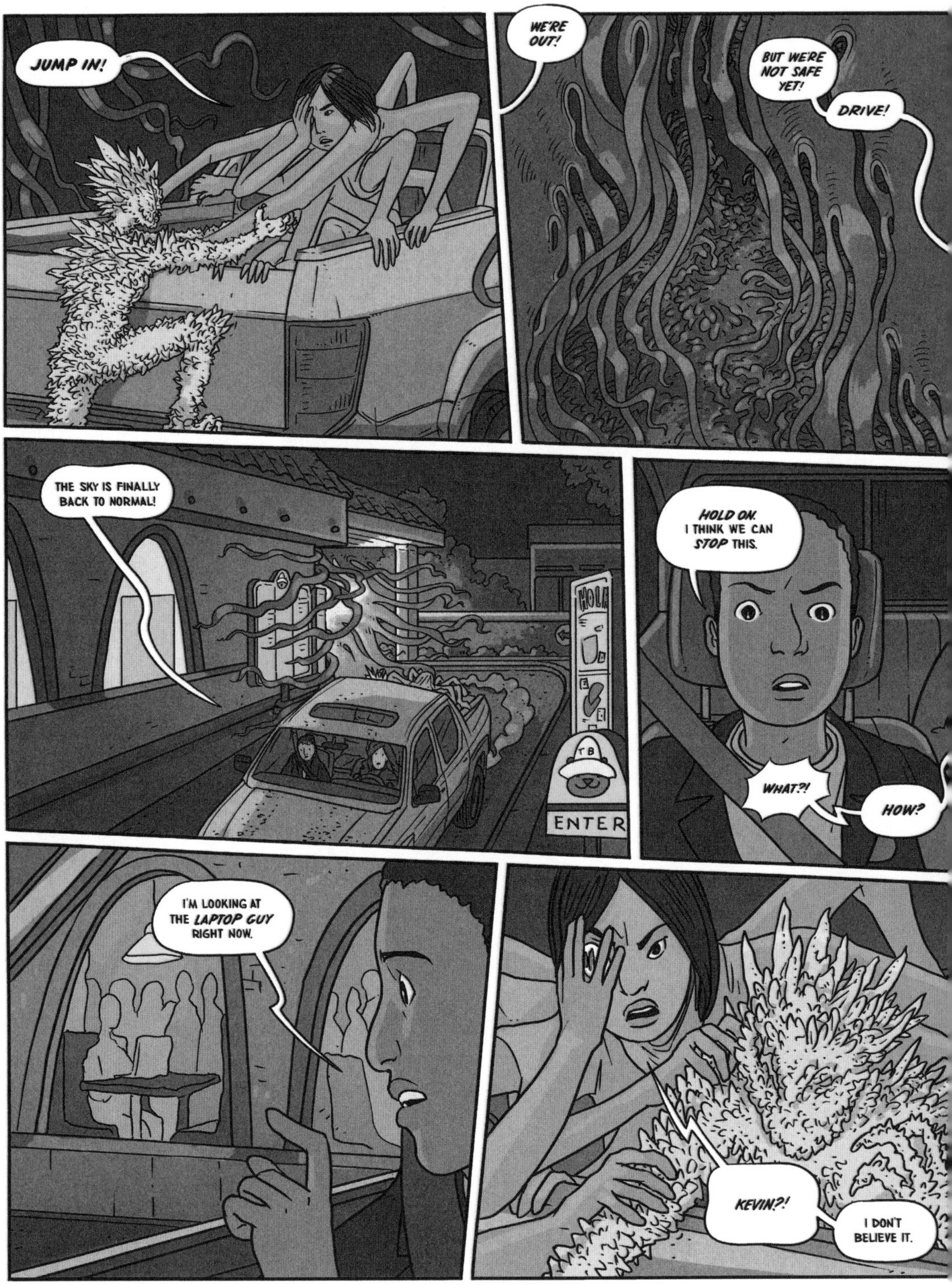
JUMP IN!
WE'RE OUT!
BUT WE'RE NOT SAFE YET!
DRIVE!
THE SKY IS FINALLY BACK TO NORMAL!
ENTER
HOLD ON. I THINK WE CAN STOP THIS.
WHAT?!
HOW?
I'M LOOKING AT THE LAPTOP GUY RIGHT NOW.
KEVIN?!
I DON'T BELIEVE IT.

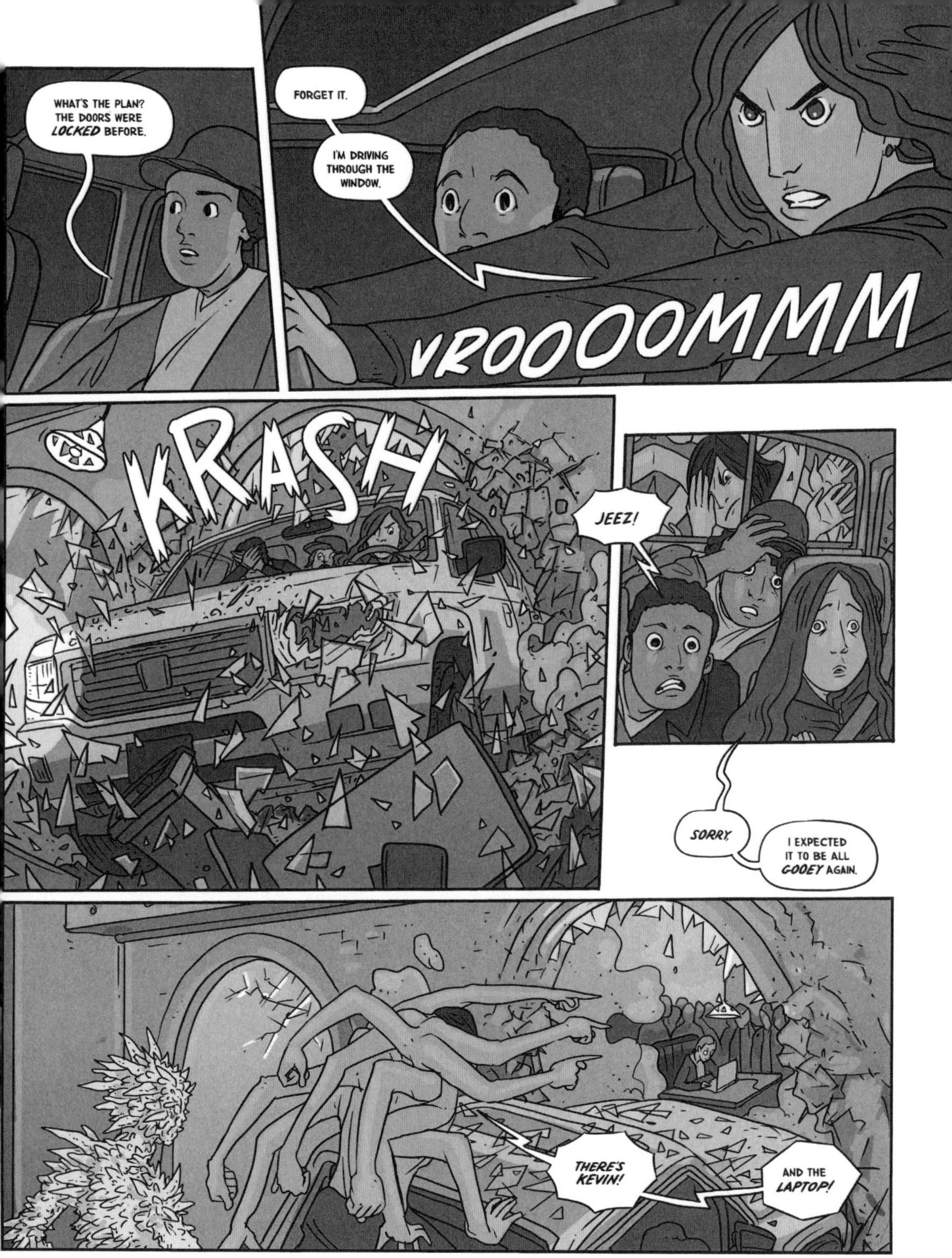
WHAT'S THE PLAN? THE DOORS WERE LOCKED BEFORE.
FORGET IT.
I'M DRIVING THROUGH THE WINDOW.
VROOOOMMM
KRASH
JEEZ!
SORRY.
I EXPECTED IT TO BE ALL GOOEY AGAIN.
THERE'S KEVIN!
AND THE LAPTOP!

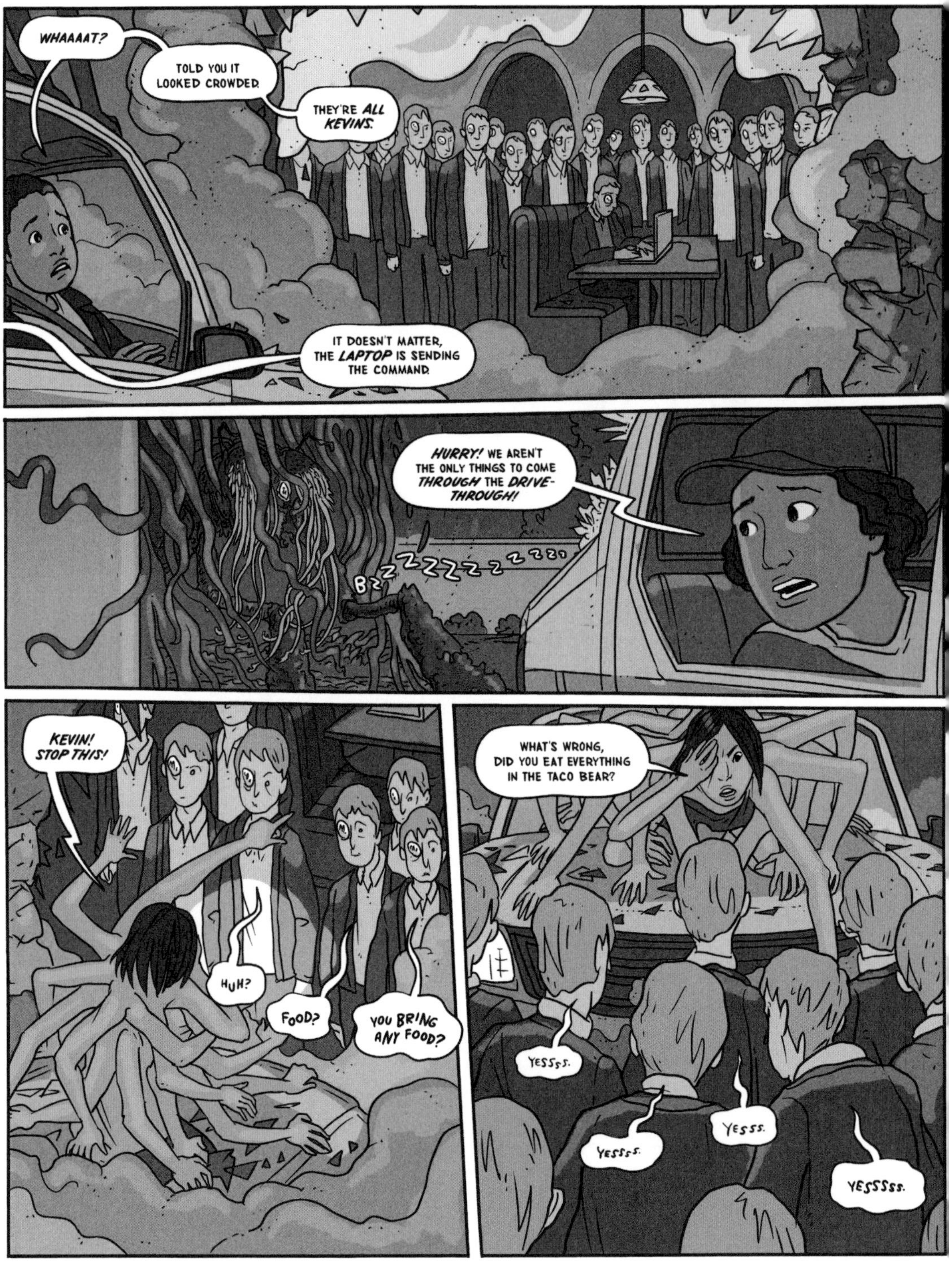
WHAAAAT?
TOLD YOU IT LOOKED CROWDED.
THEY'RE ALL KEVINS.
IT DOESN'T MATTER, THE LAPTOP IS SENDING THE COMMAND.
HURRY! WE AREN'T THE ONLY THINGS TO COME THROUGH THE DRIVE-THROUGH!
BZZZZZZZZZZZZ
KEVIN! STOP THIS!
HUH?
FOOD?
YOU BRING ANY FOOD?
WHAT'S WRONG, DID YOU EAT EVERYTHING IN THE TACO BEAR?
YESSSS.
YESSSS.
YESSS.
YESSSSS.

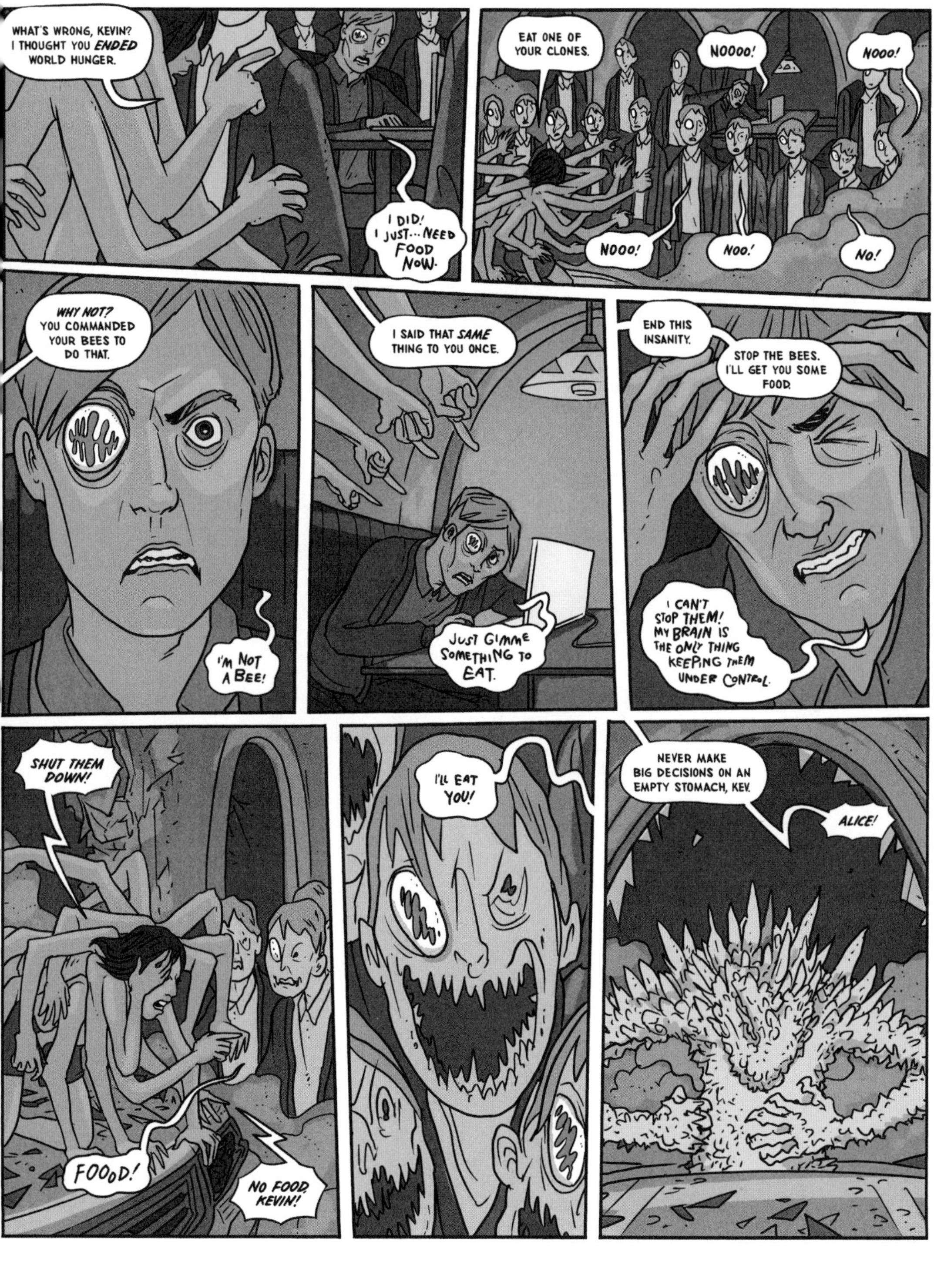

WHAT'S WRONG, KEVIN? I THOUGHT YOU ENDED WORLD HUNGER.
I DID! I JUST... NEED FOOD NOW.
EAT ONE OF YOUR CLONES.
NOOOO!
NOOO!
NOOO!
NOO!
NO!
WHY NOT? YOU COMMANDED YOUR BEES TO DO THAT.
I'M NOT A BEE!
I SAID THAT SAME THING TO YOU ONCE.
JUST GIMME SOMETHING TO EAT.
END THIS INSANITY.
STOP THE BEES. I'LL GET YOU SOME FOOD.
I CAN'T STOP THEM! MY BRAIN IS THE ONLY THING KEEPING THEM UNDER CONTROL.
SHUT THEM DOWN!
FOOOD!
NO FOOD, KEVIN!
I'LL EAT YOU!
NEVER MAKE BIG DECISIONS ON AN EMPTY STOMACH, KEV.
ALICE!

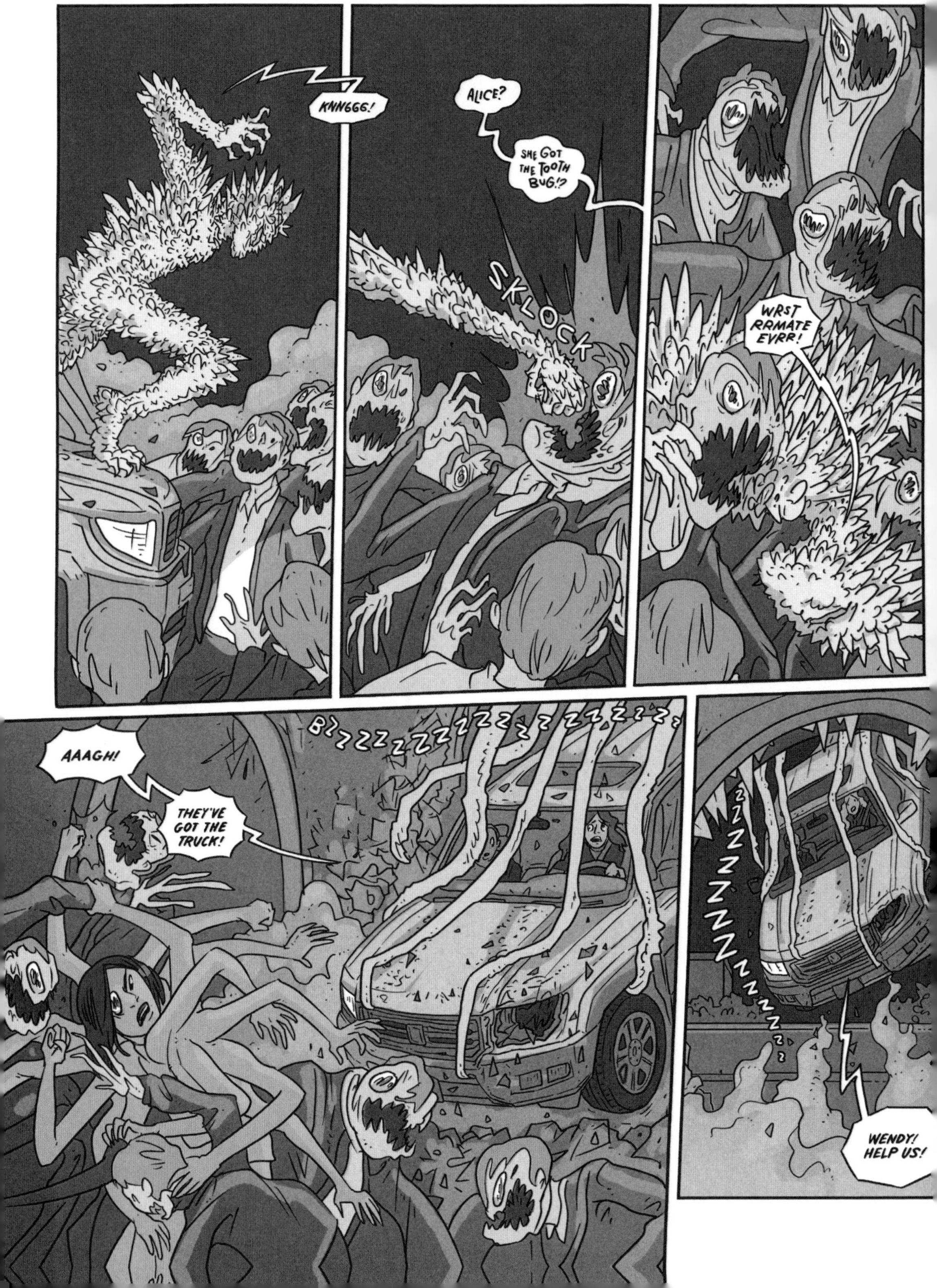
KNNGGG!
ALICE?
SHE GOT THE TOOTH BUG!?
SKLOCK
WRST RRMATE EVRR!
AAAGH!
THEY'VE GOT THE TRUCK!
BZZZZZZZZZZZZZZZZZZZ
ZZZZZZZZZZZZZ
WENDY! HELP US!

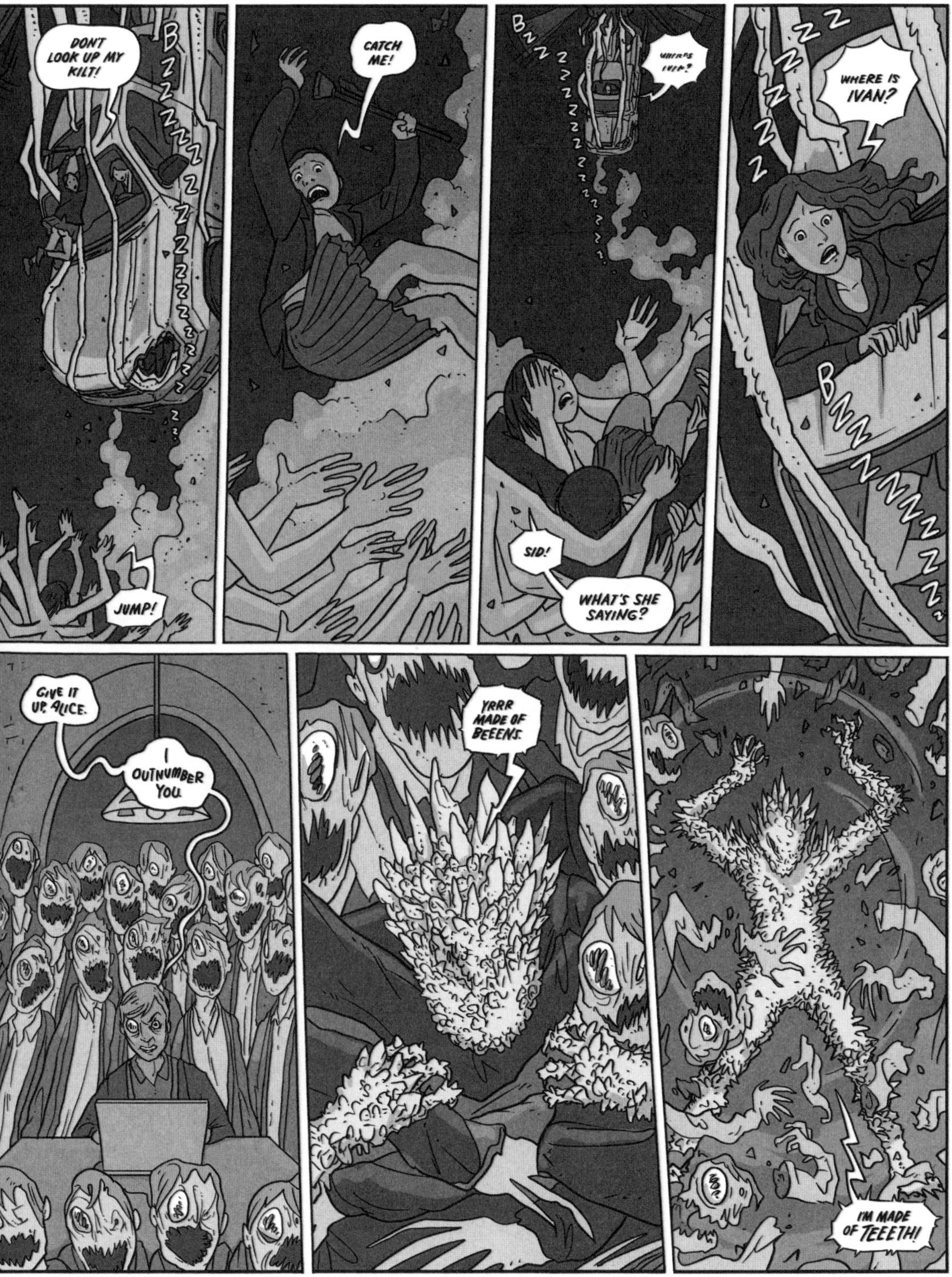

DON'T LOOK UP MY KILT!
BZZZZZZZZZZZZZZZ
JUMP!
CATCH ME!
BZZZZZZZZZZZZZ
SID!
WHAT'S SHE SAYING?
WHERE IS IVAN?
ZZZZZZ
BZZZZZZZZZZZ
GIVE IT UP, ALICE.
I OUTNUMBER YOU.
YRRR MADE OF BEEENS.
I'M MADE OF TEEETH!

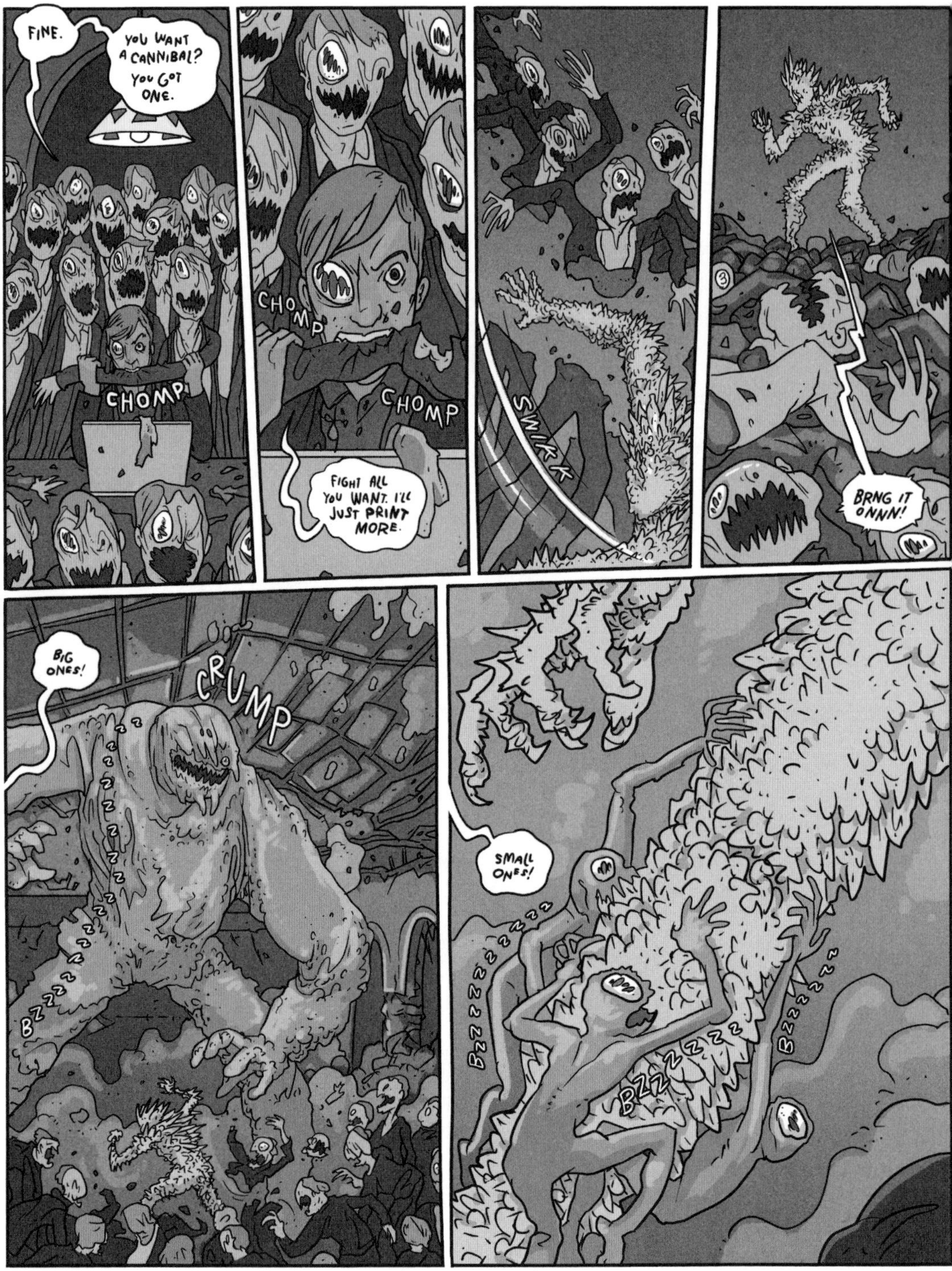
FINE.
YOU WANT A CANNIBAL? YOU GOT ONE.
CHOMP
CHOMP
CHOMP
FIGHT ALL YOU WANT. I'LL JUST PRINT MORE.
SWIKK
BRNG IT ONNN!
BIG ONES!
CRUMP
BZZZZZZZZ
SMALL ONES!
BZZZZZZZ
BZZZ
BZZZZZZ

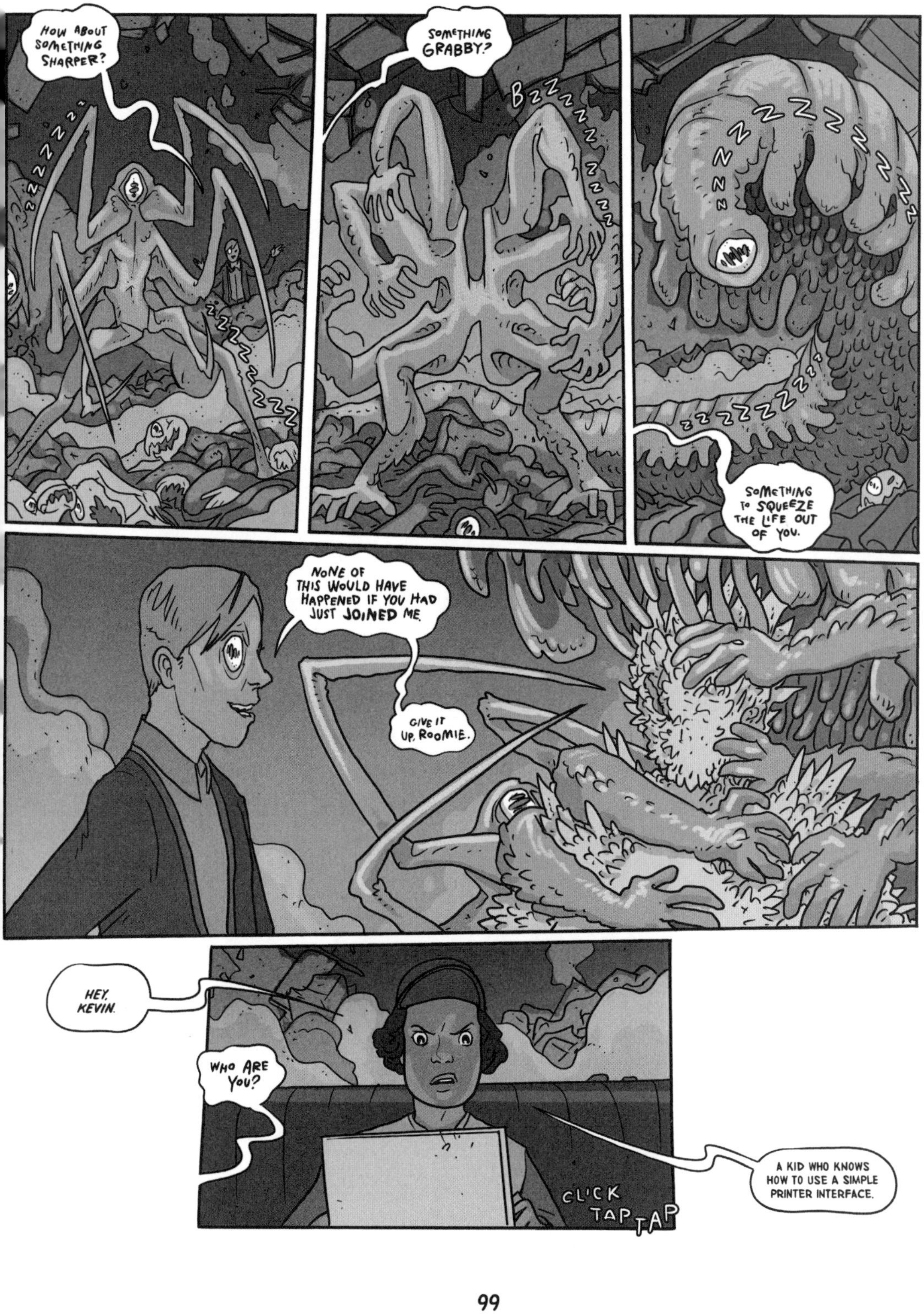

HOW ABOUT SOMETHING SHARPER?
ZZZZZZZ
SOMETHING GRABBY?
BZZZZZZZZZ
ZZZZZZZZZZ
SOMETHING TO SQUEEZE THE LIFE OUT OF YOU.
NONE OF THIS WOULD HAVE HAPPENED IF YOU HAD JUST JOINED ME.
GIVE IT UP, ROOMIE.
HEY, KEVIN.
WHO ARE YOU?
A KID WHO KNOWS HOW TO USE A SIMPLE PRINTER INTERFACE.
CLICK
TAP TAP

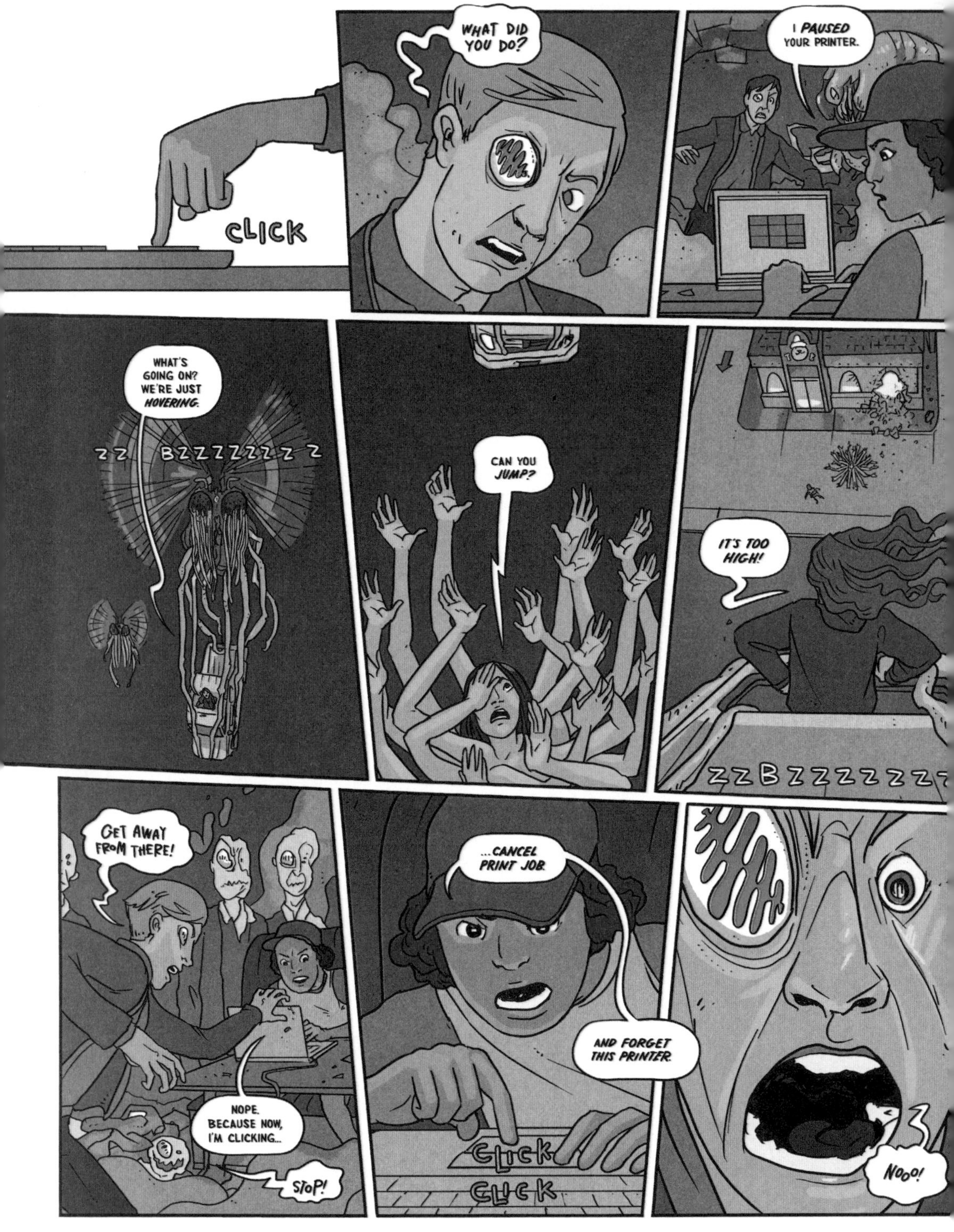
CLICK
WHAT DID YOU DO?
I PAUSED YOUR PRINTER.
WHAT'S GOING ON? WE'RE JUST HOVERING.
ZZ BZZZZZZZZ Z
CAN YOU JUMP?
IT'S TOO HIGH!
ZZBZZZZZZZ
GET AWAY FROM THERE!
NOPE. BECAUSE NOW, I'M CLICKING...
STOP!
...CANCEL PRINT JOB.
AND FORGET THIS PRINTER.
CLICK
CLICK
NOOO!

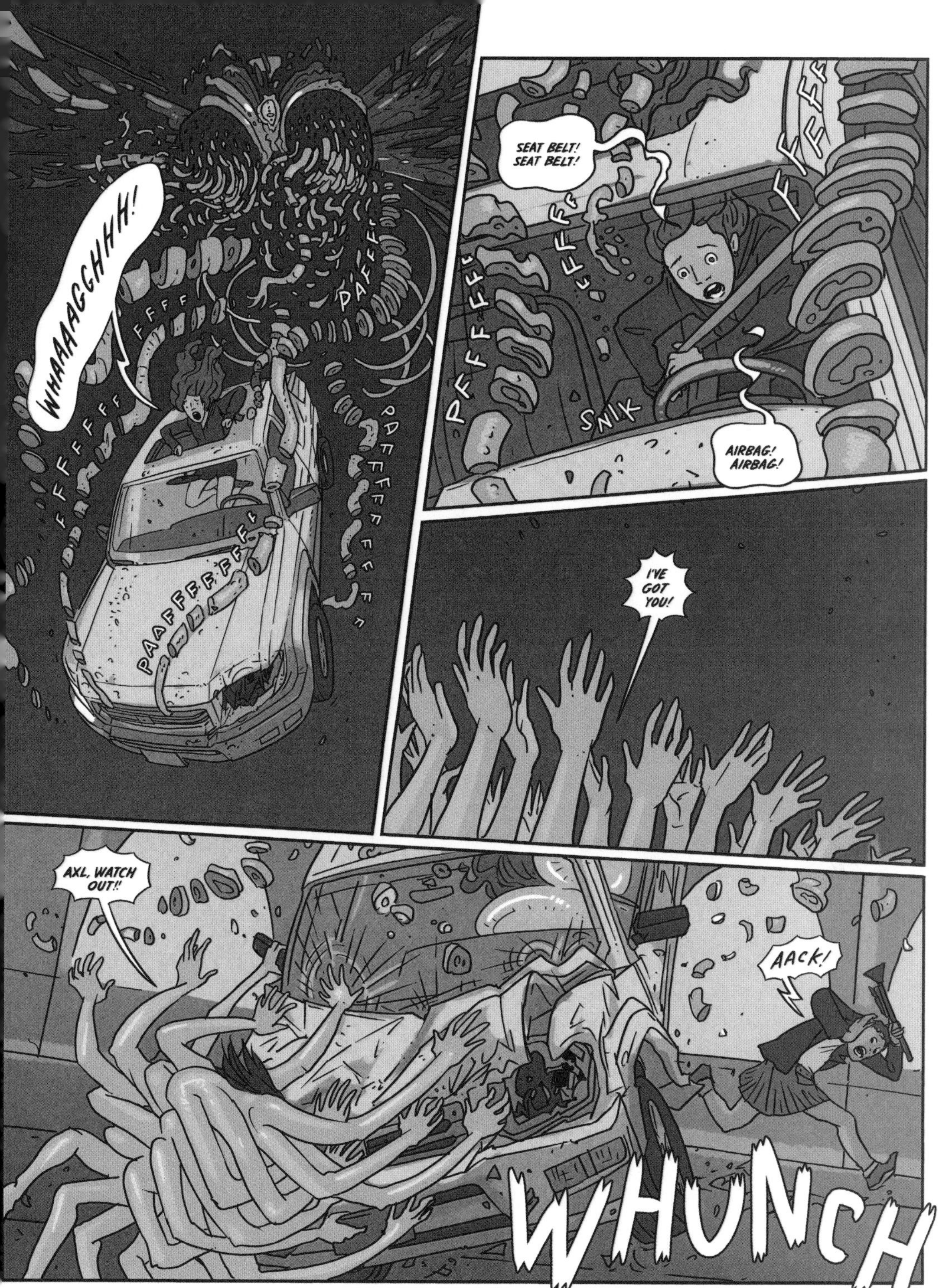

WHAAAAGCHHH!
SEAT BELT! SEAT BELT!
SNIK
AIRBAG! AIRBAG!
I'VE GOT YOU!
AXL, WATCH OUT!!
AACK!
WHUNCH

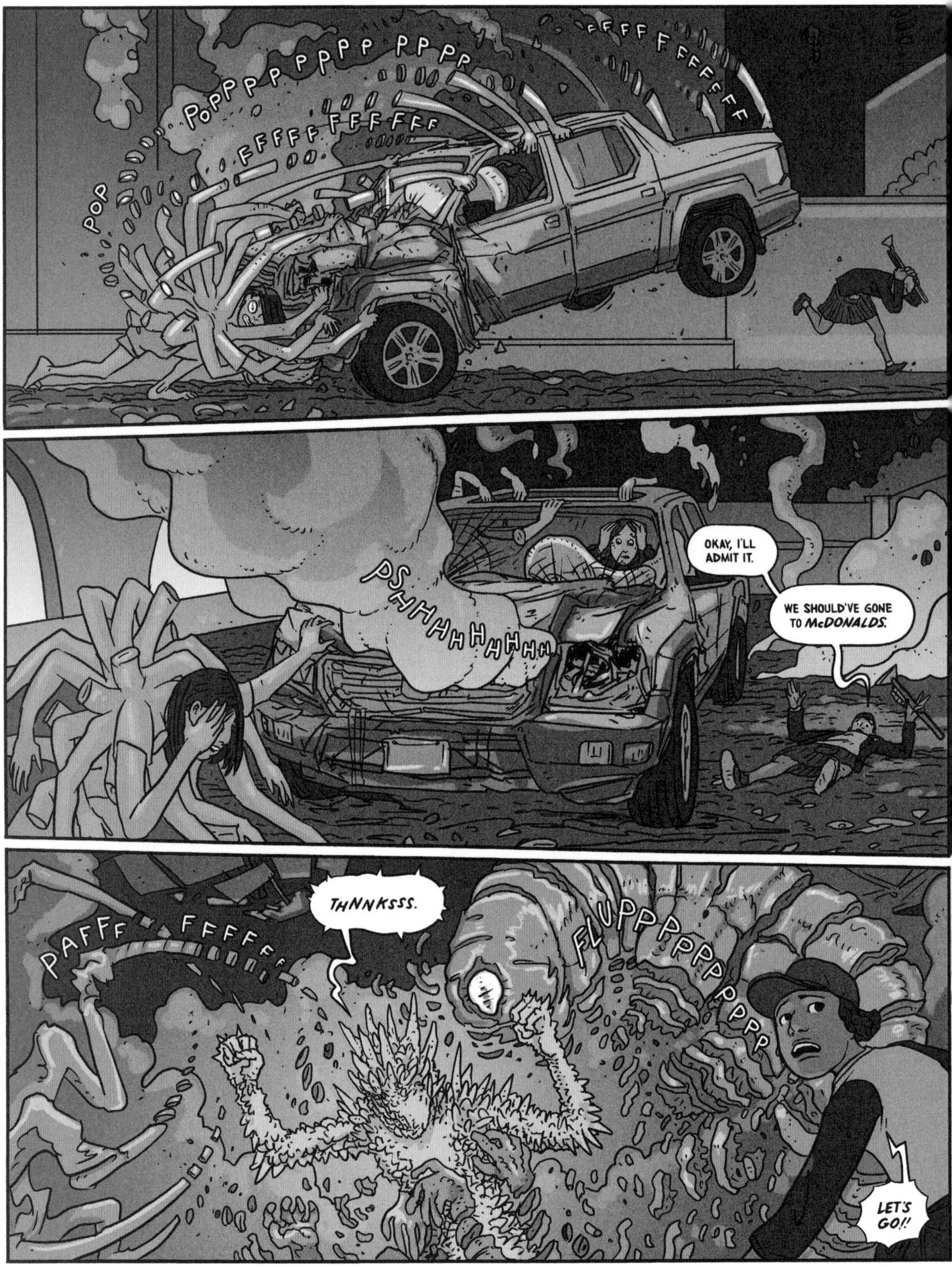
POP
POPPPP PPPPP PPPP
FFFFF FFFFFF
FFFF F FFFFFF
PSHHHHHHHHHH
OKAY, I'LL ADMIT IT.
WE SHOULD'VE GONE TO McDONALDS.
PAFFF
FFFFFF
THNNKSSS.
FLUPPPPPPPPPP
LET'S GO!!

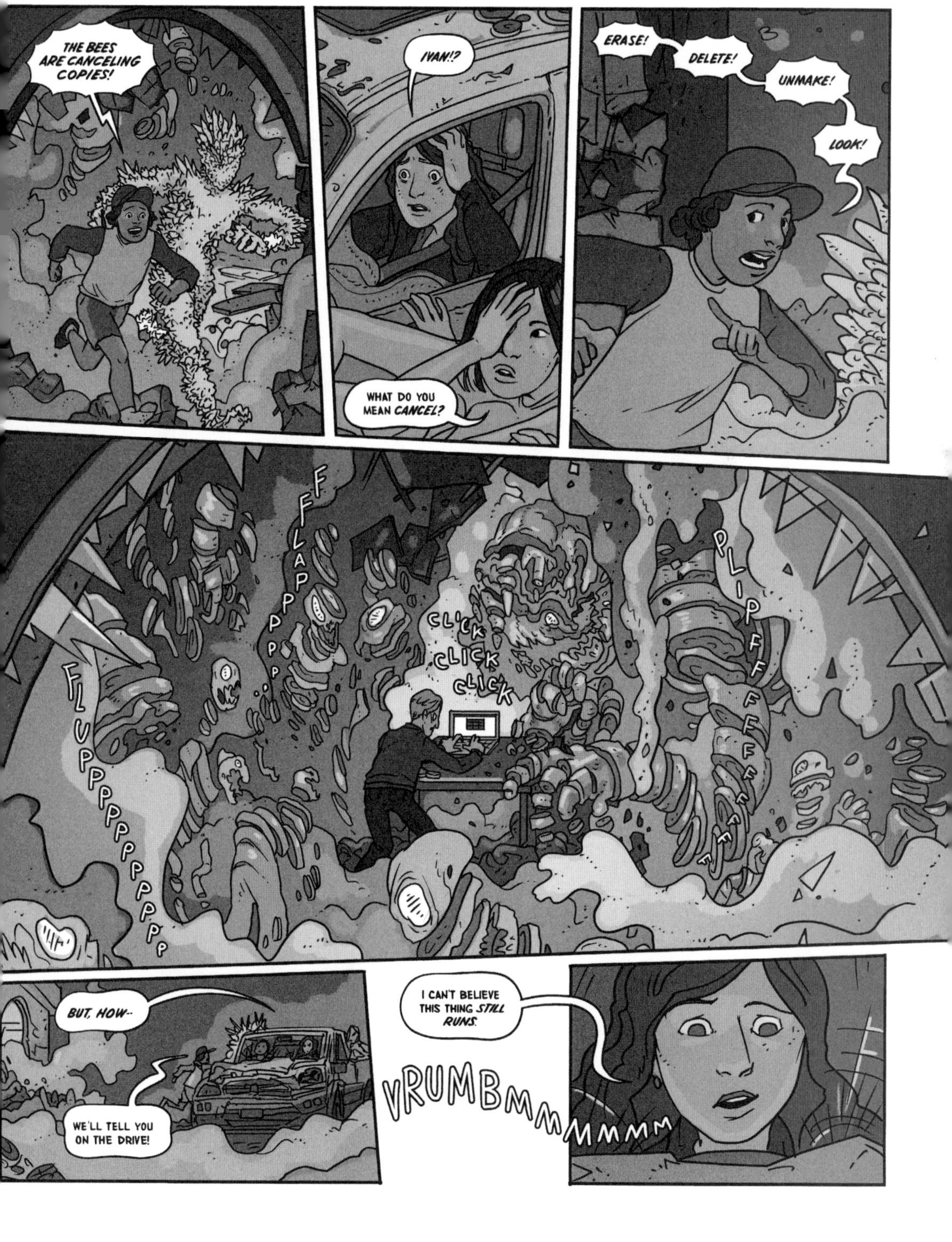
THE BEES ARE CANCELING COPIES!
IVAN!?
WHAT DO YOU MEAN CANCEL?
ERASE!
DELETE!
UNMAKE!
LOOK!
FF
FLAPPPPP
CLICK
CLICK
CLICK
PLIPFFFFFFFFFFF
FLUPPPPPPPPPPPPP
BUT, HOW--
WE'LL TELL YOU ON THE DRIVE!
I CAN'T BELIEVE THIS THING STILL RUNS.
VRUMBMMMMMMM

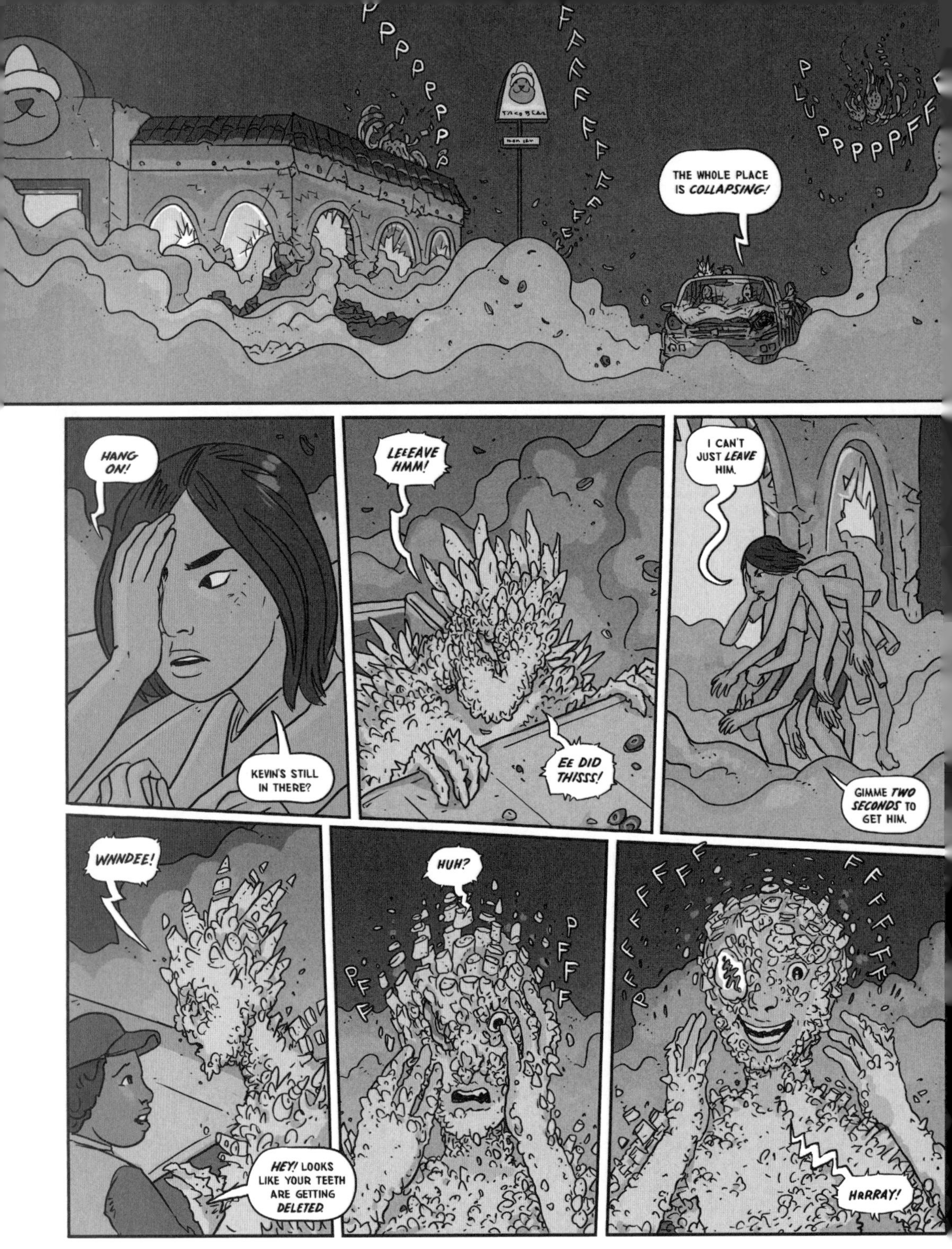
PPPPPPPPP
FFFFFFFFFFF
PLUPPPPPPFF
THE WHOLE PLACE IS COLLAPSING!
HANG ON!
KEVIN'S STILL IN THERE?
LEEEAVE HMM!
EE DID THISSS!
I CAN'T JUST LEAVE HIM.
GIMME TWO SECONDS TO GET HIM.
WNNDEE!
HEY! LOOKS LIKE YOUR TEETH ARE GETTING DELETED.
HUH?
PFF
PFFF
FFFFFF
FFFFFFF
HRRRAY!

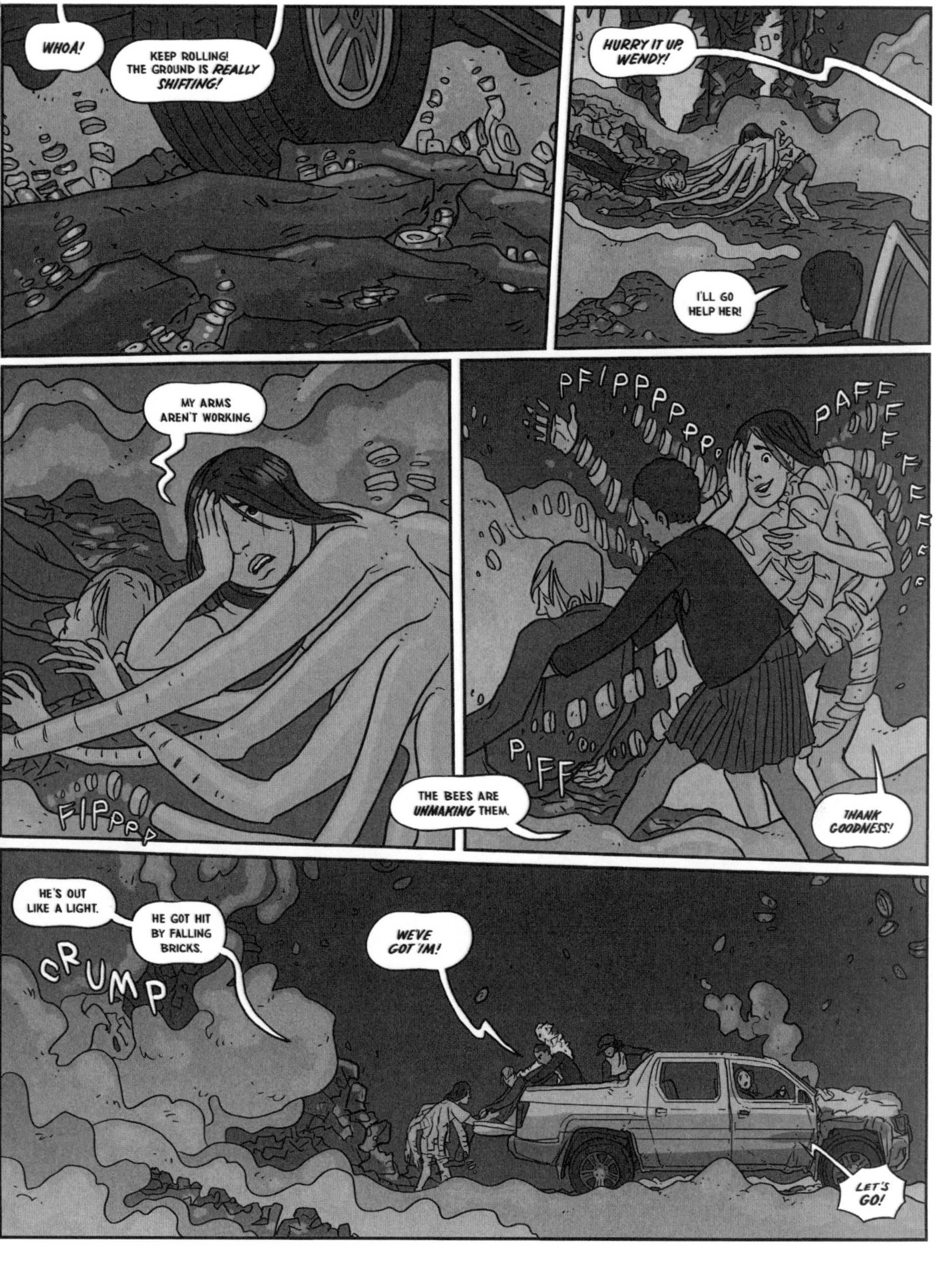
WHOA!
KEEP ROLLING! THE GROUND IS REALLY SHIFTING!
HURRY IT UP, WENDY!
I'LL GO HELP HER!
MY ARMS AREN'T WORKING.
FIPppp
PFIPPPPPPPP
PAFFFFFFFFFF
PIFF
THE BEES ARE UNMAKING THEM.
THANK GOODNESS!
HE'S OUT LIKE A LIGHT.
HE GOT HIT BY FALLING BRICKS.
CRUMP
WE'VE GOT 'IM!
LET'S GO!

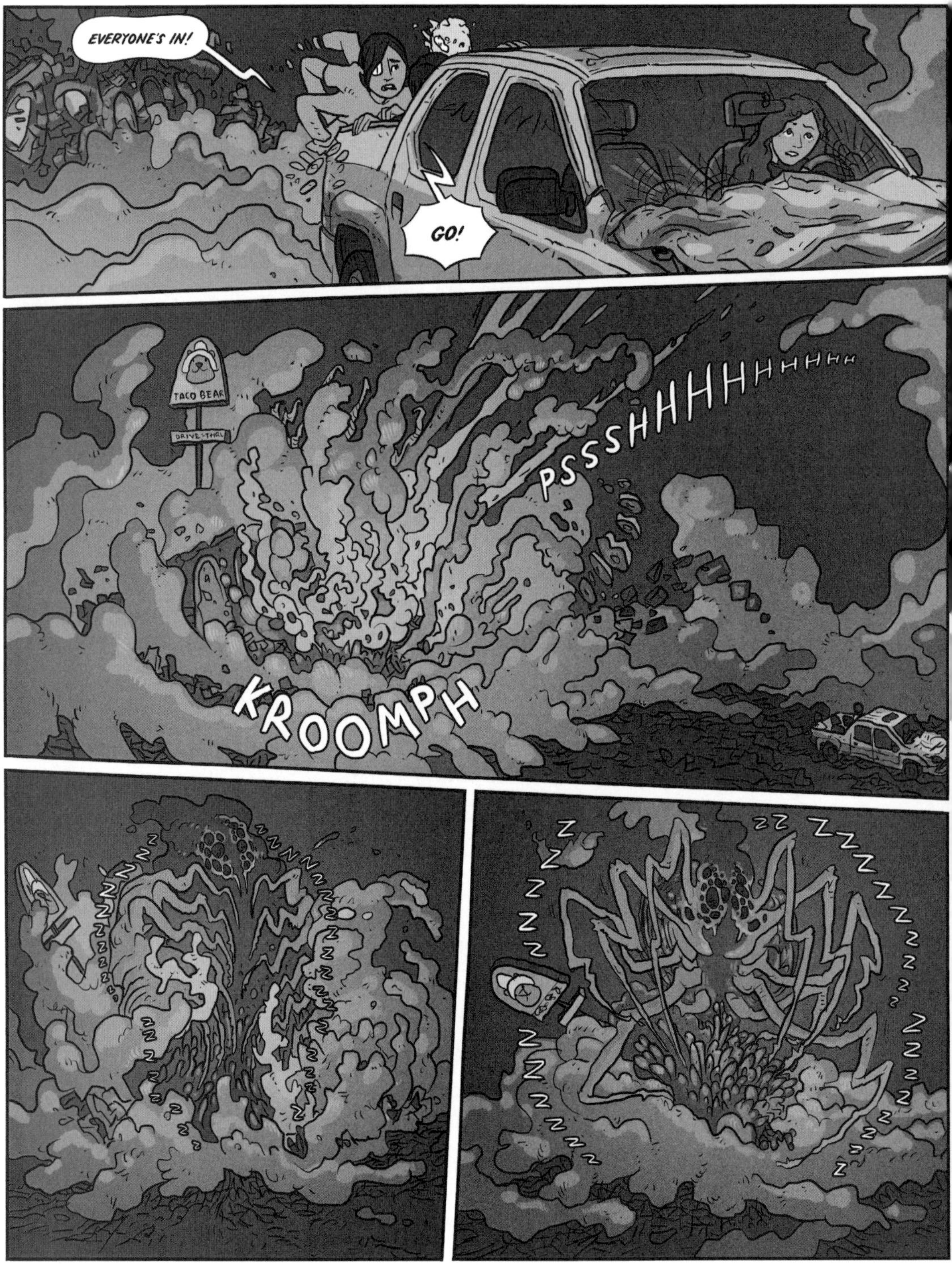
EVERYONE'S IN!
GO!
TACO BEAR
PSSSHHHHHHHHHH
KROOMPH

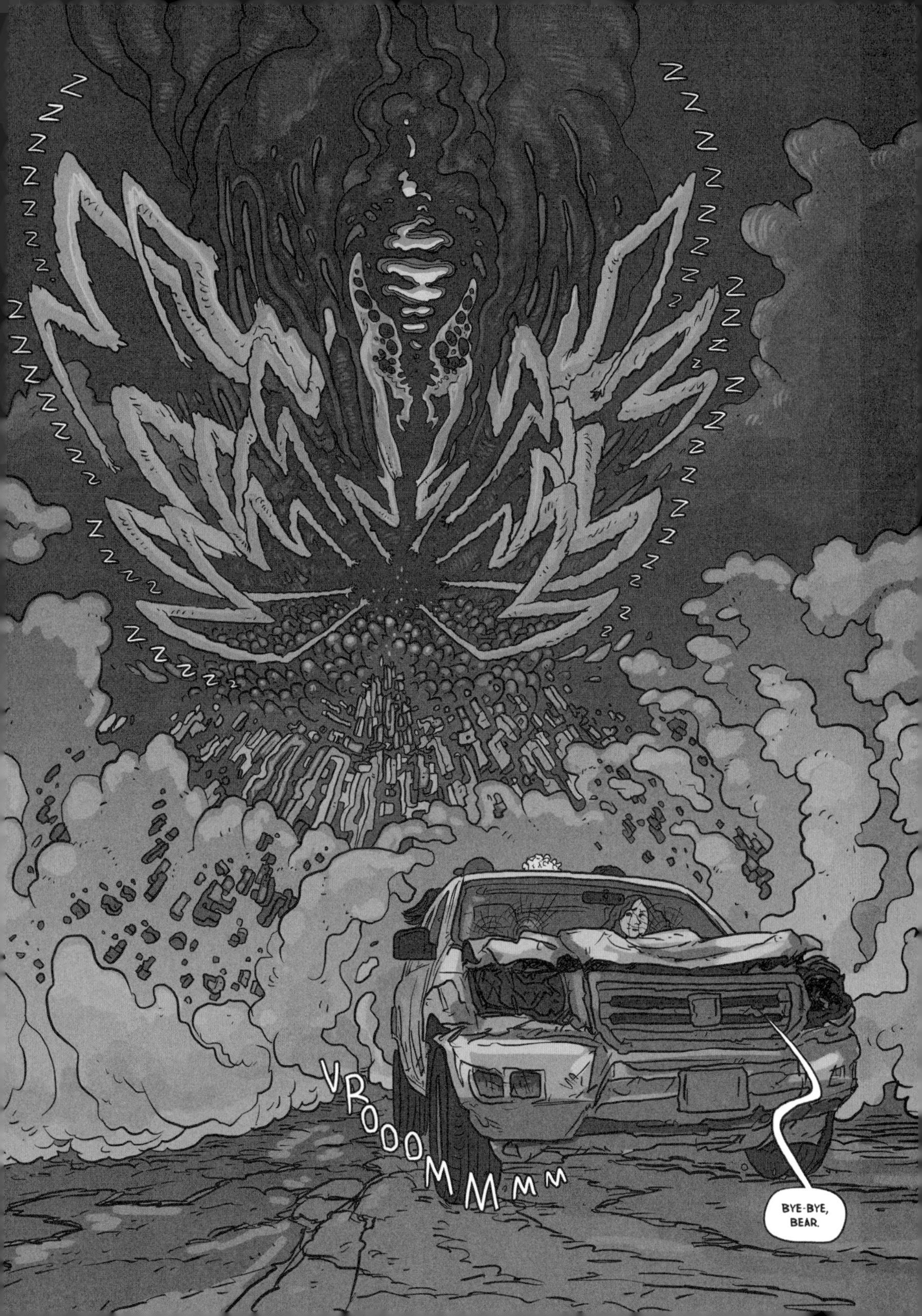

ZZZZZZZZZZ
VROOOOMMMMM
BYE-BYE, BEAR.

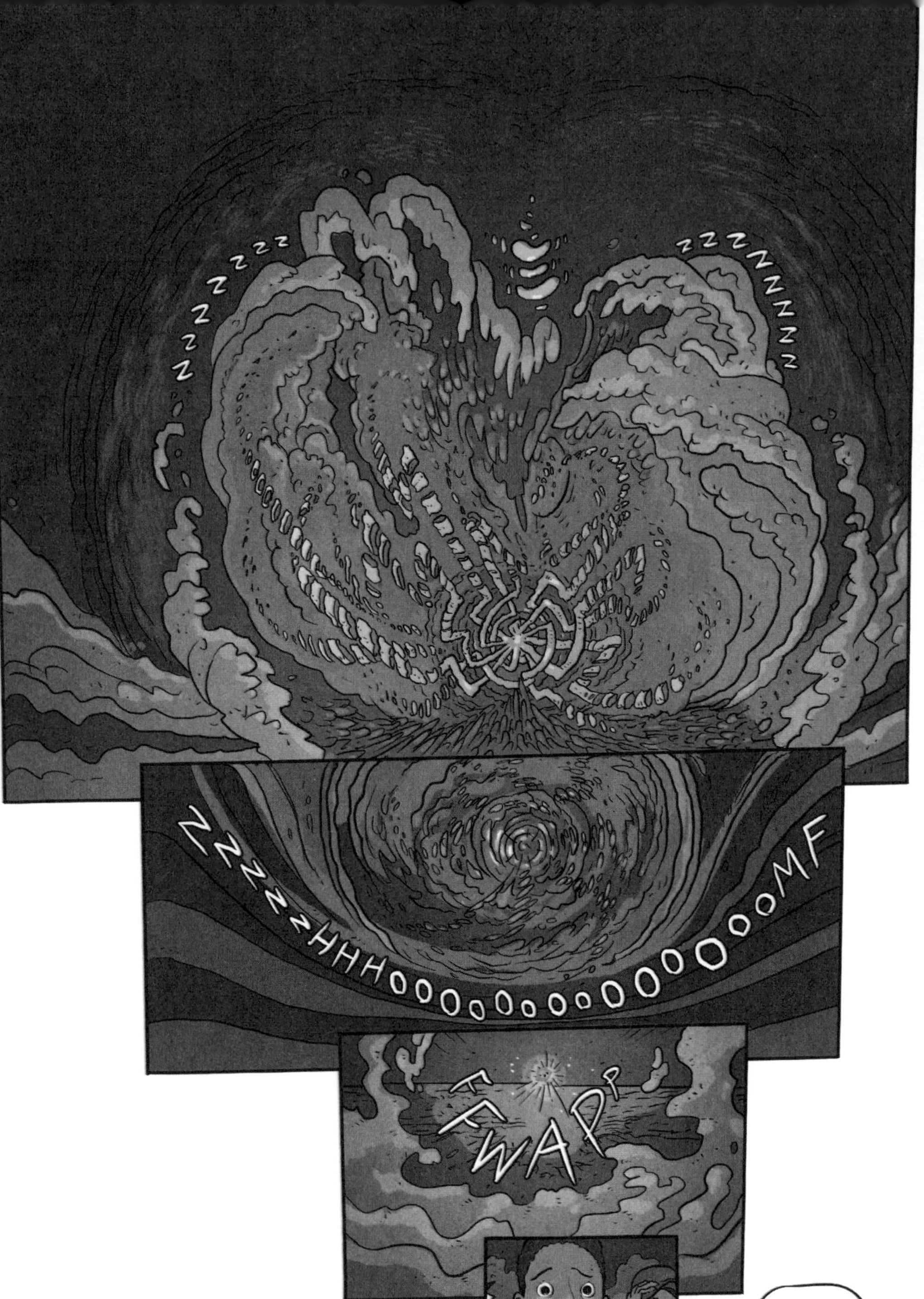

ZZZZzzHHHOOOOOOOOOOOOOOooMF
FFWAPP
THE DRIVE-THROUGH IS CLOSED.

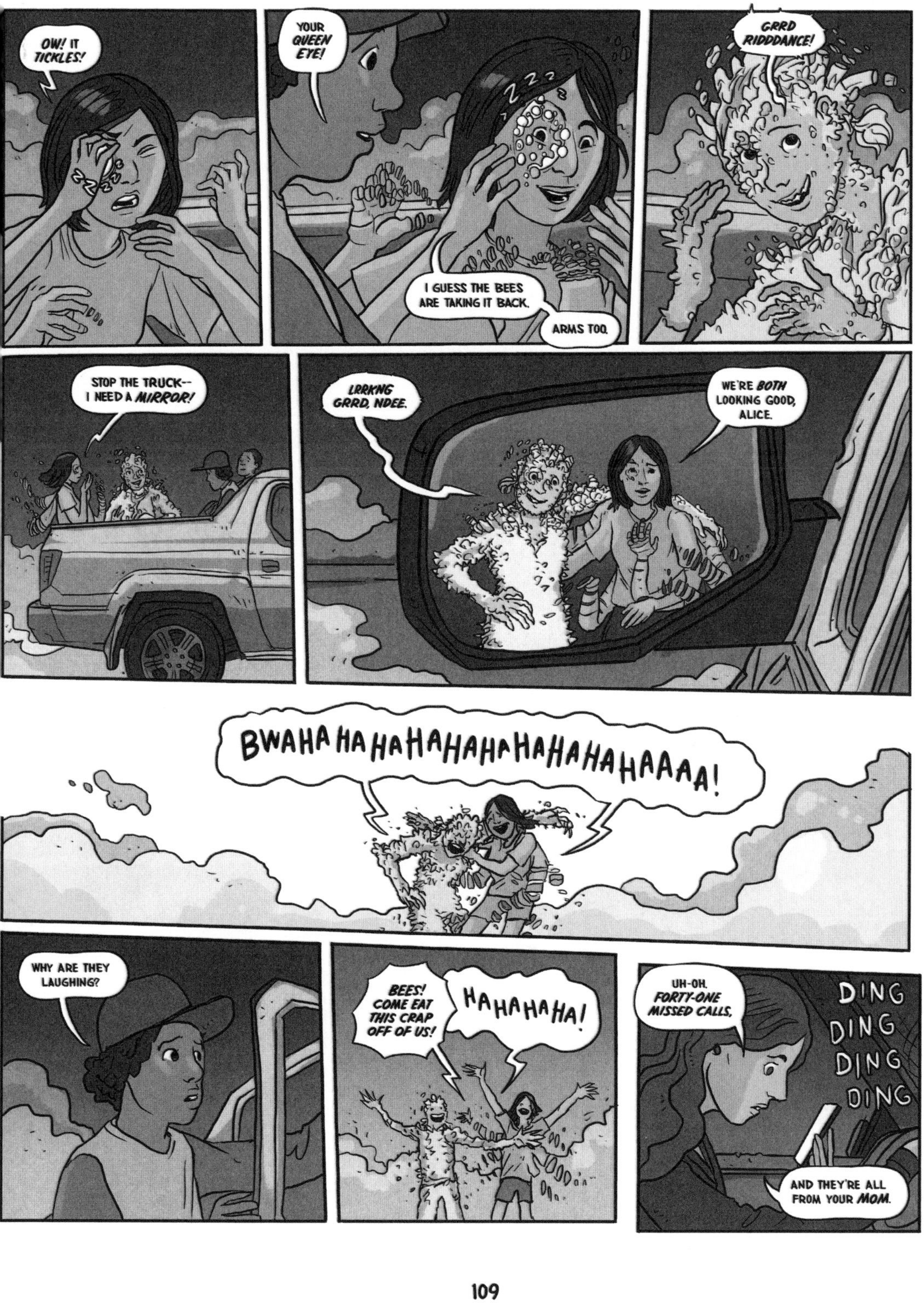
OW! IT TICKLES!
YOUR QUEEN EYE!
I GUESS THE BEES ARE TAKING IT BACK.
ARMS TOO.
GRRD RIDDDANCE!
STOP THE TRUCK-- I NEED A MIRROR!
LRRKNG GRRD, NDEE.
WE'RE BOTH LOOKING GOOD, ALICE.
BWAHAHAHAHAHAHAHAHAHAHAHAHAAAAA!
WHY ARE THEY LAUGHING?
BEES! COME EAT THIS CRAP OFF OF US!
HAHAHAHAHA!
UH-OH. FORTY-ONE MISSED CALLS.
DING DING DING DING
AND THEY'RE ALL FROM YOUR MOM.

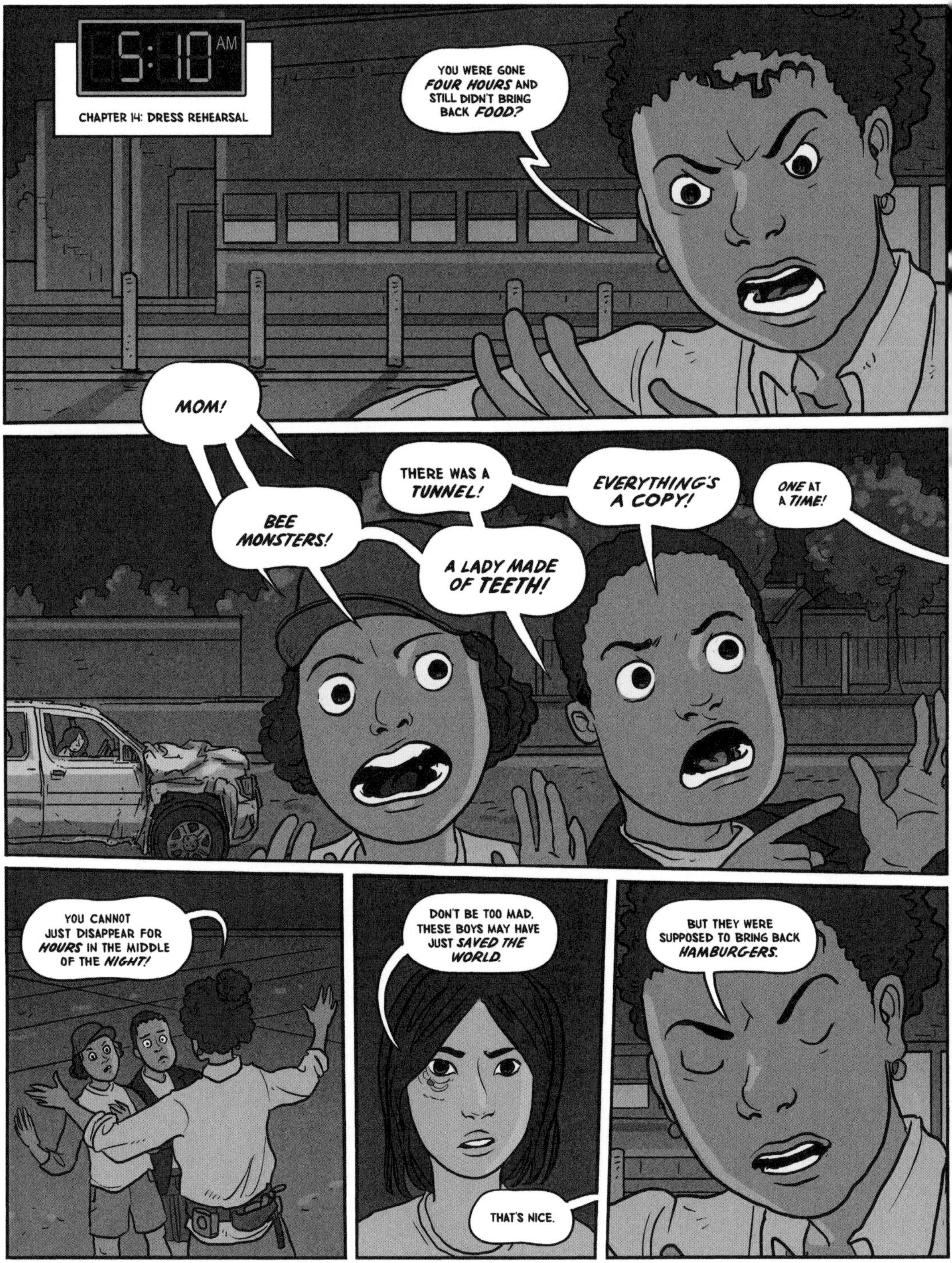

5:10 AM
CHAPTER 14: DRESS REHEARSAL
YOU WERE GONE FOUR HOURS AND STILL DIDN'T BRING BACK FOOD?
MOM!
BEE MONSTERS!
THERE WAS A TUNNEL!
A LADY MADE OF TEETH!
EVERYTHING'S A COPY!
ONE AT A TIME!
YOU CANNOT JUST DISAPPEAR FOR HOURS IN THE MIDDLE OF THE NIGHT!
DON'T BE TOO MAD. THESE BOYS MAY HAVE JUST SAVED THE WORLD.
THAT'S NICE.
BUT THEY WERE SUPPOSED TO BRING BACK HAMBURGERS.

112

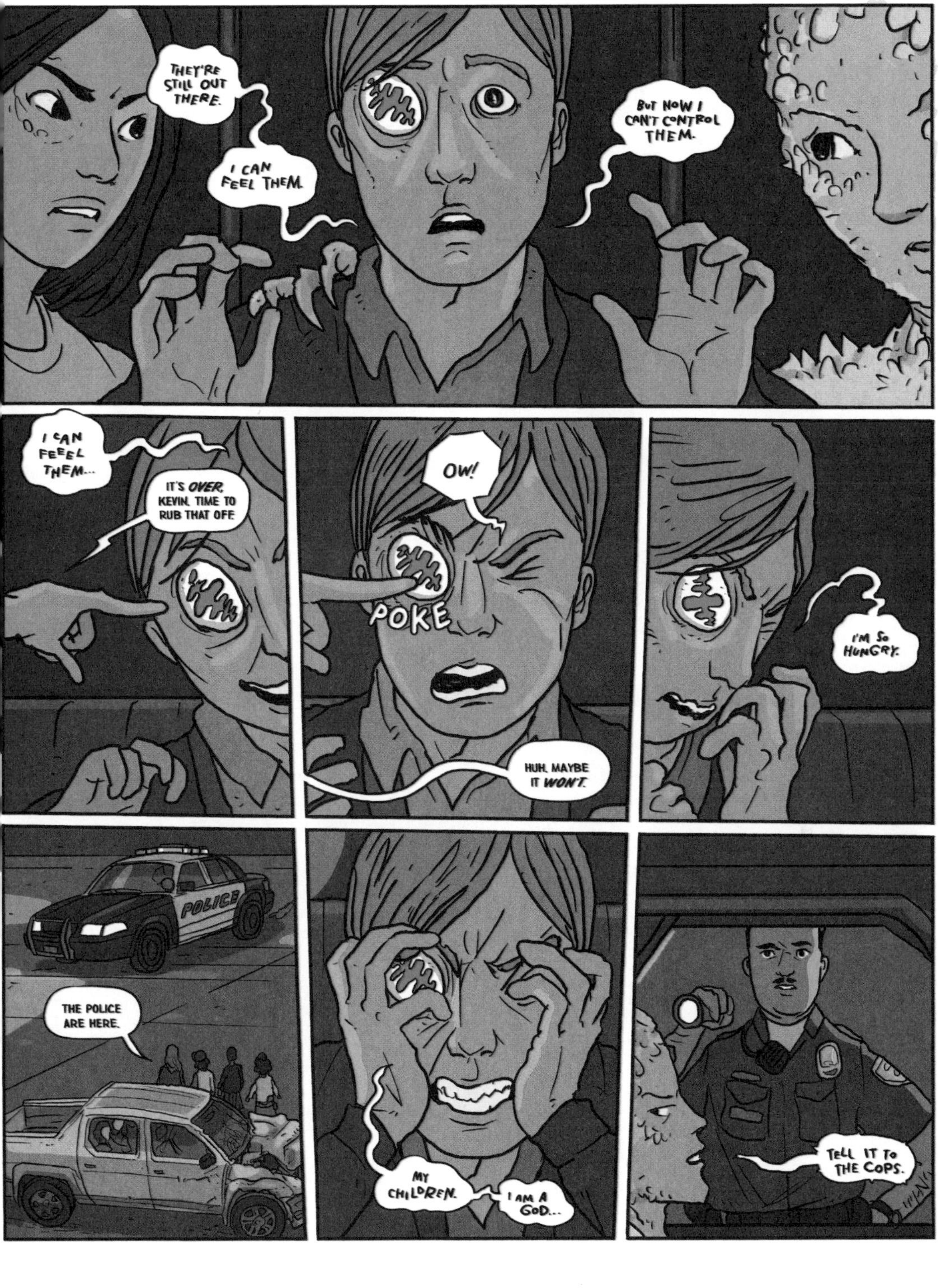
THEY'RE STILL OUT THERE.
I CAN FEEL THEM.
BUT NOW I CAN'T CONTROL THEM.
I CAN FEEEL THEM...
IT'S OVER, KEVIN. TIME TO RUB THAT OFF.
OW!
POKE
HUH, MAYBE IT WON'T.
I'M SO HUNGRY.
POLICE
THE POLICE ARE HERE.
MY CHILDREN.
I AM A GOD...
TELL IT TO THE COPS.

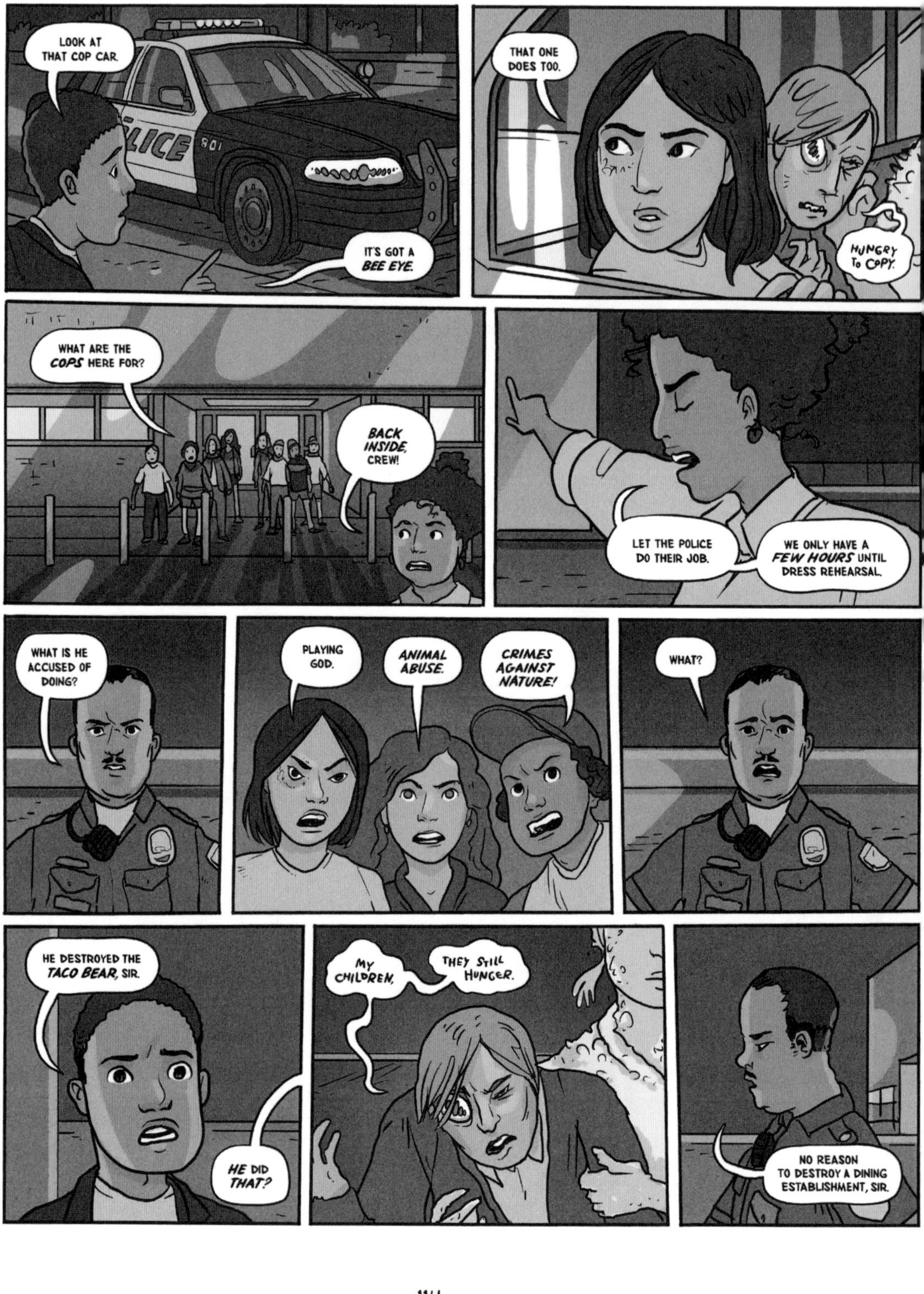

LOOK AT THAT COP CAR.
IT'S GOT A *BEE EYE.*
THAT ONE DOES TOO.
HUNGRY TO COPY.
WHAT ARE THE *COPS* HERE FOR?
BACK INSIDE, CREW!
LET THE POLICE DO THEIR JOB.
WE ONLY HAVE A *FEW HOURS* UNTIL DRESS REHEARSAL.
WHAT IS HE ACCUSED OF DOING?
PLAYING GOD.
ANIMAL ABUSE.
CRIMES AGAINST NATURE!
WHAT?
HE DESTROYED THE *TACO BEAR,* SIR.
HE DID THAT?
MY CHILDREN,
THEY STILL HUNGER.
NO REASON TO DESTROY A DINING ESTABLISHMENT, SIR.

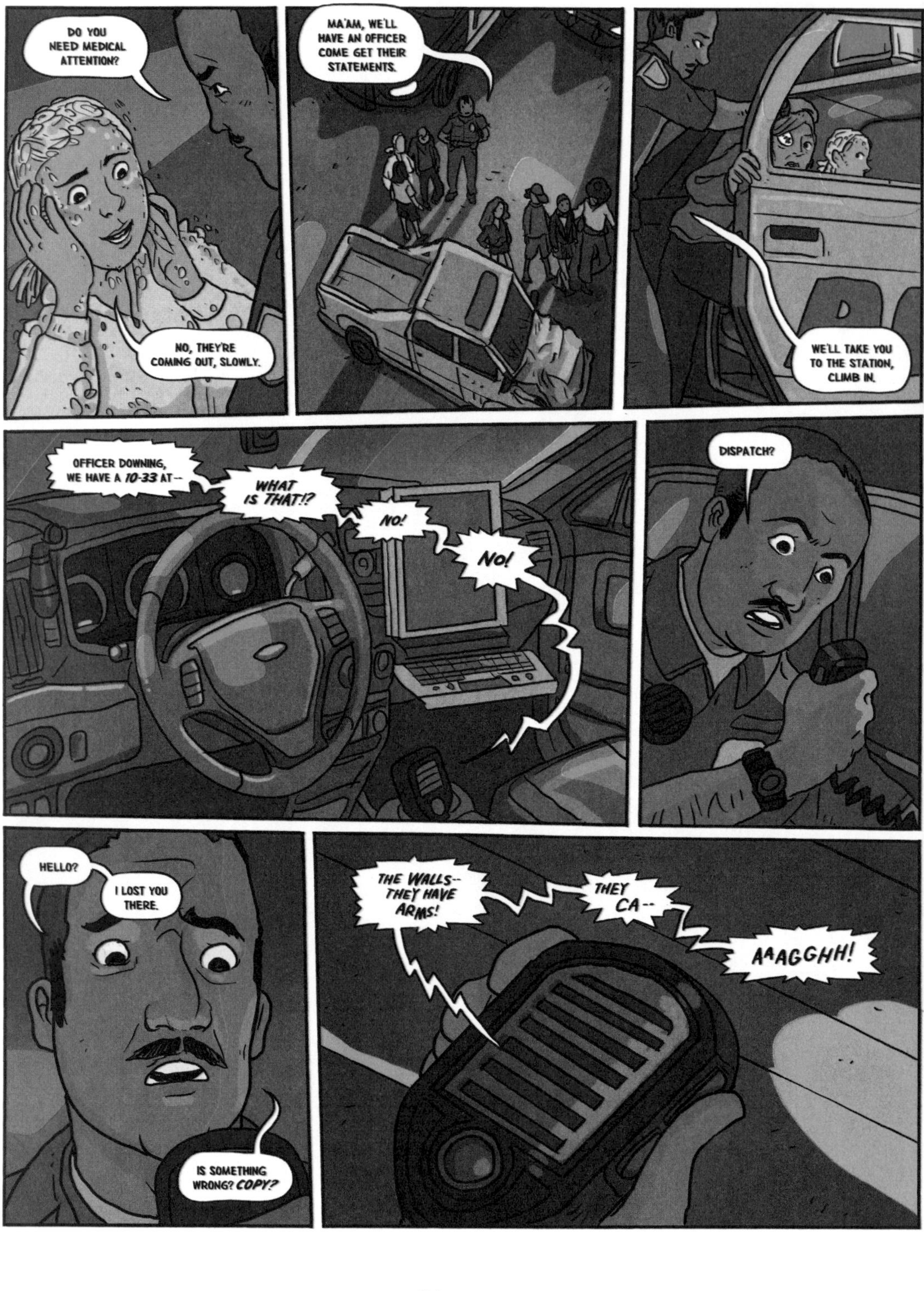
DO YOU NEED MEDICAL ATTENTION?
NO, THEY'RE COMING OUT, SLOWLY.
MA'AM, WE'LL HAVE AN OFFICER COME GET THEIR STATEMENTS.
WE'LL TAKE YOU TO THE STATION, CLIMB IN.
OFFICER DOWNING, WE HAVE A 10-33 AT--
WHAT IS THAT!?
NO!
NO!
DISPATCH?
HELLO?
I LOST YOU THERE.
IS SOMETHING WRONG? COPY?
THE WALLS-- THEY HAVE ARMS!
THEY CA--
AAAGGHH!

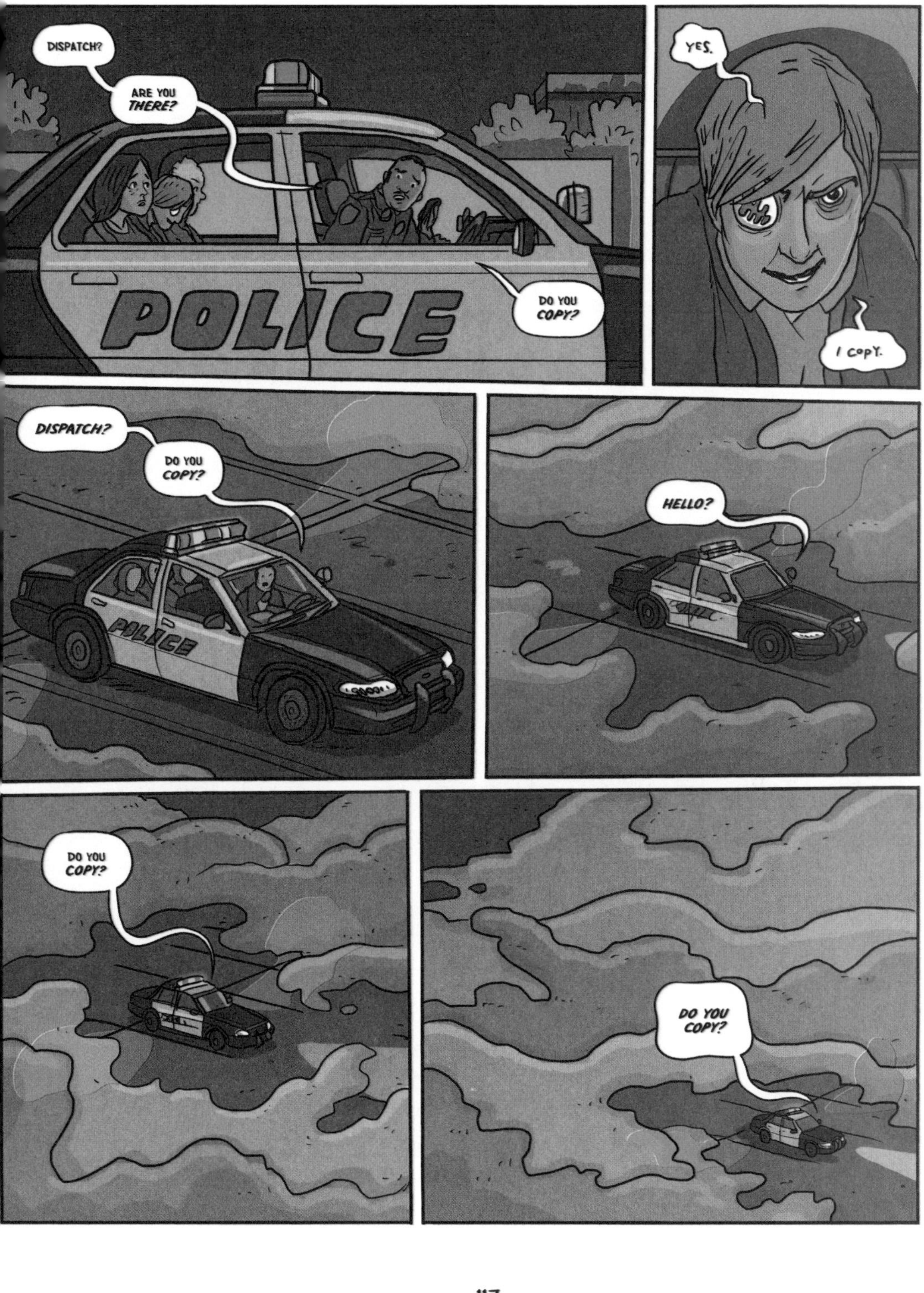
DISPATCH?
ARE YOU THERE?
DO YOU COPY?
YES.
I COPY.
DISPATCH?
DO YOU COPY?
HELLO?
DO YOU COPY?
DO YOU COPY?

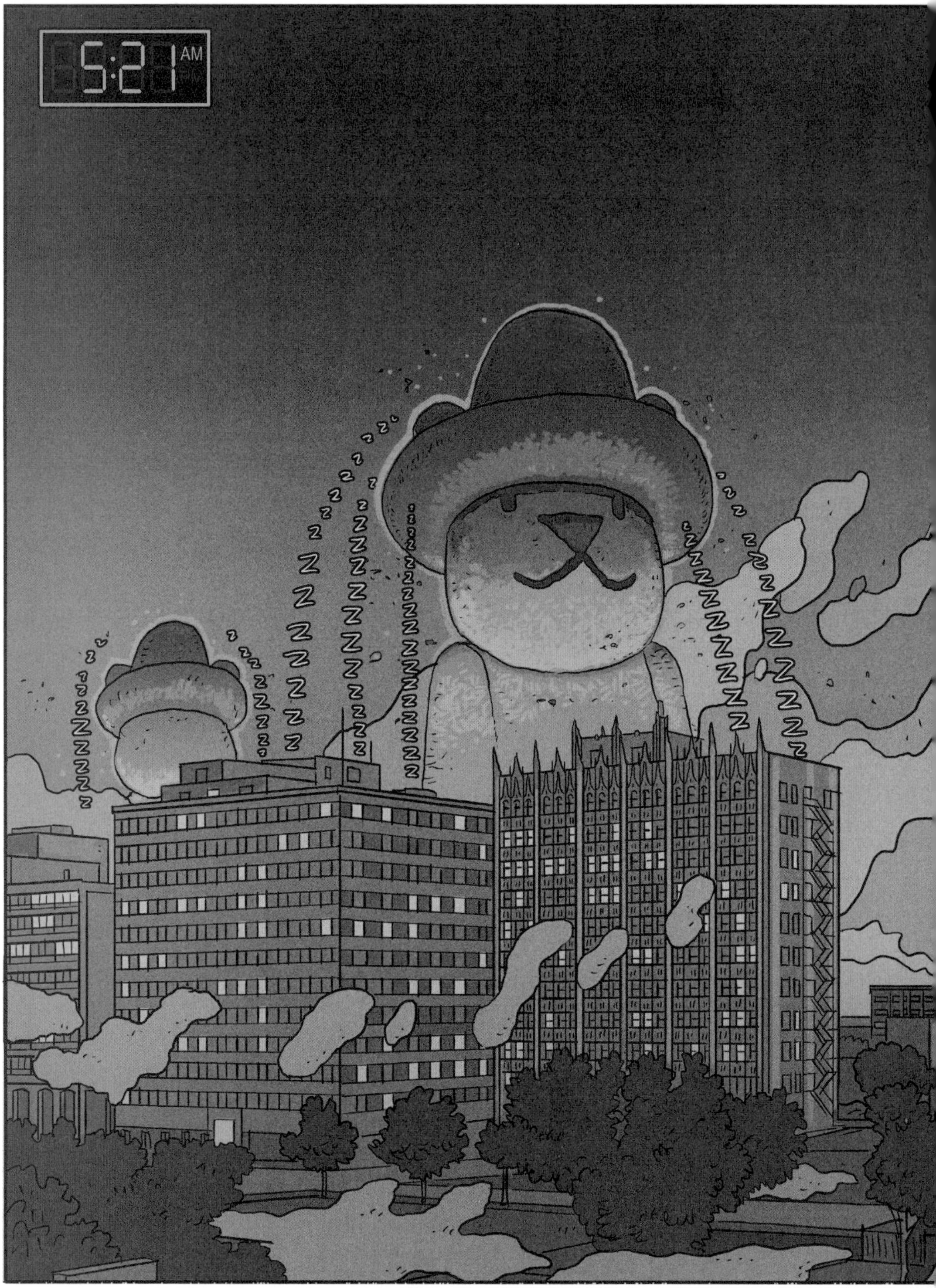
5:21 AM

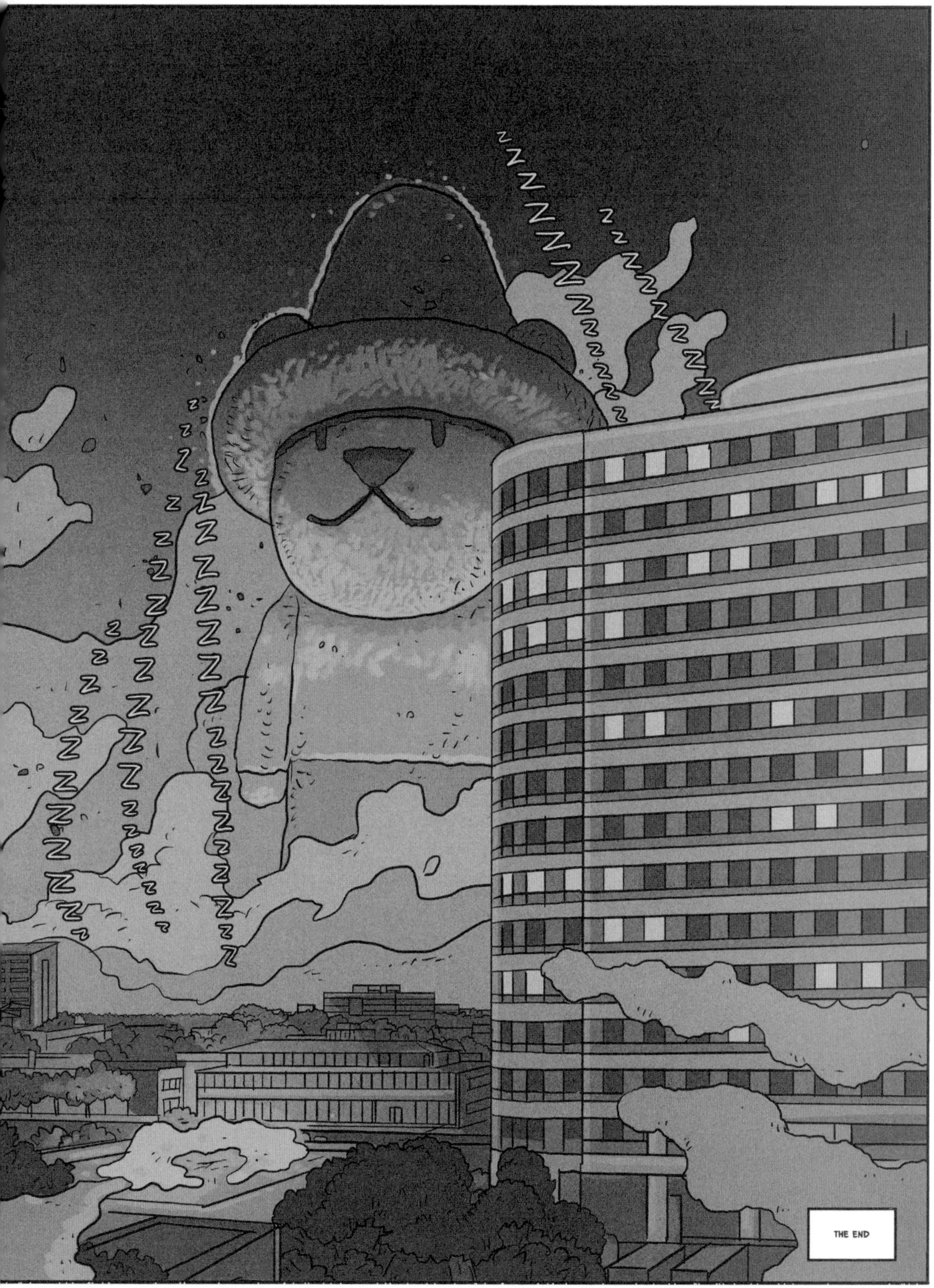
THE END

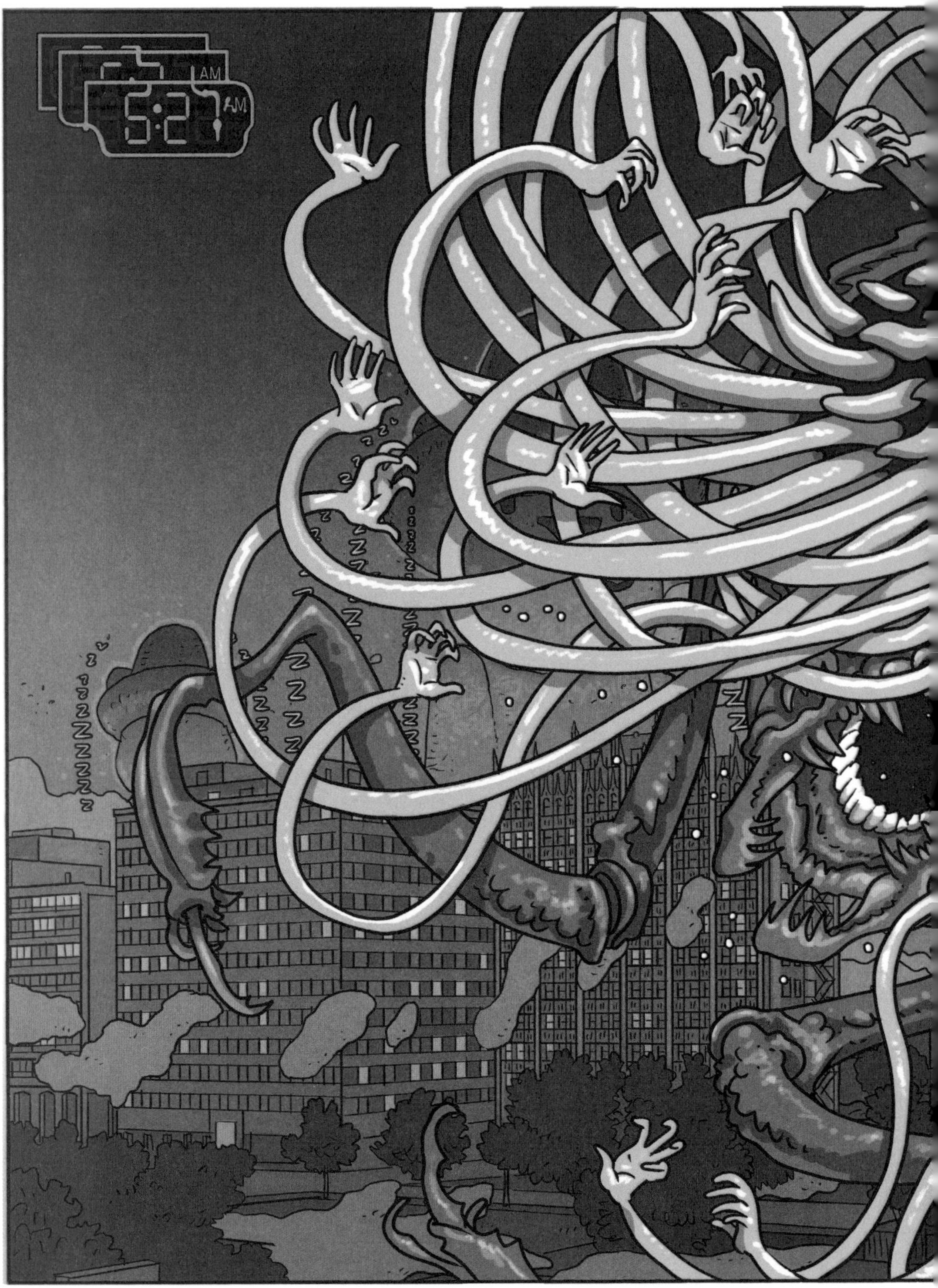
5:27 AM

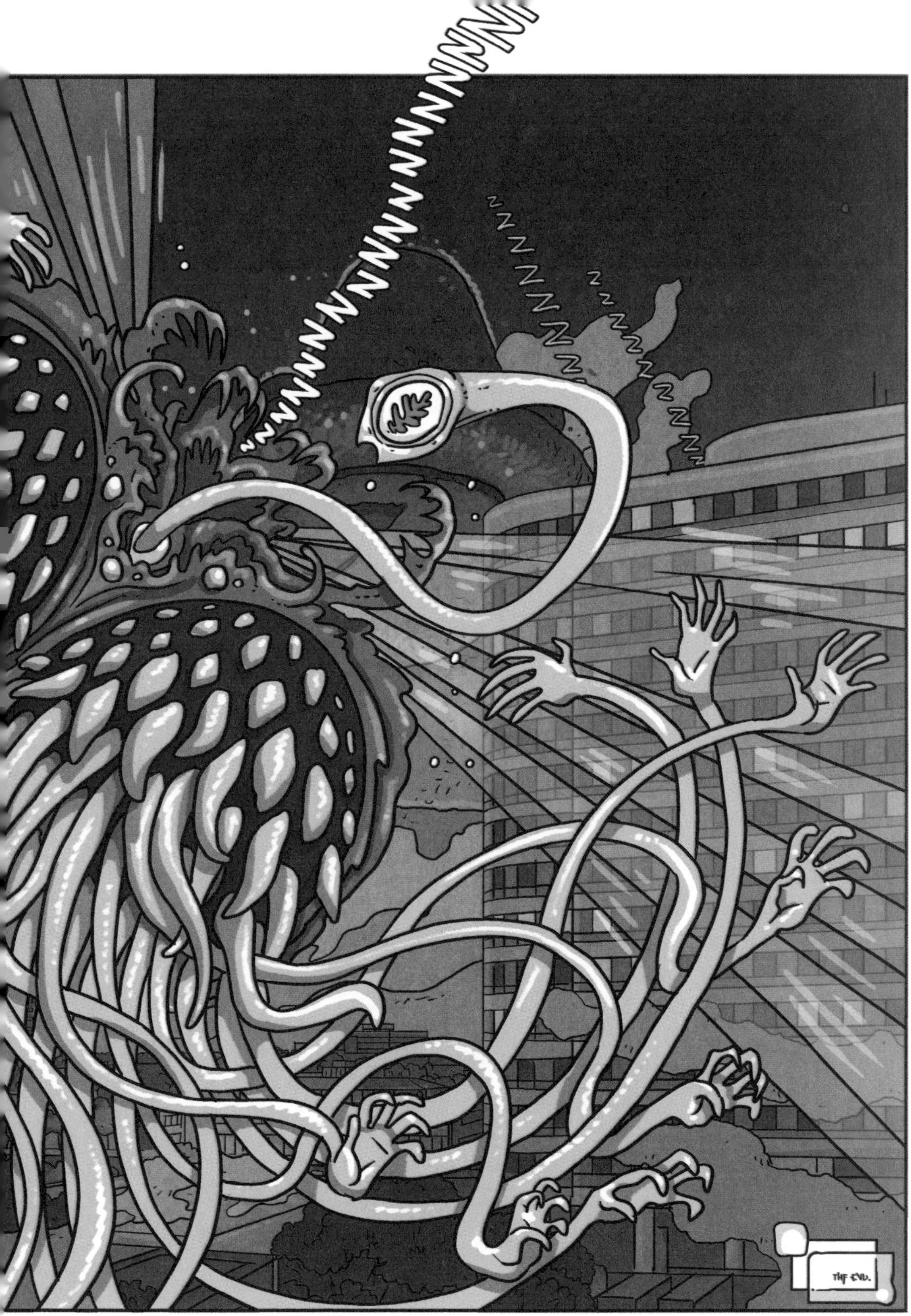
THE END.

THANK YOU FOR
READING APOCALYPSE TACO
BY NATHAN HALE.

WE HOPE YOU HAVE ENJOYED THIS TALE OF
HUNGRY INVADERS.

FOR MORE
SCIENCE FICTION TERROR, PLEASE READ
ONE TRICK PONY.

AND FOR NONFICTION THRILLS AND CHILLS,
SEE THE ONGOING AMERICAN HISTORY SERIES
NATHAN HALE'S HAZARDOUS TALES.

FOR MORE, VISIT:
NATHANHALEAUTHOR.COM

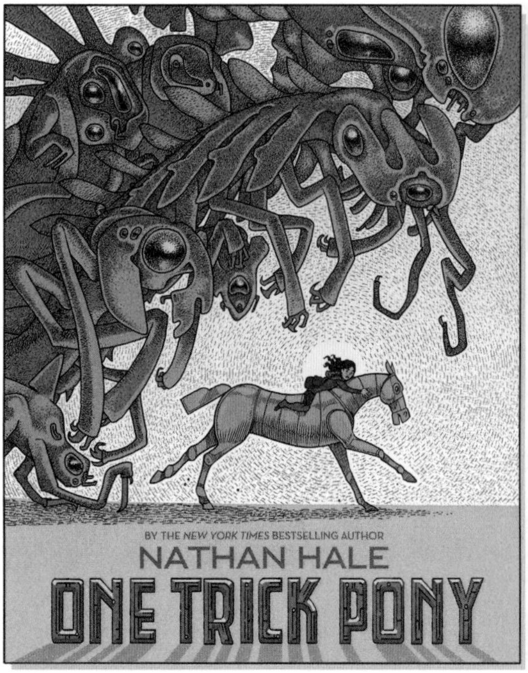
BY THE NEW YORK TIMES BESTSELLING AUTHOR
NATHAN HALE
ONE TRICK PONY

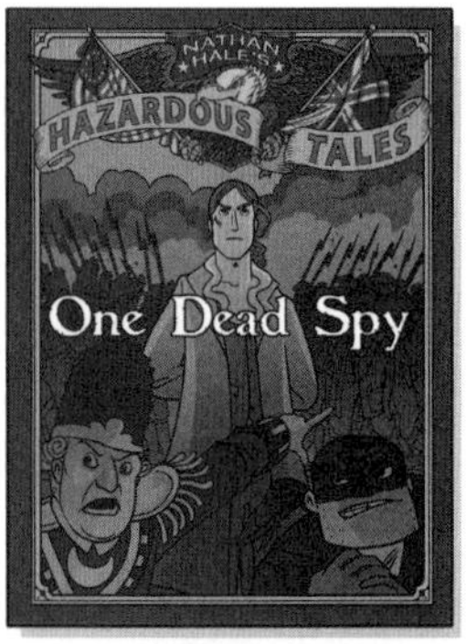
NATHAN HALE'S
HAZARDOUS TALES
One Dead Spy

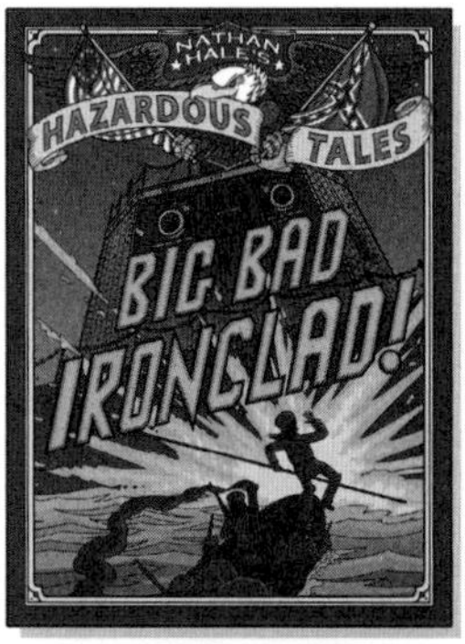
NATHAN HALE'S
HAZARDOUS TALES
BIG BAD IRONCLAD!

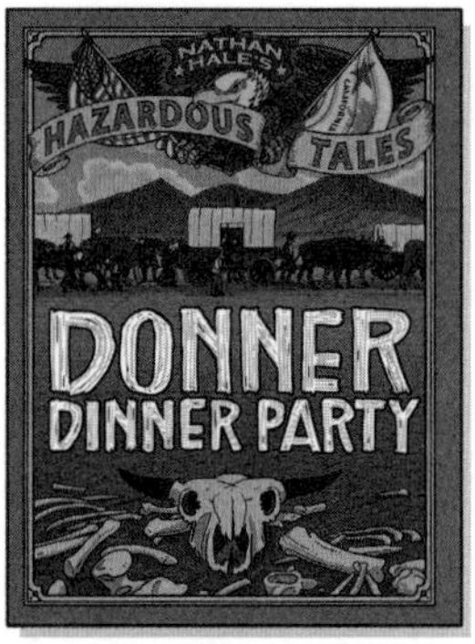
NATHAN HALE'S
HAZARDOUS TALES
DONNER DINNER PARTY

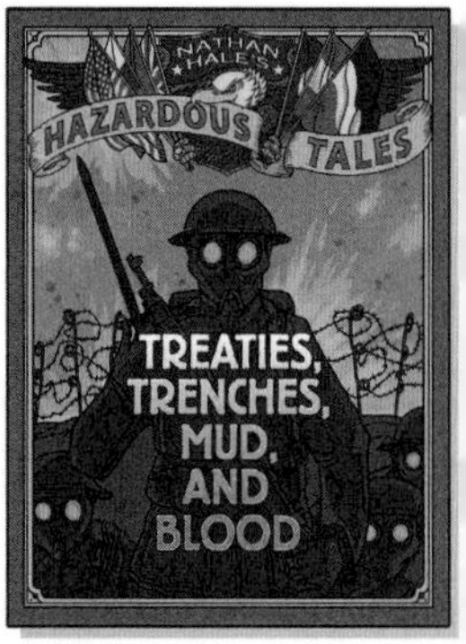
NATHAN HALE'S
HAZARDOUS TALES
TREATIES, TRENCHES, MUD, AND BLOOD

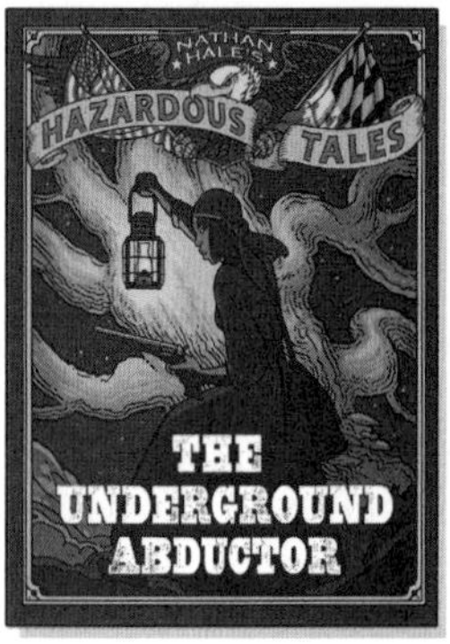
NATHAN HALE'S
HAZARDOUS TALES
THE UNDERGROUND ABDUCTOR

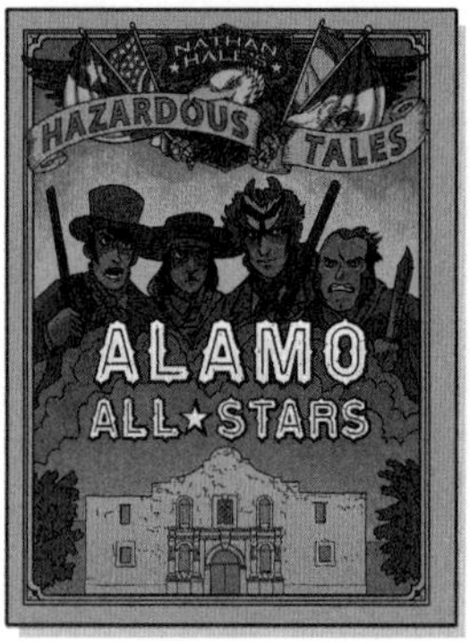
NATHAN HALE'S
HAZARDOUS TALES
ALAMO ALL★STARS

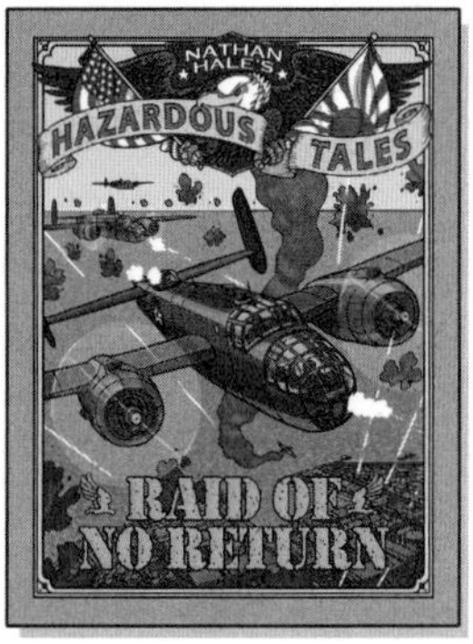
NATHAN HALE'S
HAZARDOUS TALES
RAID OF NO RETURN

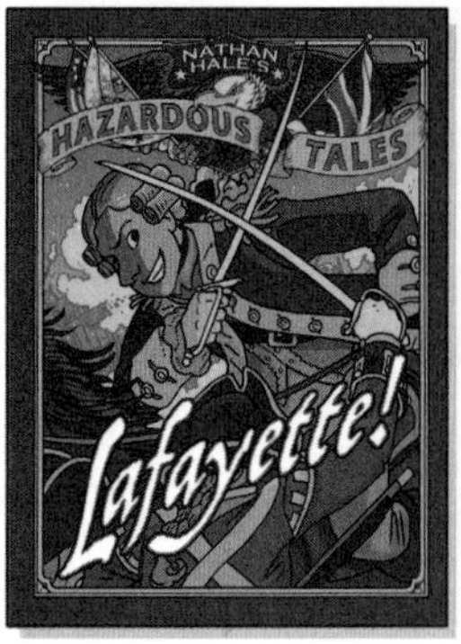
NATHAN HALE'S
HAZARDOUS TALES
Lafayette!

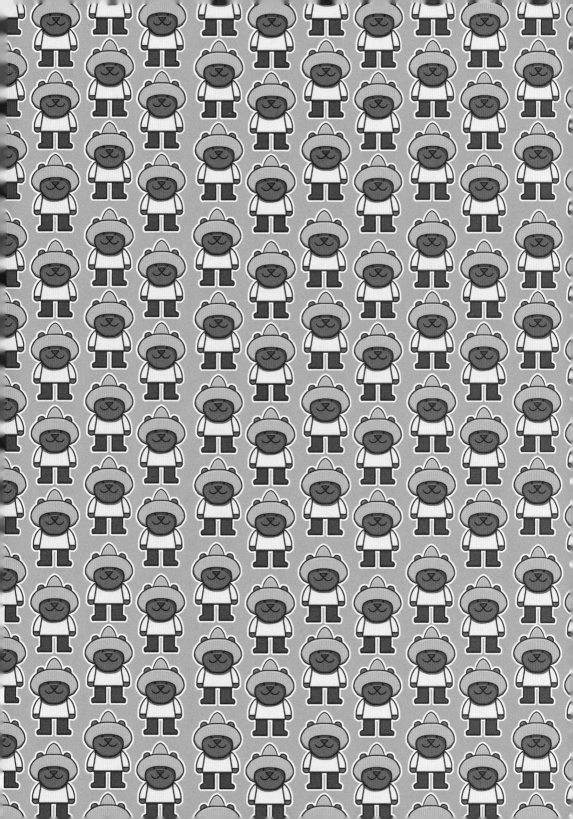

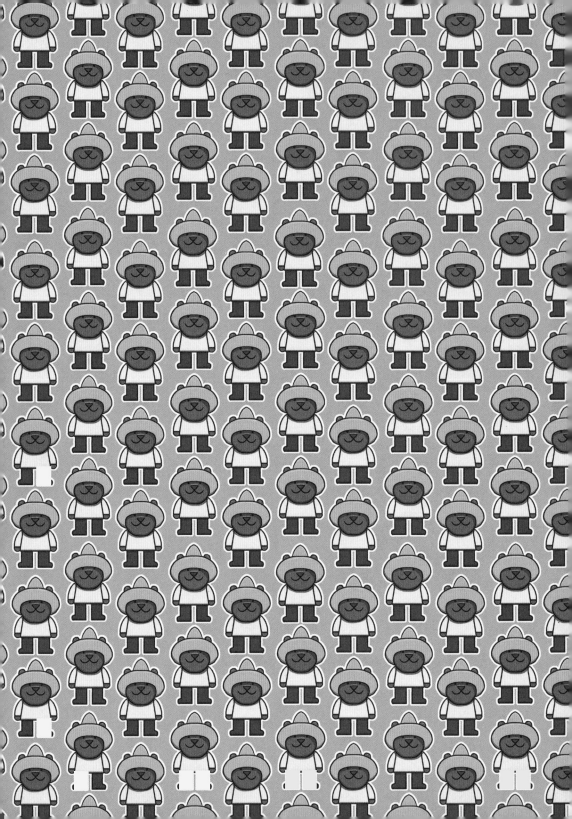